ctions, fumbling and

and there

too quickly and

hen I got off the grass on to t

so that

stand I we travelled the first few

leaps and I lurches, the bonnet go

in a storm and the springs

have been in fits. [The maid

roared at her and she stopped

handle. I roared at her to stop

slowed down I saw the maid

her to stop. At last I recognised

of fear, hers, and mine. I

it her back

Possessed of a Past

Possessed of a Past

A John Banville Reader

SELECTED BY RAYMOND BELL

PICADOR

First published 2012 by Picador
an imprint of Pan Macmillan, a division of Macmillan Publishers Limited
Pan Macmillan, 20 New Wharf Road, London N1 9RR
Basingstoke and Oxford
Associated companies throughout the world
www.panmacmillan.com

ISBN 978-1-4472-1472-4

Acknowledgments for the use of copyrighted material appear on pages 497–500,
which constitute an extension of this copyright page.

1 3 5 7 9 8 6 4 2

A CIP catalogue record for this book is available from
the British Library.

Printed and bound by CPI Group (UK) Ltd, Croydon, CR0 4YY

The past beats inside me like a second heart.

(*The Sea*, 2005)

Contents

xi *Preface*

xiii *A Note on the Texts*

xv *Chronology*

Revelations

FICTION, 1973–2012

3 Summer at Birchwood (*Birchwood*, 1973)

18 Rheticus (*Doctor Copernicus*, 1976)

27 The Harmony of the Spheres (*Kepler*, 1981)

37 Fern House (*The Newton Letter*, 1982)

45 Gabriel Swan (*Mefisto*, 1986)

55 Possessed of a Past

I 'The painting is called' (*The Book of Evidence*, 1989)

II 'I am always fascinated' (*Ghosts*, 1993)

III 'When she urged me to beat her' (*Athena*, 1995)

101 The Golden World (1992)

114 Taking Possession (*The Untouchable*, 1997)

128 The Lost Ones

I 'The telephone began to shrill, giving me a fright' (*Eclipse*, 2000)

II 'So this, she saw, was where it would end' (*Shroud*, 2002)

III 'A charming spot it was Cass chose to die in' (*Eclipse*, 2000)

IV 'We had a dreadful night' (*Ancient Light*, 2012)

158 Lady Laura and the Dowager Duchess (*Shroud*, 2002)
170 Only Dying, After All (*The Sea*, 2005)
177 O Lost, Raw World! (*The Infinities*, 2009)
185 Blest Boy (*Ancient Light*, 2012)

Playing Parts
STAGE AND RADIO PLAYS, 1994–2006

203 From *The Broken Jug* (1994)
232 *Stardust: Three Monologues of the Dead* (2002)
240 *Kepler* (2004)
283 *A World Too Wide* (2005)
294 *Conversation in the Mountains* (2006)

A Blest World
ESSAYS, LECTURES AND REVIEWS, 1990–2010

333 Survivors of Joyce (1990)
343 The Personae of Summer (1993)
349 Thou Shalt Not Kill (1997)
359 'Speaks True Who Speaks Shadow' (2001)
365 Fiction and the Dream (2005)
374 Beckett's Last Words (2006)
389 Living Ghosts (2010)

Fidgets of Remembrance
MEMOIR, 1989, 2003

403 Lupins and moth-laden nights in Rosslare (1989)
408 'It was winter the first time I saw Prague' (*Prague Pictures: Portraits of a City*, 2003)

Firstlings

EARLY FICTION, 1966–1971

425 The Party (1966)

434 Wild Wood (*Long Lankin*, 1970)

442 On *Nightspawn* (*Nightspawn*, 1971)

Begettings

IN PROGRESS / IN RETROSPECT, 2006/2009

448 'Of the things we gave them' (from *The Infinities* MS, 2006)

472 First Light (*The Infinities*, 2009)

495 *Acknowledgements*

497 *Sources*

501 *About the Author*

Preface

Possessed of a Past chiefly comprises extracts from the author's fifteen novels to date, from *Nightspawn* (1971) through to *Ancient Light* (2012). The prose pieces that make up 'Revelations' (and here the term has less to do with disclosure than it does Wallace Stevens's dictum that '[d]escription is revelation'), are each discrete and self-standing. They require neither the crutch of commentary nor any elucidation. Separately, they offer the satisfactions of a short story, without being one; collectively, they form a wider narrative of medleyed voices.

Included in the *Reader* are selections from the author's stage and radio plays, among them a few shards from *The Broken Jug* (crackpots quibbling over a cracked pot); *Conversation in the Mountains* (a fictionalised account of the famously mysterious encounter between Paul Celan and Martin Heidegger in the philosopher's mountain retreat at Todtnauberg); and *Stardust* (three short monologues voiced from beyond the grave by Copernicus, Kepler and Newton).

There are essays on the art of fiction, that 'blest world' of artifice and verisimilitude, wherein Banville expounds on 'the artistic concentration' and his own internal promptings. Homage to Beckett, and deference to Joyce, is paid in two extensive essays on Banville's great literary forebears.

Personal memoir features too, with reminiscences of childhood summers in Rosslare—card-playing in chalets, chips cooked on a Kosangas stove, girls with sun-bleached hair, a boy with webbed toes—that prefigure the author's Man Booker Prize-winning novel, *The Sea*. Recollected also is a clandestine trip to Prague, and a rendezvous with a blacklisted Professor for whom the author had volunteered to smuggle into the West a sheaf of Josef Sudek prints. 'How much of this first visit to Prague am I remembering, and how much is being invented for me?'

From first visits to 'firstlings', the nascent efforts of the tyro. Among the early works gathered here is 'The Party', written a half-century ago when the author was seventeen. Not seen in print since 1966, 'The Party' was not only Banville's first published work, but also the first writing in which he 'heard something that was in a curious way not my own. It was distinct from me, it had a strangeness about it, that strangeness which is, I think, the mark of art.'

The volume concludes where things begin for any author: the blank page, and the 'begetting' of a text. Reproduced in facsimile and transcript are the initial workings of what became the 'First Light' section of *The Infinities*. Remarkable not least of all for the author's exquisite penmanship, this early draft shows Banville sedulously shaping his sentences, striking up that all-important rhythm, the characters being limned into life.

There are myriad correspondences throughout this *Reader*, prompted in no small part by the pieces' propinquity to each other, their thrumming *nextness*. Notes sounded in the earlier fictions soar to their mellifluous apogees elsewhere; echoes sift from the air in whole flocks over this retrospective.

For Banville is a rapt and rigorous observer of the quotidian, his prose celestial, the pages salted with the 'stars of detail' via which James Wood says we navigate our darkened lives. One hopes that the limpid light which falls over these stepping-stone selections may yet lead readers to the greater corpus of this mischievous, most masterly, of artificers.

What's past is prologue: the pages turn.

A Note on the Texts

The fiction pieces assembled in 'Revelations' have all been titled for ease of revisiting, a fingerpost set upon darkling plains. The titles are drawn from the selections themselves, save for 'Possessed of a Past', a phrase from *Kepler*, but one felicitous to the trilogy of texts it now precedes. (It is also this *Reader*'s watermark.) 'Life and Art', a drab and lacklustre nameplate affixed by a hand not Banville's when this tableau first appeared in 1992, has been freshly gilded by its author to 'The Golden World', a realm that glimmeringly foreshadows that of *Ghosts*. The passages are arranged in order of first publication, except where it made for contiguous sense to disjoint the chronology and integrate pieces where best appropriate, as in the case of 'The Golden World' and the extracts which comprise 'The Lost Ones'. Regarding the latter and its fugal second section (*'So this, she saw, was where it would end'*), Cass Cleave's final moments have been italicised to set them apart from her father's unassuageable sorrowings. Ellipses, those of the plumper variety (• • •), are used to denote section breaks and, where square-bracketed ([• • •]), to stoutly signal an abridgement. Other minor excisions and emendations have been made, but these have been mere chippings, too negligible to warrant a scree of footnotes.

In 'Playing Parts', I welcome the opportunity to play my own part, and correct some regrettable errors which appeared in the original, limited edition of the radio play, *Conversation in the Mountains*. Not only were the Celan translations misattributed to the late Michael Hamburger—the excerpts were entirely from John

Felstiner's superbly nuanced *Selected Poems and Prose of Paul Celan*—but the 'Deathfugue' which opens Scene I of the play was itself an unfortunate hybrid of renderings.

The essays, lectures and reviews that form 'A Blest World'—less a world here than an archipelago: Banville's reviewery is vast—have been selected for the light they shed on work that appears elsewhere in the *Reader*. I should point out that several revolvers which smouldered notionally in some of these essays—triggered, as they were, by the word *psychology*: 'when I hear the word *psychology* applied in the area of fiction I tend to reach instinctively for my revolver ('Fiction and the Dream')'—have been mostly surrendered at Banville's behest. The American spellings that naturally quickened 'Living Ghosts' when it appeared in *The New York Review of Books* have been standardised, and admit now of their own Hiberno-hauntings.

In 'Fidgets of Remembrance' (Wallace Steven's memorable formulation may be found in his 'Credences of Summer', verses of which are excerpted by Banville in 'The Personae of Summer'), the author's reminiscences of Prague have been heavily abridged, the ellipses grown even plumper than the 'pale, tumorous and hot' *knedlíky* (Czech dumplings) he advises we 'skip smartly' over.

And skip smartly we do . . .

In 'The Party', the first of Banville's 'Firstlings'—the author's own term for those juvenilian first forays in fiction—only obvious typographical errors have been corrected.

As to the facsimile pages that constitute 'Begettings', Banville's holograph workings are perfectly decipherable and I see no need to enumerate what are self-evident transcription conventions.

The 'Chronology', although comprehensive, is not complete; it has its lapses like in any lived life. No mention is made of Banville's 'dark and twin brother', the scarcely selfsame *semblable*, Benjamin Black.

Chronology

1945 Born in Wexford, Ireland.

1962 First story, 'The Party', written.

1966 'The Party' published in *The Kilkenny Magazine*.

1970 First book, *Long Lankin* (a collection of short stories and a novella), published. Reissued in revised form in 1984.

1971 First novel, *Nightspawn*, published. Reissued in 1993.

1973 *Birchwood* published. Wins the Allied Irish Banks' Prize and the Irish Arts Council Macaulay Fellowship.

1976 *Doctor Copernicus* published. Wins the Whitbread Prize, the James Tait Black Memorial Prize, and the American Ireland Fund Literary Award.

1981 *Kepler* published. Wins the *Guardian* Prize for Fiction.

1982 *The Newton Letter* published.

1984 A film version of *The Newton Letter*, entitled *Reflections*, broadcast by Channel 4 and RTÉ.

1986 *Mefisto* published.

1988 Appointed Literary Editor of *The Irish Times*.

1989 *The Book of Evidence* published. Shortlisted for the Booker Prize. Wins the Guinness Peat Aviation Book Award and the Marten Toonder Award.

1990 Begins a long-standing tenure as reviewer-essayist with *The New York Review of Books*.

1991 *La Spiegazione dei Fatti* (the Italian translation of *The Book of Evidence*) awarded the Premio Ennio Flaiano.

1993 *Ghosts* published. Shortlisted for the Whitbread Fiction Prize.

1994 *The Broken Jug*, an adaptation of Kleist's *Der zerbrochne Krug*, premiered at the Peacock Theatre, Dublin, on 1 June. *Seachange*, a film adaptation of the author's uncollected story 'Rondo', broadcast by RTÉ.

1995 *Athena* published.

1996 *The Ark*, a story for children, published.

1997 *The Untouchable* published. Wins the Lannan Literary Award. Shortlisted for the Whitbread Fiction Prize.

1999 Adapts Elizabeth Bowen's *The Last September* for the screen.

2000 *Eclipse* published. *God's Gift*, an adaptation of Kleist's *Amphitryon*, premiered at the O'Reilly Theatre, Dublin, on 12 October. *Doctor Copernicus*, *Kepler* and *The Newton Letter* published together in a single volume under the title *The Revolutions Trilogy*.

2001 *The Book of Evidence*, *Ghosts* and *Athena* published together in a single volume under the title *Frames*.

2002 *Shroud* published. Longlisted for the Man Booker Prize. *Stardust: Three Monologues of the Dead* broadcast by BBC Radio 3's *The Verb*. *Dublin 1742*, a play for children, performed at The Ark in Dublin on 5 June. The stage production of *The Book of Evidence* premiered at the Watergate Theatre, Kilkenny, on 10 August.

2003 Awarded the Premio Nonino. *Prague Pictures: Portraits of a City* published as part of Bloomsbury's 'The Writer and the City' series.

2004 *Kepler*, a radio play, broadcast by BBC Radio 4 on 11 August.

2005 *The Sea* published. Wins the Man Booker Prize. *Love in the Wars*, an adaptation of Kleist's *Penthesilia*, published. *A World Too Wide*, a radio play about Shakespeare's 'sixth age of man', broadcast by RTÉ.

2006 Awarded the Premio Grinzane-Francesco Biamonti Prize. *The Sea* shortlisted for British Book Awards Author of the Year. *Todtnauberg*, a radio play about the 1967 meeting between Paul Celan and Martin Heidegger, broadcast by BBC Radio 4 on 20 January.

2007 *The Sea* nominated for the Man Booker International Prize. Awarded the Madeleine Zepter Prix Littéraire Européen. Made a fellow of the Royal Society of Literature.

2008 *Conversation in the Mountains*, the script of *Todtnauberg*, published.

2009 *The Infinities* published.

2010 *The Infinities* wins the Kerry Group Irish Fiction Award. *The Sea* shortlisted for the Irish Book of the Decade (Bord Gáis Energy Irish Book Awards).

2011 Awarded the Franz Kafka Prize. Co-scripts with Glenn Close and Gabriela Prekop, the film *Albert Nobbs*.

2012 *Ancient Light* published. Shortlisted for the Prince of Asturias Award for Literature.

Revelations

FICTION

1973–2012

Summer at Birchwood

The butterflies came in swarms in early summer, small blues, delicate creatures. There must have been something in the wood that attracted them, or in the garden, some rare wild plant perhaps. We got used to them, and when they found their way even into the house, and fluttered awkwardly, like clockwork flowers, around our heads at the breakfast table, it was with the tiniest frown of irritation that Mama rose to open the window, murmuring *shoo, shoo*. They were easily killed, I mean it would have been easy to kill them, while they went about their business on the lupins and the roses, but I never knowingly destroyed one of them, I don't know why. Indeed, in time I became their protector, their patron and friend, and I would carry them, throbbing in my cupped hands, out of the hall before Josie arrived with her mop to kill them. When I released them from the steps their incredulous drunken leap from my palm made the summer airs over the garden seem suddenly lighter, gayer, and as delicately tinted as the skyblue silken dust they left smeared on my fingers. Not that I had any love for them, or even liking. I wanted to kill them, but I did not. Some days my teeth ached with the desire for wanton slaughter, but I would not allow myself the pleasure, treasuring my beneficence, and knowing anyway that if the situation became desperate there was nothing to stop me taking a rolled-up newspaper into the wood one afternoon and bludgeoning to extinction a whole species of lepidoptera, small blues, while they frittered away the first glorious days of summer.

It was in summer too that I came into my kingdom. The calendar date is lost, but the occasion is still invested in my mind with the sonorous harmony of a more complex, less tangible combination of pure numbers. There was a clearing in the wood, not a clearing, but an open place under the sadly drooping, slender boughs of a big tree. Mama sat at the edge of a white cloth spread on the grass, reading a book and brushing imaginary flies away from her cheek. At her tiny feet my father lay on his back with his hands behind his head, quite still, and yet managing to give the impression of bouncing restlessly, tensely, on the springy turf. I watched, fascinated, this curious phenomenon, but soon the shifting patterns of light and leaf on the cloth distracted me, and there was another distraction, which it took me a while to identify, and it was this, that Mama had not once in ten minutes turned a page of her book. That was very strange. At last Papa stood up, stretched himself ostentatiously, and yawned. Mama's lack of interest in her book grew more intense, if that is possible, and I caught her glancing sideways at him with that furtive, mournful, altogether lovesick look which already I had come to know so well. Patting the last of his yawn with three fingertips, he considered the top of her head, the inclined pale plane of her jaw, and then turned and sauntered off into the trees, whistling through his teeth, his hands in his pockets. Soon she put her book away and followed him, as I knew she would. I was forgotten.

Our wood was one of nature's cripples. It covered, I suppose, three or four acres of the worst land on the farm, a hillside sloping down crookedly to the untended nether edge of the stagnant pond we called a lake. Under a couple of feet of soil there was a bed of solid rock, that intractable granite for which the area is notorious. On this unfriendly host the trees grew wicked and deformed, some of them so terribly twisted that they crawled horizontally across the hill, their warped branches warring with the undergrowth, while behind them, at some distance, the roots they had struggled to put down were thrust up again by the rock, queer maimed things. Here too, on the swollen trunks, were lymphatic mushrooms flourishing in sodden moss, and other things, reddish glandular blobs which I called dwarfs' ears. It was a hideous, secretive and exciting place, I liked it there, and when, surfeited on the fetid air of the lower wood, I sought the sunlight above the hill, there on a high ridge, to lift my spirit, was the eponymous patch of birches, restless gay little trees which sang in summer, and in winter winds rattled together their bare branches as delicate as lace.

Left alone, I pulled pale stalks of grass from their sockets and crushed the soft flesh in my mouth. Timidly, almost unnoticed, there came a breaking in upon me that music, palpable and tender, which a wood in summer makes, whose melody is always just beyond hearing, always enticing. Dreamily I wandered down through the trees, into the bluegreen gloom. Down there were flies, not the intricate translucent things which browsed among the birches, but vivid nightblue brutes with brittle bodies, swarming over the rot, and there were black birds too, under the bushes screaming. Somewhere afar a dog barked listlessly between precise pauses, and I heard the sound of an axe, and other sounds too numerous to name. I came to Cotter's place. This was a little house, in ruins, with everything gone under lyme grass and thorns but for one end wall with a fireplace halfway up it, and a shattered chimney with the black flue exposed, and over the fireplace a cracked mirror, a miracle of light, staring impassively over the tops of the trees. I never knew who Cotter was, but the name suggested . . . never mind. He was long gone now, and in what had been his kitchen, among the ferns that flourished there, a woman's pale hands clutched and loosed in languorous spasms a pale white arse bare below a hiked-up shirttail. She cried out softly under his thrusts, and, as I watched, a delicate arc of briar beside them, caught by a stray breeze, sprang up suddenly into the air, where two butterflies were gravely dancing. Lift your head! Look! The mirror's pale, unwavering, utterly silent gaze sent something like a deep black note booming through the wood's limpid song, and I felt, what shall I say, that I had discovered something awful and exquisite, of immense, unshakeable calm.

I wandered farther then, by unknown ways, and soon I heard Mama's voice hallooing here and there, each cry a little closer. I waited, and it was not long until she came hurrying down the hill, hands fluttering and her hair streaming behind her. She leaned over me, enfolding me in a tender weight of love and concern, murmuring incoherently into my ear, warm round words, swollen like kisses. Her cheeks burned. We found Papa pacing impatiently under the tree, kicking leaves and smoking a cigar. The picnic things were packed and stacked beside him. As we approached he bent to pick them up, and bending gave me that crooked sidelong sort of grin which is about the most I ever had from him by way of affection, which I always tried to avoid, and never could, it was so knowing, so penetrating and so cold. Mama was very busy, tying up her hair, taking things out of the basket only to put them back again, foothering around, as Granny Godkin would have said. The folded cloth slipped from under her arm and opened like an ungainly flower, and from out of its centre staggered a bruised blue butterfly. She paused, stood motionless for a moment, and then very slowly put her hands over her face and began to cry. 'Jesus,' said Papa, without any particular emotion, and walked away from us. For my part I was quite calm.

We straggled homeward. My father's long stride carried him far ahead of us, and he had to stop often and urge us on with weary silent stares. Mama laughed and chattered and exclaimed over the flowers in the hedge, trying by her gaiety to make the three of us doubt that outburst of tears. Her prattling irritated me.

Full of the secret glimpsed under Cotter's wall, I carried myself carefully, like a patient floating blissfully on a drug, forgetful of the pain biding its time outside the vacuum. O I am not saying that I had discovered love, or what they call the facts of life, for I no more understood what I had seen than I understood Mama's tears, no, all I had found was the notion of—I shall call it harmony. How would I explain, I do not understand it, but it was as if in the deep wood's gloom I had recognised, in me all along, waiting, an empty place where I could put the most disparate things and they would hang together, not very elegantly, perhaps, or comfortably, but yet together, singing like seraphs.

So it was, as I walked up the drive, I perceived in my once familiar kingdom the subtle strains of this new music. The sun shone calmly on the garden, except in the corner by the swing where daffodils blazed like trumpetblasts. Josie was polishing an upstairs window, and the glass, awash with sky, shivered and billowed under the sweep of her cloth. We climbed the steps, into the hall, and Mama, pressing a hand to her forehead, dropped a bunch of primroses on a chair and swept away to her room. The cluster of bruised flowers came slowly asunder, one fell, another, and then half of them tumbled in a flurry to the carpet, and behind me the tall clock creaked and clicked, and struck a sonorous bronze chord. Listen, listen, if I know my world, which is doubtful, but if I do, I know it is chaotic, mean and vicious, with laws cast in the wrong moulds, a fair conception gone awry, in short an awful place, and yet, and yet a place capable of glory in those rare moments when a little light breaks forth, and something is not explained, not forgiven, but merely illuminated.

[• • •]

Papa was right, the blackcurrant crop was the heaviest in years that year. Just as well, since the fruit was by now one of the last remaining sources of income at Birchwood. The land on which it flourished had been already sold, and this was the final harvest we would take. Michael and I were put in charge of the pickers, a ragged army of tenant children and their grandmothers, and a few decrepit old men no longer capable of heavier toil. They were a wild primitive bunch, the old people half crazed by the weight of their years, the children as cheerfully vicious as young animals. Their conversation dwelt almost to the exclusion of all else on sex and death, and the children managed a neat conjunction of the two by carrying on their lovelife after dark in the local graveyard. They shied away instinctively from me, found me cold, I suppose, or saw my father in me, but Michael they immediately accepted. That surprised me. They listened to his orders and, more startling still, did as he told them. They even offered to arrange a girlfriend for him. That offer he declined, for he had little interest in the sexual duet, being a confirmed soloist, and it was I who made a conquest, when I met Rosie.

In the morning I rose early and waded down through pools of sleep on the stairs to the garden, where Michael waited for me in the cart with Nockter. The lawn was drenched with light, the trees in the wood were still. A bright butterfly darned the air above the horse's head. We rattled along violet-shadowed lanes quick with blackbirds, by the edges of the meadows where the corn was bursting. Birdsong shook the wood like gushes of wind. All was still but for the small clouds sailing their courses, and it was pleasant to be abroad in that new morning, with the smell of the furze, and the grass sparkling, that hawk, all these things.

We reached the plantation. Nockter set up the huge brass scales, and Michael unharnessed the horse, whispering in its ear. I heard beyond the clatter of metal and leather the distant ring of voices, and turned and saw, down the long meadow, a concourse approaching, trembling on the mist, their cries softly falling through the air, mysterious and gay. If only, when they were beside me, when I was among them, they had retained even a fragment of the beauty of that first vision, I might have loved them. It is ever thus.

The fruit we hardly picked, but rather saved. From under their canopies of leaf the heavy purple clusters tumbled with a kind of abandon into our hands. Down in the green gloom under the bushes, where spiders swarmed, the berries were gorgeous, achingly vivid against the dusty leaves, but once plucked, and in the baskets, their burnished lustre faded and a moist whitish film settled on the skin. If they were to be eaten, and we ate them by the handful at the start, it was only in that shocked moment of separation from the stems that they held their true, their unearthly flavour. Then the fat beads burst on our tongues with a chill bitterness which left our eyelids damp and our mouths flooded, a bitterness which can still pierce my heart, for it is the very taste of time.

Rosie was there with her granny, an obese old woman whose coarse tongue and raucous cackle froze the child into a trance of embarrassment. I noticed her first when we paused at noon to eat our sandwiches. Michael and I lay in the long grass of a ditch, belching and sighing, contemplating our outstretched bare legs and grimy toes. Rosie sat a little way from us, daintily fighting three persistent flies for possession of a cream bun. She had short dark hair rolled into hideous sausage curls. A saddle of freckles sat on her nose. She wore sandals and a dress with daisies on it. She was pretty, a sturdy sunburnt creature. Having won her bun, she wiped the corners of her mouth with her fingertips and began to eat blackcurrants from the basket beside her, slowly, one by one, drawing back her lips and bursting each berry between her tiny white teeth. A trickle of crimson juice ran down her chin and dropped, plop, into her lap, staining a yellow daisy pink.

We went back to work then. I heard her granny's laughter rising over the meadow, and by some mysterious process that awful noise was transmuted into an audible expression of the excitement which was making my hands tremble and my heart race.

So at every noon we drew a little nearer to each other, treading our way like swimmers toward that bright island which we did not reach until the last day of the harvest, when the weights were totted and the wages paid, and under cover of the general gaiety she sidled up to me, stood for a long time in a tense silence, and then abruptly said,

'I made sevenanatanner.'

She opened her fist and showed me the moist coins lying on her palm. I pursed my lips and gravely nodded, and gazed away across the fields, trying to look as though I were struggling with some great and terrible thought. At our feet Michael sat with his back against the wheel of the cart, slowly munching an enormous sandwich. He glanced up at us briefly, with a faint trace of mockery. Rosie stirred and sighed, trapped her hands behind her back, and began to grind the toe of her sandal into the grass. Her knees were stippled with rich red scratches, crescents of blood-beads.

'That's fourteen stone,' she said, and added faintly, 'and two pound.'

That was more than I had picked, and I was about to admit as much when abruptly Michael bounced up between us, coughed, hitched up his trousers, and grinned at the horse. The shock of this apparition made our eyes snap back into focus, and the others around us materialised again, and the wave of jabbering voices and the jingle of money swelled in our ears. Rosie blushed and sadly, slowly, paced stiff-legged away.

I helped Nockter to dismantle the scales, and we loaded the pieces on the cart while Michael harnessed the horse. The pickers drifted off into the lowering sun. We followed them across the meadow and then turned away toward home. Nockter clicked his tongue at the horse and rattled the reins along its back. Michael and I walked in silence beside the rolling cart. He was wearing Nockter's hat pushed down on the back of his head. We reached the lane. I was thinking that if Michael had not popped up between us like that, the clown, I might have, I could have, why, I *would* have—Rosie stepped out of a bush at the side of the lane ahead of us, tugging at her dress. My heart! She gaped at us, greatly flustered, started off in one direction, turned, tried the other, stopped. The cart rumbled on. Nockter grinned. Michael began to whistle. I hesitated, doing a kind of agonised dance in my embarrassment, and finally stood still. She smiled timidly. A massed choir of not altogether sober cherubim burst into song. I felt ridiculous.

'You're gas,' said Rosie.

She came to me at Cotter's place that evening with a shower of rain behind her. The drops fell like fire through the dying copper light of day. All the wood was aflame. She had wanted me to meet her in the graveyard, like any normal swain. I drew the line there.

[• • •]

Summer ended officially with the lighting of a fire in the drawing room. Rain fell all day, big sad drops drumming on the dead leaves, and smoke billowed back down the chimneys, where rooks had nested. The house seemed huge, hollow, all emptiness and echo. In the morning Granny Godkin was discovered in the hall struggling with an umbrella which would not open. She was going down to the summerhouse, rain or no rain, and when they tried to restrain her she shook her head and muttered, and rattled the umbrella furiously. In the last weeks, after her brief vibrant interval of fanged gaiety when the prospect appeared of a peasant revolt, she had become strangely withdrawn and vague, wandering distractedly about the house, sighing and sometimes even quietly weeping. She said there was no welcome for her now at Birchwood, and spent more and more time down at the lake despite the autumnal damp. Often Michael and I would see her sitting motionless by the table in the summerhouse, her head inclined and her eyes intently narrowed, listening to the subtle shifts and subsidences within her, the mechanism of her body winding down.

'But you'll catch your death,' Mama cried. 'It's teeming.'

'What?' the old woman snapped. 'What? Leave me alone.'

'But—'

'Let me *be*, will you.'

Mama turned to my father. 'Joe, can you not . . . ? She'll get her death . . .' As always when she spoke to him now her voice dwindled hopelessly, sadly, and in silence her eyes, moist with tenderness and despair, followed him as he shrugged indifferently and turned away wearily to shut himself into the drawing room.

'*Curse you, will you open,*' Granny Godkin snarled, and thwacked the brolly like a whip. Mama, with her pathetic faith in reason, opened wide the front door to show the old woman the wickedness of the weather. 'Look, look how bad it is. You'll be drenched.'

Granny Godkin paused, and grinned slyly, wickedly, and glanced up sideways at Mama.

'You worry?' she whispered. 'Heh!'

The grin became a skeletal sneer, and she glared about her at the hall, and suddenly the umbrella flew open, a strange glossy black blossom humming on its struts, and when I think of that day it is that black flower dipping and bobbing in the gloomy hall which recalls the horror best. The old woman thrust it before her out the door, where a sudden gust of wind snatched it up and she was swept down the steps, across the lawn, and I ducked into the library to avoid Mama's inevitable, woebegone embrace.

Aunt Martha waited for me, huddled in an armchair by the empty fireplace with a shawl around her shoulders, gazing blankly at a book open in her lap and gnawing a raw carrot. She hardly looked at me, but flung the carrot into the grate and began to whine at once.

'Where have you been? I'm waiting this hour. Do you think I've nothing better to do? Your father says you're to learn Latin, I don't know why, god only knows, but there you are. Look at this book. Amo amas amat, love. Say it, amo, come on. Amo, I love.'

I sat and looked at her with that serene silent stare which never failed to drive her into a frenzy. She slapped the primer shut and bared her teeth, an unpleasant habit she had when angry, just like Papa.

'You know you really are a horrible little boy, do you know that, do you? Why do you hate me? I spend half my life in this house trying to give you some kind of an education, and all you do is gawp and grin—O yes, I've seen you grinning, you you you . . .' She clapped a hand to her forehead and closed her eyes. 'O, I, I must . . . Look, come, try to learn something, look at this lovely language, these words, Gabriel, please, for me, for your Mama, you're a dear child. Now, amo, I love . . .'

But she shut the book again, and with a low moan looked fretfully around the room, searching for something to which she might anchor her fractured attention. It occurred to me that my presence made hardly any difference to her, I mean she would have carried on like this whether I was there or not, might even have talked all that nonsense to the empty air. They were all fleeing into themselves, as fast as they could flee, all my loved ones. At the dinner table now I could gaze at any or all of them without ever receiving in return an inquiring glance, or an order to eat up and stop staring, or even a sad smile from Mama. Even Michael had since that day at the summerhouse become silent and preoccupied, had begun to avoid me, and I felt sure that he knew some secret which involved me and which I was not to know. I was like a lone survivor wandering among the wreckage, like Tiresias in the city of plague.

Papa insinuated himself into the room, slipped in at the door and tiptoed to the window without looking at us, and there stood gazing out at the dripping trees, rocking slowly on his heels, a gloomy ghost. Aunt Martha appeared not to have noticed him. She tapped my knee peremptorily with her fist.

'You must learn, Gabriel, it's no good to—'

The room shook. There was no sound, but instead a sensation of some huge thing crumpling, like a gargantuan heart attack, that part of an explosion that races out in a wave ahead of the blast and buckles the silence. But the blast did not arrive, and Aunt Martha looked at the ceiling, and Papa glanced at us querulously over his shoulder, and we said nothing. Perhaps we had imagined it, like those peals of thunder that wrench us out of sleep on calm summer nights. The world is full of inexplicable noises, yelps and howls, the echoes of untold disasters.

'It's no good to just sit and say nothing, Gabriel,' said Aunt Martha. 'You must learn things, we all had to learn, and it's not so difficult. Mensa is a table, see? Mensa . . .'

While she talked, Papa made his way across the room by slow degrees, casually, his lips pursed, until he stood behind her chair looking down over her shoulder at the book and jingling coins in his pocket. She fell silent, and sat very still with her head bent over the page, and Papa hummed a tune and walked out of the room, and she put down the primer and followed him, and I was left alone, wondering where and when all this had happened before.

I picked up the book she had dropped and thumbed glumly through it. The words lay dead in ranks, file beside file of slaughtered music. I rescued one, that verb to love, and, singing its parts in a whisper, I lifted my eyes to the window. Nockter, his elbows sawing, knees pumping, came running across the lawn. It was so perfect a picture of bad news arriving, this little figure behind the rainstippled glass looming out of wind and violence, that at first I took it to be no more than a stray fancy born of boredom. I looked again. He slipped on the grass, frantically backpedalling an imaginary bicycle, and plunged abruptly arse over tip out of my view amid a sense of general hilarity. I waited, and sure enough a few moments later the house quivered with the first groundswell of catastrophe. Nockter appeared in my window again, limping back the way he had come, with my father now by his side, his coattails flying. Next came poor Mama, struggling against the wind and, last of all, in a pink dressing gown, Aunt Martha. They dived into the wood, one after another, but when they were gone the shaking and shuddering of the stormtossed garden seemed an echo of their tempestuous panic. Michael entered quietly behind me.

'What's up?' he asked.

I did not know, and hardly cared. It was not for me to question this splendid spectacle of consternation in the adult camp. I was not a cruel child, only a cold one, and I feared boredom above all else. So we clasped our hands behind our backs and gazed out into the rain, awaiting the next act. Soon they came back, straggling despondently in reverse order, Aunt Martha, Mama, and then Nockter and my father. They passed by the window with downcast eyes.

'We should . . .' Michael began. He eyed me speculatively, biting bits off a thumbnail. 'Do you think she's . . . ?'

The hall. I remember it so well, that scene, so vividly. My father was stooped over the phone, rattling the cradle with a frenzied forefinger and furiously shaking the earpiece, but the thing would not speak to him. His hair was in his eyes, his knees trembled. Mama, with one hand on her forehead and the other stretched out to the table behind her for support, leaned backwards in a half swoon, her lips parted and eyelids drooping, her drenched hair hanging down her back. Nockter sat, caked with mud from his fall, on the edge of a little chair, looking absurdly stolid and calm, almost detached. The front door stood open. Three dead leaves were busy chasing each other round and round on the carpet. I saw all this in a flash, and no doubt that precise situation took no more than an instant to swell and flow into another, but for me it is petrified forever, the tapping finger, Mama's dripping hair, those leaves. Aunt Martha, in her ruined pink frilly, was slowly ascending the stairs backwards. The fall of her foot on each new step shook her entire frame as the tendons tugged on a web of connections, and her jaws slackened, her chest heaved, while out of her mouth there fell curious little high-pitched grunts, which were so abrupt, so understated, that I imagined them as soft furry balls of sound falling to the carpet and lodging in the nap. Up she went, and up, until there were no more steps, and she sat down on the highest one with a bump and buried her face in her hands, and at last an ethereal voice in the phone answered Papa's pleas with a shrill hoot.

My memory is curious, a magpie with perverse eyes, it fascinates me. Jewels I remember only as glitter, and the feel of glass in my beak. I have filled my nest with dross. What does it mean? That is the question I am forever asking, what can it mean? There is never a precise answer, but instead, in the sky, as it were, a kind of Jovian nod, a celestial tipping of the wink, *that's all right, it means what it means*. Yes, but is that enough? Am I satisfied? I wonder. That day I remember Nockter falling, Mama running across the garden in the rain, that scene in the hall, all those things, whereas, listen, what I should recall to the exclusion of all else is the scene in the summerhouse that met Michael and me when we sneaked down there, the ashes on the wall, that rendered purplish mass in the chair, Granny Godkin's two feet, all that was left of her, in their scorched button boots, and I do remember it, in a sense, as words, as facts, but I cannot see it, and there is the trouble. Well, perhaps it is better thus. I have no wish to make unseemly disclosures about myself, and I can never think of that ghastly day without suspecting that somewhere inside me some cruel little brute, a manikin in my mirror, is bent double with laughter. Granny! Forgive me.

(*Birchwood*, 1973)

Rheticus

I can see it now, of course, how cunning they were, the two of them, Giese and the Canon, cunning old conspirators; but I could not see it then. I woke late in the morning to find Raphaël beside me, with honey and hot bread and a jug of spiced wine. The food was welcome, but the mere presence of the lithesome lad would have been sufficient, for it broke a fast far crueller than belly-hunger—I mean the fasting from the company of youth and rosy cheeks and laughing eyes, which I had been forced to observe since leaving Wittenberg and coming among these grey-beards. We spent a pleasant while together, and he, the shy one, twisted his fingers and shifted from foot to foot, chattering on in a vain effort to stem his blushes. At length I gave him a coin and sent him skipping on his way, and although the old gloom returned once he was gone, it was not half so leaden as before. Too late I remembered that sober talk I had determined to have with him; the matter would have to be dealt with. An establishment of clerics, all men—and Catholics at that!—was a perilous place for a boy of his . . . his youth and beauty. (I was about to say innocence, but in honesty I must not, even though I know that thereby I banish the word from the language, for if it is denied to him then it has no meaning anymore. I speak in riddles. They shall be solved. My poor Raphaël! they destroyed us both.)

• • •

I rose and went in search of the Canon, and was directed to the *arboretum*, a name which conjured up a pleasant image of fruit trees in flower, dappled green shade, and little leafy paths where astronomers might stroll, discussing the universe. What I found was a crooked field fastened to a hill behind the castle, with a few stunted bushes and a cabbage patch—and, need I say, no sign of the Canon. As I stamped away, sick of being sent on false chases, a figure rose up among the cabbages and hailed me. Today Bishop Giese was rigged out again in his peasant costume. The sight of those breeches and that jerkin irritated me greatly. Do these damn Catholics, I wondered, never do else but dress up and pose? His hands were crusted with clay, and when he drew near I caught a strong whiff of horse manure. He was in a hearty mood. I suppose it went with the outfit. He said:

'*Grüss Gott*, Herr von Lauchen! The Doctor informs me that you are ill. Not gravely so, I trust? Our Prussian climate is uncongenial, although here, on Castle Hill, we are spared the debilitating vapours of the plain—which are yet not so bad as those that rise from the Frisches Haff at Frauenburg, eh, *meinherr*? Ho ho. Let me look at you, my son. Well, the nature of your ailment is plain: Saturn, malign star . . .' And he proceeded to parrot verbatim the Canon's little sermon in praise of the Graces. I listened in silence, with a curled lip. I was at once amused and appalled: amused that this clown should steal the master's words and pretend they were his own, appalled at the notion, which suddenly struck me, that the Canon may not after all have been mocking me, but may have been actually serious about that fool Ficino's cabalistic nonsense! O, I know well the baleful influence which Saturn wields over my life; I know that the Graces are good; but I also know that a hectacre of crocuses would not have eased my heartsickness one whit. *Crocuses!* However, as I was to discover, the Canon neither believed nor disbelieved Ficino's theories, no more than he believed nor disbelieved the contents of any of the score or so set speeches with which he had long ago armed himself, and from which he could choose a ready response to any situation. All that mattered to him was the saying, not what was said; words were the empty rituals with which he held the world at bay. Copernicus did not believe in truth. I think I have said that before.

Giese put his soiled hand on my arm and led me along a path below the castle wall. When he had finished his dissertation on the state of my health, he paused and glanced at me with a peculiar, thoughtful look, like that of an undertaker speculatively eyeing a sick man. The last remaining patches of the morning's mist clung about us like old rags, and the slowly ascending sun shed a damp weak light upon the battlements above. The world seemed old and tired. I wanted to find the Canon, to wrest from him his secrets, to thrust fame upon his unwilling head. I wanted *action*. I was young. The Bishop said:

'You come, I believe, from Wittenberg?'

'Yes. I am a Lutheran.'

My directness startled him. He smiled wanly, and nodded his large head up and down very rapidly, as though to shake off that dreaded word I had uttered; he withdrew his hand carefully from my arm.

'Quite so, my dear sir, quite so,' he said, 'you are a Lutheran, as you admi— as you say. Now, I have no desire to dispute with you the issues of this tragic schism which has rent our Church, believe me. I might remind you that Father Luther was not the first to recognise the necessity for reform—but, be that as it may, we shall not argue. A man must live with his own conscience, in that much at least I would agree with you. So. You are a Lutheran. You admit it. There it rests. However, I cannot pretend that your presence in Prussia is not an embarrassment. It is not to me, you understand; the world pays scant heed to events here in humble Löbau. No, Herr von Lauchen, I refer to one who is dear to us both: I mean of course our *domine praeceptor*, Doctor Nicolaus. It is to him that your presence is an embarrassment, and, perhaps, a danger even. But now I see I have offended you. Let me explain. You have not been long in Prussia, therefore you cannot be expected to appreciate the situation prevailing here. Tell me, are you not puzzled by the Doctor's unwillingness to give his knowledge to the world, to publish his masterpiece? It would surprise you, would it not, if I were to tell you that it is not doubt as to the validity of his conclusions that makes him hesitate, nothing like that, no—but fear. So it is, Herr von Lauchen: *fear*.'

He paused again, again we paced the path in silence. I have called Giese a fool, but that was only a term of abuse: he was no fool. We left the castle walls behind, and descended a little way the wooded slope. The trees were tall. Three rabbits fled at our approach. I stumbled on a fallen bough. The pines were silvery, each single needle adorned with a delicate filigree of beaded mist. How strange, the clarity with which I remember that moment! Thus, even as the falcon plummets, the sparrow snatches a last look at her world. Bishop Giese, laying his talons on my arm again, began to chant, I think that is the word, in Latin:

'Painful is the task I must perform, and tell to one—from Wittenberg!—of the storm of envy which surrounds our learned friend. *Meinherr*, I pray you, to my tale attend with caution and forbearance, and don't feel that in these few bare facts you see revealed a plot hatched in the corridors of Rome. This evil is the doing of one alone: do you know the man Dantiscus, Ermland's Bishop (Johannes Flachsbinder his name, a Danzig sop)? Copernicus he hates, and from jealousy these many years he has right zealously persecuted him. Why so? you ask, but to answer you, that is a task, I fear, beyond me. Why ever do the worst detest the best, and mediocrities thirst to see great minds brought low? It is the world. Besides, this son of Zelos, dimwitted churl though he be, thinks Prussia has but room for one great mind—that's his! The fellow's moon mad, *certes*. Now, to achieve his aims, and ruin our *magister*, he defames his name, puts it about he shares his bed with his *focaria*, whom he has led into foul sin to satisfy his lust. My friend, you stare, as though you cannot trust your ears. This is but one of many lies this Danziger has told! And in the eyes of all the world the Doctor's reputation is destroyed, and mocking condemnation, he believes, would greet his book. Some years ago, at Elbing, ignorant peasants jeered a waxwork figure of Copernicus that was displayed in a carnival farce. Thus Dantiscus wins, and our friend keeps silent, fearing to trust his brilliant theories to the leering mob. And so, *meinherr*, the work of twoscore years lies fallow and unseen. Therefore, I beg you, do not leave us yet. We must try to make him reconsider—*but hush! here is the Doctor now. Mind, do not say what secrets I have told you!*—Ah Nicolaus, good day.'

We had left the wood and entered the courtyard by a little low postern gate. Had Giese not pointed him out, I would not have noticed the Canon skulking under an archway, watching us intently with a peculiar fixed grin on his grey face. Out of new knowledge, I looked upon him in a new light. Yes, now I could see in him (so I thought!) a man enfettered, whose every action was constrained by the paramount need for secrecy and caution, and I felt on his behalf a burning sense of outrage. I would have flung myself to my knees before him, had there not been still vivid in my mind the memory of a previous genuflection. Instead, I contented myself with a terrible glare, that was meant to signify my willingness to take on an army of Dantiscuses at his command. (And yet, behind it all, I was confused, and even suspicious: what was it exactly that they required of me?) I had forgotten my declared intention of leaving that day; in fact, I had said it merely to elicit some genuine response from that night-capped oracle in my chamber, and certainly I had not imagined that this thoughtless threat would provoke the panic which apparently it had. I determined to proceed with care—but of course, like the young fool that I was, I had no sooner decided on caution than I abandoned it, and waded headlong into the mire. I said:

'*Meister*, we must return to Frauenburg at once! I intend to make a copy of your great work, and take it to a printer that I know at Nuremberg, who is discreet, and a specialist in such books. You must trust me, and delay no longer!'

In my excitement I expected some preposterously dramatic reaction from the Canon to this naked challenge to his secretiveness, but he merely shrugged and said:

'There is no need to go to Frauenburg; the book is here.'

I said:

'But but but but but—!'

And Giese said:

'Why Nicolaus—!'

And the Canon, glancing at us both with a mixture of contempt and distaste, answered:

'I assumed that Herr von Lauchen did not journey all the way from Wittenberg merely for amusement. You came here to learn of my theory of the revolutions of the spheres, did you not? Then so you shall. I have the manuscript with me. Come this way.'

We went all three into the castle, and the Canon straightway fetched the manuscript from his room. The events of the morning had moved so swiftly that my poor brain, already bemused by illness, could not cope with them, and I was in a state of shock—yet not so shocked that I did not note how the old man vainly tried to appear unconcerned when he surrendered to me his life's work, that I did not feel his trembling fingers clutch at the manuscript in a momentary spasm of misgiving as it passed between us. When the deed was done he stepped back a pace, and that awful uncontrollable grin took hold of his face again, and Bishop Giese, hovering near us, gave a kind of whistle of relief, and I, fearing that the Canon might change his mind and try to snatch the thing away from me, rose immediately and made off with it to the window.

DE REVOLUTIONIBUS ORBIUM MUNDI
—for mathematicians only—

• • •

How to express my emotions, the strange jumble of feelings kindled within me, as I gazed upon the living myth which I held in my hands, the key to the secrets of the universe? This book for years had filled my dreams and obsessed my waking hours so completely that now I could hardly comprehend the reality, and the words in the crabbed script seemed not to speak, but to sing rather, so that the rolling grandeur of the title boomed like a flourish of celestial trumpets, to the accompaniment of the wordly fiddling of the motto with its cautious admonition, and I smiled, foolishly, helplessly, at the inexplicable miracle of this music of Heaven and Earth. But then I turned the pages, and chanced upon the diagram of a universe in the centre of which stands Sol in the splendour of eternal immobility, and the music was swept away, and my besotted smile with it, and a new and wholly unexpected sensation took hold of me. It was sorrow! sorrow that old Earth should be thus deposed, and cast out into the darkness of the firmament, there to prance and spin at the behest of a tyrannical, mute god of fire. I grieved, friends, for our diminishment! O, it was not that I did not already know that Copernicus's theory postulated a heliocentric world—everyone knew that—and anyway I had been permitted to read Melanchthon's well-thumbed copy of the *Commentariolus*. Besides, as everyone also knows, Copernicus was not the first to set the Sun at the centre. Yes, I had for a long time known what this Prussian was about, but it was not until that morning at Löbau Castle that I at last realised, in a kind of fascinated horror, the full consequences of this work of cosmography. Beloved Earth! he banished you forever into darkness. And yet, what does it matter? The sky shall be forever blue, and the earth shall forever blossom in spring, and this planet shall forever be the centre of all we know. I believe it.

• • •

I read the entire manuscript there and then; that is not of course to say that I read every word: rather, I opened it up, as a surgeon opens a limb, and plunged the keen blade of my intellect into its vital centres, thus laying bare the quivering arteries leading to the heart. And there, in the knotted cords of that heart, I made a strange discovery . . . but more of that presently. When at last I lifted my eyes from those pages, I found myself alone. The light was fading in the windows. It was evening. The day had departed, with Giese and Copernicus, unnoticed. My brain ached, but I forced it to think, to seek out a small persistent something which had been lodging in my thoughts since morning, biding its time. It was the memory of how, when in the courtyard I challenged him to surrender the manuscript to me, Copernicus had for an instant, just for an instant only, cast off the timorous churchman's mask to reveal behind it an icy scorn, a cold, cruel arrogance. I did not know why I had remembered it, why it seemed so significant; I was not even sure that I had not imagined it; but it troubled me. *What is it they want me to do?* Go carefully, Rheticus, I told myself, hardly knowing what I meant . . .

I found Copernicus and Giese in the great hall of the castle, seated in silence in tall carved chairs on either side of the enormous hearth, on which, despite the mildness of the evening, stacked logs were blazing fiercely. The windows, set high up in the walls, let in but little of the evening's radiance, and in the gloom the robes of the two still figures seemed to flow and merge into the elaborate flutings of the thrones on which they sat, so that to my bruised perception they appeared limbless, a pair of severed heads, ghastly in the fire's crimson glow. Copernicus had put himself as close to the blaze as he could manage without risking combustion, but still he looked cold. As I entered the arc of flickering firelight, I found that he was watching me. I was weary, and incapable of subtlety, and once again I ignored my own injunction to go carefully. I held up the manuscript and said:

'I have read it, and find it is all I had expected it would be, more than I had hoped; will you allow me to take it to Nuremberg, to Petreius the printer?'

He did not answer immediately. The silence stretched out around us until it seemed to creak. At length he said:

'That is a question which we cannot discuss, yet.'

At that, as though he had been given a signal, the Bishop stirred himself and put an end to the discussion (discussion!). Had I eaten? Why then, I must! He would have Raphaël bring me supper in my room, for I should retire, it was late, I was ill and in need of rest. And, like a sleepy child, I allowed myself to be led away, too tired to protest, clutching the manuscript, babe's favourite toy, to my breast. I looked back at Copernicus, and the severed head smiled and nodded, as if to say: sleep, little one, sleep now. My room looked somehow different, but I could not say in what way, until next morning when I noticed the desk, amply stocked with writing implements and paper, which they installed without my knowing. O the cunning!

(*Doctor Copernicus*, 1976)

The Harmony of the Spheres

He was after the eternal laws that govern the harmony of the world. Through awful thickets, in darkest night, he stalked his fabulous prey. Only the stealthiest of hunters had been vouchsafed a shot at it, and he, grossly armed with the blunderbuss of his defective mathematics, what chance had he? crowded round by capering clowns hallooing and howling and banging their bells whose names were Paternity, and Responsibility, and Domestgod-damnedicity. Yet O, he had seen it once, briefly, that mythic bird, a speck, no more than a speck, soaring at an immense height. It was not to be forgotten, that glimpse.

The 19th of July, 1595, at 27 minutes precisely past 11 in the morning: that was the moment. He was then, if his calculations were accurate, 23 years, 6 months, 3 weeks, 1 day, 20 hours and 57 minutes, give or take a few tens of seconds, old.

Afterwards he spent much time poring over these figures, searching out hidden significances. The set of date and time, added together, gave a product 1,652. Nothing there that he could see. Combining the integers of that total he got 14, which was twice 7, the mystical number. Or perhaps it was simply that 1652 was to be the year of his death. He would be eighty-one. (He laughed: with his health?) He turned to the second set, his age on that momentous July day. These figures were hardly more promising. Combined, not counting the year, they made a quantity whose only significance seemed to be that it was divisible by 5, leaving him the product 22, the age at which he had left Tübingen. Well, that was not much. But if he halved 22 and subtracted 5 (that 5 again!), he got 6, and it was at six that he had been taken by his mother to the top of Gallows Hill to view the comet of 1577. And 5, what did that busy 5 signify? Why, it was the number of the intervals between the planets, the number of notes in the arpeggio of the spheres, the five-tone scale of the world's music! . . . if his calculations were accurate.

He had been working for six months on what was to become the *Mysterium cosmographicum*, his first book. His circumstances were easier then. He was still unmarried, had not yet even heard Barbara's name, and was living at the Stiftsschule in a room that was cramped and cold, but his own. Astronomy at first had been a pastime merely, an extension of the mathematical games he had liked to play as a student at Tübingen. As time went on, and his hopes for his new life in Graz turned sour, this exalted playing more and more obsessed him. It was a thing apart, a realm of order to set against the ramshackle real world in which he was imprisoned. For Graz was a kind of prison. Here in this town, which they were pleased to call a city, the Styrian capital, ruled over by narrow-minded merchants and a papist prince, Johannes Kepler's spirit was in chains, his talents manacled, his great speculative gift strapped upon the rack of schoolmastering—right! yes! laughing and snarling, mocking himself—endungeoned, by God! He was twenty-three.

It was a pretty enough town. He was impressed when first he glimpsed it, the river, the spires, the castle-crowned hill, all blurred and bright under a shower of April rain. There seemed a largeness here, a generosity, which he fancied he could see even in the breadth and balance of the buildings, so different from the beetling architecture of his native Württemberg towns. The people too appeared different. They were promenaders much given to public discourse and dispute, and Johannes was reminded that he had come a long way from home, that he was almost in Italy. But it was all an illusion. Presently, when he had examined more closely the teeming streets, he realised that the filth and the stench, the cripples and beggars and berserks, were the same here as anywhere else. True, they were Protestant loonies, it was Protestant filth, and a Protestant heaven those spires sought, hence the wider air hereabout: but the Archduke was a rabid Catholic, and the place was crawling with Jesuits, and even then at the Stiftsschule there was talk of disestablishment and closure.

He, who had been such a brilliant student, detested teaching. In his classes he experienced a weird frustration. The lessons he had to expound were always, always just somewhere off to the side of what really interested him, so that he was forever holding himself in check, as a boatman presses a skiff against the run of the river. The effort exhausted him, left him sweating and dazed. Frequently the rudder gave way, and he was swept off helplessly on the flood of his enthusiasm, while his poor dull students stood abandoned on the receding bank, waving weakly.

The Stiftsschule was run in the manner of a military academy. Any master who did not beat blood out of his boys was considered lax. (Johannes did his best, but on the one occasion when he could not avoid administering a flogging his victim was a great grinning fellow almost as old as he, and a head taller.) The standard of learning was high, sustained by the committee of supervisors and its phalanx of inspectors. Johannes greatly feared the inspectors. They dropped in on classes unannounced, often in pairs, and listened in silence from the back, while his handful of pupils sat with arms folded, hugging themselves, and gazed at him, gleefully attentive, waiting for him to make a fool of himself. Mostly he obliged, twitching and stammering as he wrestled with the tangled threads of his discourse.

'You must try to be calm,' Rector Papius told him. 'You tend to rush at things, I think, forgetting perhaps that your students do not have your quickness of mind. They cannot follow you, they become confused, and then they complain to me, or . . .' he smiled '. . . or their fathers do.'

'I know, I know,' Johannes said, looking at his hands. They sat in the rector's room overlooking the central courtyard of the school. It was raining. There was wind in the chimney, and balls of smoke rolled out of the fireplace and hung in the air around them, making his eyes sting. 'I talk too quickly, and say things before I have had time to consider my words. Sometimes in the middle of a class I change my mind and begin to speak of some other subject, or realise that what I have been saying is imprecise and begin all over again to explain the matter in more detail.' He shut his mouth, squirming; he was making it worse. Dr Papius frowned at the fire. 'You see, Herr Rector, it is my *cupiditas speculandi* that leads me astray.'

'Yes,' the older man said mildly, scratching his chin, 'there is in you perhaps too much . . . passion. But I would not wish to see a young man suppress his natural enthusiasm. Perhaps, Master Kepler, you were not meant for teaching?'

Johannes looked up in alarm, but the rector was regarding him only with concern, and a touch of amusement. He was a gentle, somewhat scattered person, a scholar and physician; no doubt he knew what it was to stand all day in class wishing to be elsewhere. He had always shown kindness to this strange little man from Tübingen, who at first had so appalled the more stately members of the staff with his frightful manners and disconcerting blend of friendliness, excitability and arrogance. Papius had more than once defended him to the supervisors.

'I am not a good teacher,' Johannes mumbled, 'I know. My gifts lie in other directions.'

'Ah yes,' said the rector, coughing; 'your astronomy.' He peered at the inspectors' report on the desk before him. 'You teach *that* well, it seems?'

'But I have no students!'

'Not your fault—Pastor Zimmermann himself says here that astronomy is not everyone's meat. He recommends that you be put to teaching arithmetic and Latin rhetoric in the upper school, until we can find more pupils eager to become astronomers.'

Johannes understood that he was being laughed at, albeit gently.

'They are ignorant barbarians!' he cried suddenly, and a log fell out of the fire. 'All they care for is hunting and warring and looking for fat dowries for their heirs. They hate and despise philosophy and philosophers. They they they—they do not *deserve* . . .' He broke off, pale with rage and alarm. These mad outbursts must stop.

Rector Papius smiled the ghost of a smile. 'The inspectors?'

'The . . . ?'

'I understood you to be describing our good Pastor Zimmermann and his fellow inspectors. It was of them we were speaking.'

Johannes put a hand to his brow. 'I—I meant of course those who will not send their sons for proper instruction.'

'Ah. But I think, you know, there are many among our noble families, and among the merchants also, who would consider astronomy *not* a proper subject for their sons to study. They burn at the stake poor wretches who have had less dealings with the moon than you do in your classes. I am not defending this benighted attitude to your science, you understand, but only drawing it to your attention, as it is my—'

'But—'

'—As it is my *duty* to do.'

They sat and eyed each other, Johannes sullen, the rector apologetically firm. Grey rain wept on the window, the smoke billowed. Johannes sighed. 'You see, Herr Rector, I cannot—'

'But try, will you, Master Kepler: try?'

He tried, he tried, but how could he be calm? His brain teemed. A chaos of ideas and images churned within him. In class he fell silent more and more frequently, standing stock still, deaf to the sniggering of his students, like a crazed hierophant. He traipsed the streets in a daze, and more than once was nearly run down by horses. He wondered if he were ill. Yet it was more as if he were . . . in love! In love, that is, not with any individual object, but generally. The notion, when he hit on it, made him laugh.

At the beginning of 1595 he received a sign, if not from God himself then from a lesser deity surely, one of those whose task is to encourage the elect of this world. His post at the Stiftsschule carried with it the title of calendar maker for the province of Styria. The previous autumn, for a fee of twenty florins from the public coffers, he had drawn up an astrological calendar for the coming year, predicting great cold and an invasion by the Turks. In January there was such a frost that shepherds in the Alpine farms froze to death on the hillsides, while on the first day of the new year the Turk launched a campaign which, it was said, left the whole country from Neustadt to Vienna devastated. Johannes was charmed with this prompt vindication of his powers (and secretly astonished). O a sign, yes, surely. He set to work in earnest on the cosmic mystery.

He had not the solution, yet; he was still posing the questions. The first of these was: Why are there just six planets in the solar system? Why not five, or seven, or a thousand for that matter? No one, so far as he knew, had ever thought to ask it before. It became for him the fundamental mystery. Even the formulation of such a question struck him as a singular achievement.

He was a Copernican. At Tübingen his teacher Michael Mästlin had introduced him to that Polish master's world system. There was for Kepler something almost holy, something redemptive almost, in that vision of an ordered clockwork of sun-centred spheres. And yet he saw, from the beginning, that there was a defect, a basic flaw in it which had forced Copernicus into all manner of small tricks and evasions. For while the *idea* of the system, as outlined in the first part of *De revolutionibus*, was self-evidently an eternal truth, there was in the working out of the theory an ever increasing accumulation of paraphernalia—the epicycles, the equant point, all that—necessitated surely by some awful original accident. It was as if the master had let fall from trembling hands his marvellous model of the world's working, and on the ground it had picked up in its spokes and the fine-spun wire of its frame bits of dirt and dead leaves and the dried husks of worn-out concepts.

Copernicus was dead fifty years, but now for Johannes he rose again, a mournful angel that must be wrestled with before he could press on to found his own system. He might sneer at the epicycles and the equant point, but they were not to be discarded easily. The Canon from Ermland had been, he suspected, a greater mathematician than ever Styria's calendar maker would be. Johannes raged against his own inadequacies. He might know there was a defect, and a grave one, in the Copernican system, but it was a different matter to find it. Nights he would start awake thinking he had heard the old man his adversary laughing at him, goading him.

And then he made a discovery. He realised that it was not so much in what he *had* done that Copernicus had erred: his sin had been one of omission. The great man, Johannes now understood, had been concerned only to see the nature of things demonstrated, not explained. Dissatisfied with the Ptolemaic conception of the world, Copernicus had devised a better, a more elegant system, which yet, for all its seeming radicalism, was intended only, in the schoolman's phrase, to save the phenomena, to set up a model which need not be empirically true, but only plausible according to the observations.

Then had Copernicus believed that his system was a picture of reality, or had he been satisfied that it agreed, more or less, with appearances? Or did the question arise? There was no sustained music in that old man's world, only chance airs and fragments, broken harmonies, scribbled cadences. It would be Kepler's task to draw it together, to make it sing. For truth was the missing music. He lifted his eyes to the bleak light of winter in the window and hugged himself. Was it not wonderful, the logic of things? Troubled by an inelegance in the Ptolemaic system, Copernicus had erected his great monument to the sun, in which there was embedded the flaw, the pearl, for Johannes Kepler to find.

But the world had not been created in order that it should sing. God was not frivolous. From the start he held to this, that the song was incidental, arising naturally from the harmonious relation of things. Truth itself was, in a way, incidental. Harmony was all. (Something wrong, something wrong! but he ignored it.) And harmony, as Pythagoras had shown, was the product of mathematics. Therefore the harmony of the spheres must conform to a mathematical pattern. That such a pattern existed Johannes had no doubt. It was his principal axiom that nothing in the world was created by God without a plan the basis of which is to be found in geometrical quantities. And man is godlike precisely, and only, because he can think in terms that mirror the divine pattern. He had written: The mind grasps a matter so much the more correctly the closer it approaches pure quantities as its source. Therefore his method for the task of identifying the cosmic design must be, like the design itself, founded in geometry.

Spring came to Graz and, as always, took him by surprise. He looked out one day and there it was in the flushed air, a quickening, a sense of vast sudden swooping, as if the earth had hurtled into a narrowing bend of space. The city sparkled, giving off light from throbbing windowpanes and polished stone, from blue and gold pools of rain in the muddied streets. Johannes kept much indoors. It disturbed him, how closely the season matched his present mood of restlessness and obscure longing. The Shrovetide carnival milled under his window unheeded, except when a comic bugle blast or the drunken singing of revellers shattered his concentration, and he bared his teeth in a soundless snarl.

Perhaps he was wrong, perhaps the world was not an ordered construct governed by immutable laws? Perhaps God, after all, like the creatures of his making, prefers the temporal to the eternal, the makeshift to the perfected, the toy bugles and bravos of misrule to the music of the spheres. But no, no, despite these doubts, no: his God was above all a god of order. The world works by geometry, for geometry is the earthly paradigm of divine thought.

Late into the nights he laboured, and stumbled through his days in a trance. Summer came. He had been working without cease for six months, and all he had achieved, if achievement it could be called, was the conviction that it was not with the planets themselves, their positions and velocities, that he must chiefly deal, but with the intervals between their orbits. The values for these distances were those set out by Copernicus, which were not much more reliable than Ptolemy's, but he had to assume, for his sanity's sake, that they were sound enough for his purpose. Time and time over he combined and recombined them, searching for the relation which they hid. Why are there just six planets? That was a question, yes. But a profounder asking was, why are there just these distances between them? He waited, listening for the whirr of wings. On that ordinary morning in July came the answering angel. He was in class. The day was warm and bright. A fly buzzed in the tall window, a rhomb of sunlight lay at his feet. His students, stunned with boredom, gazed over his head out of glazed eyes. He was demonstrating a theorem out of Euclid—afterwards, try as he might, he could not remember which—and had prepared on the blackboard an equilateral triangle. He took up the big wooden compass, and immediately, as it always contrived to do, the monstrous thing bit him. With his wounded thumb in his mouth he turned to the easel and began to trace two circles, one within the triangle touching it on its three sides, the second circumscribed and intersecting the vertices. He stepped back, into that box of dusty sunlight, and blinked, and suddenly something, his heart perhaps, dropped and bounced, like an athlete performing a miraculous feat upon a trampoline, and he thought, with rapturous inconsequence: I shall live forever. The ratio of the outer to the inner circle was identical with that of the orbits of Saturn and Jupiter, the furthermost planets, and here, within these circles, determining that ratio, was inscribed an equilateral triangle, the fundamental figure in geometry. Put therefore between the orbits of Jupiter and Mars a square, between Mars and earth a pentagon, between earth and Venus a . . . Yes. O yes. The diagram, the easel, the very walls of the room dissolved to a shimmering liquid, and young Master Kepler's lucky pupils were treated to the rare and gratifying spectacle of a teacher swabbing tears from his eyes and trumpeting juicily into a dirty handkerchief.

(*Kepler*, 1981)

Fern House

I was born down there, in the south, you knew that. The best memories I have of the place are of departures from it. I'm thinking of Christmas trips to Dublin when I was a child, boarding the train in the dark and watching through the mist of my breath on the window the frost-bound landscape assembling as the dawn came up. At a certain spot every time, I can see it still, day would at last achieve itself. The place was a river bend, where the train slowed down to cross a red metal bridge. Beyond the river a flat field ran to the edge of a wooded hill, and at the foot of the hill there was a house, not very big, solitary and square, with a steep roof. I would gaze at that silent house and wonder, in a hunger of curiosity, what lives were lived there. Who stacked that firewood, hung that holly wreath, left those tracks in the hoarfrost on the hill? I can't express the odd aching pleasure of that moment. I knew, of course, that those hidden lives wouldn't be much different from my own. But that was the point. It wasn't the exotic I was after, but the *ordinary*, that strangest and most elusive of enigmas.

Now I had another house to gaze at, and wonder about, with something of the same remote prurience. The lodge was like a sentry box. It stood, what, a hundred, two hundred yards from the house, yet I couldn't look out my window without spotting some bit of business going on. The acoustics of the place too afforded an alarming intimacy. I could clearly hear the frequent cataclysms of the upstairs lavatory, and my day began with the pips for the morning news on the radio in Charlotte Lawless's kitchen. Then

I would see Charlotte herself, in wellingtons and an old cardigan, hauling out a bucket of feed to the henhouse. Next comes Ottilie, in a sleepy trance, with the child by the hand. He is off to school. He carries his satchel like a hunchback's hump. Edward is last, I am at work before I spy him about his mysterious business. It all has the air of a pastoral mime, with the shepherd's wife and the shepherd, and Cupid and the maid, and, scribbling within a crystal cave, myself, a haggard-eyed Damon.

I had them spotted for patricians from the start. The big house, Edward's tweeds, Charlotte's fine-boned slender grace that the dowdiest of clothes could not mask, even Ottilie's awkwardness, all this seemed the unmistakable stamp of their class. Protestants, of course, landed, the land gone now to gombeen men and compulsory purchase, the family fortune wasted by tax, death duties, inflation. But how bravely, how beautifully they bore their losses! Observing them, I understood that breeding such as theirs is a preparation not for squiredom itself, but for that distant day, which for the Lawlesses had arrived, when the trappings of glory are gone and only style remains. All nonsense, of course, but to me, product of a post-peasant Catholic upbringing, they appeared perfected creatures. Oh, don't accuse me of snobbery. This was something else, a fascination before the spectacle of pure refinement. Shorn of the dull encumbrances of wealth and power, they were free to be purely what they were. The irony was, the form of life their refinement took was wholly familiar to me: wellington boots, henhouses, lumpy sweaters. Familiar, but, ah, transfigured. The nicety of tone and gesture to which I might aspire, they achieved by instinct, unwittingly. Their ordinariness was inimitable.

Sunday mornings were a gala performance at Ferns. At twenty to ten, the bells pealing down in the village, a big old-fashioned motor car would feel its way out of the garage. They are off to church. An hour later they return, minus Edward, with Charlotte at the wheel. Wisps of tiny music from the radio in the kitchen come to me. Charlotte is getting the dinner ready—no, she is preparing a light lunch. Not for them surely the midday feeds of my childhood, the mighty roast, the steeped marrowfat peas, the block of runny ice-cream on its cool perch on the bathroom windowsill. Edward tramps up the hill, hands in his pockets, shoulders rolling. In front of the house he pauses, looks at the broken fanlight, and then goes in, the door shuts, the train moves on, over the bridge.

My illusions about them soon began, if not to crumble, then to modify. One day I struck off past the orchard into the lands at the back of the house. All round were the faint outlines of what must once have been an ornate garden. Here was a pond, the water an evil green, overhung by a sadness of willows. I waded among hillocks of knee-high grass, feeling watched. The day was hot, with a burning breeze. Everything swayed. A huge bumble bee blundered past my ear. When I looked back, the only sign of the house was a single chimney pot against the sky. I found myself standing on the ruins of a tennis court. A flash of reflected sunlight caught my eye. In a hollow at the far side of the court there was a long low glasshouse. I stumbled down the bank, as others in another time must have stumbled, laughing, after a white ball rolling inexorably into the future. The door of the glasshouse made a small sucking sound when I opened it. The heat was a soft slap in the face. Row upon row of clay pots on trestle tables ran the length of the place, like an exercise in perspective, converging at the far end on the figure of Charlotte Lawless standing with her back to me. She wore sandals and a wide green skirt, a white shirt, her tattered sun hat. I spoke, and she turned, startled. A pair of spectacles hung on a cord about her neck. Her fingers were caked with clay. She dabbed the back of a wrist to her forehead. I noticed the tiny wrinkles around her eyes, the faint down on her upper lip.

I said I hadn't known the hothouse was here, I was impressed, she must be an enthusiastic gardener. I was babbling. She looked at me carefully. 'It's how we make our living,' she said. I apologised, I wasn't sure for what, and then laughed, and felt foolish. There are people to whom you feel compelled to explain yourself. 'I got lost,' I said, 'in the garden, believe it or not, and then I saw you here, and . . .' She was still watching me, hanging on my words; I wondered if she were perhaps hard of hearing. The possibility was oddly touching. Or was it simply that she wasn't really listening? Her face was empty of all save a sense of something withheld. She made me think of someone standing on tiptoe behind a glass barrier, every part of her, eyes, lips, the gloves that she clutches, straining to become the radiant smile that awaits the beloved's arrival. She was all potential. On the bench where she had been working lay an open pair of secateurs, and a cut plant with purple flowers.

We went among the tables, wading through a dead and standing pool of air, and she explained her work, naming the plants, the strains and hybrids, in a neutral voice. Mostly it was plain commercial stuff, apple treelets, flower bulbs, vegetables, but there were some strange things, with strange pale stalks, and violent blossoms, and bearded fruit dangling among the glazed, still leaves. Her father had started the business, and she had taken it over when her brother was killed. 'We still trade as Grainger Nurseries.' I nodded dully. The heat, the sombre hush, the contrast between the stillness here and the windy tumult pressing against the glass all around us, provoked in me a kind of excited apprehension, as if I were being led, firmly, but with infinite tact, into peril. Ranked colours thronged me round, crimson, purples, and everywhere green and more green, glabrous and rubbery and somehow ferocious. 'In Holland,' she said, 'in the seventeenth century, a nurseryman could sell a new strain of tulip for twenty thousand pounds.' It had the flat sound of something read into a recorder.

She looked at me, her hands folded, waiting for my comment. I smiled, and shook my head, trying to look amazed. We reached the door. The summer breeze seemed a hurricane after the silence within. My shirt clung to my back. I shivered. We walked a little way down a path under an arch of rhododendrons. The tangled arthritic branches let in scant light, and there was a smell of mossy rot reminiscent of the tang of damp flesh. Then at once, unaccountably, we were at the rear of the house. I was confused; the garden had surreptitiously taken me in a circle. Charlotte murmured something, and walked away. On the drive under the sycamores I paused and looked back. The house was impassive, except where a curtain in an open upstairs window waved frantically in the breeze. What did I expect? Some revelation? A face watching me through sky-reflecting glass, a voice calling my name? There was nothing—but something had happened, all the same.

• • •

The child's name was Michael. I couldn't fit him to the Lawlesses. True, he was given, like Edward, to skulking. I would come upon him in the lanes roundabout, poking in the hedge and muttering to himself, or just standing, with his hands behind him as if hiding something, waiting for me to pass by. Sitting with a book under a tree in the orchard one sunny afternoon, I looked up to find him perched among the branches, studying me. Another time, towards twilight, I spotted him on the road, gazing off intently at something below the brow of the hill where he stood. He had not heard me behind him, and I paused, wondering what it was that merited such rapt attention. Then with a pang I heard it, rising through the stillness of evening, the tinny music of a carnival in the village below.

One evening Edward stopped at the lodge on his way up from the village. He had the raw look of a man lately dragged out of bed and thrust under a cold tap, his eyes were red-rimmed, his hair lank. He hummed and hawed, scuffing the gravel of the roadside, and then abruptly said: 'Come up and have a bite to eat.' I think that was the first time I had been inside the house. It was dim, and faintly musty. There was a hurley stick in the umbrella stand, and withered daffodils in a vase on the hall table. In an alcove a clock feathered the silence and let drop a single wobbly chime. Edward paused to consult a pocket watch, frowning. In the fussy half-light his face had the grey sheen of putty. He hiccuped softly.

Dinner was in the big whitewashed kitchen at the back of the house. I had expected a gaunt dining room, linen napkins with a faded initial, a bit of old silver negligently laid. And it was hardly dinner, more a high tea, with cold cuts and limp lettuce, and a bottle of salad cream the colour of gruel. The tablecloth was plastic. Charlotte and Ottilie were already halfway through their meal. Charlotte looked in silence for a moment at my midriff, and I knew at once I shouldn't have come. Ottilie set a place for me. The barred window looked out on a vegetable garden, and then a field, and then the blue haze of distant woods. Sunlight through the leaves of a chestnut tree in the yard was a ceaseless shift and flicker in the corner of my eye. Edward began to tell a yarn he had heard in the village, but got muddled, and sat staring blearily at his plate, breathing. Someone coughed. Ottilie pursed her lips and began to whistle silently. Charlotte with an abrupt spastic movement turned to me and in a loud voice said:

'Do you think we'll give up neutrality?'

'Give up . . . ?' The topic was in the papers. 'Well, I don't know, I—'

'Yes, tell us now,' Edward said, suddenly stirring himself and thrusting his great bull head at me, 'tell us what you think, I'm very interested, we're all very interested, aren't we all very interested? A man like you would know all about these things.'

'I think we'd be very—'

'Down here of course we haven't a clue. Crowd of bogtrotters!' He grinned, snorting softly and pawing the turf.

'I think we'd be very unwise to give it up,' I said.

'And what about that power station they want to put up down there at Carnsore? Bloody bomb, blow us all up, some clown with a hangover press the wrong button, we won't need the Russians. What?' He was looking at Charlotte. She had not spoken. 'Well what's wrong with being ordinary,' he said, 'like any other country, having an army and defending ourselves? Tell me what's wrong with that.' He pouted at us, a big resentful baby.

'What about Switzerland?' Ottilie said; she giggled.

'Switzerland? *Switzerland*? Ha. Milkmen and chocolate factories, and, what was it the fellow said, cuckoo clocks.' He turned his red-rimmed gaze on me again. 'Too many damn neutrals,' he said darkly.

Charlotte sighed, and looked up from her plate at last.

'Edward,' she said, without emphasis. He did not take his eyes off me, but the light went out in his face, and for a moment I almost felt sorry for him. 'Not that I give a damn anyway,' he muttered, and meekly took up his spoon. So much for current affairs.

I cursed myself for being there, and yet I was agog. A trapdoor had been lifted briefly on dim thrashing forms, and now it was shut again. I watched Edward covertly. The sot. He had brought me here for an alibi for his drinking, or to forestall recriminations. I saw the whole thing now, of course: he was a waster, Charlotte kept the place going, everything had been a mistake, even the child. It all fitted, the rueful look and the glazed eye, the skulking, the silences, the tension, that sense I had been aware of from the beginning of being among people facing away from me, intent on something I couldn't see. Even the child's air of sullen autonomy was explained. I looked at Charlotte's fine head, her slender neck, that hand resting by her plate. Leaf-shadow stirred on the table like the shimmer of tears. How could I let her know that I understood everything? The child came in, wrapped in a white bath-towel. His hair was wet, plastered darkly on his skull. When he saw me he drew back, then stepped forward, frowning, a robed and kiss-curled miniature Caesar. Charlotte held out her hand and he went to her. Ottilie winked at him. Edward wore a crooked leer, as if a smile aimed at the centre of his face had landed just wide of the target. Michael mumbled goodnight and departed, shutting the door with both hands on the knob. I turned to Charlotte eagerly. 'Your son,' I said, in a voice that fairly throbbed, 'your son is very . . .' and then floundered, hearing I suppose the tiny tinkle of a warning bell. There was a silence. Charlotte blushed. Suddenly I felt depressed, and . . . prissy, that's the word. What did I know, that gave me the right to judge them? I shouldn't be here at all. I ate a leaf of lettuce, at my back that great rooted blossomer, before me the insistent enigma of other people. I would stay out of their way, keep to the lodge—return to Dublin even. But I knew I wouldn't. Some large lesson seemed laid out here for me.

Ottilie came with me out on the step. She said nothing, but smiled, at once amused and apologetic. And then, I don't know why, the idea came to me. Michael wasn't their child: he was, of course, hers.

(*The Newton Letter*, 1982)

Gabriel Swan

I don't know when it was that I first heard of the existence, if that's the word, of my dead brother. From the start I knew I was the survivor of some small catastrophe, the shock-waves were still reverberating faintly inside me. The mysterious phenomenon that produced us is the result, the textbooks tell me, of a minor arrest in the early development of a single egg, so that the embryonic streak begins dividing by binary fission. I prefer to picture something like a scene from a naughty seaside postcard, the fat lady, apple cheeks, big bubs and mighty buttocks, cloven clean in two by her driven little consort. However, the cause is no matter, only the effect. The perils we had missed were many. We might have been siamese. One of us might have exsanguinated into the other's circulation. Or we might simply have strangled one another. All this we escaped, and surfaced at last, gasping. I came first. My brother was a poor second. Spent swimmer, he drowned in air. My father, when Jack Kay fetched him home at last, looked in dull wonderment at the scene: the infant mewling in its mother's arms, and that lifeless replica of it laid out on the sheet.

My mother feared I too would die. Jack Kay reminded her how his brothers, her homuncles, had succumbed after a day. She nursed me with a kind of vehemence, willing me to live. She would not let me out of her sight. She made a nest for me in the big drawer of the wardrobe in her bedroom. I see myself lying there, unnaturally silent, slowly flexing my bandy arms and legs, like a tortoise stranded on its back. When she leans over me I look at her gropingly and frown. My vague, bleached gaze is that of a traveller come back from somewhere immensely far and strange. At night she lay awake and listened to the furtive noises this new life made, the shufflings and soft sighs, and now and then what sounded like a muffled exclamation of impatience. Later on, when I had learned to walk, and could get away by myself, I developed a private language, a rapid, aquatic burbling, which made people uneasy. It sounded as if I were conversing with someone. Hearing me, my mother would pause outside my door, on the stairs, and I in turn, hearing her, would immediately fall silent. Thus we would remain, the two of us, for a long time, alert, motionless, listening to our own inexplicably palpitant heartbeats. Jack Kay, moustache twitching, wondered aloud if maybe I was wrong in the head.

I feel a tender, retrospective concern, mixed with a trace of contempt, it's true, for this baffled little boy who moves through my memories of those first years in watchful solitude, warily. I clung to the house. My bedroom looked down through two tiny windows into the square, it was like hiding inside a head. I seemed to myself not whole, nor wholly real. Fairy tales fascinated me, there was something dismayingly familiar in them, the mad logic, the discontinuities, the random cruelty of fate. I was brought to a circus, I remember it, the noise, the flashing lights, the brass farts of the band, the incongruous scent of crushed grass coming up between the seats. There were tumbling midgets, and a woman with a snake, and a brilliantined contortionist, thin as a blade, who sat down on his coccyx and assembled a series of agonised tableaux with the stony detachment of a pornographer displaying his wares. It was the clowns, though, that really unnerved me, with their pointy heads and rubber feet and oddly diffused yells, the way they kept tormenting each other, the way the short one would stand bawling in frustration and seeming pain and then whirl round suddenly and smash his lanky companion full in the face with terrible, steely insouciance. I sat without a stir throughout the show, gazing down into the lighted ring with wistful avidity, like that boy in the story who longed to learn how to shudder.

My mother took me for walks, first in a pram, then tottering ahead of her on a sort of reins, then dawdling farther and farther behind her along the hedgerows. Sometimes we went as far as Ashburn and wandered through the unkempt grounds. She showed me the cottage where she was born, behind the stables. Ashburn would be for her always an idyll. The life of the big house, at the far fringes of which she had hovered longingly, she remembered as a languorous mime to the music of tick-tocking tennis balls across green lawns and the far-off bleat of the huntsman's horn on frosty mornings, a scene small and distant, yet perfectly, preciously detailed, atinkle with tiny laughter, like a picture glimpsed of eighteenth-century aristocrats at play in a dappled glade. In the midst of this pretty pastoral stood the cottage, where the frog king Jack Kay had reigned. Here her memories were more precise, of whitewash, and rats in the thatch, the tin bath in front of the fire on Saturday nights, a speckled hen standing on one leg in a patch of sun in the kitchen doorway. And the endless squabbles, of course, the shouting, the boxed ears. Now the stables were falling, the forge where Jack Kay had worked was silent. One day, on an overgrown path, under a huge tree, we met Miss Kitty, the last of the Ashburns of Ashburn Park, a distracted and not very clean maiden lady with a great beaked nose and tangled hair, who talked to us calmly enough for a bit, then turned abruptly and ordered us off the estate, waving her arms and shouting.

There were other spectacles, other frights. I have only a single recollection of Grandfather Swan, a big effigy sitting up in bed laughing in the little house in Queen Street. It was Easter morning, and I was five years old. The sick-room smelled of pipe tobacco and piss. There was a window open beside the bed. The sunlight outside glittered after a recent shower. Grandfather Swan had been shaving, the bowl and cut-throat and bit of looking-glass were still beside him, and there was a fleck of fresh blood on the collar of his nightshirt. His hands trembled, apart from that he seemed quite hale. But he was dying. I was conscious of the solemnity of the occasion. Hard fingers prodded me between the shoulder-blades, and I stepped forward, gazing in awe at the old man's taut white brow and big moustache, the agate nails, the swept-back spikes of iron-grey hair that made it seem as if some force were dragging the head away and up, to the window, to the shining roofs, to the spring sky itself, pale blue and chill like his eyes. He must have talked to me, but I remember only his laugh, not so much a sound as something that surrounded him, like an aura, and not at all benign. For a long time death was to seem a sort of disembodied, sinister merriment sitting in wait for me in that fetid little room.

And yet, I wonder. Is this really a picture of Grandfather Swan, or did I in my imagination that Easter morn wishfully substitute another, tougher old man for this one who was doomed? I mean Jack Kay. The laugh, the alarming fingernails, the wirebrush moustache stained yellow in the middle, all these are his, surely? Jack Kay. To me he was always eighty. He wore his years like a badge of tenacity, grimly, with a kind of truculence. But let me have done with him. He lived at Ashburn, and worked the forge. He was an intermittent drunkard. He married Martha somebody, I forget the name, a scullery maid at the big house. They had children. They were unhappy.

Or at least Martha was. I do not see her clearly. She and Granny Swan died about the same time. They blur into each other, two put-upon old women, somehow not quite life-sized, dropsical, dressed in black, always unwell, always complaining. Their voices are a faint, background murmur, like the twittering of mice behind a wainscot. They must have had some effect, must have contributed a gene or two, yet there remains almost nothing of them. In the matter of heredity they were no match for their menfolk. All the same, there is a memory, which, though neither woman is really in it, is their inspiration. One of those windy damp days of early autumn, with a sky of low, dove-grey cloud, the shining pavements plastered with leaves, and an empty dustbin rolling on its side in the middle of the road. Someone had told me my granny was dead. The news, far from being sad, was strangely exhilarating, and there on that street suddenly I was filled with a snug excitement, which I could not explain, but which was somehow to do with life, with the future. I was not thinking of the living woman, she had been of scant significance to me. In death, however, she had become one with those secret touchstones the thought of which comforted and mysteriously sustained me: small lost animals, the picturesque poor, warnings of gales at sea, the naked feet of Franciscans.

I don't know which of the two women it was that had died. Let the image of that silvery light on that rainy road be a memorial, however paltry, to them both.

• • •

My father in these early memories is a remote, enigmatic and yet peculiarly vivid figure. He worked as a tallyman for a grain merchant. He smelled of chaff, dust, jute, all dry things. He had asthma, and a bad leg. His silences, into which a remark about the weather or a threat of death would drop alike without trace, were a force in our house, like a dull drumming that has gone on for so long it has ceased to be heard but is still vaguely, disturbingly felt. His presence, diffident and fleeting, lent a mysterious weight to the most trivial occasion. He took me to the Fort mountain one day on the bar of his bicycle. It was September, clear and still. The heather was in bloom. We sat on a ditch eating sandwiches, and drinking tepid milk out of lemonade bottles that my mother had filled for us and corked with twists of paper. The sanatorium was high up behind us, hidden among pines except for the steep-pitched roof and a tall cluster of chimneys, closed, silent, alluring. I toyed dreamily with the thought of myself reclining in a timeless swoon on the veranda up there, swaddled in blankets, with the dazzling white building at my back and the sun slowly falling down the sky in front of me, and a wireless somewhere quietly playing danceband music. My father wore a flat cap and a heavy, square-cut overcoat, a size too big for him, that smelled of mothballs. He pointed out a hawk wheeling in the zenith.

—Take the eye out of you, he said, one of them lads.

He was a short man, with long arms and bowed legs. His head was small, which made his trunk seem weightier than it was. With those limbs, that sharp face, the close-set dark eyes, he had something of those stunted little warriors, the dark-haired ones, Pict or Firbolg, I don't know, who stalk the far borders of history. I can see him, in pelts and pointed shoon, limping at twilight through the bracken. A small man, whom the vengeful gods have overlooked. A survivor.

• • •

Sometimes I catch myself dreaming that dream in which childhood is an endless festival, with bands of blond children sweeping through the streets in sunlight, laughing. I can almost see the tunics, the sandalled feet, the white-robed elders watching indulgently from the olive tree's shade. Something must have fed this Attic fantasy, a game of tag, perhaps, on a Sunday evening in summer, the houses open to the tender air, and mothers on the doorsteps, talking, and someone's sister, in her first lipstick, leaning at gaze out of an upstairs window.

The town was twelve thousand souls, three churches and a Methodist hall, a narrow main street, a disused anthracite mine, a river and a silted harbour. Fragments of the past stuck up through the present, rocks in the stream of time: a Viking burial mound, a Norman tower, a stump of immemorial wall like a broken molar. History was rich there. Giraldus Cambrensis knew that shore. The Templars had kept a hospice on the Spike peninsula. The region had played its part in more than one failed uprising. By now the splendour had faded. There was too, I almost forgot, the great war against the Jehovah's Witnesses, I had watched the final rout: a priest punching in the belly a skinny young man in a mac, the crowd shouting, the bundles of *The Watchtower* flying in the air. And there was a celebrated murder, never solved, an old woman battered to death one dark night in her sweetshop down a lane. It was the stuff of nightmares, the body behind the counter, the bottled sweets, the blood.

A picture of the town hangs in my mind, like one of those priceless yet not much prized medieval miniatures, its provenance uncertain, its symbols no longer quite explicable, the translucency of its faded colours lending it a quaint, accidental charm. Can it really all be so long ago, so different, or is this antique tawny patina only the varnish which memory applies even to a recent past? It's true, there is a lacquered quality to the light of those remembered days. The grey of a wet afternoon in winter would be the aptest shade, yet I think of a grocer's brass scales standing in a beam of dusty sunlight, a bit of smooth blue china—they were called chaynics—found in the garden and kept for years, and there blooms before my inward gaze the glow of pale gold wings in a pellucid, Limbourg-blue sky.

Along with the tower and the broken wall there were the human antiquities, the maimed and the mad, the hunchbacks, the frantic old crones in their bonnets and black coats, and the mongols, with their little eyes and bad feet and sweet smiles, gambolling at the heels of touchingly middle-aged mothers. They were all of them a sort of brotherhood, in which I was a mere acolyte. It had its high priests too. There was the little man who came one summer to stay with relatives on the other side of our square. He wore blue suits and shiny shoes, pearl cufflinks, a ruby ring. He had a large handsome head and a barrel chest. His hair was a masterpiece, black and smooth as shellac, as if a gramophone record had been moulded to his skull. He rode an outsize tricycle. Astride this machine he held court under the trees of the square, surrounded by a mesmerized crowd of children, his arms folded and one gleaming toecap touching the ground with balletic delicacy. He was in a way the ideal adult, bejewelled, primped and pomaded, magisterially self-possessed, and just four feet tall. His manners were exquisite. Such tact! In his presence I felt hardly different from ordinary children.

• • •

I went to the convent school. Corridors painted a light shade of sick, tall windows with sash cords taut as a noose, and nuns, a species of large black raptor, swooping through the classrooms, their rosaries clacking like jesses. I feared my classmates, and despised them too. I can see them still, their gargoyle faces, the kiss curls, the snot. My name for some reason they found funny. They would bring their brothers or their big sisters to confront me in the playground.

—There he is, ask him.

—You, what's your name?

—Nobody.

—Come on, say it!

And they would get me by the scruff.

—Gabriel . . . ow! . . . Gabriel Swan.

It sent them into fits, it never failed.

In my class there was another pair of, yes, of identical twins, listless little fellows with pale eyes and knobbly, defenceless knees. I was fascinated. They were so calm, so unconcerned, as if being alike were a trick they had mastered long ago, and thought nothing of any more. They could have had such a time, playing pranks, switching places, fooling everybody. That was what fascinated me, the thought of being able to escape effortlessly, as if by magic, into another name, another self—that, and the ease too with which they could assert their separate identities, simply by walking away from each other. Apart, each twin was himself. Only together were they a freak.

But I, I had something always beside me. It was not a presence, but a momentous absence. From it there was no escape. A connecting cord remained, which parturition and even death had not broken, along which by subtle tugs and thrums I sensed what was not there. No living double could have been so tenacious as this dead one. Emptiness weighed on me. It seemed to me I was not all my own, that I was being shared. If I fell, say, and cut my knee, I would be aware immediately of an echo, a kind of chime, as of a wine-glass shattering somewhere out of sight, and I would feel a soft shock like that when the dreamer on the brink of blackness puts a foot on a step which is not there. Perhaps the pain was lessened—how would I have known?

Sometimes this sense of being burdened, of being somehow imposed upon, gave way to a vague and seemingly objectless yearning. One wet afternoon, at the home of a friend of my mother's who was a midwife, I got my hands on a manual of obstetrics which I pored over hotly for five tingling minutes, quaking in excitement and fear at all this amazing new knowledge. It was not, however, the gynaecological surprises that held me, slack-jawed and softly panting, as if I had stumbled on the most entrancing erotica, but that section of glossy, Rubenesque colour plates depicting some of mother nature's more lavish mistakes, the scrambled blastomeres, the androgynes welded at hip or breast, the bicipitous monsters with tiny webbed hands and cloven spines, all those queer, inseverable things among which I and my phantom brother might have been one more.

It seems out of all this somehow that my gift for numbers grew. From the beginning, I suppose, I was obsessed with the mystery of the unit, and everything else followed. Even yet I cannot see a one and a zero juxtaposed without feeling deep within me the vibration of a dark, answering note. Before I could talk I had been able to count, laying out my building blocks in ranked squares, screaming if anyone dared to disturb them. I remember a toy abacus that I treasured for years, with multicoloured wooden beads, and a wooden frame, and little carved feet for it to stand on. My party piece was to add up large numbers instantly in my head, frowning, a hand to my brow, my eyes downcast. It was not the manipulation of things that pleased me, the mere facility, but the sense of order I felt, of harmony, of symmetry and completeness.

(*Mefisto*, 1986)

Possessed of a Past

I

The painting is called, as everyone must know by now, *Portrait of a Woman with Gloves*. It measures eighty-two centimetres by sixty-five. From internal evidence—in particular the woman's attire—it has been dated between 1655 and 1660. The black dress and broad white collar and cuffs of the woman are lightened only by a brooch and gold ornamentation on the gloves. The face has a slightly Eastern cast. (I am quoting from the guidebook to Whitewater House.) The picture has been variously attributed to Rembrandt and Frans Hals, even to Vermeer. However, it is safest to regard it as the work of an anonymous master.

None of this means anything.

I have stood in front of other, perhaps greater paintings, and not been moved as I am moved by this one. I have a reproduction of it on the wall above my table here—sent to me by, of all people, Anna Behrens—when I look at it my heart contracts. There is something in the way the woman regards me, the querulous, mute insistence of her eyes, which I can neither escape nor assuage. I squirm in the grasp of her gaze. She requires of me some great effort, some tremendous feat of scrutiny and attention, of which I do not think I am capable. It is as if she were asking me to let her live.

She. There is no she, of course. There is only an organisation of shapes and colours. Yet I try to make up a life for her. She is,

I will say, thirty-five, thirty-six, though people without thinking still speak of her as a girl. She lives with her father, the merchant (tobacco, spices, and, in secret, slaves). She keeps house for him since her mother's death. She did not like her mother. Her father dotes on her, his only child. She is, he proclaims, his treasure. She devises menus—Father has a delicate stomach—inspects the kitchen, she even supervises his wine cellar. She keeps an inventory of the household linen in a little notebook attached to her belt by a fine gold chain, using a code of her own devising, for she has never learned to read or write. She is strict with the servants, and will permit no familiarities. Their dislike she takes for respect. The house is not enough to absorb her energies, she does good works besides: she visits the sick, and is on the board of visitors of the town's almshouse. She is brisk, sometimes impatient, and there are mutterings against her among the almsfolk, especially the old women. At times, usually in spring and at the beginning of winter, everything becomes too much for her. Notice the clammy pallor of her skin: she is prey to obscure ailments. She takes to her bed and lies for days without speaking, hardly breathing, while outside in the silvery northern light the world goes about its busy way. She tries to pray, but God is distant. Her father comes to visit her at evening, walking on tiptoe. These periods of prostration frighten him, he remembers his wife dying, her terrible silence in the last weeks. If he were to lose his daughter too—But she gets up, wills herself to it, and very soon the servants are feeling the edge of her tongue again, and he cannot contain his relief, it comes out in little laughs, roguish endearments, a kind of clumsy skittishness. She considers him wryly, then turns back to her tasks. She cannot understand this notion he has got into his head: he wants to have her portrait painted. I'm old, is all he will say to her, I am an old man, look at me! And he laughs, awkwardly, and avoids her eye. My portrait? she says, mine?—I am no fit subject for a painter. He shrugs, at which she is first startled, then grimly amused: he might at least have attempted to contradict her. He seems to realise what is going through her mind, and tries to mend matters, but he becomes flustered, and, watching him fuss and fret and pluck at his cuffs, she realises with a pang that it's true, he has aged. Her father, an old man. The thought has a touch of bleak comedy, which she cannot account for. You have fine hands, he says, growing testy, annoyed both at himself and her, your mother's hands—we'll tell him to make the hands prominent. And so, to humour him, but also because she is secretly curious, she goes along one morning to the studio. The squalor is what strikes her first of all. Dirt and daubs of paint everywhere, gnawed chicken bones on a smeared plate, a chamber-pot on the floor in the corner. The painter matches the place, with that filthy smock, and those fingernails. He has a drinker's squashed and pitted nose. She thinks the general smell is bad until she catches a whiff of his breath. She discovers that she is relieved: she had expected someone young, dissolute, threatening, not this pot-bellied old soak. But then he fixes his little wet eyes on her, briefly, with a kind of impersonal intensity, and she flinches, as if caught in a burst of strong light. No one has ever looked at her like this before. So this is what it is to be known! It is almost indecent. First he puts her standing by the window, but it does not suit, the light is wrong, he says. He shifts her about, grasping her by the upper arms and walking her backwards from one place to another. She feels she should be indignant, but the usual responses do not seem to function here. He is shorter than her by a head. He makes some sketches, scribbles a colour note or two, then tells her to come tomorrow at the same time. And wear a darker dress, he says. Well! She is about to give him a piece of her mind, but already he has turned aside to another task. Her maid, sitting by the door, is biting her lips and smirking. She lets the next day pass, and the next, just to show him. When she does return he says nothing about the broken appointment, only looks at her black dress—pure silk, with a broad collar of Spanish lace—and nods carelessly, and she is so vexed at him it surprises her, and she is shocked at herself. He has her stand before the couch. Remove your gloves, he says, I am to emphasise the hands. She hears the note of amused disdain in his voice. She refuses. (*Her* hands, indeed!) He insists. They engage in a brief, stiff little squabble, batting icy politenesses back and forth between them. In the end she consents to remove one glove, then promptly tries to hide the hand she has bared. He sighs, shrugs, but has to suppress a grin, as she notices. Rain streams down the windows, shreds of smoke fly over the rooftops. The sky has a huge silver hole in it. At first she is restless, standing there, then she seems to pass silently through some barrier, and a dreamy calm comes over her. It is the same, day after day, first there is agitation, then the breakthrough, then silence and a kind of softness, as if she were floating away, away, out of herself. He mutters under his breath as he works. He is choleric, he swears, and clicks his tongue, sending up sighs and groans. There are long, fevered passages when he works close up against the canvas, and she can only see his stumpy legs and his old, misshapen boots. Even his feet seem busy. She wants to laugh when he pops his head out at the side of the easel and peers at her sharply, his potato nose twitching. He will not let her see what he is doing, she is not allowed even a peek. Then one day she senses a kind of soundless, settling crash at his end of the room, and he steps back with an expression of weary disgust and waves a hand dismissively at the canvas, and turns aside to clean his brush. She comes forward and looks. For a second she sees nothing, so taken is she by the mere sensation of stopping like this and turning: it is as if—as if somehow she had walked out of herself. A long moment passes. The brooch, she says, is wonderfully done. The sound of her own voice startles her, it is a stranger speaking, and she is cowed. He laughs, not bitterly, but with real amusement and, so she feels, a curious sort of sympathy. It is an acknowledgement, of—she does not know what. She looks and looks. She had expected it would be like looking in a mirror; but this is someone she does not recognise, and yet knows. The words come unbidden into her head: Now I know how to die. She puts on her glove, and signals to her maid. The painter is speaking behind her, something about her father, and money, of course, but she is not listening. She is calm. She is happy. She feels numbed, hollowed, a walking shell. She goes down the stairs, along the dingy hall, and steps out into a commonplace world.

Do not be fooled: none of this means anything either.

I had placed the string and the wrapping-paper carefully on the floor, and now stepped forward with my arms outstretched. The door behind me opened and a large woman in a tweed skirt and a cardigan came into the room. She halted when she saw me there, with my arms flung wide before the picture and peering wildly at her over my shoulder, while I tried with one foot to conceal the paper and the ball of twine on the floor. She had blue-grey hair, and her spectacles were attached to a cord around her neck. She frowned. You must stay with the party, she said loudly, in a cross voice—really, I don't know how many times I have to say it. I stepped back. A dozen gaudily dressed people were crowding in the doorway behind her, craning to get a look at me. Sorry, I heard myself say meekly, I got lost. She gave an impatient toss of the head and strode to the middle of the room and began at once to speak in a shouted singsong about Carlin tables and Berthoud clocks, and weeks later, questioned by the police and shown my photograph, she would deny ever having seen me before in her life. Her charges shuffled in, jostling surreptitiously in an effort to stay out of her line of sight. They took up position, standing with their hands clasped before them, as if they were in church, and looked about them with expressions of respectful vacancy. One grizzled old party in a Hawaiian shirt grinned at me and winked. I confess I was rattled. There was a knot in the pit of my stomach and my palms were damp. All the elation I had felt on the way here had evaporated, leaving behind it a stark sense of foreboding. I was struck, for the first time, really, by the enormity of what I was embarked on. I felt like a child whose game has led him far into the forest, and now it is nightfall, and there are shadowy figures among the trees. The guide had finished her account of the treasures in the room—the picture, *my* picture, was given two sentences, and a misattribution—and walked out now with one arm raised stiffly above her head, still talking, shepherding the party behind her. When they had gone I waited, staring fixedly at the doorknob, expecting her to come back and haul me out briskly by the scruff of the neck. Somewhere inside me a voice was moaning softly in panic and fright. This is something that does not seem to be appreciated—I have remarked on it before—I mean how timorous I am, how easily daunted. But she did not return, and I heard them tramping away up the stairs. I set to work again feverishly. I see myself, like the villain in an old three-reeler, all twitches and scowls and wriggling eyebrows. I got the picture off the wall, not without difficulty, and laid it flat on the floor—shying away from that black stare—and began to tear off lengths of wrapping-paper. I would not have thought that paper would make so much noise, such scuffling and rattling and ripping, it must have sounded as if some large animal were being flayed alive in here. And it was no good, my hands shook, I was all thumbs, and the sheets of paper kept rolling back on themselves, and I had nothing to cut the twine with, and anyway the picture, with its thick, heavy frame, was much too big to be wrapped. I scampered about on my knees, talking to myself and uttering little squeaks of distress. Everything was going wrong. Give it up, I told myself, oh please, please, give it up now, while there's still time! but another part of me gritted its teeth and said, no you don't, you coward, get up, get on your feet, do it. So I struggled up, moaning and snivelling, and grasped the picture in my arms and staggered with it blindly, nose to nose, in the direction of the french window. Those eyes were staring into mine, I almost blushed. And then—how shall I express it—then somehow I sensed, behind that stare, another presence, watching me. I stopped, and lowered the picture, and there she was, standing in the open window, just as she had stood the day before, wide-eyed, with one hand raised. This, I remember thinking bitterly, this is the last straw. I was outraged. How dare the world strew these obstacles in my path. It was not fair, it was just not fair! Right, I said to her, here, take this, and I thrust the painting into her arms and turned her about and marched her ahead of me across the lawn. She said nothing, or if she did I was not listening. She found it hard going on the grass, the picture was too heavy for her, and she could hardly see around it. When she faltered I prodded her between the shoulder-blades. I really was very cross. We reached the car. The cavernous boot smelled strongly of fish. There was the usual jumble of mysterious implements, a jack, and spanners and things—I am not mechanically minded, or handed, have I mentioned that?—and a filthy old pullover, which I hardly noticed at the time, thrown in a corner with deceptive casualness by the hidden arranger of all these things. I took out the tools and threw them behind me on to the grass, then lifted the painting from the maid's arms and placed it face-down on the worn felt matting. This was the first time I had seen the back of the canvas, and suddenly I was struck by the antiquity of the thing. Three hundred years ago it had been stretched and sized and left against a lime-washed wall to dry. I closed my eyes for a second, and at once I saw a workshop in a narrow street in Amsterdam or Antwerp, smoky sunlight in the window, and hawkers going by outside, and the bells of the cathedral ringing. The maid was watching me. She had the most extraordinary pale, violet eyes, they seemed transparent, when I looked into them I felt I was seeing clear through her head. Why did she not run away? Behind her, in one of the great upstairs windows, a dozen heads were crowded, goggling at us. I could make out the guide-woman's glasses and the American's appalling shirt. I think I must have cried aloud in rage, an old lion roaring at the whip and chair, for the maid flinched and stepped back a pace. I caught her wrist in an iron claw and, wrenching open the car door, fairly flung her into the back seat. Oh, why did she not run away! When I got behind the wheel, fumbling and snarling, I caught a whiff of something, a faint, sharp, metallic smell, like the smell of worn pennies. I could see her in the mirror, crouched behind me as in a deep glass box, braced between the door and the back of the seat, with her elbows stuck out and fingers splayed and her face thrust forward, like the cornered heroine in a melodrama. A fierce, choking gust of impatience surged up inside me. Impatience, yes, that was what I felt most strongly—that, and a grievous sense of embarrassment. I was mortified. I had never been so exposed in all my life. People were looking at me—she in the back seat, and the tourists up there jostling at the window, but also, it seemed, a host of others, of phantom spectators, who must have been, I suppose, an intimation of all that horde who would soon be crowding around me in fascination and horror. I started the engine. The gears shrieked. In my agitation I kept getting ahead of myself and having to go back and repeat the simplest actions. When I had got the car off the grass and on to the drive I let the clutch out too quickly, and the machine sprang forward in a series of bone-shaking lurches, the bonnet going up and down like the prow of a boat caught in a wash and the shock absorbers grunting. The watchers at the window must have been in fits by now. A bead of sweat ran down my cheek. The sun had made the steering-wheel almost too hot to hold, and there was a blinding glare on the windscreen. The maid was scrabbling at the door handle, I roared at her and she stopped at once, and looked at me wide-eyed, like a rebuked child. Outside the gate the bus driver was still sitting in the sun. When she saw him she tried to get the window open, but in vain, the mechanism must have been broken. She pounded on the glass with her fists. I spun the wheel and the car lumbered out into the road, the tyres squealing. We were shouting at each other now, like a married couple having a fight. She pummelled me on the shoulder, got a hand around in front of my face and tried to claw my eyes. Her thumb went up my nose, I thought she would tear off the nostril. The car was going all over the road. I trod with both feet on the brake pedal, and we sailed in a slow, dragging curve into the hedge. She fell back. I turned to her. I had the hammer in my hand. I looked at it, startled. The silence rose around us like water. Don't, she said. She was crouched as before, with her arms bent and her back pressed into the corner. I could not speak, I was filled with a kind of wonder. I had never felt another's presence so immediately and with such raw force. I saw her now, really saw her, for the first time, her mousy hair and bad skin, that bruised look around her eyes. She was quite ordinary, and yet, somehow, I don't know—somehow radiant. She cleared her throat and sat up, and detached a strand of hair that had caught at the corner of her mouth.

You must let me go, she said, or you will be in trouble.

It's not easy to wield a hammer in a motor car. When I struck her the first time I expected to feel the sharp, clean smack of steel on bone, but it was more like hitting clay, or hard putty. The word *fontanel* sprang into my mind. I thought one good bash would do it, but, as the autopsy would show, she had a remarkably strong skull—even in that, you see, she was unlucky. The first blow fell just at the hairline, above her left eye. There was not much blood, only a dark-red glistening dent with hair matted in it. She shuddered, but remained sitting upright, swaying a little, looking at me with eyes that would not focus properly. Perhaps I would have stopped then, if she had not suddenly launched herself at me across the back of the seat, flailing and screaming. I was dismayed. How could this be happening to me—it was all so *unfair*. Bitter tears of self-pity squeezed into my eyes. I pushed her away from me and swung the hammer in a wide, backhand sweep. The force of the blow flung her against the door, and her head struck the window, and a fine thread of blood ran out of her nostril and across her cheek. There was blood on the window, too, a fan-shaped spray of tiny drops. She closed her eyes and turned her face away from me, making a low, guttural noise at the back of her throat. She put a hand up to her head just as I was swinging at her again, and when the blow landed on her temple her fingers were in the way, and I heard one of them crack, and I winced, and almost apologised. Oh! she said, and suddenly, as if everything inside her had collapsed, she slithered down the seat on to the floor.

There was silence again, clear and startling. I got out of the car and stood a moment, breathing. I was dizzy. Something seemed to have happened to the sunlight, everywhere I looked there was an underwater gloom. I thought I had driven only a little way, and expected to see the gates of Whitewater, and the tour bus, and the driver running towards me, but to my astonishment the road in both directions was empty, and I had no idea where I was. On one side a hill rose steeply, and on the other I could see over the tops of pine trees to far-off, rolling downs. It all looked distinctly improbable. It was like a hastily painted backdrop, especially that smudged, shimmering distance, and the road winding innocently away. I found I was still clutching the hammer. With a grand sweep of my arm I flung it from me, and watched it as it flew, tumbling slowly end over end, in a long, thrilling arc, far, far out over the blue pinetops. Then abruptly I bent forward and vomited up the glutinous remains of the breakfast I had consumed an age ago, in another life.

I crawled back into the car, keeping my eyes averted from that crumpled thing wedged behind the front seat. The light in the windscreen was a splintered glare, I thought for a second the glass was smashed, until I put a hand to my face and discovered I was crying. This I found encouraging. My tears seemed not just a foretoken of remorse, but the sign of some more common, simpler urge, an affect for which there was no name, but which might be my last link, the only one that would hold, with the world of ordinary things. For everything was changed, where I was now I had not been before. I trembled, and all around me trembled, and there was a sluggish, sticky feel to things, as if I and all of this—car, road, trees, those distant meadows—as if we had all a moment ago struggled mute and amazed out of a birthhole in the air. I turned the key in the ignition, bracing myself, convinced that instead of the engine starting something else would happen, that there would be a terrible, rending noise, or a flash of light, or that slime would gush out over my legs from under the dashboard. I drove in second gear along the middle of the road. Smells, smells. Blood has a hot, thick smell. I wanted to open the windows, but did not dare, I was afraid of what might come in—the light outside seemed moist and dense as glair, I imagined it in my mouth, my nostrils.

I drove and drove. Whitewater is only thirty miles or so from the city, but it seemed hours before I found myself in the suburbs. Of the journey I remember little. That is to say, I do not remember changing gears, accelerating and slowing down, working the pedals, all that. I see myself moving, all right, as if in a crystal bubble, flying soundlessly through a strange, sunlit, glittering landscape. I think I went very fast, for I recall a sensation of pressure in my ears, a dull, rushing blare. So I must have driven in circles, round and round those narrow country roads. Then there were houses, and housing estates, and straggling factories, and supermarkets big as aircraft hangars. I stared through the windscreen in dreamy amazement. I might have been a visitor from another part of the world altogether, hardly able to believe how much like home everything looked and yet how different it was. I did not know where I was going, I mean I was not going anywhere, just driving. It was almost restful, sailing along like that, turning the wheel with one finger, shut off from everything. It was as if all my life I had been clambering up a steep and difficult slope, and now had reached the peak and leaped out blithely into the blue. I felt so free. At the first red traffic light the car drifted gently to a stop as if it were subsiding into air. I was at the junction of two suburban roads. On the left there was a little green rise with a chestnut tree and a neat row of new houses. Children were playing on the grassy bank. Dogs gambolled. The sun shone. I have always harboured a secret fondness for quiet places such as this, unremarked yet cherished domains of building and doing and tending. I leaned my head back on the seat and smiled, watching the youngsters at play. The lights changed to green, but I did not stir. I was not really there, but lost somewhere, in some sunlit corner of my past. There was a sudden rapping on the window beside my ear. I jumped. A woman with a large, broad, horsy face—she reminded me, dear God, of my mother!—was peering in at me and saying something. I rolled down the window. She had a loud voice, it sounded very loud to me, at any rate. I could not understand her, she was talking about an accident, and asking me if I was all right. Then she pressed her face forward and squinnied over my shoulder, and opened her mouth and groaned. Oh, she said, the poor child! I turned my head. There was blood all over the back seat now, far too much, surely, for just one person to have shed. For a mad instant, in which a crafty spark of hope flared and died, I wondered if there *had* been a crash, which somehow I had not noticed, or had forgotten, if some overloaded vehicle had ploughed into the back of us, flinging bodies and all this blood in through the rear window. I could not speak. I had thought she was dead, but there she was, kneeling between the seats and groping at the window beside her, I could hear her fingers squeaking on the glass. Her hair hung down in bloodied ropes, her face was a clay mask streaked with copper and crimson. The woman outside was gabbling into my ear about telephones and ambulances and the police—the police! I turned to her with a terrible glare. Madam! I said sternly (she would later describe my voice as *cultured* and *authoritative*), will you please get on about your business! She stepped back, staring in shock. I confess I was myself impressed, I would not have thought I could muster such a commanding tone. I rolled up the window and jammed the car into gear and shot away, noticing, too late, that the lights had turned to red. A tradesman's van coming from the left braked sharply and let out an indignant squawk. I drove on. However, I had not gone more than a street or two when suddenly an ambulance reared up in my wake, its siren yowling and blue light flashing. I was astonished. How could it have arrived so promptly? In fact, this was another of those appalling coincidences in which this case abounds. The ambulance, as I would later learn, was not looking for me, but was returning from—yes—from the scene of a car crash, with—I'm sorry, but, yes—with a dying woman in the back. I kept going, haring along with my head down, my nose almost touching the rim of the wheel. I do not think I could have stopped, locked in fright as I was. The ambulance drew alongside, swaying dangerously and trumpeting like a frenzied big beast. The attendant in the passenger seat, a burly young fellow in shirt-sleeves, with a red face and narrow sideburns, looked at the blood-streaked window behind me with mild, professional interest. He conferred briefly with the driver, then signalled to me, with complicated gestures, nodding and mouthing, to follow them. They thought I was coming from the same crash, ferrying another victim to hospital. They surged ahead. I followed in their wake, befuddled with alarm and bafflement. I could see nothing but this big square clumsy thing scudding along, whooshing up dust and wallowing fatly on its springs. Then abruptly it braked and swung into a wide gateway, and an arm appeared out of the side window and beckoned me to follow. It was the sight of that thick arm that broke the spell. With a gulp of demented laughter I drove on, past the hospital gate, plunging the pedal to the floor, and the noise of the siren dwindled behind me, a startled plaint, and I was free.

I peered into the mirror. She was sitting slumped on the seat with her head hanging and her hands resting palm upwards on her thighs.

Suddenly the sea was on my left, far below, blue, unmoving. I drove down a steep hill, then along a straight cement road beside a railway track. A pink and white hotel, castellated, with pennants flying, rose up on my right, enormous and empty. The road straggled to an end in a marshy patch of scrub and thistles, and there I stopped, in the midst of a vast and final silence. I could hear her behind me, breathing. When I turned she lifted her sibyl's fearsome head and looked at me. *Help me*, she whispered. *Help me*. A bubble of blood came out of her mouth and burst. *Tommy!* she said, or a word like that, and then: *Love*. What did I feel? Remorse, grief, a terrible—no no no, I won't lie. I can't remember feeling anything, except that sense of strangeness, of being in a place I knew but did not recognise. When I got out of the car I was giddy, and had to lean on the door for a moment with my eyes shut tight. My jacket was bloodstained, I wriggled out of it and flung it into the stunted bushes—they never found it, I can't think why. I remembered the pullover in the boot, and put it on. It smelled of fish and sweat and axle-grease. I picked up the hangman's hank of rope and threw that away too. Then I lifted out the picture and walked with it to where there was a sagging barbed-wire fence and a ditch with a trickle of water at the bottom, and there I dumped it. What was I thinking of, I don't know. Perhaps it was a gesture of renunciation or something. Renunciation! How do I dare use such words. The woman with the gloves gave me a last, dismissive stare. She had expected no better of me. I went back to the car, trying not to look at it, the smeared windows. Something was falling on me: a delicate, silent fall of rain. I looked upwards in the glistening sunlight and saw a cloud directly overhead, the merest smear of grey against the summer blue. I thought: I am not human. Then I turned and walked away.

(*The Book of Evidence*, 1989)

II

I am always fascinated by the way the things that happen happen. I mean the ordinary things, the small occurrences that keep adding themselves on to all that went before in the running total of what I call my life. I do not think of events as discrete and discontinuous; mostly there is just what seems a sort of aimless floating. I am not afloat at all, of course, it only feels like that: really I am in free fall. And I come to earth repeatedly with a bump, though I am surprised every time, sitting in a daze on the hard ground of inevitability, like Tom the cat, leaning on my knuckles with my legs flung wide and stars circling my poor sore head. When Billy stopped the van we sat and listened for a while to the engine ticking and the water gurgling in the radiator, and I was like my wife in that hotel room that I had conjured up for her imaginary tryst, looking about her in subdued astonishment at the fact of being where she was. I had not intended that we should come this way, I had left it to Billy to choose whatever road he wished; yet here we were. Was it another sign, I asked myself, in this momentous day of signs? Billy looked out calmly at the stretch of country road before us and drummed his fingers on the steering wheel.

'Where's this?' he said.

'Home.' I laughed. The word boomed like a foghorn.

'Nice,' Billy said. 'The trees and all.' I marvelled anew at his lack of curiosity. Nothing, it seems, can surprise him. Or am I wrong, as I usually am about people and their ways? For all I know he may be in a ceaseless fever of amazement before the spectacle of this wholly improbable world. He twitches a lot, and sometimes he used to wake up screaming in his bunk at night; but then, we all woke up screaming in the night, sooner or later, so that proves nothing. All the same, I am probably underestimating him; underestimating people is one of my less serious besetting sins. 'Your family still here?' he said. 'Your mam and dad?'

He frowned. I could see him trying to imagine them, big, bossy folk with loud voices clattering down this road astride their horses, as outlandish to him as medieval knights in armour.

'No,' I said. 'All dead, thank God. My wife lives here now.'

I opened the door of the van and swung my legs out and sat for a moment with my head bowed and shoulders sagging and the gin bottle dangling between my knees. When I lifted my eyes I could see the roof of the house beyond the ragged tops of the hedge. I found myself toying with the notion that this was all there was, just a roof put up there to fool me, like something out of the *Arabian Nights*, and that if I stood up quickly enough I would glimpse under the eaves a telltale strip of silky sky and a shining scimitar of moon floating on its back.

'Did I ever tell you, Billy,' I said, still gazing up wearily at those familiar chimney-pots, 'about the many worlds theory?'

Of the few scraps of science I can still recall (talk about another life!), the many worlds theory is my favourite. The universe, it says, is everywhere and at every instant splitting into a myriad versions of itself. On Pluto, say, a particle of putty collides with a lump of lead and another, smaller particle is created in the process and goes shooting off in all directions. Every single one of those possible directions, says the many worlds theory, will produce its own universe, containing its own stars, its own solar system, its own Pluto, its own you and its own me: identical, that is, to all the other myriad universes except for this unique event, this particular particle whizzing down this particular path. In this manifold version of reality chance is an iron law. Chance. Think of it. Oh, it's only numbers, I know, only a cunning wheeze got up to accommodate the infinities and make the equations come out, yet when I contemplate it something stirs in me, some indistinct, fallen thing that I had thought was dead lifts itself up on one smashed wing and gives a pathetic, hopeful cheep. For is it not possible that somewhere in this crystalline multiplicity of worlds, in this infinite, mirrored regression, there is a place where the dead have not died, and I am innocent?

'What do you think of that, Billy?' I said. 'That's the many worlds theory. Isn't that something, now?'

'Weird,' he answered, shaking his head slowly from side to side, humouring me.

Spring is strange. This day looked more like early winter, all metallic glitters and smooth, silver sky. The air was cool and bright and smelled of wet clay. An odd, unsteady sort of cheerfulness was gradually taking hold of me—the gin, I suppose.

'What's the first thing you noticed when you got out, Billy?' I said.

He hardly had to think at all.

'The quiet,' he said. 'People not shouting all the time.'

The quiet, yes. And the breadth of things, the far vistas on every side and the sense of farther and still farther spaces beyond. It made me giddy to think of it.

I got myself up at last, feet squelching in the boggy verge, and walked a little way along the road. I had nothing particular in mind. I had no intention as yet of going near the house—the gate was in the other direction—for in my heart I knew my wife was right, that I should stay away. All the same, now that I was here, by accident, I could not resist looking over the old place one more time, trying my feet in the old footprints, as it were, to see if they still fitted. Yet I could not feel the way one is supposed to feel amid the suddenly rediscovered surroundings of one's past, all swoony and tearful, in a transport of ecstatic remembrance, clasping it all to one's breast with a stifled cry and a sudden, sweet ache in the heart, that kind of thing. No; what I felt was a sort of glazed numbness, as if I were suspended in some thin, transparent stuff, like one of those eggs my mother used to preserve in waterglass when I was a child. This is what happens to you in prison, you lose your past, it is confiscated from you, along with your bootlaces and your belt, when you enter through that strait gate. It was all still here, of course, the ancient, enduring world, suave and detailed, standing years-deep in its own silence, only beyond my touching, as if shut away behind glass. There were even certain trees I seemed to recognise; I would not have been surprised if they had come alive and spoken to me, lifting their drooping limbs and sighing, as in a children's storybook. At that moment, as though indeed this were the enchanted forest, there materialised before me on the road, like a wood-sprite, a little old brown man in big hobnailed boots and a cap, carrying, of all things, a sickle. He had long arms and a bent back and bandy legs, and progressed with a rolling gait, as if he were bowling himself along like a hoop. As we approached each other he watched me keenly, with a crafty, sidewise, leering look. When we had drawn level he touched a finger to his cap and croaked an incomprehensible greeting, peering up at me out of clouded, half-blind eyes. I stopped. He took in my white suit with a mixture of misgiving and scornful amusement; he probably thought I was someone of consequence.

'Grand day,' I said, in a loud voice hollow with false heartiness.

'But hardy, though,' he answered smartly and looked pleased with himself, as if he had caught me out in some small, deceitful stratagem.

'Yes,' I said, abashed, 'hardy indeed.'

He stood bowed before me, bobbing gently from the waist as if his spine were fitted with some sort of spring attachment at its base. The sickle dangled at the end of his long arm like a prosthesis. We were silent briefly. I considered the sky while he studied the roadway at my feet. I was never one for exchanging banter with the peasantry, yet I was loath to pass on, I do not know why. Perhaps I took him for another of this day's mysterious messengers.

'And are you from these parts yourself, sir?' he said, in that wheedling tone they reserve for tourists and well-heeled strangers in general.

For answer I made a broad, evasive gesture.

'Do you know that house?' I asked, pointing over the hedge.

He passed a hard brown hand over his jaw, making a sandpapery noise, and gave me a quick, sly look. His eyes were like shards from some large, broken, antique thing, a funerary jar, perhaps.

'I do,' he said. 'I know it well.'

Then he launched into a long rigmarole about my family and its history. I listened in awed astonishment as if to a tale of the old gods. It was all invention, of course; even the few facts he had were upside-down or twisted out of shape. 'I knew the young master, too,' he said. (*The young master?*) 'I seen him one day kill a rabbit. Broke its neck: like that. A pet thing, it was. Took it up in his hands and—' he made a crunching noise out of the side of his mouth '—kilt it. He was only a lad at the time, mind, a curly-headed little fellow you wouldn't think would say boo to a goose. Oh, a nice knave. I wasn't a bit surprised when I heard about what he done.'

What was this nonsense? I had never wrung the neck of any rabbit. I was the most innocuous of children, a poor, shivering mite afraid of its own shadow. Why had he invented this grotesque version of me? I felt confusion and a sort of angry shame, as if I had been jostled aside in the street by some ludicrously implausible imposter claiming to be me. The old man was squinting up at me with a slackmouthed grin, a solitary, long yellow tooth dangling from his upper gums. 'I suppose you're looking for him too, are you?' he said.

A cold hand clutched my heart.

'Why?' I said. 'Who else was looking for him?'

His grin turned slyly knowing. 'Ah,' he said, 'there's always fellows like that going around, after people.'

He winked and touched a finger to his cap again, with the smug, self-satisfied air of a man who has properly settled someone's hash, and bowled himself off on his way. I looked after him but saw myself, a big, ragged, ravaged person, flabby as a porpoise, standing there in distress on the windy road, dangling from an invisible gibbet in my incongruous white suit, arms limp, with my mouth open and my bell-bottoms flapping and the neck of the gin bottle sticking out of my pocket. I do not know why I was so upset. There came over me then that sense of dislocation I experience with increasing frequency these days, and which frightens me. It is as if mind and body had pulled loose from each other, or as if the absolute, essential *I* had shrunk to the size of a dot, leaving the rest of me hanging in enormous suspension, massive and yet weightless, like a sawn tree before it topples. I wonder if it is incipient epilepsy, or some other insinuating cerebral malady? But I do not think the effect is physical. Perhaps this is how I shall go mad in the end, perhaps I shall just fly apart like this finally and be lost to myself forever. The attack, if that is not too strong a word for it, the attack passed, as it always does, with a dropping sensation, a sort of general lurch, as if I had been struck a great, soft, padded punch and somehow had fallen out of myself even as I stood there, clenched in fright. I looked about warily, blinking; I might have just landed from somewhere entirely different. Everything was in its place, the roof beyond the hedge and the old man hobbling away and the back of Billy's seal-dark head motionless in the car, as though nothing had happened, as though that fissure had not opened up in the deceptively smooth surface of things. But I know that look of innocence the world puts on; I know it for what it is.

I found a gap in the hedge and pulled myself through it, my shoes sinking to the brim in startlingly cold mud. Twigs slapped my face and thorns clutched at my coat. I had forgotten what the countryside is like, the blank-faced, stolid malevolence of bush and briar. When I got to the other side I was panting. I had the feeling, as so often, that all this had happened before. The house was there in front of me now, quite solid and substantial after all and firmly tethered to its roof. Yet it seemed changed, seemed smaller and nearer to the road than it should be, and for a panicky moment I wondered if my memory had deceived me and this was not my house at all. (*My* house? Ah.) Mother's rose bushes were still flourishing under the big window at the gable end. They were in bud already. Poor ma, dead and gone and her roses still there, clinging on in their slow, tenacious, secret way. I started across the lawn, the soaked turf giving spongily under my tread. The past was gathering ever more thickly around me, I waded through it numbly like a greased swimmer, waiting to feel the chill and the treacherous undertow. I veered away from the front door—I do not naturally go in at front doors any more—and skirted round by the rose bushes, squinting up at the windows for a sign of life. How frowningly do empty windows look out at the world, full of blank sky and oddly arranged greenery. At the back of the house I skulked about for a while in the clayey dampness of the vegetable garden, feeling like poor Magwitch on the run. A few big stalks of last year's cabbages, knobbed like backbones, leaned this way and that, and there were hens that high-stepped worriedly away from me in slow motion, or stood canted over on one leg with their heads inclined, shaking their wattles and uttering mournful croaks of alarm. (What strange, baroque creatures they are, hens; there is something Persian about them, I always feel.) I was not thinking of anything. I was just feeling around blindly, like a doctor feeling for the place that pains. I would have welcomed pain. Dreamily I advanced, admiring the sea-green moss on the door of the disused privy, the lilac tumbling over its rusted tin roof. A breeze swooped down and a thrush whistled its brief, thick song. I paused, light-headed and blinking. At last the luminous air, the bird's song, that particular shade of green, all combined to succeed in transporting me back for a moment to the far, lost past, to some rain-washed, silver-grey morning like this one, forgotten but still somehow felt, and I stood for a moment in inexplicable rapture, my face lifted to the light, and felt a sort of breathlessness, an inward staggering, as if an enormous, airy weight had been dropped into my arms. But it did not last; that tender burden I had been given to hold, whatever it was, evaporated at once, and the rapture faded and I was numb again, as before.

I put my face to the kitchen window and peered inside. I could see little except shadows and my own eyes reflected in the glass, fixed and hungry, like the eyes of a desperate stranger. Crouched there with my breath steaming the pane and the bilious smell of drains in my nostrils, I felt intensely the pressure of things behind me, the garden and the fields and the far woods, like an inquisitive crowd gathering at my back, elbowing for a look. I am never really at ease in the open; I expect always some malignity of earth or air to strike me down or, worse, to whirl me up dizzyingly into the sky. I have always been a little afraid of the sky, so transparent and yet impenetrable, so deceptively harmless-looking in its bland blueness.

The back door was locked. I was turning to go, more relieved I think than anything else, when suddenly, in a sudden swoon of anger, or proprietorial resentment, or something, I don't know what, I turned with an elbow lifted and bashed it against one of the panes of frosted glass in the door. These things are not as easy as the cinema makes them seem: it took me three good goes before I managed it. The glass gave with a muffled whop, like a grunt of laughter, guttural and cruel, and the splinters falling to the floor inside made a sinister little musical sound, a sort of elfin music. I waited, listening. What a connoisseur of silences I have become over the years! This one had astonishment in it, and warm fright, and a naughty child's stifled glee. I took a breath. I was trembling, like a struck cymbal. How darkly thrilling it is to smash a pane of glass and reach through the jagged hole into the huge, cool emptiness of the other side. I pictured my hand pirouetting all alone in there, in that shocked space, doing its little back-to-front *pas de deux* with the key. The door swung open abruptly and I almost fell across the threshold; it was not so much the suddenness that made me totter but the vast surprise of being here. For an instant I saw myself as if lit by lightning, a stark, crouched figure, vivid and yet not entirely real, an emanation of myself, a hologram image, pop-eyed and flickering. Shakily I stepped inside, and recalled, with eerie immediacy, the tweedy and damply warm underarm of a blind man I had helped across a street somewhere, in some forgotten city, years ago.

I shut the door behind me and stood and took another deep breath, like a diver poised on the springboard's thrumming tip. The furniture hung about pretending not to look at me. Stillness lay like a dustsheet over everything. There was no one at home, I could sense it. I walked here and there, my footsteps falling without sound. I had a strange sensation in my ears, a sort of fullness, as if I were in a vessel fathoms deep with the weight of the ocean pressing all around me. The objects that I looked at seemed insulated, as if they had been painted with a protective coating of some invisible stuff, cool and thick and smooth as enamel, and when I touched them I could not seem to feel them. I thought of being here, a solemn little boy in a grubby jersey, crop-headed and frowning, with inky fingers and defenceless, translucent pink ears, sitting at this table hunched over my homework on a winter evening and dreaming of the future. Can I really ever have been thus? Can that child be me? Surely somewhere between that blameless past and this grim present something snapped, some break occurred without my noticing it in the line I was paying out behind me as I ran forward, reaching out an eager hand towards all the good things that I thought were waiting for me. Who was it, then, I wonder, that picked up the frayed end and fell nimbly into step behind me, chuckling softly to himself?

I went into the hall. There was the telephone she had delayed so long before answering. The machine squatted tensely on its little table like a shiny black toad, dying to speak, to tell all, to blurt out everything that had been confided to it down the years. Where had everyone gone to? Had they fled at the sound of my voice on the line, had she dropped everything and bundled the child in her arms and run out to the road and driven away with a shriek of tyres? I realised now why it was I could touch nothing, could not feel the texture of things: the house had been emptied of me; I had been exorcised from it. Would she know I had been here? Would she sense the contamination in the air? I closed my eyes and was assailed anew by that feeling of both being and not being, of having drifted loose from myself. I have always been convinced of the existence somewhere of another me, my more solid self, more weighty and far more serious than I, intent perhaps on great and unimaginable tasks, in another reality, where things are really real; I suppose for him, out there in his one of many worlds, I would be no more than the fancy of a summer's day, a shimmer at the edge of vision, something half-glimpsed, like the shadow of a cloud, or a gust of wind, or the hover and sudden flit of a dragonfly over reeded, sun-white shallows. And now as I stood in the midst of my own absence, in the birthplace that had rid itself of me utterly, I murmured a little prayer, and said, Oh, if you are really there, bright brother, in your more real reality, think of me, turn all your stern attentions on me, even for an instant, and make *me* real, too.

(Of course, at times I think of that other self not as my better half but my worse; if he is the bad one, the evil, lost twin, what does that make me? That is an avenue down which I do not care to venture.)

I climbed the stairs. I felt oddly, shakily buoyant, as if there were springs attached to the soles of my shoes and I must keep treading down heavily to prevent them from bouncing me over the banisters. On the first landing I stopped and turned from side to side, poor baffled minotaur, my head swinging ponderously on its thick tendons, a bullish weight, my humid, blood-dark glower groping stubbornly for something, for some smallest trace of my past selves lurking here, like the hidden faces in a comic-book puzzle. As a child I loved to be alone in the house; it was like being held loosely in the friendly clutches of a preoccupied, mute and melancholy giant. Something now had happened to the light, some sort of gloom had fallen. It was not raining. Perhaps it was fog; in these parts fog has a way of settling without warning and as quickly lifting again. At any rate I recall a clammy and crepuscular glow. I walked down the corridor. It was like walking in a dream, a sort of slow stumbling, weightless and yet encumbered. At the end of the corridor there was an arched window with a claret-coloured pane that had always made me think of cold churches and the word *litany*. The door to one of the bedrooms was ajar; I imagined someone standing behind it, breathless and listening, just like me. I hesitated, and then with one finger pushed the door open and stepped in sideways and stood listening in the softly thudding silence. The room was empty, a large, high, white chamber with a vaulted ceiling and one big window looking out into the umbrage of tall trees. There was no furniture, there were no pictures on the walls, there was nothing. The floorboards were bare. Whose room had this been? I did not remember it; that elaborate ceiling, for instance, domed and scooped like the inner crown of a priest's biretta: there must have been a false ceiling under it in my time that now had been removed. I looked up into the soft shadows and felt everything fall away from me like water. How cool and calm all was, how still the air. I thought how it would be to live here in this bone-white cell, in all this emptiness, watching the days ascend and fall again to darkness, hearing faintly the wind blow, seeing the light edge its way across the floor and die. And then to float away, to be gone, like dust, dispersed into the vast air. Not to be. Not to be at all. Deep down, deep beyond dreaming, have I ever desired anything other than that consummation? Sometimes I think that satyr, what's-his-name, was right: better not to have been born, and once born to have done with the whole business as quick as you can.

A bird like a black bolt came flying straight out of the trees and dashed itself with a bang against the windowpane.

Something jogged my memory then, the bird, perhaps, or the look of those trees, or that strange, misty light in the glass: once, when I was sick, they had moved me here from my own room,

I cannot think why—for the view, maybe, or the elevation, I don't know. I saw again the bed at the window, the tall, fluted half-columns of the curtains rising above me, the tops of the autumnal trees outside, and the child that I was then, lying quietly with bandaged throat, grey-browed and wan, my hands resting on the turned-down sheet, like a miniature warrior on his tomb. How strangely pleasurable were the illnesses of those days. Afloat there in febrile languor, with aching eyes and leaden limbs and the blood booming in my ears, I used to dream myself into sky-bound worlds where metallic birds soared aloft on shining loops of wire and great clouded glass shapes sailed ringingly through the cool, pellucid air. Perhaps this is how children die; perhaps still pining somehow for that oblivion out of which they have so lately come they just forget themselves and quietly float away.

A faint reflection moved on the glass before me and I turned to find my son standing in the doorway, watching me with a placid and enquiring smile. I thought, *I met Death upon the road*. I sat down on the window-sill. I felt feeble suddenly.

'Van!' I said and laughed breathlessly. 'How you've grown!'

Did he know me, I wonder? He must be seventeen now, or eighteen—in my confusion I could not remember his birthday, or even what month it falls in. I had not seen him for ten years. Would it upset him to come upon me suddenly here like this? Who knows what upsets him. Maybe nothing does, maybe he is perfectly at peace, locked away inside himself. I picture a far, white country, everything blurred and flat under a bleached sky, and, off on the horizon, a bird, perhaps, tiny as a toy in all that distance, flying steadily away. But how huge he was!—I could do nothing at first except sit leaning forward with my hands on my knees, gaping at him. He was a good half head taller than I, with a barrel chest and enormous shoulders and a great, broad brow, incongruously noble, like that of a prehistoric stone statue standing at an angle on a hillside above the shore of some remote, forgotten island. The blond curls that I remembered had grown thick and had turned a rusty shade of red; that is from me. He had his mother's dark colouring, though, and her dark, solemn eyes. His gaze, even at its steadiest, kept pulling away distractedly to one side, which created a curious, flickering effect, as if within that giant frame a smaller, frailer version of him, the one that I remembered, were minutely atremble. In my imagination I got up out of myself, like a swimmer clambering out of water, and took a staggering step towards him, my arms outstretched, and pressed him to my breast and sobbed. Poor boy, my poor boy. This is awful. In reality I am still sitting on the window-sill, with my hands with their whitened knuckles clamped on my knees, looking up at him and inanely, helplessly smiling; I never was one for embraces. He made a noise deep in his throat that might have been a chuckle and walked forward with a sort of teetering and unexpectedly light, almost dancing step, and peered at the stunned blackbird perched outside on the sill, glazed and motionless and all puffed up around its puzzlement and pain. It kept heaving shuddery little sighs and slowly blinking. There was blood on its beak. What a shock the poor thing must have had when what looked like shining air turned suddenly to solid glass and the world snapped shut. Is that how it is for my boy all the time, a sort of helpless blundering against darkly gleaming, impenetrable surfaces? He pointed to the bird and glanced at me almost shyly and did that chuckle again. He had a musty, faintly sweet smell that made me think of wheelchairs and those old-fashioned, cloth-padded wooden crutches. He was always fascinated by birds. I remembered, years ago, when he was a child, walking with him one blustery autumn day through the grounds of a great house we had paid a shilling to see. There was a peacock somewhere, we could hear its uncanny, desolate cry above the box hedges and the ornamental lawns. Van was beside himself and kept running agitatedly back and forth with his head lifted in that peculiar, angled way that he had when he was excited, looking to see what could be making such extravagant sounds. But we never did find the peacock, and now the day came back to me weighted with that little absence, that missed, marvellous bird, and I felt the pang of it, distant and piercing, like the bird's cry itself.

'Are you all right?' I said to him. That curious, dense light was in the trees and pressing like gauze against the windowpanes. 'Are you happy?'

What else could I say? His only response was a puzzled, fleeting frown, as if what he had heard was not my voice but only a familiar and yet as always incomprehensible, distant noise, another of the squeaks and chirrups thronging the air of his white world. I have never been able to rid myself of the notion that his condition was my fault, that even before he was born I damaged him somehow with my expectations, that my high hopes made him hang back inside himself until it was too late for him to come out properly and be one with the rest of us. And no matter what I may tell myself, I did have hopes. Of what? Of being saved through him, as if the son by his mere existence might absorb and absolve the sins of the father? Even that grandiloquent name I insisted on hanging around his neck—Vanderveld! for God's sake, after my mother's people—even that was a weight that must have helped to drag him down. When he was still an infant I used to picture us someday in the far future strolling together down a dappled street in the south somewhere, he a grown man and I still miraculously youthful, both of us in white, my hand lightly on his shoulder and him smiling: father and son. But while I had my face turned away, dreaming of that or some other, equally fatuous idyll, the Erl King got him.

Suddenly, as if nothing at all had happened, the blackbird with a sort of clockwork jerk rose up and flexed its wings and flew off swiftly into the cottony white light. Van made a little disappointed mewling noise and pressed his face to the glass, craning to see the last of the bird, and for a second, as he stood with his face turned like that, I saw my mother in him. Dear Jesus, all my ghosts are gathering here.

Things are sort of smeared and splintery after that, as if seen through an iridescent haze of tears. I walked here and there about the house, with Van going along softly behind me with that dancer's dainty tread. I poked about in bedrooms and even looked through drawers and cupboards, but it was no good, I could make no impression. Everything gave before me like smoke. What was I looking for, anyway? Myself still, the dried spoor of my tracks? Not to be found here. I gathered a few bits of clothes together and took down from the top of a wardrobe an old cardboard suitcase to put them in. The clasps snapped up with a noise like pistol shots and I opened the lid and caught a faint smell of something that I almost recognised, some herb or fragrant wood, a pallid sigh out of the past. When I looked over my shoulder Van was gone, leaving no more than a fading shimmer on the air. I saw myself, kneeling on the floor with the case open before me, like a ravisher hunched over his splayed victim, and I stuffed in the last of my shirts and shut the lid and rose and hurried off down the stairs. In the kitchen the back door with its broken pane still stood open; it had a somehow insolent, insinuating look to it, like that of a tough lounging with his elbow against the wall and watching me with amusement and scorn. I went out skulkingly, clutching my suitcase and flushed with an inexplicable shame. I shall never, not ever again, go back there. It is lost to me; all lost. As I emerged from the gap in the hedge I felt myself stepping out of something, as if I had left a part of my life behind me, snagged on the briars like an old coat, and I experienced a spasm of blinding grief; it was so pure, so piercing, that for a moment I mistook it for pleasure; it flooded through me, a scalding serum, and left me feeling almost sanctified, holy sinner.

I was surprised to find Billy still waiting for me. After all I had been through I thought he would be gone, taken by the whirlwind like everything else I seemed to have lost today. Someone was leaning in the window of the van, talking to him, a thin, black-haired man who, seeing me approach, straightened up at once and legged it off around the bend in the road, stepping along hurriedly in a peculiarly comic and somehow ribald way, one arm swinging and the other hand inserted in his jacket pocket and the cuffs of his trousers flapping.

The air in the van was thick with cigarette smoke.

'Who was that?' I said.

Billy shrugged and did not look at me. 'Some fellow,' he said. He threw his fag end out of the window and started up the engine and we lurched on our way. When we drove around the bend there was no sign of the black-haired man.

'See the family?' Billy asked.

'I told you,' I said, 'I have no family. I had a son once, but he died.'

(*Ghosts*, 1993)

III

When she urged me to beat her I should have known the game was up, or at least that it soon would be. After such knowledge, and so on. There are moments—yes, yes, despite anything I may have said in the past, there are moments when a note sounds such as never has been heard before, dark, serious, undeniable, a strand added to the great chord. That was the note I heard the day she clutched my wrist and whispered, '*Hit me, hit me like you hit her.*' I stopped at once what I was doing and hung above her, ears pricked and snout aquiver, like an animal caught on open ground. Her head was lifted from the pillow and her eyes were filmy and not quite focused. Sweat glistened in the hollow of her throat. A vast, steel-blue cloud was sneaking out of the frame of the window and the rooftops shone. At just that moment, with what seemed bathetic discontinuity, I realised what the smell was that I had caught in the basement that first day when she brought me there. My heart now seemed to have developed a limp. In a frightened rush I asked her what she meant and she gave her head a quick, impatient shake and closed her eyes and took a deep breath and pressed herself to me and sighed. I can still feel the exact texture of her skin against mine, taut and slightly clammy and somehow both chill and hot at the same time.

In the closing days of November a false spring blossomed. (That's it, talk about the weather.) Bulbs recklessly sprouted in the parks and birds tried out uncertain warblings and people wearing half-smiles walked about dazedly in the steady, thin sunshine. Even A. and I were enticed outdoors. I see us in those narrow streets, a pair of children out of a fairy tale, wandering through the gingerbread village unaware of the ogres in their towers spying on us. (One of us, certainly, was unaware.) We sat in dank public houses and behind the steamed-up windows of greasy cafés. A. held on tightly to my arm, trembling with what seemed a sort of hazy happiness. I was happy, too. Yes, I will not equivocate or qualify. I was happy. How hard it is to say such a simple thing. Happiness for me now is synonymous with boredom, if that is the word for that languorous, floating sense of detachment that would come over me as I strolled with her through the streets or sat in some fake old-fashioned pub listening to her stories of herself and her invented lives.

It was she who first spotted Barbarossa. He was living in a cardboard box in the doorway of a cutler's shop in Fawn Street, a fat, ginger-bearded fellow in a knitted tricolour cap, that must have been left over from some football match, and an old brown coat tied about the middle with a bit of rope. We studied his habits. By day he would store his box down a lane beside the knife shop and pack up his stuff in plastic bags and set off on his rounds. Amongst the gear he carried with him was a mysterious contraption, a loose bundle of socketed metal pipes of varying thicknesses, like the dismantled parts of a racing bicycle or a chimney sweep's brushes, which he guarded with especial circumspection. Rack our brains though we might we could not think what use the thing could be to him, and though we came up with some ingenious possibilities we rejected them all. Obviously it was precious, though, and despite the considerable transportation problems it posed for him he lugged it everywhere, with the care and reverence of a court official bearing the fasces in solemn procession. His belongings were too much for him to carry all together and so he had devised a remarkable method of conveyance. He would take the pipes and three of his six or seven bulging plastic bags and shuffle forward hurriedly for fifteen yards or so and set down the bags in a doorway or propped against a drainpipe; then, still carrying the precious pipes, he would retrace his steps and fetch the remaining bags and bring them forward and set them down along with the others. There would follow then a brief respite, during which he would check the plastic bags for wear and tear, or rearrange the bundle of pipes, or just stand gazing off, thinking who knows what thoughts, combing stubby fingers through his tangled beard, before setting off again. Of all our derelicts—by the end we had assembled a fine collection of them, wriggling on their pins—Barbarossa was A.'s favourite. She declared she would have liked to have had him for a dad. I make no comment.

One afternoon we found ourselves, I don't know how, in a little square or courtyard somewhere near the cathedral—we could see the bell-tower above us, massive, crazy and unreal—and when we stopped and looked about, something took hold in me, a feeling of unfocused dread, as if without knowing it we had crossed invisible barriers into a forbidden zone. The day was grey and still. A few last leaves tinkled on the soot-black boughs of a spindly, theatrical-looking tree standing in a wire cage. There was no one about but us. Windows in the backs of tall houses looked down on us blankly. I had the sense of some vast presence, vigilant and malign. I wanted to leave, to get away from that place, but A. absently detached her arm from mine and stepped away from me and stood in silence, almost smiling, with her face lifted, listening, somehow, and waiting. Thus the daughter of Minos must have stood at the mouth of the maze, feeling the presence of her terrible brother and smelling the stink of blood and dung. (But if I am Theseus, how is it that I am the one who is left weeping on this desolate shore?) Nothing happened, though, and no one came, and presently she let me take her hand and lead her away, like a sleepwalker. Someday I must see if I can pick up the thread and follow it into the heart of that labyrinth again.

Often in the middle of these outings we would turn without a word and hurry back to the room, swinging along together like a couple in a three-legged race, and there throw off our clothes and fall on the couch as if to devour each other. I hit her, of course; not hard, but hard enough, as we had known I would, eventually. At first she lay silent under these tender beatings, her face buried in the pillow, writhing slowly with her limbs flung out. Afterwards she would have me fetch her the hand-mirror from my work-table so that she could examine her shoulders and hips and the backs of her flanks, touching the bruises that in an hour would have turned from pink to muddy mauve, and running a fingertip along the flame-coloured weals that my belt had left on her. At those times I never knew what she was thinking. (Did I ever?) Perhaps she was not thinking anything at all.

And I, what did I think, what feel? At first bemusement, hesitancy and a sort of frightful exultation at being allowed such licence. I was like the volunteer blinking in the spotlight with the magician's gold watch and mallet in his hands; what if I broke something (*'Go ahead, hit it!'*) and the trick did not work and it stayed broken? From some things there is no going back—who should know that better than I? So I slapped at her gingerly, teeth bared wincingly and my heart in my mouth, until she became exasperated and thrust her rump at me impatiently like an urgent cat. I grew bolder; I remember the first time I drew a gasp from her. I saw myself towering over her like a maddened monster out of Goya, hirsute and bloody and irresistible, Morrow the Merciless. It was ridiculous, of course, and yet not ridiculous at all. I was monster and at the same time man. She would thrash under my blows with her face screwed up and fiercely biting her own arm and I would not stop, no, I would not stop. And all the time something was falling away from me, the accretion of years, flakes of it shaking free and falling with each stylised blow that I struck. Afterwards I kissed the marks the tethers had left on her wrists and ankles and wrapped her gently in the old grey rug and sat on the floor with my head close to hers and watched over her while she lay with her eyes closed, sleeping sometimes, her breath on my cheek, her hand twitching in mine like something dying. How wan and used and lost she looked after these bouts of passion and pain, with her matted eyelashes and her damp hair smeared on her forehead and her poor lips bruised and swollen, a pale, glistening new creature I hardly recognised, as if she had just broken open the chrysalis and were resting a moment before the ordeal of unfolding herself into this new life I had given her. I? Yes: I. Who else was there, to make her come alive?

The whip was our sin, our secret. We never spoke of it, never mentioned it at all, for that would have been to tamper with the magic. And it was magic, more wand than whip, working transfigurations of the flesh. She did not look at me when I was wielding it, but shut her eyes and rolled her head from side to side, slack-mouthed in ecstasy like Bernini's St Theresa, or stared off steadily into the plush torture chamber of her fantasies. She was a devotee of pain; nothing was as real to her as suffering. She had a photograph, torn from some book, that she kept in her purse and showed me one day, taken by a French anthropologist sometime at the turn of the century, of a criminal being put to death by the ordeal of a thousand cuts in a public square in Peking. The poor wretch, barefoot, in skullcap and black pyjama pants, was lashed to a stake in the midst of a mildly curious crowd who seemed merely to have paused for a moment in passing to have a look at this free treat before going on about their busy business. There were two executioners, wiry little fellows with pigtails, also in black, also wearing skullcaps. They must have been taking the job in turns, for one of them was having a stretch, with a hand pressed to the small of his back, while his fellow was leaning forward cutting a good-sized gouge into the flesh of the condemned man's left side just under the ribcage with a small, curved knife. The whole scene had a mundane if slightly festive, milling look to it, as if it were a minor holiday and the execution a familiar and not very interesting part of the day's entertainments. What was most striking was the victim's expression. His face was lifted and inclined a little to one side in an attitude at once thoughtful and passionate, the eyes cast upward so that a line of white was visible under the pupils; the tying of his hands had forced his shoulders back and his knobbled, scrawny chest stuck out. He might have been about to deliver himself of a stirring address or burst out in ecstatic song. Yes, ecstasy, that's it, that's what his stance suggested, the ecstasy of one lost in contemplation of a transcendent reality far more real than the one in which his sufferings were taking place. One leg of his loose trousers was hitched up where the executioner—the one with the crick in his back, no doubt—had been at work on the calf and the soft place at the back of the knee; a rivulet of black blood extended in a zigzag from his narrow, shapely foot and disappeared among the feet of the crowd.

I asked her why she kept such a terrible thing. She was sitting cross-legged on the couch with the photograph in her lap, running a blindman's fingertips over it. I took it from her. The once-glossy surface, cross-hatched with a fine craquelure, had the flaky, filmed-over texture of a dead fish's eye.

'Are you shocked?' she said, peering at me intently; when she looked at me like that I understood how it would feel to be a mirror. Her gaze shifted and settled on the space between us. What did she know? The penumbra of pain, the crimson colour of it, its quivering echo. She did not know the thing itself, the real thing, the flash and shudder and sudden heat, the body's speechless astonishment. I handed her back the photograph. It struck me that we were both naked. All that was needed was an apple and a serpent. Light from the window gave her skin a leaden lustre.

'Tell me about that man you knew,' she said. 'The one that killed the woman.'

She was so still she seemed not even to breathe.

'You know nothing,' I said.

She nodded; her breasts trembled. She found her cigarettes and lit one with a hand that shook. She resumed her cross-legged perch on the end of the couch and gave herself a sort of hug. A flake of ash tumbled softly into her lap.

'Then tell me,' she said, not looking at me.

I told her: midsummer sun, the birds in the trees, the silent house, that painted stare, then blood and stench and cries. When I had recounted everything we made love, immediately, without preliminaries, going at each other like—like I don't know what. '*Hit me*,' she cried, '*hit me!*' And afterwards in the silence of the startled room she cradled my head in the hollow of her shoulder and rocked me with absent-minded tenderness.

'I went to No. 23 the other day after you were gone,' she said. I knew that dreamily thoughtful tone. I waited, my heart starting up its club-footed limp. 'I went to see Rosie,' she said. 'Remember Rosie? There was this fellow there who wanted two women at the same time. He must have been a sailor or something, he said he hadn't had it for months. He was huge. Black hair, these very black eyes, and an earring.'

I moved away from her and lay with my back propped against the curved head of the couch and my hands resting limply on my bare thighs. A soft grey shadow was folded under the corner of the ceiling nearest the window. Dust or something fell on the element of the electric fire and there was a brief crackle and then a dry hot smell.

'Did you open your legs for him?' I said. I knew my lines.

'No,' she said, 'my bum. I lay with my face in Rosie's lap and held the cheeks of my bum apart for him and let him stick it into me as far as it would go. It was beautiful. I was coming until I thought I would go mad. While he was doing it to me he was kissing Rosie and licking her face and making her say filthy things about me. And then when he was ready again I sucked him off while Rosie was eating me. What do you think of that?'

I could feel her watching me, her little-girl's gloating, greedy eye. This was her version of the lash.

'Did you let him beat you?'

'I asked him to,' she said, 'I begged him to. While he was doing me and Rosie he was too busy but afterwards he got his belt and gave me a real walloping while Rosie held me down.'

I reached out gropingly and took one of her feet in my hand and held it tightly. It might have been one huge raw rotten stump of tooth.

'And did you scream?'

'I howled,' she said. 'And then I howled for more.'

'And there was more.'

'Yes.'

'Tell me.'

'No.'

We sat and listened to the faint, harsh sound of our breathing. I shivered, feeling a familiar blank of misery settle on my heart. It was an intimation of the future I was feeling, I suppose, the actual future with its actual anguish, lying in wait for me, like a black-eyed sailor with his belaying-pin. I am not good at this kind of suffering, this ashen ache in the heart, I am not brave enough or cold enough; I want something ordinary, the brute comfort of not thinking, of not being always, always . . . I don't know. I looked at the photograph of the execution where she had dropped it on the floor; amongst that drab crowd the condemned man was the most alive although he was already dying. A. squirmed along the couch, keeping her eyes averted, and lay against me with her knees drawn up and her fists clenched under her chin and her thin arms pressed to her chest.

'I'm sorry,' she said, a sort of sigh, her breath a little weight against my neck. 'I'm sorry.'

We parted hurriedly on those occasions, not looking at each other, like shamefaced strangers who had been forced for a time into unwilling intimacy and now were released. I would stop on the doorstep, dazed by light, or the look of people in the street, the world's shoddy thereness. Or perhaps it was just the sense of my suddenly recovered self that shocked me. As I set off through the streets I would skulk along, wrapped up in my misery and formless dismay, a faltering Mr Hyde in whom the effects of the potion have begun to wear off. Then all my terrors would start up in riotous cacophony.

Aunt Corky said there were people watching the flat. She had rallied in the unseasonably vernal weather. The brassy wig was combed and readjusted, the scarlet insect painted afresh but crooked as ever on her mouth. In the afternoons she would get herself out of bed, a slow and intricate operation, and sit in her rusty silk tea-gown at the big window in the front room watching the people passing by down in the street and the cars vying for parking spaces like bad-tempered seals. When she tired of the human spectacle she would turn her eyes to the sky and study the slow parade of clouds the colour of smoke and ice passing above the rooftops. Surprising how quickly I had got used to her presence. Her smell—her out-of-bed smell, compounded of face powder, musty clothes, and something slightly rancid—would meet me when I came in the door, like someone else's friendly old pet dog. I would loiter briefly in the porch, clearing my throat and stamping my feet, in order to alert her to my arrival. Often in the early days I was too precipitate and would come upon her lost in a reverie from which she would emerge with a start and a little mouse-cry, blinking rapidly and making shapeless mouths. Sometimes even after I had noisily announced my arrival I would enter the room and find her peering up at me wildly with her head cocked and one eyebrow lifted and a terrified surmise in her eye, not recognising me, this impudently confident intruder. I think half the time she imagined the flat was her home and that I was the temporary guest. She talked endlessly when I was there (and when I was not there, too, for all I know); now and then I would find myself halting in my tracks and shaking my head like a horse tormented by flies, ready to hit her if she said one word more. She would stop abruptly then and we would stare at each other in consternation and a sort of violent bafflement. 'I am telling you,' she would declare, her voice quivering with reproach, 'they are down there in the street, every day, watching.' With what a show of outraged frustration she would turn from me then, fierce as any film goddess, swivelling at the waist and tightening her mouth at the side and lifting one clenched and trembling fist a little way and letting it fall again impotently to the arm of her chair. I would have to apologise then, half angry and half rueful, and she would give her shoulders a shake and toss her gilt curls and fish about blindly for her cigarettes.

As it turned out, she was right; we were being watched. I do not know at what stage my incredulity changed to suspicion and suspicion to alarm. The year was darkening. The Vampire was still about his fell business and another mutilated corpse had been discovered, folded into a dustbin in a carpark behind a church. The city was full of rumour and fearful speculation, clutching itself in happy terror. There was talk of satanism and ritual abuse. In this atmosphere the imagination was hardly to be trusted, yet the signs that I was being stalked were unmistakable: the car parked by the convent gates with its engine running that pulled out hurriedly and roared away when I approached; the eye suddenly fixed on me through a gap in a crowd of lunchtime office workers hurrying by on the other side of the street; the figure behind me in the hooded duffle-coat turning on his heel a second before I turned; and all the time that celebrated tingling sensation between the shoulder-blades. I was I think more interested than frightened. I assumed it must be Inspector Hackett's men keeping an eye on me. Then one morning I arrived home still shivery with the afterglow of an early tryst with A. and found the Da's big mauve motor car double-parked outside the front door. Young Popeye was at the wheel. I stopped, but he would not turn his eyes and went on staring frowningly before him through the windscreen, professional etiquette forbidding any sign of recognition, I suppose. He was growing a small and not very successful moustache of an unconvinced reddish tint, which he fingered now with angry self-consciousness as I leaned down and peered at him through the side window. I let myself into the house and mounted the stairs eagerly. I pictured Aunt Corky bound and gagged with a knife to her throat and one of the Da's heavies sitting with a haunch propped on the arm of the couch and swivelling a toothpick from one side of his mouth to the other. Cautiously I opened the door of the flat—how it can set the teeth on edge, the feel of a key crunching into a lock—and put in my head and listened, and heard voices, or a voice, at least: Aunt Corky, spilling invented beans, no doubt.

She was sitting by the fire in her best dress—you should have seen Aunt Corky's best dress—balancing a teacup and saucer on her knee. Facing her, in the other armchair, the Da sat, arrayed in a somewhat tatty, full-length mink coat and a dark-blue felt toque with a black veil (another one!) that looked like a spider-web stuck with tiny flies. He was wearing lumpy, cocoa-coloured stockings—who makes them any more?—and county shoes with a sensible heel. A large handbag of patent leather rested against the leg of his chair. Tea-things were set out on a low table between them. A half-hearted coal fire flickered palely in the grate. 'Ah!' said Aunt Corky brightly. 'Here he is now.'

I came forward hesitantly, feeling an ingratiating smile spreading across my face like treacle. What would be the rules of comportment here?

'I was just passing,' the Da said and did that cracked laugh of his, making a sound like that of something sharp and brittle being snapped, and his veil trembled. Dressed up like this he bore a disconcerting resemblance to my mother in her prime.

'I believe you're working together,' Aunt Corky said and gave me a smile of teasing admonishment, shaking her head, every inch the *grande dame*; she turned back to the Da. 'He never tells me anything, of course.'

The Da regarded me calmly.

'Is Cyril still out there?' he said. 'The son,' he told Aunt Corky; 'he's a good lad but inclined to be forgetful.'

'Oh, don't I know!' Aunt Corky said and cocked her head at me again. 'Will you take off your coat,' she said, 'and join us?'

I drew up a chair and sat down. I kept my coat on.

Cyril.

The Da took a draught of tea. He was having trouble with his veil.

'He was to blow the horn when you arrived,' he said. 'Did he not see you, or what?'

I shrugged, and said he must not have noticed me; I felt suddenly protective towards young Popeye, now that I knew his real name, and had seen that moustache.

There was a silence. A coal in the fire whistled briefly. The Da stared before him with a bilious expression, pondering the undependability of the young, no doubt. Really, it was uncanny how much he reminded me of my mother, God rest her fierce soul; something in the stolid way he sat, with feet apart and planted firmly on the rug, was her to the life.

Aunt Corky's attention had wandered; now she gave a little start and looked about her guiltily.

'We were discussing art,' she said. 'Those pictures.' She smiled dreamily with eyes turned upward and sighed. 'How I would love to see them!'

The Da winked at me and with mock gruffness said, 'Why don't you take your auntie down to that room and let her have a look?' He turned to Aunt Corky. 'They're all the same,' he said, 'no regard.' He put down his cup and heaved himself from the chair with a grunt and walked to the window, stately, imperious and cross. 'Look at him,' he said disgustedly, glaring down into the street. 'The pimply little get.'

While his back was turned I looked at Aunt Corky with an eyebrow arched but she only gazed at me out of those hazed-over eyes and smiled serenely. Her head, I noted, had developed a distinct tremor. I had a vision of her dying and the Da and me carrying her downstairs to the ambulance, I at the head and the Da, his hat raked at a comical angle and his veil awry, clutching her feet and walking backwards and shouting for Cyril.

The Da came back and resumed his seat, arranging his skirts deftly about his big, square knees. His fur coat fell open to reveal a black velvet dress with bald patches. He eyed me genially.

'Have you seen our friend at all?' he said. 'Mr Morden.' I shook my head. He nodded. 'They seek him here, they seek him there,' he said.

I considered for a moment and then asked him if he realised that the police were on to him. He only beamed, lifting his veil to get a better look at me.

'You don't say!' he said. 'Well now.'

I mentioned Hackett's name.

'I know him!' he cried happily, slapping his knee. 'I know him well. A decent man.'

'He asked me about the pictures,' I said.

His shoulders shook. 'Of course he did!' he said, as if this were the best of news.

Aunt Corky had been following these exchanges like a spectator at a tennis match. Now she said, 'A headache for the police, I am sure, such valuable things.' We looked at her. 'Guarding them,' she said. 'And then there would be the question of insurance. I remember dear Baron Thyssen saying to me . . .'

The Da was watching her brightly, with keen attention, like Prince the dog.

'Oh, we don't need that,' he said, 'the Guards, or insurance, any of that. No, no. We can look after our own things by ourselves.' He turned to me again. 'That right, Mr M.?' M for Marsyas, slung upside-down between two bent laurels with his innards on show and blood and gleet dripping out of his hair. 'By the way,' he said, 'I had a dream about you last night.' He lifted a finger and circled it slowly in the air above his head. 'I see things in my dreams. You were in a little room with your books. You weren't happy. Then you were outside and this fellow came along and offered you a job. He knew you were a man he could trust.'

I think of fear as a sort of inner organ, something like a big pink and purple bladder, that suddenly swells up and squeezes everything else aside, heart, liver, lights. It is always a surprise, this sudden, choking efflorescence, I can't say why; God knows, I should be familiar with it by now. The Da's pale eye in its pachydermous folds was fixed on me, and now something in it flashed and it was as if his face were a disguise within a disguise and behind it someone else entirely had stepped up and put a different eye to the empty socket and looked out at me with casual and amused contempt, taking the measure of me, and I flinched and heard myself catch my breath sharply.

The doorbell rang, two short bursts and then a long, and Aunt Corky's teacup rattled. The Da, become his genial self again, grasped his handbag and stood up, grunting. 'There's my call,' he said. Aunt Corky smiled up at him sweetly, her faltering mind elsewhere by now. He took her hand and shook it solemnly. 'Goodbye now, missus,' he said. 'And remember what I say—water, that's the thing for you. Take five or six good big glasses of water a day and you'll be right as rain. I'm a great believer in it.' He nodded slowly, still shaking her hand, his head and arm moving in unison; then he turned and stumped to the door. On the way he paused and peered at himself in the mirror above the sideboard and adjusted his hat and veil. He winked at me over his shoulder and said, 'Are my seams straight?' I opened the door for him. It felt as massive as a bulkhead. My hand on the latch would not be steady. 'Well, ta ta for now,' he said, and wiggled his broad rump and went off cackling down the stairs.

When I came back into the room Aunt Corky gave me a roguish little grin and shook her head.

'The company you keep!' she said.

(*Athena*, 1995)

The Golden World

He arrived in Paris for the first time huddled on a hay cart. That was a morning in the May of 1702, blustery and wet, with silk in the air and Dutch clouds piled up and a dull pewter shine on the river. He was on the run: something to do with a woman. The authorities in Utrecht were looking for him. His mother had wept; his father the roofer, that rude man, had swung a punch at him. He was eighteen and already had a cough—Gillot, his first teacher, told him he sounded like a crow. What was his name then? Faubelin, Vanhoblin, Van Hobellijn: take your pick. He changed his name, his nationality, everything, covering his tracks. He never lost those Dutch gutturals though, at which his fancy friends laughed behind their hands.

For a week he lay on a pallet wrapped in his cloak in a dirty little room above Gérin's print shop on the Pont Notre Dame, shaking with fever and grumbled at by the *maître*. Below him the other student hacks copied holy pictures all day long, lugubrious madonnas, St Jeromes with book and lion, ill-proportioned depositions from the cross. The stink of turpentine and pigments seeped up through the floorboards, and he would say that forever afterwards all studios smelled to him faintly of sickness. There was a war going on and the streets were thronged with beggars showing off their stumps.

He worked at the Opéra, painting sets, and even acted in the drama on occasion. Acting did not suit him, though: too much like life for him, who did not know how else to live except by playing parts. He went to the Comédie and stood in the pit amid the ceaseless noise and bustle and the stench of bodies, lost in contemplation of that glowing world above him on the stage. He never followed the plots, those ridiculous farragos, but watched the actors, studying their movements, their stylised, outlandish gestures. Afterwards he sat alone for hours in the Café Procope, sketching from memory. One of his first submissions to the Academy was a harlequinade in oils, very prettily done, he thought, with just the right balance of gaiety and menace. Second prize. Well.

Le grand hiver

It is the winter of 1709, after the disaster of Malplaquet. There was famine in Paris: mothers would not let their children out alone for fear they would be taken and eaten by the poor. Ice on the Seine, and that strange, thin, sour smell in the air for months that everyone said was the smell of the dead on the battlefield, blowing on the wind all the way down from Valenciennes. In the Tuileries one black night a tree exploded in the frost. Vaublin had been studying with Gillot for four years and was sick of it, the nagging and the sneers, the petty jealousies. Gillot was another like himself, watchful and secretive, a misanthrope. In the end they quarrelled, unforgivable things were shouted and Vaublin left and went to work with his friend Claude Audran at the Luxembourg Palace. Audran was the curator of the palace gallery. Vaublin sat every afternoon for hours, until the light faded and his fingers seized up from the cold, copying Rubens's series on the life of Marie de' Medici, plundering all that old master's secrets. Such silence around him there in those vast, gilded rooms, as if the entire city were dead. He stood at the windows and watched the winter twilight coming on, the icy mist turning the same shade of pink as the big-bummed figures on the canvases behind him.

He was living in the rue Dauphine then, with an excitingly sluttish girl he had picked up one night at the Veuve Laurent and who had stayed because she had nowhere else to go; he knew that as soon as she could find a rich protector she would leave him. Her name was Léonie: my lion, he called her, in his ironical way. He brought her to the comedies but they bored her; she was deficient in a sense of humour. She complained of having to stand in the pit and spent the time watching with envy and resentment the jewelled ladies with their gallants up in the boxes. He painted her as a court beauty, in a borrowed gown and hat.

She stood before the finished portrait for a long time, wrinkling her nose and frowning, and at last pronounced it bad: her waist was too deep (it is true, his female figures are always long-waisted), and he had got her nose all wrong. Why had he made her expression so mournful? And what was she supposed to be looking back at, with her head turned like that, in that awkward way?

The past, he said, and laughed?

That night he coughed blood for the first time, a frighteningly copious flow. Léonie surprised him with her tenderness. She swabbed the blood where it had soaked the sheet, and made a tisane for him, and sat and rocked him like a baby in her arms. Her brother, she said, had suffered from consumption. When he asked her what had become of him she was silent, which was the answer he had feared. He lay against her breast and shivered, light-headed with terror and a sort of shocked hilarity, watching the candle flame shake and sway as if it were the little palpitant flame of his own suddenly frail, enfeebled life.

His friend Antoine La Roque had lost a leg at Malplaquet. Tell me, Antoine, Vaublin asked him, did you think you were going to die? What was it like?

But Antoine only laughed and claimed he could not remember anything except lying on the field and watching a huge thick gold cloud in the zenith floating slowly out of his view. La Roque occasionally contributed art criticism to the *Nouveau Mercure*. Don't worry, Jean, he said gaily, I'll write your obituary.

Fête galante

Living people were too much for Vaublin: he preferred his figures fixed. These strange moments that he painted, so still, so silent, what did they signify for him? He has put a stop to things; here in these twilight glades the helpless tumbling of things through time comes to a halt. His people will not die, even if they have never lived. They exist in stillness; if they were to stir they would vanish.

I like in particular the faint but ever-present air of the perverse that hangs over all his work. From a certain angle these polite arcadian scenes can seem a riotous bacchanal. How lewdly his ladies look, their eager eyes shiny as marbles and their cheeks pinkly aglow, as if from a gentle smacking. Even the props have something tumescent about them, these smooth pillars and tall, thick trees, these pendulous and rounded clouds, these dense bushes where the Marquis's men are lurking, hung like stallions, waiting to be summoned into service.

The parks, the great parks, how he must have loved them, at Anet and Chantilly and Montmorency and Sceaux, above all Sceaux. One summer midnight there he came upon a girl sitting weeping on a stone bench in the park and took her hand without a word and led her through the shrubbery to a little moonlit clearing and made love to her beside a broken statue, smelling her faintly musty, mossy smell and tasting the salt of her tears. She clasped him to her flat little breast and crushed her mouth against his cheek and gasped a word he did not catch—the name of whoever it was she had been weeping for, he supposed—and in a moment it was over and she lay against him in a kind of languorous exhaustion. Over her shoulder he saw in the moonlight an enormous toad come flopping towards them over the grey grass. He never saw the girl again; she remained in his memory only as a scrap of lace, a sharply indrawn breath, the salt taste of tears. The toad he would remember always.

Another war was dragging to a close. The peace was signed at Utrecht. Vaublin was amused; he did not associate his birthplace with peacemaking. He recalled his father standing in the street one summer morning drunk, locked out of the house, in his shirt and boots and no breeches, shouting up abuse at the window of the bedroom where Vaublin's mother cowered on the bed and wept with Vaublin and his little brothers clutched about her (Lancret, Vaublin thought, would do the scene nicely, with his taste for sentiment). That was Utrecht for him.

The Swede Carl Gustaf Tessin called on him and bought a score of counterproofs and ten originals. Vaublin was living then on the quai de Conti, alone, in big, shabby rooms with a good north light. Tessin wrote of him in one of his lively letters home:

> He has promised to paint me a *Festival of the Lenten Fair*, for which I have advanced one hundred livres of the agreed three hundred. It will be his masterpiece, provided he puts the final touches to it, but if he falls into his black humour and his mind is possessed, then away he'll go and it's goodbye masterpiece.

Vaublin went daily to the Fair and wandered among the crowds, looking, looking. He liked the marionette shows and the coarse burlesques, the clumsier the better. He had his favourite characters and painted them again and again: Mezzetin, the scheming valet; poor Gilles, who clowned on the tightrope and always got beaten; and, of course, Polichinelle, that spiteful hunchback. There was something frankly malignant in these spectacles that appealed to Vaublin. He detected the same note, much refined, in the smooth, cruel little comedies of Regnard and Dancourt. The actors from the Comédie sat for him in costume. Paul Poisson, La Thorillière, old Baron, all the leading figures. They were perfect for his purposes, all pose and surface brilliance. They would strike an attitude and hold it for an hour without stirring, in a trance of self-regard. They brought him backstage to the first-night parties, frantic efforts presided over sometimes by Dancourt himself, a plump, self-satisfied cynic. He painted Dancourt's wanton daughter Mimi in the figure of Finette, in a silver gown—how he loved the nacreous sheen and shimmer of those heavy silks!—with a little hat, playing her lute and turning towards the viewer a glance at once wistful and lascivious.

You have made me seem very stout, Mimi said, and looked at him peculiarly, with shining eyes, as if she might be on the point of tears, and gathered up her things and hurried from the studio.

He thought he had offended her, but when next he encountered Dancourt at the theatre the playwright regarded him with cold merriment and said, My daughter, poor doe, is quite smitten with you, you know. Was it a joke? It came to him yet again how little he understood of people.

The double

A curious episode. It was in the summer of 1717, when the dolts in the Academy had at last accepted him as a member—he had presented his *Pélegrinage à l'île joyeuse*; even they could not find much fault with that—and he was moving in exalted company, that he first began to be aware of the presence in the city of this shadowy counterpart. At first it was amusing, when an acquaintance would meet him on the Pont Neuf and stare in surprise, saying he had seen him not five minutes ago in Saint Germain with a lady on his arm and wearing a scarlet cloak. He suspected a conspiracy among his friends to play a hoax on him. Then he began to notice the pictures. There were *Fêtes galantes* and *Amusements champêtres*, and even theatrical scenes, his speciality, the figures in which seemed to look at him with suppressed merriment, knowingly. They were done in a style uncannily like his own, but hastily, with technical lapses and scant regard for quality of surface. Yet they were good—they were alarmingly good, in their hurried, slipshod way. No Lancret or Pater would be capable of such mingled delicacy and power, such dash and daring. They looked like the rushed work of a great master, tossed off in an afternoon or two for an impatient and not very discriminating patron. At times, though, he had the feeling that they were aimed directly at him, an elaborate, monstrous gibe meant to mock his pretensions and the flaws in his technique. But who would be so lavishly gifted that he could afford to squander so much effort on a pointless joke? He tried to get a good look at them, but somehow they always eluded him: he would glimpse a *Récréation galante* being carried between two aproned porters out of a dealer's shop, or a gold and green *Île enchantée* over the fireplace of a fashionable salon just as he was being ushered from the room; when he made enquiries of the collectors that he knew, even the most expert among them could not help him, and only shrugged and said that what he was describing sounded remarkably like his own work. One night at a carnival ball in the Comtesse de Verrue's house on the rue du Cherche-Midi he elbowed his way through the crush and managed to station himself near an interesting little *Fête champêtre*, but the light was poor and the air thick with candle smoke and the fug of bodies, and he could not even make out the signature, a slanted scrawl done with a loaded brush and underscored by a broad black line; at first he thought, with a spasm of something that was almost fright, that the initial was V, but it might as easily have been a U or a W. His nose was almost touching the varnish as he searched for a familiar face among the figures, or a telltale quirk of the brush that might reveal the painter's identity, when Madame Verrue, the *Dame de Volupté* herself, came up to him in that languorously suggestive way that she had and took his arm and led him off to talk to some bore about money.

Everyone must have been talking money in those early days of the System. Law's bank had opened on the rue Quincampoix, and cargoes were on their way from the Indies and Africa and China, and suddenly it seemed everyone was rich in paper money. Vaublin, with his peasant's love of substance, preferred gold. He kept it under the floorboards and sewn into the lining of his cloaks. He discovered in himself a distressing inclination towards gambling, though; almost every other night he would find himself seated at cards at the house of the Loyson sisters, watching in a hot sweat, a terrible smile fixed on his face and the air whistling in his papery lungs as the pile of yellow coins at his elbow steadily dwindled. It was an escape from the studio, from the waiting canvas, from that daytime world of meticulous, mad labours. It was risk against caution, abandon against care, chance against rule. Let it go, let it all go; what did he care.

He was thirty-three that year. His health was worse than ever. Someone told him—he would believe anything—that fresh air was debilitating, and for weeks he did not venture out of doors during daylight hours. He was painting pure dreams now, locked in the solitude of his studio. He did not use models, he could not bear the presence of another near him when he worked; it had always filled him with silent fury, the way they sighed and shifted and tried to make idiotic conversation. Now he no longer needed them. When he wanted a face or a gesture he went to his old sketch-books, or cannibalised his finished work from the past. He was not interested in the individual: he would have been content to have given the same features to all his figures, it did not matter, a nose, eyes, mouth, all the same. What he was after was something intangible, some simple, essential thing that perhaps was not human at all. He came increasingly to recognise that the centre of a painting, that point of equilibrium from which every element of the composition flows and where at the same time all is somehow ingathered, was never where it seemed it should be. The challenge was to find it and work from there. It could be a patch of sky, the fold of a gown, a dog scratching its ear, anything. He was in a hurry all the time. He had never believed in himself, never thought of what he was doing as art; that was what the masters did, real work, while he played. Now he would leave pieces unfinished, thrust them into a corner face to the wall, disgusted with them, and rush on to new subjects, new scenes. He had a feeling constantly of being hindered; some days he had almost to fight his way to the easel, as if there really were an invisible double there before him, crowding him aside. The light dazzled him, the air rattled like stones in his chest.

He witnessed the deportation of wives for the colonists in Louisiana. Women had been rounded up from the stews and the prisons and given a cotton shift and put on board ship in hundreds at the quayside below his windows. There were riots, all night the sky was red with fires. Next day he began work on the *Embarquement pour l'île d'amour*.

That summer was hot. He went out in the pale nights, mingling with the masked, excited crowds at the public balls in the Palais Royal. He liked crowds, liked the clamour and the crush and the feeling of being in the grip of a vast, shapeless, flowing force. He even enjoyed in his bleak way the breathlessness, the sense of teetering on the very brink of panic and suffocation. He could bear it all only for a little while; often he would end up clinging to a pillar in the tree-scented darkness of the Allée d'Argenson, doubled up and coughing out his life. His friend Madame de Caylus nagged at him to have more care.

Look at you! she would cry, when he came hobbling into one of her soirées at midnight, ashen-faced and panting harshly, look at you, Jean Vaublin, you are killing yourself! And she would take his chill, trembling hands in hers and sit down with him on a divan and smile at him chidingly and peer into his face, until he too smiled despite himself and looked away from her and bit his lip like a little boy scolded by his *maman*. Her sympathy irritated him. Sometimes it frightened him, too. She had a way of turning aside from him and letting her face go hard and blank like the face of one turning aside from a deathbed. She plied him with all sorts of crazy cures; it was ice-cold baths one week and cold compresses the next. He tried them all, of course; they seemed only to make him worse. Once, when she pressed him to let her doctor bleed him—as if he were not bleeding enough already!—he flew into a rage.

There is no help for me! he shouted at her, don't you know that?

The summer ended. Autumn was damp and chill that year, with week-long fogs. His strength was failing. When he stepped to the canvas another, heavier arm seemed to lift alongside his. No help, no help on earth.

L'embarquement

He went to England at the end of 1719. Where did he sail from, where did he land? So many things I do not know about him and never will. That must have been the beginning of his final period of hectic wanderings. He had intended to spend a month in London but stayed for half a year. He saw the celebrated Doctor Mead and allowed himself to believe his lungs could be cured. Mead put him on a regimen of quinine and fresh oxblood and took him to Old Slaughter's in St Martin's Lane where he drank Dutch gin and water and ate a pig's foot boiled in brine.

We must fatten you up, sir, the doctor said, and clapped a big soft hand on his meagre shoulder and laughed in his jolly way.

Vaublin grinned uncontrollably into his glass and blushed; how childish these hearty, capable people made him feel. Will I live, doctor? he asked, direct as ever, and the doctor stared at him in consternation and laughed even louder.

Live, man? he roared. Of course you'll live! But he did not say for how long.

Mead was the author of a scholarly work, *The Influence of the Sun and the Moon on the Human Body*, and bored Vaublin with enthusiastic talk of tides and ecliptics and cosmic harmony.

The moon only reminds me of Pierrot, Vaublin said dreamily—and Pierrot, of course, reminds me of myself. A silence followed and then the doctor cleared his throat and changed the subject.

He was an authority also on poisons.

One bright day in April, when Vaublin had coughed up what seemed to him must be at least a litron of blood, he asked the doctor shyly if he would prepare a fatal draught for him, in concentrated form, so that he could carry it with him for use if life at the last should become unbearable—not worth the candle, he said, smiling wryly, pleased with the English phrase. The doctor refused, of course, and grew quite indignant. Things were never the same between them after that.

In June Vaublin returned to France, sicker now than when he had left. Paris was silent, dazed with the great heat of that summer and the shock of economic collapse: the System had failed, Law's bank was closed, the speculators had been ruined. In July came news of the plague in Marseille; the city was declared officially dead. Vaublin had thought he would not live to see the decade change, yet here he was, still hanging on while others all around him died. In January his father had succumbed to the purpural fever; in his heart he was glad that man had not outlived him.

Self-portrait

Poor Vaublin at the end dragging himself all over Paris with the angel after him; that was dying, no mistaking it. He was terrified they would bury him before he was absolutely dead, since after all, as he said, he had never been absolutely alive. Wait for the green spot, he urged them, only half in jest, wait for the gangrenous green spot, as they used to do with the ancient kings. And he laughed, on the verge of tears, as he always seemed to be in those last weeks. He experienced strange periods of euphoria standing before that enormous canvas, lost in the picture surface, almost a part of the paint, his hands working faster than his brain could follow. And then the terrible, sweat-soaked nights, and the recurring dream: the figures in the picture coming dazedly to life like the survivors of some huge catastrophe. And in the mornings shivering at the window in the thin dawn-light, amazed it was all still there, large as life, the roofs, the river, the quayside wreathed in mist, all there and not caring anything for him. Paris! he cried, Paris, I'm dying! And wiped his nose on his knuckles. The figure at his back in the corner always now, watching him with quiet interest, waiting.

He had rented a little attic room on the Île in the house of an old Jew who prayed aloud in the night, keening and sighing. In the mornings a girl from the bakery next door brought him bread and apples, a flask of wine, saying nothing, standing big-eyed in the doorway while he delved for pennies in his purse. When she was there he heard his breathing, how bad it was.

What month is it? he asked her one day.

July!

It was hot. He was so tired, so tired. He left the door open and she began to come in, venturing a little farther each day. She stood by the wall with her hands behind her and watched him work. She was so quiet he could forget she was there. She came back in the night and slept with him, held him shaking in her thin, pale arms. When he woke in the morning she was gone. He put on his smock and walked to the canvas barefoot. It was so much bigger than he. He felt as if he were afloat on some dense, brimming surface. Each brush stroke dragged with a liquid weight. He drifted amongst the figures, bumping softly against this one or that, feeling their insubstantial thereness. Once, working up close against the canvas, he coughed and stippled a patch of sky with blood. He gave Pierrot the girl's face and then painted over it with his own. A self-portrait, the only one he ever did. That night from his pallet, the girl asleep with her bum pressed against his side, he lay and looked at the great pale figure glimmering above him and grinned in the dark. My monster. Me. And then suddenly, without realising it, died.

('The Golden World', 1992)

NOTE The author wishes to acknowledge the great catalogue on the life and works of Antoine Watteau, *Watteau: 1684–1721*, by Margaret Morgan Grasselli and Pierre Rosenberg, with the assistance of Nicole Parmantier (National Gallery of Art, Washington, 1984).

Taking Possession

To take possession of a city of which you are not a native you must first of all fall in love there. I had always known London; my family, although they hardly ever went there, considered it our capital, not dour Belfast, with its rain-coloured buildings and bellowing shipyard sirens. It was only in that summer I spent in London with Nick, however, that the place came fully alive for me. I say I spent the summer with him but that is wishful exaggeration. He was working—another exaggeration—for his father at Brevoort & Klein, and had moved down from Oxford to a flat above a newsagent's shop off the Fulham Road. I remember that flat with remarkable clarity. There was a small living room at the front with two peaked mansard windows that made an incongruously ecclesiastical effect; the first time Boy came there he clapped his hands and cried: 'Fetch me my surplice, we must have a black mass!' The flat was known as the Eyrie, a word neither Nick nor I was sure how to pronounce, but it suited, for certainly it was eerie—Nick favoured tall candles and Piranesi prints—and airy, too, especially in spring, when the windows were filled with flying sky and the timbers creaked like the spars of a sailing ship. Nick, who was by nature a unique mix of the aesthete and the hearty, let the place run to appalling squalor: I still shudder when I think of the lavatory. At the back was a poky bedroom with a sharply canted ceiling, in which there was wedged skew-ways an enormous brass bed Nick claimed to have won in a poker game in a gambling den behind Paddington Station. It was one of Nick's stories.

He did not often sleep at the flat. His girls refused to stay there, because of the filth, and anyway in those times girls rarely stayed overnight, at least not the kind of girl that Nick consorted with. Mostly it was a place to throw parties in, and to recover in from the resulting hangovers. On these occasions he would take to his bed for two or three days, surrounded by an accumulating clutter of books and boxes of sweets and bottles of champagne, supplied by a succession of friends whom he would summon to him by telephone. I can still hear his voice on the line, an exaggeratedly anguished whisper: 'I say, old man, do you think you could come round? I do believe I'm dying.' Usually when I arrived a small crowd would already have assembled, another party in embryo, sitting about on that vast raft of a bed eating Nick's chocolates and drinking champagne from tooth-glasses and kitchen cups, with Nick in his nightshirt propped against a bank of pillows, pale as ivory, his black hair standing on end, all eyes and angles, a figure out of Schiele. Boy would be there, of course, and Rothenstein, and girls called Daphne and Brenda and Daisy, in silks and cloche hats. Sometimes Querell would come round, tall, thin, sardonic, standing with his back against the wall and smoking a cigarette, somehow crooked, like the villain in a cautionary tale, one eyebrow arched and the corners of his mouth turned down, and a hand in the pocket of his tightly buttoned jacket that I always thought could be holding a gun. He had the look of a man who knew something damaging about everyone in the room. (I realise that I am seeing him not as he was then, young, and gauche, surely, like the rest of us, but as he was in his late thirties, when the Blitz was on, and he seemed the very personification of the times: embittered, tense, offhand, amusedly despairing, older than his, and our, years.)

Those parties: did anyone really enjoy them? What I chiefly recall is the air of suppressed desperation that pervaded them. We drank a lot, but drink seemed only to make us frightened, or despairing, so that we must shriek all the louder, as if to scare off demons. What was it that we feared? Another war, yes, the world-wide economic crisis, all that, the threat of Fascism; there was no end of things to be afraid of. We felt such deep resentments! We blamed all our ills on the Great War and the old men who had forced the young to fight in it, and perhaps Flanders really did destroy us as a nation, but—But there I go, falling into the role of amateur sociologist that I despise. I never thought in terms of *us*, or *the nation*; none of us did, I am convinced of it. We *talked* in those terms, of course—we never *stopped* talking thus—but it was all no more than a striking of attitudes to make ourselves feel more serious, more weighty, more authentic. Deep down—if we did, indeed, have deeps—we cared about ourselves and, intermittently, one or two others; isn't that how it always is? *Why did you do it?* that girl asked me yesterday, and I replied with parables of philosophy and art, and she went away dissatisfied. But what other reply could I have given? *I* am the answer to her question, the totality of what I am; nothing less will suffice. In the public mind, for the brief period it will entertain, and be entertained by, the thought of me, I am a figure with a single salient feature. Even for those who thought they knew me intimately, everything else I have done or not done has faded to insignificance before the fact of my so-called treachery. While in reality all that I am is all of a piece: all of a piece, and yet broken up into a myriad selves. Does that make sense?

So what we were frightened of, then, was ourselves, each one his own demon.

Querell when he phoned the other day had the grace not to pretend to be shocked. He knows all about betrayal, the large variety and the small; he is a connoisseur in that department. When he was at the height of his fame (he has slipped somewhat from the headlines, since he is old and no longer the hellion he once was) I used to chuckle over newspaper photographs of him hobnobbing with the Pope, since I knew that the lips with which he kissed the papal ring had most likely been between some woman's thighs a half-hour previously. But Querell too is in danger of being shown up for what he really is, whatever that might be. That fishy look he always had is becoming more pronounced with age. In yet another interview recently—where did he ever get the reputation for shunning publicity?—he made one of those seemingly deep but in fact banal observations that have become his trademark. 'I don't know about God,' he told the interviewer, 'but certainly I believe in the Devil.' Oh yes, one always needed a long spoon to sup with Querell.

He was genuinely curious about people—the sure mark of the second-rate novelist. At those parties in the Eyrie he would stand for a long time leaning with his back against the wall, diabolical trickles of smoke issuing from the corners of his mouth, watching and listening as the party took on an air of monkey-house hysteria. He drank as much as the rest of us, but it seemed to have no effect on him except to make those unnervingly pale-blue eyes of his shine with a kind of malicious merriment. Usually he would slip away early, with a girl in tow; you would glance at the spot where he had been standing and find him gone, and seem to see a shadowy after-image of him, like the paler shadow left on a wall when a picture is removed. So I was surprised when during a party one August afternoon he accosted me in the corridor.

'Listen, Maskell,' he said, in that insinuatingly truculent way of his, 'I can't take any more of this filthy wine—let's go and have a real drink.'

My head felt as if it were stuffed with cotton wool and the sunlight in the mansard windows had taken on the colour of urine, and for once I was content to leave. A girl was standing weeping in the bedroom doorway, her face in her hands; Nick was not to be seen. Querell and I walked in silence down the clattery stairs. The air in the street was blued with exhaust fumes; strange to think of a time when one still noticed the smell of petrol. We went to a pub—was it Finch's then, or had it another name?—and Querell ordered gin and water, 'the tart's tipple', as he said with a snicker. It was just after opening time and there were few customers. Querell sat with one foot hooked on the rung of his stool and the other delicately braced *en pointe* on the floor; he did not undo the buttons of his jacket. I noticed the frayed shirt cuffs, the shine on the knees of his trousers. We were of an age, but I felt a generation younger than him. He had a job on the *Express*, or perhaps it was the *Telegraph*, writing juicy tidbits for the gossip column, and as we drank he recounted office anecdotes, drolly describing the eccentricities of his fellow journalists and the public-school asininity of the editor of the day in what were obviously pre-prepared paragraphs of admirable fluency and precision. Tight though I was I saw clearly that this was a performance, from behind which he was studying me with the detached intentness that was to become his trademark as a novelist. He was already an expert at putting up smokescreens (literally as well as figuratively: he smoked without cease, apparently the same, everlasting cigarette, for I never seemed able to catch him in the act of lighting up).

He came to the end of his stories and we were silent for a while. He ordered more drinks, and when I tried to pay for them he waved my money away with that matter-of-fact assumption of superiority that was another of his characteristics. I don't know why he should have assumed I was broke; on the contrary, I was comparatively well-off at the time, thanks to my column for the *Spectator* and occasional lectures at the Institute.

'You're pretty fond of the Beaver, aren't you,' he said.

It was said with such studied casualness that I grew wary, despite the gin.

'I haven't known him for very long,' I said.

He nodded. 'Of course, you were a Cambridge man. Not that I saw a great deal of him at Oxford.' Nick had said to me of Querell that in their college days he had been too busy whoring to bother much with friendships. Despite recent rumours to the contrary, Querell was an incorrigible hetero, whose fascination with women ran almost to the level of the gynaecological. I thought he always *smelled* faintly of sex. I hear he is still chasing girls, in his seventies, down there on the Côte d'Azur. 'Quite a boy, the Beaver,' he said, and paused, and then gave me a peculiar, sidelong look and asked: 'Do you trust him?' I did not know what to answer, and mumbled something about not being sure that I thought that anyone was really to be trusted. He nodded again, seemingly satisfied, and dropped the subject and began to talk instead about a fellow he had bumped into recently, whom he had known at Oxford.

'He'd interest you,' he said. 'He's a red-hot Sinn Féiner.'

I laughed.

'I'm from the other side of the fence, you know,' I said. 'My people are black Protestants.'

'Oh, Protestants in Ireland are all Catholics, really.'

'Rather the opposite, I should have thought. Or we're all just plain pagans, perhaps.'

'Well, anyway, the place is interesting, isn't it? I mean the politics.'

I wonder—good lord, I wonder if he was putting out feelers with a view to recruiting me, even then? That was the summer of 'thirty-one; was he already with the Department, that early? Or maybe it was just the question of religion that interested him. Although none of us knew it, he was already taking instruction at

Farm Street. (Querell's Catholicism, by the way, has always seemed to me far more of an anachronism than my Marxism.) And in fact now he dropped the subject of politics and went on to talk about religion, in his usual oblique way, telling me a story about Gerard Manley Hopkins preaching at some sort of women's gathering in Dublin and scandalising the congregation by comparing the Church to a sow with seven teats representing the seven sacraments. I laughed, and said what a sad poor fool Hopkins was, trying for the common touch like that and failing ridiculously, but Querell gave me another long, measuring look and said: 'Yes, he made the mistake of thinking that the way to be convincing is to put on a false front,' and I felt obscurely confounded.

We finished our drinks and left the pub, I very bleary indeed by now, and Querell hailed a taxi and we went to Curzon Street, where there was an opening at Alighieri's. The work, by an émigré White Russian whose name I have forgotten, was hopeless trash, a combination of supremacist sterility and Russian-icon kitsch that turned my already drink-insulted stomach. He was all the rage, though, this Supremavitch, and the crowd was so large it had overflowed from the gallery, and people were standing about the pavement in the evening sunshine, drinking white wine and sneering at passers-by, and producing that self-congratulatory low roar that is the natural collective voice of imbibers at the fount of art. Ah, what heights of contempt I was capable of in those days! Now, in old age, I have largely lost that faculty, and I miss it, for it was passion of a sort.

Nick's party seemed to have transferred itself here intact. There was Nick himself, still tousled, still barefoot, with a pair of trousers pulled on over his nightshirt, and Leo Rothenstein in his three-piece suit, and the silken Daphnes and Daisys, and even the weeping girl, red eyed but laughing now, all of them drunk and embarrassingly loud. When they saw Querell and me approaching they turned on us, and someone shouted something at which everyone laughed, and Querell swore and turned on his heel and stalked away in the direction of the park, narrow head held aloft and elbows pressed tightly to his sides; in his high-shouldered dark-brown suit he reminded me of an HP Sauce bottle.

Remarkable how sobering it is to arrive in the midst of people more drunk than oneself; within minutes of stopping on the pavement among that sodden, billowing crowd I began to taste copper at the back of my mouth and felt a headache starting up and knew that I must have more drink or face the rest of the evening in a state of ashen melancholy. Boy had buttonholed me and was shouting into my ear some outrageous tale about an encounter with a negro sailor ('. . . like a length of bloody hawser!') and breathing garlic fumes all over me. I wanted to talk to Nick but the girls had got him, and were hilariously admiring his bare and extremely dirty feet. I broke away from Boy at last and plunged into the interior of the gallery, where, though crowded, it seemed less confined than outside on the pavement. A glass of wine materialised in my hand. I was at that clear-eyed yet hallucinatory stage of inebriation in which the commonplace takes on a sort of comically transfigured aspect. The people standing about seemed the most bizarre of creatures; it struck me how amazing, and amazingly droll, it was that human beings should go about upright and not on all fours, which would surely be more natural, and that of those gathered here, practically everyone, including myself, was equipped with a glass which he or she must hold upright while at the same time talking at the highest possible speed and volume. It all seemed quite mad and laughable and at the same time acutely, achingly moving. I turned away from the Russian's daubs, which everyone else was ignoring anyway, and made my way into the back rooms, where Wally Cohen had his offices. Wally, a little roly-poly fellow with curls ('Shylock's shy locks'—Boy), made a sort of running gag of his Jewishness, rubbing his hands and smiling oilily and referring to his co-religionists as Jewboys and snipcocks. I suspect he was at heart an anti-Semite, as a lot of the Jews whom I knew were, in those pre-war days. I came upon him in a storeroom, one ham perched on the corner of a table, swinging a chubby little leg and talking animatedly to a dark-haired young woman whom I seemed vaguely to recognise.

'Victor, my boy!' he cried. 'You have a haunted, hungry look.'

Wally had been a Marxist since his teens, one of the first of us to contract the virus.

'I've been drinking with Querell,' I said.

He chuckled. 'Ah, the pontiff; yes.'

The young woman, whom he had not bothered to introduce, was regarding me with a sceptical eye, trying, so it seemed to me, not to laugh. She was short and dark and compactly made, with bruised shadows under her eyes. She wore one of those tube-shaped dresses of the time, made of layers of bronze-black silk along which the light darkly shimmered and flashed, and I thought of a scarab beetle, locked in its brittle, burnished carapace. Wally resumed his conversation with her and she turned her attention slowly away from me. He was going on about some painter whose work he had lately discovered—José Orozco, someone like that. Wally was one of those genuine enthusiasts the world at the time was still capable of producing. He was to die seven years later, with Cornford's brigade, at the siege of Madrid.

'It's the only thing that's possible any longer,' he was saying. 'People's art. The rest is bourgeois self-indulgence, masturbation for the middle classes.'

I glanced at the young woman: words like masturbation were not uttered as lightly then as now. She gave a jaded laugh and said:

'Oh, do shut up, Wally.'

He grinned and turned to me. 'What do you say, Victor? Sure

and begorrah, isn't it the revolution itself that's coming to this land of the oppressor?'

I shrugged. Bumptious Jews like Wally were hard to stomach; the camps had not yet made his tribe into the chosen people once again. Besides, he had never liked me. I suspect he knew how much I hated my name—only bandleaders and petty crooks are called Victor—for he used it at every opportunity.

'If you're so much in favour of Socialist art,' I said, 'why are you exhibiting that White trash out there?'

He lifted his shoulders, grinning, and showed me his merchant's palms. 'It sells, my boy; it sells.'

Nick came wandering in then, his bare feet slapping the floorboards and his drunken smile askew. He exchanged a sardonic and, as it seemed to me, curiously complicit glance with the young woman and a second later I realised who she was.

'Look at us,' he said happily, sweeping his wineglass in an unsteady arc that encompassed himself and the party behind him, as well as Wally and his sister and me. 'What a decadent lot.'

'We were just anticipating the revolution,' Wally said.

Nick laughed at that. I turned to Baby.

'I'm sorry,' I said, 'I knew I knew you but . . .'

She lifted an eyebrow at me and answered nothing.

The room was painted greyish white and the ceiling was a shallow dome. Two filthy windows side by side looked out on a cobbled yard thick with evening sunlight shining straight from Delft. Pictures were stacked against the walls under a fur of mouse-grey dust. Unnerved by Baby's challenging, slightly bulbous gaze, I went and poked amongst them. Failed fashions of past years, tired, sad and shamefaced: orchards in April, the odd wan nude, some examples of English cubism that were all soft angles and pastel planes. And then there it was, in its chipped gilt frame, with a cracked coating of varnish that made it seem as if hundreds of shrivelled toenails had been carefully glued to the surface. It was unmistakable what it was, even at first glance, and in poor light. I laid it back quickly against the wall, and a sort of hot something began swelling outward from a point in the centre of my breast; whenever I look at a great picture for the first time I know why we still speak of the heart as the seat of the emotions. My breathing grew shallow and my palms were moist. It was as if I had stumbled on something indecent; this was how I used to feel as a schoolboy when someone would pass me a dirty picture under the desk. I am not exaggerating. I have never cared to examine the roots of my response to art; too many tendrils coiling about each other down there in the dark. I waited a moment, telling myself to be calm—the alcohol in my system had suddenly all evaporated—and then, taking a deep breath, I lifted out the picture and carried it to the window.

Definitely.

Wally was on to me at once.

'Seen something you like, Victor?' he said.

I shrugged, and peered closely at the brushwork, trying to appear sceptical.

'Looks like *The Death of Seneca*, by what's-his-name,' Nick said, surprising me. 'We saw it in the Louvre, remember?' I imagined myself kicking him, hard, on the shin.

Wally came and stood at my shoulder, breathing. 'Or another working of the same subject,' he said thoughtfully. 'When he found a subject he liked, he stuck to it until it was done to death.' He was interested now; my reviews annoyed him, but he respected my eye.

'Well, I think it's school of,' I said, and put the picture back in its place, with its face to the wall, expecting it to cling to my hand like a child about to be abandoned. Wally was eyeing me with malicious speculation. He was not fooled.

'If you want it,' he said, 'make me an offer.'

Nick and Baby were sitting side by side on Wally's table in an oddly crumpled attitude, heads hanging and legs limply dangling, graceful and lifeless as a pair of marionettes. Suddenly I was shy in their presence, and said nothing, and Wally looked at them and then at me and nodded, closing his eyes and slyly smiling, as if he understood my predicament of the moment, which I did not: something to do with art, and embarrassment, and desire, all mixed together.

'Tell you what,' he said. 'Five hundred quid and it's yours.'

I laughed; that was a fortune in those days.

'I could manage a hundred,' I said. 'It's an obvious copy.'

Wally put on one of his shtetl expressions, narrowing his eyes and setting his head to the side and hunching a shoulder. 'What are you saying to me, my man—a copy, is it, a copy?' Then he straightened up again and shrugged. 'All right: three hundred. That's as low as I'll go.'

Baby said: 'Why don't you get Leo Rothenstein to buy it for you? He has pots of money.'

We all looked at her. Nick laughed, and jumped down nimbly from the table, suddenly animated.

'That's a good idea,' he said. 'Come on, let's find him.'

My heart sank (odd formulation, that; the heart does not seem to fall, but to *swell*, rather, I find, when one is alarmed). Nick would turn the thing into a rag, and Wally would get peeved, and I would lose my chance, the only one I was ever likely to have, to take possession of a small but true masterpiece. I followed him and Baby (I wonder, by the way, why she was called that—her name was Vivienne, cool and sharp, like her) out to the pavement, where the crowd had thinned. Leo Rothenstein was there still, though, we heard his booming, plummy tones before we saw him. He was talking to Boy and one of the blonde, diaphanous girls. They were discussing the gold standard, or the state of Italian politics, something like that. Small talk on large topics, the chief characteristic of the time. Leo had the matt sheen of the very rich. He was handsome, in an excessively masculine way, tall, full-chested, with a long, swarth, Levantine head.

'Hello, Beaver,' he said. I got a nod, Baby a sharp, appraising look and the shadow of a smile. Leo was parsimonious with his attentions.

'Leo,' Nick said, 'we want you to buy a picture for Victor.'

'Oh, yes?'

'Yes. It's a Poussin, but Wally doesn't know it. He's asking three hundred, which is a snip. Think of it as an investment. Better than bullion, a picture is. You tell him, Boy.'

Boy, for reasons that I could never understand, was considered to have something of a feeling for pictures, and on occasion had advised Leo's family on its art collection. It amused me to imagine him in the company of Leo's father, an august and enigmatic gentleman with the look of a Bedouin chieftain, the two of them pacing the showrooms and gravely pausing before this or that big brown third-rate canvas, Boy all the while struggling to suppress a laugh. Now he did his gargoyle grin: eyes bulging, nostrils flared, the thick, fleshy mouth turned down at the corners. '*Poussin?*' he said. 'Sounds tasty.'

Leo was measuring me with genial distrust.

'I have a hundred,' I said, with the sense of setting a foot down firmly on a sagging tightrope. When Leo laughed his big, soft laugh you could almost see the sound coming out of his mouth spelled out in letters: *Ha, Ha, Ha*.

'Oh, go on,' Nick said and scowled in tipsy petulance from Leo to me and back again, as if it were his game and we were laggards. Leo looked at Boy and something passed between them, then he turned his measuring eye back on me.

'You say it's genuine?' he said.

'If I had a reputation I'd stake it on it.'

The tightrope thrummed. Leo laughed again and shrugged.

'Tell Wally I'll send him a cheque,' he said, and turned away.

Nick punched me softly on the shoulder. 'There,' he said; 'told you.' He seemed suddenly quite drunk. I had a sensation of helpless, happy falling. Baby squeezed my arm. The blonde girl stepped close to Boy and whispered, 'What's a Poussin?'

(*The Untouchable*, 1997)

The Lost Ones

I

The telephone began to shrill, giving me a fright. I had not known it was still connected. After a flustered search I found it in the hall, on the floor behind a disembowelled sofa. It was an old-fashioned model made of Bakelite; the receiver had the osseous heft of a tribal artefact, shaped and polished by long and murderous use. I took a moment to register Lydia's voice on the line. I heard her dry laugh.

'Have you forgotten us already?' she said.

'I didn't know the telephone still worked.'

'Well, it does.' A beat of breathing silence. 'And how is the hermit?'

'Hungover.' I could see through into the kitchen; the window there had a flaw in one of its panes, and when I made the tiniest movement of my head a tree in the garden seemed to ripple, as if refracted under water. 'I was drinking with Quirke,' I said.

'With what?'

'Quirke. Our so-called caretaker.'

'Much care he's taken.'

'He brought a bottle of whiskey.'

'To launch you on your new life. Did he break it over your head?'

I could see the scene, the morning light like heavy pale gas and Lydia standing in the living room of the big old dark house by the sea that had been part of her inheritance from her father, with the receiver wedged between shoulder and jaw, a trick that I have never been able to master, talking sideways into it as if it were a sleepy infant cradled beside her face. There is the briny smell of the sea, the far cry of gulls. It all seemed so clear and yet so far away it might have been a vision of life on another planet, unimaginably distant from this one, yet similar in every detail.

'Cass called again,' Lydia said.

'Yes?' Slowly I sat down on the sofa, sinking so low my chin almost touched my knees, the sofa's horsehair guts spilling out from underneath and tickling my bare ankles.

'She has a surprise for you.'

She breathed a brief laugh.

'Oh?'

'You'll be amazed.'

No doubt I shall; a surprise from Cass is a formidable prospect. The tree beyond the flawed pane in the kitchen window rippled. Lydia made a sound that to my consternation seemed a sob; when she spoke again her voice was husky with reproach. 'I think you should come home,' she said. 'I think you should be here when she arrives.' I had nothing to say to that. I was remembering the day my daughter was born. She sprang into the world, a smeared and furious fingerling, bearing the generations with her. I had not been prepared for so many resemblances. She was my mother and father, and Lydia's father and dead mother, and Lydia herself, and a host of shadowy ancestors, all of them jostling together, as in the porthole of a departing emigrant ship, in that miniature face contorted upon the struggle for breath. I was present for the birth—oh, yes, I was very progressive, went in for all that kind of thing; it was another performance, of course, inwardly I quailed before the bloody spectacle. By the time the baby came I was in a sort of daze, and did not know where to turn. They put the infant in my arms before they had even washed her. How light she was, yet what a weight. A doctor in bloodied green rubber boots spoke to me but I could not understand him; the nurses were brisk and smug. When they lifted Cass away from me I seemed to hear the twang of an umbilical cord, one that I had paid out of myself, severing. We brought her home in a basket, like some precious piece of shopping we could not wait to unwrap. It was winter, and there was an alpine sting to the air. I recall the pallid sunlight on the car park—Lydia blinking like a prisoner led up from the dungeons—and the cold fresh fragrant breeze coming down from the high hills behind the hospital, and nothing to be seen of the baby but a patch of vague pink above a satin blanket. When we got her home we had no cot for her, and had to put her in the open bottom drawer of a tallboy in our bedroom. I could hardly sleep for fear of getting up in the night and forgetting she was there and slamming it shut. Triangles of watery light from the headlamps of passing motor cars kept opening across the ceiling only to be folded smartly again and dropped, like so many ladies' fans, into the drawer where she was asleep. We had a nickname for her, what was it? Hedgehog, I think; yes, that was it, because of the tiny snuffling noises she made. Bright, innocent-seeming days, in my memory of them, though the clouds were already massing behind the horizon.

'I am talking to myself here,' Lydia said, with a tight, exasperated sigh.

I allowed my eyes to close, feeling the rims of the inflamed lids hotly touch. My head ached. 'When is she arriving?' I said.

'Oh, she won't say, of course—that would be too simple.' Lydia's voice always takes on a bridling tone when she speaks of our difficult daughter. 'She'll probably just appear one day out of the blue.'

Another silence then, in which I could hear the rustle of my own breathing in the mouthpiece. I opened my eyes and looked out to the kitchen again. What struck me first about the image, vision, hallucination—I would not have known what to call it, had I thought to call it anything—that I glimpsed out there was the ordinariness of it: the figure of a woman, tall, young, turning from the range, abruptly handing something, it looked like, to what seemed a seated child. Slowly I set the receiver down on the arm of the sofa. No sound at all, except for a faint, a very faint hissing, that might have been no more than the sound of my own self, blood, lymph, labouring organs, making its low susurrus in my ears. I was given only that glimpse—the woman, if it was a woman, turning, the arm extending, the child unmoving, if it was a child—and then it was gone. I squeezed my sore eyes shut again, trying to retain the image. It was all inexplicably, achingly familiar.

I walked softly out to the kitchen and stood and looked about. No one was there. Everything was as it had been a minute ago, before the phone rang, except for a sense of general suspension, as of things holding themselves in stillness, not daring to breathe. I returned to the hall and sat down again on the sofa, a sort of collapse, and exhaled a shuddery sigh. Lydia was still on the line.

'What?' she said snappishly. 'What did you say?'

I felt a piercing cold.

'I said, the place is haunted.' I was laughing now, unmanageable, feathery gasps of laughter burbling out of me.

Another silence.

'You are your own ghost,' Lydia said, with angry haste, and I heard the receiver drop with a crash into its cradle an instant before the connection broke, she too all at once become phantom, fading into air and distance.

• • •

It was not the first time I had seen a ghost in this house. One day, when I was a boy, in the dreamy boredom of a summer afternoon

I climbed up the unlit steep stairs to the garret, drawn there at who knows what behest. The room was hot under the slanted, low ceiling. Someone, my mother, I suppose, in one of her periodic doomed attempts at thriftiness, had spread shallots on the bare wooden floor to preserve them for a winter that now was long past, and the air was spiced with their sweet decayed dry odour, stirring in me a tangle of indistinct rememberings. There was a single, small window here, round, like a porthole, at which I was leaning, peering out vacantly through the dusty pane into an immensity of dense blue air, when something, not a sound but a sort of tightening in the atmosphere of the room, made me turn my head. I expected it would be one of the lodgers; sometimes on my prowls I would meet one of the more peculiar among them, creeping about, looking for something to spy on or to steal, I suppose. But it was not a lodger. It was my dead father, standing in the open doorway, as real as in life, dressed in striped pyjamas and shoes without laces and an old wheat-coloured cardigan, the same attire that he had worn every day in the long last months of his dying. He held himself stooped in an attitude of indecision, not looking at me, apparently unaware of me, with his head inclined a little, listening, it might be, or trying to recollect something, to capture some stray thought. After a moment he seemed to give up the effort, whatever it was, and shrugged, letting one shoulder droop in that way that he had, and turned and ducked through the doorway out to the stairs and was gone.

I was not frightened. I would have been, I am sure, had he looked directly at me, or given some sign that he knew I was there. As it was, I was only puzzled, and curious, too, of course. Afterwards, I supposed I had been asleep somehow, in some kind of waking sleep, or trance, although there had been no moment at which I had felt myself coming to. I thought of telling my mother what I had seen, and even went down through the house in search of her, but when I found her I was overcome by a sort of shyness, and knew that I must preserve the visit, or haunting, or whatever it had been, against the contamination of a mere recounting of it. For I believed I had been privileged, a privileged witness to some bit of intimate and perhaps momentous business, as when at school one day passing by an empty classroom I had glimpsed a teacher, a youngish man with red hair—I can still see him, so clearly—standing by the blackboard with a letter in his hands, weeping lavishly, his shoulders shaking, with dark stains on his soutane where the tears were splashing.

For a long time after I saw my father everything was bathed in a faint glow of strangeness, an unearthly radiance. The world seemed tilted slightly out of true. Now, all these years later, when I saw the woman in the kitchen, I thought at once that I must have conjured up the apparition in order that it might have the same effect, that is, to make me disoriented, and alienate me from my surroundings and from myself. For I had determined, from the moment Lydia had left me on the doorstep and driven away with tears in her eyes, that I would not let myself become accustomed to the new life I had entered into on the site of the old, and had been angry to discover straight away that I was failing. To be watchful and attentive of everything, to be vigilant against complacency, to resist habituation, these were my aims in coming here. I would catch myself, red-handed, in the act of living; alone, without an audience of any kind, I would cease from performing and simply *be*. And what would be my register of being if not things, the more commonplace the better? Yet almost immediately I found myself settling down in these once familiar surroundings and letting them be so again, with all my plans and pledges forgotten. Even the first sight of my old room had affected me hardly at all; what makes for presence if not absence?—I mean the presence of oneself as a remembered other—and I might as well never have gone away, so little of me was there, to be pondered on or grasped. *Making strange*, people hereabouts say when a child wails at the sudden appearance of a visitor; how was I to make strange now, and not stop making strange? How was I to fight the deadening force of custom? In a month, in a week, I told myself, the old delusion of belonging would have re-established itself irremediably.

So if the purpose of the appearance of this ghost is to dislocate me and keep me thrown off balance, am I indeed projecting it out of my own fancy, or does it come from some outside source? Both, somehow, it seems, although I do not understand how that can be. That glimpse through the kitchen doorway was the first of many such sightings, brief, diaphanous, gleamingly translucent, like a series of photographs blown up to life-size and for a moment made wanly animate. What happens in them continues to be remarkable only in its being unremarkable, the woman going about what seem to be commonplace tasks—nothing is definite in the dimension in which she exists—or just standing, silent, lost in reverie. It is not possible to make out her features properly. That is, I see the scenes in photographic sharpness, but the figures themselves are not finally realised, their features not fully developed, as if they had moved a fraction while the plate was still being exposed. The child in particular is unfixed; I do not know why I even call it a child, so vague and amorphous is its form; it is the mere idea of a child, no more. They are still growing into existence, these shadows made of light, or perhaps they existed once and are fading now. Whatever they are engaged in, whatever attitude they strike, they seem always somehow guardedly at attention. Have they, I wonder, on their side, an intimation of my presence? Am I to them what they are to me, a fleeting brightness glimpsed out of the corner of the eye, through a doorway, or pausing for a second on the stairs and then vanishing with a noiseless sigh? And it is not just these two—that is, they are the ones I see, if see is the word, but there is the sense of others, too, a world of unseen others, through which this woman and her formless child move, and in which they have their life, if life is the word.

I am not afraid of them, just as I was not afraid when my father appeared to me that day in the garret. There is too much the sense of striving, of large and melancholy effort on their part, for them to be truly frightening. Some intricate system, elaborate yet mundane, an unknown unity, some little lost and desolated order, is trying to put itself into place here, to assemble itself within the ill-fitting frame of the house and its contents. I am convinced they are making the effort not only out of an unavoidable compulsion—these creatures are struggling somehow to *come to being*—but that it is for my benefit, too. I believe these phenomena are in some way concentrated on me and my state, intricately involved in the problem of whatever it is that has gone wrong with me. There is pathos in the notion of this poor half-developed world struggling blindly, in bafflement, perhaps in pain, to come fully to life, so that I might . . . what? Have something demonstrated to me? Be a witness? Be instructed? Or is it, I ask myself, is it that something is trying to exist *through me*, to find some form of being, *in me*? For although I speak of them appearing outside of me, a moving spectacle, like figures on a stage, in fact—in fact!—I am amongst them, I am of them, and they are of me, my familiars.

[• • •]

I am thinking of my daughter. At once an angry buzzing of emotions starts up in my breast. She exasperates me, I confess it. I do not trust her. I know, I know, there is even a name for the syndrome from which she suffers, yet half the time I think there is nothing at all the matter with her, that her fits and fallings, her obsessions, her black days and violent sleepless nights, are all no more than a strategy to make me pay for some enormity she imagines I visited on her in the far past. At times she has a look, a fleeting, sidelong, faintly smiling look, in which I seem to glimpse a wholly other she, cold and sly and secretly laughing. With such ingenuity does she connect the workings of the world to her own fate. Everything that happens, she is convinced, carries a specific and personal reference to her. There is nothing, not a turn in the weather, or a chance word spoken in the street, that does not covertly pass on to her some profound message of warning or encouragement. I used to try to reason with her, talking myself into spluttering, head-shaking, wildly laughing transports of frustration and rage, while she stood silently before me, as if in the stocks, shoulders up and arms hanging and her chin drawn down to her collarbone, frowning in sullen refusal and defiance. There was no keeping track of her moods, I never knew when she might veer aside and turn and confront me with a new version of herself, a whole new map of that strange, intense and volatile world that she alone inhabits. For that is how she makes it seem, that she lives in a place where there is no one else. What an actor she is! She puts on a character with an ease and persuasiveness that I could never match. Yet perhaps she is not feigning, perhaps that is her secret, that she does not act, but variously is. Like the sorcerer's assistant, she steps smiling into the spangled casket and comes out the other side transfigured.

Lydia never shared my doubts. This is, of course, another source of annoyance to me. How she would run to Cass, breathless with forced enthusiasm, and try to press her into the latest game she had devised to divert the child's attention from herself and her manias. And Cass would play along for a while, all smiles and trembling enthusiasm, only to turn away in the end and retreat again listlessly into herself. Then Lydia would seem the crestfallen child and Cass the withholding adult.

She was five or six when she displayed the first symptoms of her condition. I came home late one night after a performance and she was standing in her nightdress in the darkness at the top of the stairs, talking. Even yet, as I remember her there, a slow shiver crawls across the back of my scalp. Her eyes were open and her face was empty of expression; she looked like a waxwork model of herself. She was speaking in a low, uninflected voice, the voice of an oracle. I could not make out what she was saying except that it was something about an owl, and the moon. I thought she must be rehearsing in her sleep a nursery rhyme or jingle out of infancy. I took her by the shoulders and turned her about and walked her back to her room. She is the one who at such times is supposed to experience strange auras, but that night it was I who noticed the smell. It was the smell, I am convinced, of what was, is, wrong with her. It is not at all extraordinary, just a dull flat grey faint stink, like that of unwashed hair, or a garment left in a drawer and gone stale. I recognised it. I had an uncle, he died when I was young, I barely remember him, who played the accordion, and wore his hat in the house, and walked with a crutch. He had that smell, too. The crutch was an old-fashioned one, a single thick rough stave and a curved crosspiece padded with sweat-stained cloth; the part of the upright where his hand grasped it was polished to the texture of grey silk. I thought it was this crutch that smelled, but now I think it was the very odour of affliction itself. Cass's room in the lamplight was obsessively neat, as always—there is a touch of the nun to our Cass—yet to my alarmed heart it seemed a site of wild disorder. I made her lie down on the bed, still murmuring, her eyes fixed on my face, her hands clutching mine, and it was as if I were letting her sink into some dark deep pool, under a willow, at dead of night. Sleepily Lydia appeared in the doorway behind us, a hand in her hair, wanting to know what was the matter. I sat down on the side of the narrow bed, still holding Cass's cold pale hands. I looked at the toys on the shelves, at the lampshade stuck with faded transfers; on the wallpaper, cartoon characters pranced and grinned. I felt the darkness pressing around our cave of lamplight like the ogre in a fairy tale. A gloating moon hung crookedly in the window above the bed and when I looked up it seemed to tip me a fat wink, knowing and horrible. Cass's voice when she spoke was scratchy and dry, a fall of dust in a parched place.

'They're telling me things, Daddy,' she said, and her fingers holding mine tightened like wires. 'They're telling me things.'

What things the voices told her, what actions they urged, she would never say. They were her secret. She had periods of respite, weeks, months, even, when of their own accord they would go silent. How still the house seemed then, as if a clamour audible to all had lapsed. But presently, when my ears had adjusted, I would become aware again of that sustained note of anxiety that was always there, in every room, thin and piercing enough to shatter the frail glass of any hope. Of the three of us, Cass was the calmest in face of these disorders. Indeed, such was her calm at times that she would seem to be not there at all, to have drifted off, lighter than air. It is a different air in which she moves, a separate medium. For her I think the world is always somewhere other, an unfamiliar place where yet she has always been. This is for me the hardest thing, to think of her out there, standing on some far bleak deserted shore, beyond help, in unmoving light, with an ocean of lostness all before her and the siren voices singing in her head. She was always alone, always outside. One day when I was collecting her from school I came upon her looking down the length of a long, green-painted corridor to where at the far end a raucous group of girls was gathered. They were preparing for some game or outing, and their laughter and sharp cries made the deadened air ring. Cass stood with her schoolbag clasped to her breast, leaning forward a little, with her head on one side, frowning, helplessly eager, like a naturalist glimpsing some impossible, brilliant-hued new species that had alighted on the far bank of an unfordable river and in a moment would rise and fly away again, into the deeps of the forest, where she could not hope to follow. When she heard my step she looked up at me and smiled, my Miranda, and her eyes did that trick they had of seeming to turn over in their sockets like two flat metal discs to show their blank, defensive backs. We walked together in silence out to the street, where she stopped and stood for a moment motionless, looking at the ground. A March wind grey as her school overcoat whipped up an eddy of dust on the pavement at our feet. The cathedral bell had been ringing, the last reverberations fell about us, wrinkling the air. She told me how in history class they had learned about Joan of Arc and her voices. She raised her eyes and narrowed them and smiled again, looking off toward the river.

'Do you think they'll burn me at the stake, too?' she said. It was to become one of her jokes.

Memory is peculiar in the fierce hold with which it will fix the most insignificant-seeming scenes. Whole tracts of my life have fallen away like a cliff into the sea, yet I cling to seeming trivia with a pop-eyed tenacity. Often in these idle days, and in the wakeful nights especially, I pass the time picking over the parts of this or that remembered moment, like a blackbird grubbing among dead leaves, searching for the one telling thing lurking in the clay, among the wood-scurf and dried husks and discarded wing casings, the morsel that will give meaning to a meaningless remembrance, the fat grub concealed in open sight under the camouflage of the accidental. There are times with Cass that should be burned into the inner lining of my skull, times that I thought as I endured them I would never be so fortunate as to forget—the nights by the telephone, the hours spent watching over the crouched unmoving form under the tangled sheets, the ashen waits in anonymous consulting rooms—that yet seem to me now no more than the vague remnants of bad dreams, while an idle word of hers, a look thrown back from a doorway, an aimless car journey with her slumped silent beside me, resonate in my mind, rife with significance.

There is the icy Christmas afternoon when I took her to the park to try out her first pair of roller skates. The trees were white with hoar-frost and a crepuscular pinkish mist hung in the motionless air. I was not in a pretty mood; the place was full of screaming children and their irritatingly forbearing fathers. Cass on her skates clung to me with trembling fierceness and would not let go. It was like teaching a tiny invalid the rudiments of mobility. In the end she lost her balance and the edge of her skate struck me on the ankle and I swore at her and furiously shook off her clutching hand and she teetered this way and that for a moment and then her legs shot out from under her and she sat down suddenly on the cindered path. What a look she gave me.

There was another day when she fell again, a day in April, it was, and we were walking together in the hills. The weather was wintry still. There had been a brief fall of soft wet snow, and now the sun had come infirmly out, and the sky was made of pale glass, and the gorse was a yellow flame against the whiteness, and all about us water was dripping and trickling and covertly running under the lush, flattened grass. I remarked that the snow was icy, and she pretended to think I had said icing, and wanted to know where the cake was, and held her sides in exaggerated hilarity, doing her snuffly laugh. She was never a gainly girl, and that day she was wearing rubber boots and a heavy padded coat that made the going all the harder, and when we were coming down a stony track between two walls of blue-black pines she tripped and fell over and cut her lip. The drops of her blood against the patchwork snow were a definition of redness. I snatched her up and held her to me, a bulky warm ball of woe, and one of her quicksilver tears ran into my mouth. I think of the two of us there, among the shivering trees, the birdsong, the gossipy swift whisperings of trickling water, and something sags in me, sags, and rebounds with a weary effort. What is happiness but a refined form of pain?

(*Eclipse*, 2000)

II

So this, she saw, was where it would end. There was nowhere farther for her to go, and she was glad. She had watched from the deck of the little ferry boat the five towns receding into the evening vaguenesses of sea and sky and the humped night rising plum-blue behind the headlands, and thought how she too was disappearing, into the dark. That was how it had been all along, since she had left Turin, if not before, if not long before, a secret, gradual process of thinning and fading. The world was letting her go, as he too had let her go. She understood clearly what was happening, what must happen, so that the pattern would be complete. She had tried to explain it to Kristina Kovacs, the way everything was a part of everything else, the way it was all ordained, but Kristina had not understood. Kristina, she saw clearly, was trying to save her, as once she in turn had thought it was her task to save him. But that was not it, that was not it at all. Now they were docking, and she had a moment almost of bliss as the boat glided in silence toward the quayside, where shadowy figures waited, strangely still, until an old man in a seaman's cap stepped forward nimbly and caught the rope one of the sailors threw to him. The water swayed, smooth as oil, its surface running with coloured lights, peach and mauve and rose. Bats flitted in the sombre air. There were cafés and bars and little restaurants all along the quay, and, behind that, the village climbed the hillside, lamps in the windows of the houses, so many lives. There was a lamp too, or a lantern, above the door of the church that stood on its jagged promontory outlined against the darkening sky. A sailor from the ferry carried her bag all the way up to the hotel. How simply everything was happening.

She wrote again in her notebook, calm now, sitting under a lamp by the open window of her room, a moth making its tiny soft racket around the bulb and the small waves breathing below on the shingle. Columbine is sick. The Doctor is called. Oh, save me, save me, Dottore! Columbine is going to have a baby. The Old Man is angry. *She smiled and put away the notebook and folded her arms on the table and laid her head on her arms. She felt herself slipping gradually down a dark, immense incline. That is time, she thought, time is the curve, it steepens. Everything she had ever done, her smallest acts, even in earliest infancy, had brought her to this moment, these unavoidable moments, the last. So strange, and yet so simple. She lifted her head with an effort, for she was tired, and sat for a while, listening to the drowsy noises of the night. She had gone to see the doctor, the elegant old doctor with the dyed hair. He had been kind, moving his priestly hand over her belly, sighing. She saw the numbers on his wrist and understood. He had wanted her to go into a clinic, to end it, to have it ended. 'What will you do?' he had asked. 'Where will you turn?' And he had looked at her for a long time. 'Ah,* signorina*!'*

The postcard would arrive tomorrow. She was glad she had sent him the pen along with it. She wanted him to know all that she knew.

In the bedroom in Franco Bartoli's apartment after she had collapsed that night Kristina Kovacs had got into bed beside her. So hot, there, and airless, and yet how cool Kristina's hand had felt, resting on her heart. She had slept, knowing the woman was lying awake, watching over her. She could feel Kristina's fear, it was like a living presence, a third person lying with them, veiled, silent, unappeasable. Later she woke, and Kristina had talked to her, soothingly, as if she were talking through an open window to a madwoman out on a ledge. Well, what else are you, she asked herself now, what else are you, but a madwoman, on a ledge? She smiled into the darkness outside the window. She had looked in Kristina's handbag and found a phial of sleeping pills and thought of stealing them, but did not. She knew Kristina was watching her. She wondered if that was what he had asked her to do, to watch over her, and make sure she did not take the pills, or leap from the ledge.

She opened her guidebook at random and read about Shelley's death. He had been to Livorno to see Lord Byron. The schooner was the Ariel. *The poet, and Edward Williams, and a boy to tend the sail. Why did they give the other names, even the name of the boat, and not say what the boy's name was? They burned Shelley's body on the beach. She put the book away and rose from the chair and stood a moment motionless, listening; not a sound, anywhere, except the little waves. She went out and locked the door behind her and went as quietly as she could down the stairs and out into the night. Who was it she was afraid would hear her, try to hold her back? There was no one. The man at the desk with the grey hair and the moustache did not even lift his eyes as she went past.*

The air outside was warm, and had a strong, astringent smell, like the smell of iodine. It was the sea. She could taste salt on her lips. All these vivid things, as if they knew they were the last. She walked down through the hushed streets to the harbour. She knew where she was going. On the quayside people were out strolling, not many, the last of the tourist boats had left long ago. She was aware of glances, women's, mostly. Did they know, just by looking at her? Would they remember her? The sea was invisible, just a blackness, with no horizon, as if half the world out there had fallen clean away. Tomorrow the sun's eclipse, tonight her own. There were no voices in her head any more; they had said all they had to say, had done all they had to do. She imagined them behind her, the horde of them, standing back, big-eyed, their hands over their mouths, staring in gleeful expectation, unable to credit that she was doing at last what they had been urging for so long that she must do.

She climbed the steep, cobbled hill to the church. The lantern was still burning over the stone lintel. The door was open, the doorway hung with a heavy leather curtain worn smooth along one edge by the generations of hands pushing it aside. Penny candles, a vaulted roof, stone floor, a statue of the Virgin all blues and pinks and creams, her eyes uplifted in a transport of sorrow. Such quiet. She sat in the corner of a bench. Every tiniest act, all adding up, bringing her to this. A priest came in, an elderly man, short and fat and perfectly bald. He looked at her in surprise and went out again. Father. There was a door at the side behind the altar. She rose from the bench and went forward. The door was old, its wood chill and damp to the touch, slimed by the night air. It opened, squealing on its hinges. How simply! Here was a little square stone balcony under a gaping sky, with white water snarling around the rocks far, far below. She scrambled on to the parapet, dislodging a piece of stone and grazing her knee. A night breeze pressed her skirt against her legs, so cool, so soft. She put her hands over her womb, feeling the warmth that was not hers. If only she knew the boy's name, the boy on the Ariel*. He was drowned too. All the lost ones. Her knee smarted where she had grazed it; so insistent, everything, demanding to be noticed, to be noted. She heard someone enter the church behind her and say something, she did not understand the words. Hurry, now. She saw herself falling before she fell, falling down that quickening curve. Someone right there now, it was the priest, the old priest, she saw the light glint on his bald brow and remembered the waiter, the statue of the horseman in the dark; remembered everything.* Signorina! *She took a big breath, and for an instant was a child again, her father behind her, saying,* Jump*. Slowly, swooningly, her eyes ecstatically lifted, like the eyes of the statue of the Madonna, she* *leaned out into the nothing, as the priest at her back in vain reached forward his restraining hands. Time. Night. Water.*

(*Shroud*, 2002)

III

A charming spot it was Cass chose to die in, we saw it first from a turn of the coast road, an untidy amphitheatre of white and ochre and terracotta little houses on a stepped hill at the end of a promontory thrusting out into a white-capped sea of a deep, malignant blueness. It was like something in a travel brochure, only a little more wild of aspect. Byron supposedly did one of his marathon swims from here, thrashing away, club foot and all, to another headland a good five miles off across the strait. There were real fishermen on the harbour mending real nets, and real bars with bead curtains and men in white shirts playing clackety board games, and real *ragazzi* kicking a soccer ball under the dusty lime trees in the Piazza Cavour. Lydia parked our hired car outside the police station—at the airport I had realised that I had lost the ability to drive, simply could not work the pedals, change the gears—and we sat for a moment motionless side by side gazing blankly through the windscreen at a torn advertising poster from which an unreally perfect young woman poutingly proffered her half-naked breasts. 'I can't,' Lydia said, without emphasis. I laid a hand on her wrist but she shrugged it off, jadedly. We got out of the car, unfolding ourselves from our seats with the caution and infirm laboriousness of the sole survivors of a fatal accident. The square was strikingly familiar—that tree, that stark white wall—and I felt all this had happened before. There was the usual smell of fish and oil and dust and bad drains. A neat little man in a neat, expensive suit came out on the steps of the police station to meet us. Everything about him was made in miniature. He had a small moustache, and wonderfully small feet shod in spotless patent-leather pumps, and very black hair oiled and combed smooth and severely parted at the side. He shook hands gravely with both of us, his mouth pursed in a sympathetic moue, and ushered us inside the station. The building was incongruously grand, an echoing high square temple with pillars of pitted stone and a chequered black-and-white marble floor. Heads were briefly lifted from desks, dark eyes looked on us with remote inquisitiveness. The little man was skipping ahead, urging us on with soft clickings of tongue and lips, as if we were a pair of prize horses. I was never to make out exactly who or what he was; he may have been the chief of police, or the coroner, or Death himself, even. He could not be still, even when we had come to the mortuary and were standing helpless by the bier, but kept bowing from the shoulders, and reaching out but not quite touching Lydia's hand, or my elbow, and stepping back quickly and delicately clearing his throat behind the raised first knuckle of a tiny brown fist. It was he who took me aside, out of Lydia's hearing, and told me in a hurried whisper, husky with embarrassment, that my daughter had been pregnant when she died. Three months gone, as they say. He clapped a hand histrionically to his breast. *'Ah, signore, mi dispiace . . .'*

The sheet was drawn back. *Stella maris*. Her face was not there, the rocks and the sea had taken it. We identified her by a ring, and a little scar on her left ankle that Lydia remembered. But I would have known her, my Marina, even if all that was left of her was the bare, wave-washed bones.

What was she doing in this place, what had brought her here? As if the mystery of her life were not enough, now I must deal with the mystery of her death. We climbed the narrow streets to the little hotel where she had stayed. It was the siesta hour, and all was eerily still in the flat, airless heat, and as we laboured up those cobbled steeps we gaped about in a blear of disbelief, unable to credit the cruelty of the picturesqueness all around us. There were sleepy cats in doorways, and geraniums on window sills, and a yellow canary was singing in its cage, and we could hear the voices of children at play somewhere, in some sequestered courtyard, and our daughter was dead.

The hotel proprietor was a swarthy, big-chested old fellow with greased grey hair and a manicured moustache, a dead ringer for the film star Vittorio De Sica, if anyone now remembers him. He greeted us circumspectly, staying resolutely behind the protective barrier of the reception desk, looking at everything except us and humming to himself. He kept on nodding at everything we asked him, but the nods seemed more like shrugs, and he would tell us nothing. His fat wife, round and thick as a totem pole, had planted herself behind him with her hands implacably folded on her stomach, her Mussolini scowl fixed on the back of his head, willing him to caution. He was sorry, he could tell us nothing, he said, nothing. Cass had arrived two days ago, he said, and paid in advance. They had hardly seen her since she came, she had spent her days in the hills above the town, or walking on the beach. As he spoke he was fiddling with things on the desk, pens, cards, a sheaf of folded maps. I asked if anyone had been with her, and he shook his head too quickly, I thought. I noticed his shoes—tassels, little gold buckles—and the fine silk of his too-white shirt. Quite the dandy. He led us up the narrow stairs, past a set of mildly indecent eighteenth-century prints in plastic frames, and applied a large, mock-antique key to the door of Cass's room and opened it for us. We hung back, Lydia and I, looking incompetently in. Big bed, washstand and pitcher, straight chair with a straw seat, a narrow window squinting down on the sunstruck harbour. There was, incongruously, a smell of suntan lotion. Cass's suitcase was open on the floor, still half unpacked. A dress, a pair of shorts, her remembered shoes, mute things clamouring to speak. 'I can't,' Lydia said, as listlessly as before, and turned aside. I looked at De Sica and he looked at his nails. His lumpy wife was still there at his shoulder. She would once have been as young as Cass, and as lissom too, most likely. I gazed full into her face, beseeching her silently to tell us what had happened here to our poor damaged daughter, our eclipsed light, that had driven her to death, but she just stood and stared back at me stonily and offered not a word.

We lodged there at the hotel that night, it seemed the simplest thing to do. Our room was eerily similar to the one Cass had been in, with the same washstand and chair, and the same window framing what seemed an identical view of the harbour. We ate dinner in the silent dining room, and then went down to the harbour and walked up and down the quayside for what seemed hours. It was quiet, there at the season's end. We held hands, for the first time since the days of the Hotel Halcyon. A gold and smoke-grey sunset sank out at sea like a slow catastrophe, and the warm night came on, and the lamps on the harbour glowed, and the bristling masts tilted, and a bat swooped and swerved soundlessly about us. In the room we lay sleepless side by side on the big high bed, like a pair of long-term hospital patients, listening to the faint far whisperings of the sea. Softly I sang the little song I used to sing for Cass, to make her laugh:

I've got tears in my ears
From lying on my back,
In my bed,
While I cry,
Over you.

'What did that man say to you?' Lydia asked out of the darkness. 'The one at the police station.' She rose up on an elbow, making the mattress wobble, and peered at me. In the faint glow from the window the whites of her eyes glittered. 'What was it, that he didn't want me to hear?'

'He told me her surprise,' I said, 'the one she told you not to tell me. You were right: I am amazed.' She said nothing to that, only gave what might have been an angry sigh, and laid her head down again. 'I suppose,' I said, 'we don't know who the father is?' I could see him, a lost one like herself, most probably, some pimply young savant haggard with ambition and the weight of useless knowledge agonisingly acquired; I wonder if he knew how close he had come to replicating himself. 'Not that it matters, now.'

In the morning there was no sea, just a pale gold glare stretching off to the non-horizon. Lydia stayed in bed, with her face turned away from me, saying nothing, although I knew she was not asleep; I crept down the stairs, feeling, I am not sure why, like a murderer leaving the scene of the crime. Perfect day, sun, sea-smell, all that. As I walked through the morning quiet I felt that I was walking in her footsteps; before, she had inhabited me, now I was inhabiting her. I went up to the old church standing on its crag at the far end of the harbour, tottering over the stones shined by the feet of generations of the devout, as if I were climbing to Golgotha. The church was built by the Templars on the site of a Roman shrine dedicated to Venus—yes, I had bought a guidebook. Here Cass performed her last act. In the porch, drifts of confetti were lodged in crevices between the flagstones. The interior was sparsely adorned. There was a Madonna, attributed to Gentileschi—the father, that is, not the notorious daughter—stuck away in a side chapel, a dark piece, badly lit and in need of cleaning, but displaying the master's luminous touch, all the same. Candles burned on a black iron stand with a tin box for offerings slung beneath it, and a big pot of sickly smelling flowers stood on the flags before the bare altar. A priest appeared, and knew at once who I was. He was squat and brown and bald. He had not a word of English, and I not many of Italian, but he babbled away happily, making elaborate gestures with his hands and head. He steered me out through an arched doorway by the side of the altar, to a little stone bower that hung a hundred feet above rocks and foaming sea, where by tradition, so my trusty guidebook tells me, newly-weds come directly after the marriage ceremony, so that the bride may fling her bouquet as a sacrifice to the seething waters far below. A breeze was blowing upward along the rocks; I held my face out into its strong, iodine-smelling draught and shut my eyes. The Lord tempers the wind to the shorn lamb, says the Psalmist, but I am here to tell you that the Psalmist is wrong. The priest was showing me the place where Cass must have scrambled up on to the stone parapet and launched herself out upon the salt-bruised air, he even demonstrated how she would have done it, miming her actions for me, nimble as a goat and smiling all the while and nodding, as if it were some bold foolhardy prank he was describing, the initiatory swallow dive performed by George Gordon himself, perhaps. I picked up a jagged piece of stone newly dislodged from the parapet, and feeling its sharp weight in my hand, I wept at last, plunging headlong helplessly into the suddenly hollow depths of myself, while the old priest stood by, patting me on the shoulder and murmuring what seemed a series of soft, mild reproaches.

So I began that day the painstaking trek back over our lives, I mean our lives when Cass was there, the years she was with us. I was searching for the pattern, the one I am searching for still, the set of clues laid out like the dots she used to join up with her crayon to make a picture of the beautiful fairy with wand and wings. Was Lydia right when she accused me of somehow knowing what was to happen? I do not want to think so. For if I knew, if the ghosts were a premonition that this was what was to come, why did I not act? But then, I have always had the greatest difficulty distinguishing between action and acting. Besides, I was looking the wrong way, I was looking into the past, and that was not where those phantoms were from, at all. I used to daydream, in those first weeks I spent alone in the house, that Cass would come to live with me, that we would set up together some new version of the old life I had misled here, that we would somehow redeem the lost years. Was it out of these fantasies I conjured her? And did my conjurations weaken her hold on the real life she might have had, the life that now she will never live? The lives.

I have not begun to feel guilty, yet, not really; there will be ample time for that. That night, after my visit to the church, I had a strange and strangely affecting dream, one that almost comforted me. I was in the circus tent. Goodfellow was there, and Lily, and Lydia, and I knew too that everyone in the audience, although I could not properly see it, out there in the gloom, was known to me, or was a relative of some kind. We were all gazing upward in rapt silence, watching Cass, who was suspended motionless in midair, without support, her arms outstretched, her calm face lit by a beam of strong white soft light. As I watched, she started her descent toward me, faster and faster, still impassive, still holding up her arms as if in a blessing, but the nearer she drew, instead of growing larger in my sight, she steadily shrank, so that when at the end I reached out to catch her she was hardly there at all, was hardly more than a speck of light, that in a moment was extinguished.

I woke, clear-headed, the weariness of the past days all gone, and rose and went and stood in the darkness by the window for a long time, looking down on the deserted harbour, and the sea, whose little, lapsing waves seemed something that was being sleepily spoken, over and over.

(*Eclipse*, 2000)

IV

We had a dreadful night, the two of us, Lydia suffering one of those nocturnal bouts of mania that have beset her at irregular intervals over the past ten years. She wakes, or at least leaps from the bed, and goes dashing in the dark through all the rooms, upstairs and down, calling out our daughter's name. It is a kind of sleepwalking, or sleeprunning, in which she is convinced our Catherine, our Cass, is still alive and a child again and lost somewhere in the house. I get up groggily and follow her, only half awake myself. I do not try to restrain her, heeding the old wives' caution against interfering in any way with a person in that state, but I keep close in case she should trip over something and I might be able to catch her before she falls and save her from injuring herself. It is eerie, scurrying through the darkened house—I do not dare switch on the lights—in desperate pursuit of this fleeting figure. The shadows throng us round like a silent chorus, and at intervals a patch of moonlight or the radiance from a street-lamp falling in at a window will seem a dimmed spotlight, and I am reminded of one of those tragic queens in the Greek drama, raging through the king her husband's palace at midnight shrieking for her lost child. Eventually she tires herself out, or comes to her senses, or both, as she did last night, sinking down on a step of the stairs, all in a heap, shedding terrible tears and sobbing. I hovered about her helplessly, not knowing quite how to get my arms around her, so amorphous a shape did she appear, in her sleeveless black nightdress, her head hanging and her hands plunged in her hair that in the dark looked as black as it was the first time I saw her, walking out into summer through the revolving door of her father's hotel, the Halcyon of happy memory, the tall glass panels of the door throwing off repeated glancing bursts of blue and gold—yes, yes, the crest of the wave!

The worst part, for me, of these extravaganzas of anguished hue and cry comes at the end, when she is all contrition, berating herself for her foolishness and begging to be forgiven for waking me so violently and causing such needless panic. It is just, she says, that in her sleepwalking state it seems to her so real a thing that Cass is alive, her living daughter, trapped in one of the rooms of the house, terrified and unable to make herself heard as she calls for help. Last night she was so ashamed and angry that she swore at herself, using horrible words, until I hunkered down beside her and held her in an awkwardly simian embrace and made her lay her head in the hollow of my shoulder, and at last she grew quiet. Her nose was running and I let her wipe it on the sleeve of my pyjamas. She was shivering, but when I offered to fetch her dressing-gown or a blanket she clung to me the more tightly and would not let me leave her. The faintly stale smell of her hair was in my nostrils and the ball of her bare shoulder was chill and smooth as a marble globe under my cupped hand. Around us the hall furniture stood dimly in the gloom like shocked and speechless attendants.

I think I know what it is that torments Lydia, besides the unassuageable grief she has been nursing in her heart throughout the ten long years since our daughter died. Like me, she was never a believer in any of the worlds to come, yet I suspect she fears that through a cruel loophole in the laws of life and death Cass did not fully die but is somehow existing still, a captive in the land of the shades and suffering there, half of the pomegranate seeds still unswallowed in her mouth, waiting in vain for her mother to come and claim her back to be among the living again. Yet what is now Lydia's horror was once her hope. *How could anyone die who was so much alive?* she demanded of me that night in the hotel in Italy where we had come to claim Cass's body, and so fierce was her tone and so compelling her look that for a moment I too thought that a mistake might have been made, that it might be someone else's unrecognisable daughter who had smashed herself to death on those wave-washed rocks below the bare little church of San Pietro.

As I have said, we had not ever believed in the immortal soul, Lydia and I, and would smile in gentle condescension when others spoke of their hopes of someday seeing again departed loved ones, but there is nothing like the loss of an only child to soften the wax of sealed convictions. After Cass's death—to this day I cannot see those words written down without a disbelieving shock, they seem so unlikely, even as I grave them on the page—we found ourselves venturing, tentatively, shamefacedly, to entertain the possibility not of the next world, exactly, but of a world next to this one, contiguous with it, where there might linger somehow the spirits of those no longer here and yet not entirely gone, either. We seized on what might be signs, the vaguest portents, wisps of intimation. Coincidences were not now what they had been heretofore, mere wrinkles in the otherwise blandly plausible surface of reality, but parts of a code, large and urgent, a kind of desperate semaphoring from the other side that, maddeningly, we were unable to read. How we would begin to listen now, all else suspended, when, in company, we overheard people speaking of having been bereaved, how breathlessly we hung on their words, how hungrily we scanned their faces, looking to see if they really believed their lost one not entirely lost. Certain dispositions of supposedly chance objects would strike us with a runic force. In particular those great flocks of birds, starlings, I think they are, that gather out over the sea on certain days, amoebically swooping and swirling, switching direction in perfect, instantaneous co-ordination, seemed to be inscribing on the sky a series of ideograms directed exclusively at us but too swiftly and fluidly sketched for us to interpret. All this illegibility was a torment to us.

I say us, but of course we never spoke of these pathetic hopes of a hint from the beyond. Bereavement sets a curious constraint between the bereaved, an embarrassment, almost, that is not easy to account for. Is it the fear that such things if spoken of will take on an even greater weight, become an even heavier burden? No, that is not it, not quite. The reticence, the tactfulness, that our mutual grieving imposed on Lydia and me was at once a measure of magnanimity, the same that makes the gaoler tiptoe past the cell in which the condemned man on his last night is asleep, and a mark of our dread of stirring up and provoking to even more inventive exercises those demonic torturers whose special task it was, is, to torment us. Yet even without saying, each knew what the other was thinking, and, more acutely, what the other was feeling—this is a further effect of our shared sorrow, this empathy, this mournful telepathy.

I am thinking of the morning after the very first one of Lydia's nocturnal rampages when she had started up from the pillow convinced our recently dead Cass was alive and in the house somewhere. Even when the panic was over and we had dragged ourselves back to bed we did not get to sleep again, not properly—Lydia doing hiccuppy after-sobs and my heart tom-tomming away—but lay on the bed on our backs for a long time, as if practising to be the corpses that one day we shall be. The curtains were thick and drawn tightly shut, and I did not realise the dawn had come up until I saw forming above me a brightly shimmering image that spread itself until it stretched over almost the entire ceiling. At first I took it for an hallucination generated out of my sleep-deprived and still half-frantic consciousness. Also I could not make head or tail of it, which is not surprising, for the image, as after a moment or two I saw, was upside-down. What was happening was that a pinhole-sized opening between the curtains was letting in a narrow beam of light that had turned the room into a camera obscura, and the image above us was an inverted, dawn-fresh picture of the world outside. There was the road below the window, with its blueberry-blue tarmac, and, nearer in, a shiny black hump that was part of the roof of our car, and the single silver birch across the way, slim and shivery as a naked girl, and beyond all that the bay, pinched between the finger and thumb of its two piers, the north one and the south, and then the distant, paler azure of the sea, that at the invisible horizon became imperceptibly sky. How clear it all was, how sharply limned! I could see the sheds along the north pier, their asbestos roofs dully agleam in the early sunlight, and in the lee of the south pier the bristling, amber-coloured masts of the sailboats jostling together at anchor there. I fancied I could even make out the little waves on the sea, with here and there a gay speckle of foam. Thinking still that I might be dreaming, or deluded, I asked Lydia if she could see this luminous mirage and she said yes, yes, and reached out and clutched my hand tightly. We spoke in whispers, as if the very action of our voices might shatter the frail assemblage of light and spectral colour above us. The thing seemed to vibrate inside itself, to be tinily atremble everywhere, as if it were the teeming particles of light itself, the streaming photons, that we were seeing, which I suppose it was, strictly speaking. Yet surely, we felt, surely this was not entirely a natural phenomenon, for which there would be a perfectly simple scientific explanation, preceded by a soft little cough and followed by an apologetic hum—surely this was a thing given to us, a gift, a greeting, in other words a sure sign, sent to comfort us. We lay there watching it, awestruck, for, oh, I do not know how long. As the sun rose the inverted world above us was setting, retreating along the ceiling until it developed a hinge at one edge and began sliding steadily down the far wall and poured itself at last into the carpet and was gone. Straight away we got up—what else was there to do?—and started our dealings with the day. Were we comforted, did we feel lightened? A little, until the wonder of the spectacle to which we had been treated began to diffuse, to slip and slide and be absorbed into the ordinary, fibrous texture of things.

(*Ancient Light*, 2012)

Lady Laura and the Dowager Duchess

The route of my escape—I do not like the word, it sounds so cloak-and-daggerish, but what else can I call it?—took me initially in a sharp diagonal across France to the south-east corner of the Bay of Biscay. It was not such hard going; there were Schaudeine's people to help me at each knot of the network along which I made my way, they offered food, shelter, forged documents, cautionary advice. I stole things, even from those who were aiding me. I became quite a skilled thief; there is an art to stealing, as there is to everything, if one's approach is pure enough, disinterested enough. That especially is something I learned, that one must be disinterested, or at least present a credible semblance of being so, if one is to succeed in the tricky business of survival. The farther south I travelled, though, the more heartsick I became. I was not despairing, I was not even afraid, really, any more, only I could see no end to this flight I was embarked upon, and felt sometimes that this would be my life forever, just this endless journeying, and that eventually I would find myself retracing this same route from the start, seeing this same spider, and this same moonlight between the trees, over and over. I reached my lowest point on a December twilight in Hendaye, where I sat in a tenebrous bar listening to the flags flapping mournfully along the deserted sea front and realised with a sad start that it was Christmas Eve. Matters lightened next day, however—even the pendent sky lifted a little—when I met my contact in the town, a crop-haired girl in a beret and an outsized black coat whom I took for a boy until she spoke. She and her father were to drive me that night in her father's truck across the border to San Sebastián. Meantime she looked me over with a bright gleam in her dark eye—remember, I was young then, and large, and vigorous, still sound in limb and whole of sight—and brought me to her tiny room overlooking the sea, where we took off our clothes in the fish-coloured marine light, and she clambered all over me, lithe and quick as a minnow, nosing into cracks and crevices as if in search of some elusive tidbit. When we had finished, and I was finally, utterly empty, she sprang up and sat on my chest like a gymnast straddling the wooden horse, and I saw a silvery filament of my semen strung for a second between her open lips as she grinned and said in her hot, high little voice, *'Joyeux Noël, mon petit!'*

She was called, quaintly, Josette. I am ashamed to say I stole her watch, a chunky, cheap thing, but remarkably sturdy, for I have it still, and it still keeps time, of a sort. It had been given to her by one of my predecessors along this route, which probably for him too had included a detour through that bedroom above the sea front. Josette. In manner as well as stature she was an eerie prefigurement of my Lady Laura, whom some weeks later, in an English spring all sleet and spiked, wet sunlight, I met on a train travelling up to London from the port of Southampton. I had arrived that morning on a boat from Lisbon, a city of which I recall only the smell of tar and the rank taste of raw olive oil, and the aluminium-bright sheets of rain undulating across the docks at dawn when I was leaving. At Southampton a military official of indeterminate rank sitting behind a table had glared crossly for a long moment at my passport, lovingly made for me by an octogenarian forger in Liège, then with a snort of unamused laughter had snapped it shut and dealt it to me across the table, my winning card. I was supposed to be a pilot with the Free French forces, I had a paper to prove it. There was no heating on the train. The compartment was crowded with army officers, and smelled of cigarette smoke and wet wool. Lady Laura was huddled in a corner diagonally across from me, wearing a huge coat, just like Josette's only much more costly, and a drooping black hat with a drooping, pavonian plume. It was hard to make out her features under all that felt and feather, except for a pair of darkly glowing eyes, which I sensed settling upon me now and then, speculatively. I noticed her silk-stockinged white little feet in their expensive shoes with the strap buttoned tightly across the instep. Her tiny hands were pale as polished bone, and came out of the coat's wide sleeves like the claws of an animal's skeleton peeping out of its pelt. She was hardly bigger than a child. The soldiers, fizzing with battle fatigue, talked loudly among themselves and paid her no heed. Beads of melting sleet ran slantwise like spit across the fogged windows. The ticket collector came, and breathed worriedly over my ticket, and told me in a tone of awkward regret, for which I remember him with a warm spot of fondness even yet, that I was in a first class carriage and would have to move. Before I could get my things together the coat in the corner stirred and a hand dipped into a purse made of woven miniature silver chains and came up with a large white bank note and wagged it languidly back and forth in the air. The ticket collector took the money and clipped my ticket and tipped his cap and withdrew, giving me a wink as he went. From under the wing of the feathered hat those eyes, big and dark and velvety as pansies, held me briefly, without expression, and looked away.

She had been seeing one of her men off to the war. He had signed them into a hotel in Southampton the night before as Major and Mrs Smith. 'I felt quite the tart,' she said, and laughed. The man was afraid he would be killed in battle, and had wept in the night and clung to her. 'Honestly,' she said in wonderment, 'just like a baby.' She was sorry now she had not said goodbye to him in

London and avoided seeing him go to pieces like that. She had told me all this before we were off the train. She asked if I thought she was awful, and gave me an appraising, a testing, look. We stood in the drizzle outside the station waiting for a taxi. The crown of her hat, sprinkled all over with gemlike drops of rain, was level with the centre of my chest. 'I did not think the French were made on your scale,' she said. I said I was not French but she paid no heed; I would come to know well her capacity for not hearing things she considered inconvenient. For my part I was already suffering my first London headache. A taxi came. She offered to drop me at my destination but I said I had nowhere to go, which was true. She pursed her lips at that and frowned into the middle distance, thinking. We went and had a late breakfast in a hotel in Knightsbridge, which she paid for. From the dining room window we could look down on the traffic creeping through the rain. Under her overcoat she was dressed in dove-grey silk. She sipped at a cup of lemon tea and ate nothing. 'They do fresh eggs here, for me,' she said. 'Would you like some?' And for the first time she smiled. When I had finished my food—dear me, how I could eat in those days!—she said that she would go home to sleep now, but that I must come and visit her in the afternoon. She produced another big bank note and wrote her address on it with a little silver pencil on a fine black cord. 'It is a test of chivalry,' she said. 'If you spend it you will not know where I live.' I walked around the city for hours, feeling nothing very much. There are times like that, every refugee knows them, when one seems to hang suspended, without volition, neither despairing nor hopeful, but waiting, merely, for what will come next. Daylight was already waning when I rang the bell at her tall, narrow little house in Belgravia. She came to the door in a crimson crêpe-de-chine dressing-gown and smoking a cigarette in an ebony holder, a perfect parody of the stage vamp. Her very black hair was fixed elaborately with many pearl-headed pins, and she wore a mask of clay-white make-up and crimson lipstick that gave to her delicate features an excitingly oriental cast. All these preparations had been made to welcome someone, but not me, and for the first moment after she had opened the door she looked at me in blank consternation, before remembering who I was. She led me down the hall. 'Damn Southampton,' she said over her shoulder, 'I have caught a cold.' I could see, under the make-up, the delicate pink bloom along the edges of her nostrils and in the little groove above her upper lip. Her drawing room was furnished in the chilly, angular modern style of the day: there were low steel-and-glass tables, stick-insect chairs, a chandelier of menacing crystal spikes; the walls were covered with a black woven material that kept shimmering troublingly at the side of my vision. There was the thick heat of a hothouse, but she kept complaining that she was cold. Without asking she gave me gin to drink, and sat in the corner of an uncomfortable-looking, cuboid white sofa, hugging herself and shivering delicately. 'I feel terrible about Eddie, now,' she said, 'the poor pet.' Eddie was the pseudonymous Major Smith, he of the cowardly tears. 'I should not have told you those things about him. You must think me horribly unfeeling.' And she looked at me from under her long and matted lashes, then dropped her gaze and bit her lip delicately in an almost-smiling travesty of contrition and remorse. The doorbell rang, adding a further theatrical touch to the proceedings. She made no move to answer it, gave no sign of having heard it, even. No doubt it was the man she had been expecting instead of me. The bell went again. We sat in silence. Calmly she considered me. My stomach, still struggling with the remains of that unaccustomedly rich breakfast, growled and rumbled. The one at the door gave the bell a last, brief, half-hearted push, and then went away. Lady Laura was running a fingertip along a seam of the sofa covering. A swatch of her hair had come loose from its pins and hung down by her ear like a shiny black seashell. In a small voice she said that perhaps we should go to bed—'even though I have only just got up.'

She really was tiny; had it occurred to me I might have felt some disquiet at the ease with which I had attracted in rapid succession these two distinctly boyish little persons. When she took off her gown, under which she was conveniently naked, and lay down before me on the bed I was nervous of putting my hands on her for fear of breaking something. Where women are concerned I have always been, as you can attest, the bull in the china shop. So many I have caused to shatter in pieces, like Meissen figurines. Even the great, glazed urn that was Magda in the end was smashed under my stamping hoofs. Lady Laura was excited by the prospect of exquisite damage. She lifted her affectingly frail knees and opened her arms and smiled up into my face with slitted eyes. 'Come on,' she said, in a cat's thick gurgle, 'break me in two, and make a wish.'

She kept me, more or less, on and off, for nigh on two years. The arrangement between us she set out clearly from the start; it was to be entirely on her terms. There was no question, for instance, of my having exclusive rights to her bed; in fact, I was to have no rights at all, worth speaking of, to anything that was hers. She already had many admirers, and went on accumulating more of them all the time. She moved in a narrow, rackety milieu where aristocratic black sheep met and mingled with the art world crowd. She had a very great deal of money from her dead father, who had been a duke, but although she was a spendthrift, she was not generous. She bought me good clothes, handmade shoes, wearable trinkets of all kinds, but they were less an adornment for me than for her, by proxy. She continued to insist on my being French—'Really, darling, *no one* comes from your country'—and introduced me everywhere as *my Frog*. I liked her, really, I did; perhaps I more than liked her. There was something unwholesome about her, something acrid, discoloured, used, that I found deeply appealing;

I am remembering the stale smell of her hair, the raspy touch of her shaven legs, the deep hollows under her eyes, with their bruised, plum-brown shadows. Yet no one I have ever known, not even you, dear Cass, was as tender, as delicate, as voluptuously helpless as she was, when she chose to be. She loved, she said, my size, the improbable, impossible bulk of me, her blond, contraband brute with big square jaw and killer's paws and ridiculous, unplaceable accent.

We knew nothing about each other, I mean nothing of any consequence. She led me briefly, her slim, cool hand lying lightly in mine, into the pages of one of those smart and amusingly cruel novels which were fashionable in that era, whole shelves of which I read, to improve my English, and the echo of which, I suspect, can be detected still in the colder, primmer interiors of my lamentably heterogeneous prose style. All I saw of Laura was the brittle, bright façade she chose to present to the world at large, that undistinguished, commonplace world in which, and she was careful that I should make no mistake about it, I was as far as she was concerned just another commoner. Who knows what she saw in me, beyond the merely physical. She took me everywhere, to parties and clubs, to artists' studios, to hunt balls in huge houses, even to court, once. She knew all sorts of shady people. We went to dog races, gambling dens, to a place in the East End where cock fights were held, and where, at the end of one particularly sanguinary contest, she turned to me with a terrible, glittering smile and I saw a crescent-shaped stipple of cockerel's blood on her cheek and thought inconsequently of the bramble scratches I used to get as a child picking blackberries on my grandfather's farm. She ate too much, smoked too much, slept too late and with too many lovers. Most of all, though, she drank.

It was on a visit to her mother's house in the country that I discovered the secret of her drinking, I mean her serious, full-time dipsomania. We had motored down, as the saying went, for the weekend. It was the first time I had been shown to the Dowager Duchess, and her daughter was nervous, I could tell by the metallic brightness of her voice and the altogether too brilliant smiles she kept flashing at me as she manoeuvred her dashing little car at breakneck speed along the verdant byways of Berkshire. This hitherto unsuspected vulnerability I found affecting, and I felt protective toward her, and determined to defend her against the Dowager, who in my indignant imaginings was growing by the moment to the dimensions and ferocity of a fairy-tale dragon. She lived in grand if somewhat faded style in a stone mansion set on a hill above a tiny hamlet, from the huddled roofs of which the house's many windows averted their haughty gaze. The lady herself, like her abode, was large and stately and fascinatingly ugly. My first sight of her did nothing to contradict my expectations of fierceness and flame, for she was standing in gumboots beside a bonfire into which she was poking a mattock-like implement with scowling vigour. In greeting her daughter she consented to receive a dry kiss on the cheek. Me she took in with instant cognisance and grimly set her jaw. Beside me Laura drooped perceptibly, all her brightness dimming. I realised at once that I had been brought here as a gesture of defiance against her mother—to whom my status as semi-paid lover would have been immediately obvious—but of course the old bag had the hide of a rhino and was not in the least surprised or shocked. For a long moment we regarded each other, she and I, and for all that I was half a foot higher than her I felt that she might be about to place the heel of her rubber boot on my brow and press me without effort into the earth, like a giant tent peg. A gust of wood-smoke from the fire blew in my face and made my eyes water. I said something about the journey, commended the weather, admired the house. 'Are you a German?' the Dowager said loudly, with frowning incredulity. Laura muttered something and strode off toward the house, head down and hands jammed in the pockets of her long leather car-coat.

Matters grew steadily worse as the afternoon ground on. At four o'clock tea was served in the conservatory, under the leaning fronds of a giant fern. A grandfather clock directly behind my chair clicked its tongue in large, slow, monotonous disapproval. The Dowager complained of the land girls who had been sent down from London to dig up the lawns and plant potatoes; they knew nothing of country ways, she said, and cared only for cigarettes and going to dances; she suspected them of immoral carryings-on with the village men. I nodded sympathetically and inclined my face over my tea cup; the giddy urge to laugh kept bubbling up. Laura sat wordless between her mother and me in what seemed an agony of anger and violent disgust, as if she were a child being forced to endure the torment of adult company. Eventually she flung herself from her chair and slouched off, supposedly to tell the maid to bring fresh tea. She had been gone for a considerable time, and I had begun to wonder uneasily how long such an errand could take in even so large a house as this—had she fled altogether, got in the car and driven away, abandoning me here, with this hideous termagant?—when I heard from far within and high up in the house a thin, ululant cry that made my backbone tingle. I put down my cup; no doubt I had a look of alarm. The Dowager, who also had heard the scream, folded her large, mannish hands on her thigh and considered me keenly, with, I thought, a certain gratified amusement. 'For how long, Mr Vandal,' she asked, 'have you known my daughter?'

After a search, I found Laura upstairs, locked in a little bathroom attached to what turned out to have been the nursery. She would not open the door at first, and I had to wait, looking somewhat desperately out of a circular window at a far field with grazing cows. At last I heard the lock turning. She had a gin bottle, half empty, the neck of which she had somehow managed to break off, cutting her hand quite badly. She sat on the wooden lid of the lavatory and I knelt before her and tore my handkerchief into strips and bound the wound while she mewled and wept. The fittings in the room, the lavatory, the rust-stained bath, the hand-basin, the towel rail, were all made in miniature, to a child's scale, and I had a distracting sense of grotesque disproportion; we were back in a fairy tale again, I the worried giant now, and she the tiny, hysterical princess. She was already drunk, thoroughly, comprehensively, in a way I had not seen nor drunk before. She kept alternating between clawing apologies and accusatory, hair-shaking rages, big, iridescent bubbles of saliva forming and bursting between her slack, gin-raw lips. She said it was all my fault, she should never have brought me here, what had she been thinking of, it was mad, mad, she should have known, oh, how could I ever forgive her, she was sorry, so sorry, so very sorry . . . I took her in my arms, still kneeling before her, and she twined her legs around my waist and pressed her hot temple so hard against my cheek I thought a molar might crack. She wailed in my ear and dribbled on my shoulder. If I ever loved her, it was in that moment.

She slept until evening, there in the nursery, crouched in the narrow little bed with a cushion clutched to her stomach. The Dowager, in her gumboots again, and a suit of tweed that looked as heavy as chain-mail, glanced in nonchalantly and said she must be off to attend to some pressing agricultural matter; it was apparent she had long ago become inured to her daughter's distresses. She gave me an ironical little half grin and was gone. I sat by the bed, feeling strangely at peace. The April afternoon outside was quick with running shadows and sudden sun.

I listened to the life of the house going on around me, the clocks chiming the hours, one of the maids singing down in the kitchens, a delivery boy whistling, and seemed to see it all from far above, all clear and detailed, like one of those impossible distances glimpsed through an arched window in a van Eyck setpiece, the house and fields, the village, and roads winding away, and little figures standing at gaze, and then here, in the foreground, this room, the bed, the sleeping child-woman, and I, the wakeful watcher, keeping vigil. Tell me this world is not the strangest place, stranger even than what the gods would have invented, did they exist. She woke eventually and smiled at me, and sat up, plucking away a strand of hair that had caught at the corner of her mouth. She said nothing, only put out her arms, like a child asking wordlessly to be lifted from the cradle. The little bed would not accommodate us both so we lay on the floor on an old worn rug. I had never known her so mild, so attentive, so undefended. She gave off a strong sweet smell of gin. Halfway through our slow-motion love-making she squirmed out from under me and made me turn on my back, and flipped herself upside down and lay with her belly on my chest and took me into her mouth and would not let me go until I had spent myself against the burning bud of her epiglottis. Then she swivelled right way up again—such an agile girl!—and balanced the length of herself along me, a sprat riding on a shark, and for a second I saw Josette, with her bobbed hair and upturned small breasts, smiling at me in the fish-scale light of Hendaye, and something went through me, needle-sharp, that was surprisingly like pain. Laura rested her swollen face in the hollow of my shoulder. A last, thin shaft of sunlight from the window fell across her thigh, sickle-shaped. 'I am all mouth, aren't I,' she said with a sigh. 'You, the bottle, fags, food. Weaned too early, I imagine.'

I have one last memory of that weekend to record. The next day, Sunday, in the morning, when Laura and her mother were off performing some bucolic ritual—distributing bibles to the cottagers, perhaps, or administering gruel to their children—in the performance of which, it was firmly made clear, my company was not required, I took the opportunity to explore the Dowager's domain. On a short flight of uncarpeted, well-worn wooden stairs down at the back of the house, near what I supposed were the servants' quarters, I encountered a maid, whose name was Daisy, or Dottie, a fine, strong, big-boned girl with the arms of a ploughman and a charming overlap in her front incisors, who smelled of loaves and soap, and who cheerfully allowed me to kiss her, and put my hand on her warm bodice. There had been a shower but it was stopped now, and the light was like watered silk, and the wind was blowing, and big shivery raindrops clung to the many panes of a tall window above us. I think of her often, even yet, dear Dot or Daise. I was not then the brute that I have since become. I hope that she has had a good life, and that she is living still, tended by the third or even the fourth generation. I hope too, with small confidence, that she has not altogether forgotten me. When she had freed herself from my embrace and turned aside, laughing, and tripped away up the steps, plucking up her long skirts between two fingers and two thumbs as daintily as any fine lady, I took out of my pocket a netsuke of clouded green-white jade that I had pinched from the drawing room, and, surprised at myself, went back and replaced it on the mantelpiece among its fellows.

(*Shroud*, 2002)

Only Dying, After All

The consultant's name was Mr Todd. This can only be considered a joke in bad taste on the part of polyglot fate. It could have been worse. There is a name De'Ath, with that fancy medial capital and apotropaic apostrophe which fool no one. This Todd addressed Anna as Mrs Morden but called me Max. I was not at all sure I liked the distinction thus made, or the gruff familiarity of his tone. His office, no, his rooms, one says rooms, as one calls him Mister not Doctor, seemed at first sight an eyrie, although they were only on the third floor. The building was a new one, all glass and steel—there was even a glass-and-steel tubular lift shaft, aptly suggestive of the barrel of a syringe, through which the lift rose and fell hummingly like a giant plunger being alternately pulled and pressed—and two walls of his main consulting room were sheets of plate glass from floor to ceiling. When Anna and I were shown in my eyes were dazzled by a blaze of early-autumn sunlight falling down through those vast panes. The receptionist, a blonde blur in a nurse's coat and sensible shoes that squeaked—on such an occasion who would really notice the receptionist?—laid Anna's file on Mr Todd's desk and squeakingly withdrew. Mr Todd bade us sit. I could not tolerate the thought of settling myself on a chair and went instead and stood at the glass wall, looking out. Directly below me there was an oak, or perhaps it was a beech, I am never sure of those big deciduous trees, certainly not an elm since they are all dead, but a noble thing, anyway, the summer's green of its broad canopy hardly silvered yet with autumn's hoar. Car roofs glared. A young woman in a dark suit was walking away swiftly across the car park, even at that distance I fancied I could hear her high heels tinnily clicking on the tarmac. Anna was palely reflected in the glass before me, sitting very straight on the metal chair in three-quarters profile, being the model patient, with one knee crossed on the other and her joined hands resting on her thigh. Mr Todd sat sideways at his desk riffling through the documents in her file; the pale-pink cardboard of the folder made me think of those shivery first mornings back at school after the summer holidays, the feel of brand-new schoolbooks and the somehow bodeful smell of ink and pared pencils. How the mind wanders, even on the most concentrated of occasions.

I turned from the glass, the outside become intolerable now.

Mr Todd was a burly man, not tall or heavy but very broad: one had an impression of squareness. He cultivated a reassuringly old-fashioned manner. He wore a tweed suit with a waistcoat and watch chain, and chestnut-brown brogues that Colonel Blunden would have approved. His hair was oiled in the style of an earlier time, brushed back sternly from his forehead, and he had a moustache, short and bristly, that gave him a dogged look. I realised with a mild shock that despite these calculatedly venerable effects he could not be much more than fifty. Since when did doctors start being younger than I am? On he wrote, playing for time; I did not blame him, I would have done the same, in his place. At last he put down his pen but still was disinclined to speak, giving the earnest impression of not knowing where to begin or how. There was something studied about this hesitancy, something theatrical. Again, I understand. A doctor must be as good an actor as physician. Anna shifted on her chair impatiently.

'Well, Doctor,' she said, a little too loudly, putting on the bright, tough tone of one of those film stars of the Forties, 'is it the death sentence, or do I get life?'

The room was still. Her sally of wit, surely rehearsed, had fallen flat. I had an urge to rush forward and snatch her up in my arms, fireman-fashion, and carry her bodily out of there. I did not stir. Mr Todd looked at her in mild, hare-eyed panic, his eyebrows hovering halfway up his forehead.

'Oh, we won't let you go quite yet, Mrs Morden,' he said, showing big grey teeth in an awful smile. 'No, indeed we will not.'

Another beat of silence followed that. Anna's hands were in her lap, she looked at them, frowning, as if she had not noticed them before. My right knee took fright and set to twitching.

Mr Todd launched into a forceful disquisition, polished from repeated use, on promising treatments, new drugs, the mighty arsenal of chemical weapons he had at his command; he might have been speaking of magic potions, the alchemist's physic. Anna continued frowning at her hands; she was not listening. At last he stopped and sat gazing at her with the same desperate, leporine look as before, audibly breathing, his lips drawn back in a sort of leer and those teeth on show again.

'Thank you,' she said politely in a voice that seemed now to come from very far off. She nodded to herself. 'Yes,' more remotely still, 'thank you.'

At that, as if released, Mr Todd gave his knees a quick smack with two flat palms and jumped to his feet and fairly bustled us to the door. When Anna had gone through he turned to me and gave me a gritty, man-to-man smile, and the handshake, dry, brisk, unflinching, which I am sure he reserves for the spouses at moments such as this.

The carpeted corridor absorbed our footsteps.

The lift, pressed, plunged.

We walked out into the day as if we were stepping on to a new planet, one where no one lived but us.

• • •

Arrived home, we sat outside the house in the car for a long time, loath of venturing in upon the known, saying nothing, strangers to ourselves and each other as we suddenly were. Anna looked out across the bay where the furled yachts bristled in the glistening sunlight. Her belly was swollen, a round hard lump pressing against the waistband of her skirt. She had said people would think she was pregnant—'At my age!'—and we had laughed, not looking at each other. The gulls that nested in our chimneys had all gone back to sea by now, or migrated, or whatever it is they do. Throughout that drear summer they had wheeled above the rooftops all day long, jeering at our attempts to pretend that all was well, nothing amiss, the world continuous. But there it was, squatting in her lap, the bulge that was big baby De'Ath, burgeoning inside her, biding its time.

At last we went inside, having nowhere else to go. Bright light of midday streamed in at the kitchen window and everything had a glassy, hard-edged radiance as if I were scanning the room through a camera lens. There was an impression of general, tight-lipped awkwardness, of all these homely things—jars on the shelves, saucepans on the stove, that breadboard with its jagged knife—averting their gaze from our all at once unfamiliar, afflicted presence in their midst. This, I realised miserably, this is how it would be from now on, wherever she goes the soundless clapping of the leper's bell preceding her. *How well you look!* they would exclaim, *Why, we've never seen you better!* And she with her brilliant smile, putting on a brave face, poor Mrs Bones.

She stood in the middle of the floor in her coat and scarf, hands on her hips, casting about her with a vexed expression. She was still handsome then, high of cheekbone, her skin translucent, paper-fine. I always admired in particular her Attic profile, the nose a line of carven ivory falling sheer from the brow.

'Do you know what it is?' she said with bitter vehemence. 'It's inappropriate, that's what it is.'

I looked aside quickly for fear my eyes would give me away; one's eyes are always those of someone else, the mad and desperate dwarf crouched within. I knew what she meant. This was not supposed to have befallen her. It was not supposed to have befallen us, we were not that kind of people. Misfortune, illness, untimely death, these things happen to good folk, the humble ones, the salt of the earth, not to Anna, not to me. In the midst of the imperial progress that was our life together a grinning losel had stepped out of the cheering crowd and sketching a parody of a bow had handed my tragic queen the warrant of impeachment.

She put on a kettle of water to boil and fished in a pocket of her coat and brought out her spectacles and put them on, looping the string behind her neck. She began to weep, absent-mindedly, it might be, making no sound. I moved clumsily to embrace her but she drew back sharply.

'For heaven's sake don't fuss!' she snapped. 'I'm only dying, after all.'

The kettle came to the boil and switched itself off and the seething water inside it settled down grumpily. I marvelled, not for the first time, at the cruel complacency of ordinary things. But no, not cruel, not complacent, only indifferent, as how could they be otherwise? Henceforth I would have to address things as they are, not as I might imagine them, for this was a new version of reality. I took up the teapot and the tea, making them rattle—my hands were shaking—but she said no, she had changed her mind, it was brandy she wanted, brandy, and a cigarette, she who did not smoke, and rarely drank. She gave me the dull glare of a defiant child, standing there by the table in her coat. Her tears had stopped. She took off her glasses and dropped them to hang below her throat on their string and rubbed at her eyes with the heels of her hands. I found the brandy bottle and tremblingly poured a measure into a tumbler, the bottle-neck and the rim of the glass chattering against each other like teeth. There were no cigarettes in the house, where was I to get cigarettes? She said it was no matter, she did not really want to smoke. The steel kettle shone, a slow furl of steam at its spout, vaguely suggestive of genie and lamp. Oh, grant me a wish, just the one.

'Take off your coat, at least,' I said.

But why at least? What a business it is, the human discourse.

I gave her the glass of brandy and she stood holding it but did not drink. Light from the window behind me shone on the lenses of her spectacles where they hung at her collar bone, giving the eerie effect of another, miniature she standing close in front of her under her chin with eyes cast down. Abruptly she went slack and sat down heavily, extending her arms before her along the table in a strange, desperate-seeming gesture, as if in supplication to some unseen other seated opposite her in judgment. The tumbler in her hand knocked on the wood and splashed out half its contents. Helplessly I contemplated her. For a giddy second the notion seized me that I would never again be able to think of another word to say to her, that we would go on like this, in agonised inarticulacy, to the end. I bent and kissed the pale patch on the crown of her head the size of a sixpence where her dark hair whorled. She turned her face up to me briefly with a black look.

'You smell of hospitals,' she said. 'That should be me.'

I took the tumbler from her hand and put it to my lips and drank at a draught what remained of the scorching brandy. I realised what the feeling was that had been besetting me since I had stepped that morning into the glassy glare of Mr Todd's consulting rooms. It was embarrassment. Anna felt it as well, I was sure of it. Embarrassment, yes, a panic-stricken sense of not knowing what to say, where to look, how to behave, and something else, too, that was not quite anger but a sort of surly annoyance, a surly resentment at the predicament in which we grimly found ourselves. It was as if a secret had been imparted to us so dirty, so nasty, that we could hardly bear to remain in one another's company yet were unable to break free, each knowing the foul thing that the other knew and bound together by that very knowledge. From this day forward all would be dissembling. There would be no other way to live with death.

Still Anna sat erect there at the table, facing away from me, her arms extended and hands lying inert with palms upturned as if for something to be dropped into them.

'Well?' she said without turning. 'What now?'

(*The Sea*, 2005)

O Lost, Raw World!

Old Adam plunges, a pearl-diver, into the past, going down deeper with each dive. There is a lost world there, he sees the sunken roofs and spires, the streets where currents glide, the people phosphorescent as fish, drifting in and out of houses, through half-familiar rooms, their seahorse eyes wide open. He is frightened; he does not want to drown, as they have drowned; he knows that he soon will. He feels the tide drawing him on, drawing him on. He grasps at tendrils but they slip through his hands, slimy and cold. There is a gleam, a glint, but when he scrabbles in the sand he finds nothing, only shells and jagged coral and bits of bone, and all around him is soon obscured. His breath is running out. He feels his heart beat, hears the blood in his veins, a hollow, rushing roar. He struggles. The water coils around him, heavy as chains and ungraspable. A great bubble bursts from his mouth. *Mother!*—

He wakes, but what he wakes to is not waking.

He is once again in the humpbacked town above the estuary, with its church, its ruined tower, its steep-roofed, jostling houses. He sees it in raw April weather, a rinsed blue sky with smudges of cloud, ice-white, bruise-grey, fawn. From all the chimneys flaws of smoke fly back, as if a close-packed flotilla were putting out to sea from here. The wind ruffles the widening river, pricking up white-caps. It is all there, compact and tiny, like a toy town in a snow-globe. He is a child trudging up a hill beside a high, grey-stone wall. He wears a tweed coat with a half-belt at the back, and a peaked cap, and thick woollen stockings the tops of which are turned down to hide homemade, soiled white elastic garters. He has his satchel on his back. It is four o'clock. There are houses on the other side of the sharply tilted street, each one set a step higher up than the other. On the front door of one a black crape bow is tied to the knocker with a pasteboard card attached with a name on it, and dates, written in black ink. The door is ajar. Someone has died and anyone may go in to view the corpse. The town drunks are always there first, for a free drink in which to toast the dead man on his way. He stops and stands for a moment, looking at the house. He could go in. He could just push open the door and walk straight into the parlour. There would be someone there, a woman wearing black, standing with her hands folded in front of her, her eyes pink-rimmed and her nostrils inflamed along the edges. He would shake her thin, chilly hand and murmur something; it need not even be words. He would cross the room, his school shoes squeaking, and gaze down stonily at the dead person laid out in the coffin in his unreal-looking suit, his waxen knuckles wound round with a rosary. There would be that smell, of lilies and ashes, which the recently dead give off, or which at least is always there when someone has died. The woman would offer him cake on a plate and a tumbler of tepid lemonade. There would be others there before him, sitting in the gloom on straight chairs ranged against the walls, gripping whiskey glasses in red fists or balancing cups and saucers on their knees, sighing and shifting, murmuring pious complacencies that set his teeth on edge.

But he does not cross the road. Instead he turns and walks on up the long hill towards home.

Spring winds flow through the streets like weightless water. The blued air of April. The trees tremble, their wet black branches powdered with puffs of green. The tarmac shines. A strong gust pummels the windowpanes, making them shiver and throw off lances of light. The priest's car passes, its tyres fizzing on the wet road. The boy salutes dutifully and in return is gravely blessed, as a reflected cloud slides smoothly, fish-like, over the windscreen.

A fellow in an old black coat and corduroy trousers that are bald on the knees comes out of the church gate with a spade over his shoulder. Without stopping he leans sideways and shuts one nostril with a finger pressed along the side of it and from the other expertly ejects a bolus of snot.

O lost, raw world!

The house stands in a crooked street, wedged narrowly between its taller neighbours as if it had sidled in there one day and stayed put. He slides his hand through the letter box—it gives him a shiver of terror every time—and fishes up the key that hangs inside on a string. In the hall the familiar smells meet him: floor polish, blacklead, soap, gas from the kitchen stove. He hangs his coat and cap on a hook, throws his satchel on the floor. His mother, in her apron, a strand of hair come loose from its bun, wipes the back of a hand across her cheek; she gives him the look that she always does, suspicious, sceptical, faintly desperate. He walks his fingers along the table edge. His father is in the back room, propped against pillows on a makeshift bed made up for him on the brown leather sofa in the corner, his big hands spread out flat in front of him on the blanket. The boy thinks of the crape bow on the door-knocker, and of himself standing in the parlour here, in his Sunday suit, amid the smell of ashes and lilies. His father stirs, sighs, and makes a slithering sound in his throat. The banked fire in the grate has a frightening glare at its heart, and the coke gives off a hot reek of cat. Low in the window there is a patch of late-afternoon sky, milk-blue, and a bit of the mossed wall on top of which his mother's hens make illicit nests and hide their eggs. Gooseberry bushes out there, potato drills, cabbages gone to seed and grown as tall as paschal candles. Then the fields, and behind them the rocky hills, and then, beyond that again, elsewhere.

The first present that he can remember getting is a clay pipe. It must have been his birthday. His sister took him to the tobacconist's shop and bought it for him with money their mother had given her. It came with a waxed-cardboard pot of soapy stuff for blowing bubbles. In the garden by the hen-house he tried it out. At first he could not get the hang of it then suddenly did. The bubbles hesitated on the rim of the pipe-bowl, wobbling flabbily, then broke free and floated sedately away. They seemed to be rotating inside themselves, as if the top was always too heavy and the iridescent surplus kept cascading down the sides. Sometimes two of them stuck together and formed a fat, trembling shape something like an hourglass only squatter. They were made of an unearthly substance, a transparent quicksilver, impossibly fine and volatile, rainbow-hued. They popped against his skin like wet, cold kisses. They were another kind of elsewhere.

His father died at Christmastime. In the back room the bed in the corner was dismantled, leaving the stripped sofa standing in what seemed a gaping hole in the air, and no more fires were lit and as the December days went on the light in the room congealed and grew steadily dimmer. At the end the dying man had suddenly lifted himself up from the pillows with starting eyes and called out something in a voice so strong and deep it shocked everyone. It was not his voice, but as if someone else had spoken through him, and Adam's sister burst into tears and ran from the room, and his two brothers with their greyish bloated damp-looking faces glanced at each other quickly and their eyes seemed to swell. What their father had shouted had seemed a name but no one had been able to make it out. He had kept on glaring upwards, his head shaking and his lips thrust out like a trumpet player's, and then had fallen back and there was a noise as if he were drowning.

His mother said they must have Christmas as usual. She said

his father would want it so, that Christmas was his favourite time of all the year.

She baked a cake. Adam helped her, measuring out the ingredients on the black iron weighing-scales with the brass weights that were cool and heavy as he imagined doubloons would be. It was night, all outside a frozen stillness, the leaning roofs purplish-grey with hoarfrost and the jagged stars glittering like splintered ice and the moon high up in the middle of a glistening, blue-black sky and small as if shrunken by the cold. His mother stood at the table with her sleeves rolled, mixing in a brown bowl the dry ingredients he had weighed out for her. Her head was bent and he did not realise she was crying until he saw the tears fall into the bowl, first one and then quickly two more, making three tiny grey craters in the white mixture. Without a word she handed him the wooden spoon and went and sat down by the fireplace with her face turned away from him, making no sound. He held the bowl by the rim, encircling it with his forearm in the way that he had seen her do. When he swirled the spoon in the flour mixture the tears became three grey pellets but they were quickly absorbed. He did not think that he had ever seen his mother cry before—even beside his father's grave she had stood dry-eyed—and now he felt embarrassed and uneasy and wished she would stop. Neither spoke. They were alone in the house. He wondered how long it would take before everything in the bowl was completely mixed. But what did that mean, *completely mixed*? Every grain of the ingredients would have to be distributed perfectly, the particles of salt and baking soda spaced just so throughout the flour, each one a fixed distance from all the rest. He tried to picture it, a solid, three-dimensional white field supporting a dense and uniform lattice of particles of other shades of white. And what about the flour itself, no two grains of which were alike—how could that be *completely mixed*, even if there were no other ingredients present in it, making their own pattern?

And how would he know when that moment of perfect distribution had been achieved?—how would he know the instant to stop mixing in order not to upset the equilibrium and throw everything back into disorder? He watched the spoon going round and round, making troughs and peaks and crumbling cliffs in the soft pale powdery mixture. Where were those three tears now? How well into the mixture were they mixed? Was everything in the world so intricately linked and yet resistantly disparate? His mother stood up and blew her nose on her apron and without a word took back from him the bowl and the wooden spoon and began mixing again.

His aunt came down from the city for the funeral and stayed on for Christmas. She took over the house, directed the putting up of the decorations and the trimming of the tree, ordered in a crate of stout and bottles of port-wine and whiskey, oversaw the distribution of presents, even carved the turkey, while his mother hung back, tight-lipped and watchful, saying nothing. His aunt was not married, and worked in the city for a solicitor. She wore a dove-grey coat with a fox-fur collar and fox-fur trim on the hem, and a black toque with a pearl pin and a piece of stiff black veil at the front, and big shoes with chunky high heels. She had an air about her always of angry sorrow. She was lavishly ugly, with a long horse-face and a mouthful of outsized teeth the front ones of which were always flecked with lipstick. Her Christmas present to him was a box of puzzles made from lengths of shiny steel bent into intricate shapes and linked together seemingly inextricably, though it took him only a moment of motionless concentration to see the trick of each pair and to separate them, which caused his aunt to sniff and frown and make a humming sound. It was voluptuously satisfying the way the two gleaming skeins of metal slid apart so smoothly, with what seemed an oiled ease, and his mind would become for a moment a limitless blue space, calmly radiant, through which transparent forms moved and met and locked and unlocked and passed on through each other in a vast silence, endlessly.

His mother, not to be outdone by his aunt, gave him a little clothbound book of curious and amusing facts about numbers. Here he first encountered the magic square. How strange it was, to add up the numbers in the boxes along each side and down each diagonal and come out every time with the same result, the same and yet, for him, always somehow new. This impression of novelty among identical values he could not account for. How could fifteen be different from fifteen? And yet the difference was there, a sort of aura, unseen but felt, like air, like warmth—yes, yes, we gods were there with him even then—like the breath he breathed, the breath that sometimes caught and swelled suffocatingly in his lungs, so avid was he for more facts, more conundrums, more solutions. He borrowed books from the library, by people with letters after their unpronounceable names. He tried to devise puzzles and problems of his own. The terms eluded him, they squirmed and writhed, slipping through the mesh of his mind. He would close his eyes and seem to be seeing into clear depths, where the figures glinted, but when he reached down he would grasp nothing but shards, shards and surds, and all would become clouded and thick with murk.

He counts. How many steps it takes him to walk to school. How many times in the course of a class the teacher will say a certain word. On the way home he counts how many cracks there are in the pavement, how many men he will meet and how many women, how many counted beats it will take to get from one telegraph pole to the next, how often that bird on that bough will chirp before he has passed underneath the tree. At night in bed he counts his heartbeats. The impossibility of accuracy torments him. So many this, so many that, but what before anything is the unit?

And then there is the question of time. What for instance is an instant? Hours, minutes, seconds, even, these are comprehensible, since they can be measured on a clock, but what is meant when people speak of a moment, a while—a tick—a jiffy? They are only words, of course, yet they hang above soundless depths. Does time flow or is it a succession of stillnesses—instants—moving so swiftly they seem to us to join in an unbreaking wave? Or is there only one great stillness, stretching everywhere, in all directions, through which we move like swimmers breasting an infinite, listless sea? And why does it vary? Why is toothache time so different from the time when he is eating a sweet, one of the many sweets that in time will cause another cavity? There are lights now in the sky that set out from their sources a billion years ago. But are there lights? No, only light, flowing endlessly, moving, every instant.

Everything blurs around its edges, everything seeps into everything else. Nothing is separate.

Has the early train gone by yet? Has his wife paid her morning visit?

The waters of time muddy, the figures flicker in silence.

(*The Infinities,* 2009)

Blest Boy

It was a spring day of wintry gales and spitting sleet, and we were the only two abroad in Fishers Walk, a laneway of whitewashed cottages that ran under the high granite wall of the railway station. She was struggling against the wind with her head down, the bat-wings of her umbrella snapping, and it would have been she who passed me by, seeing nothing of me above the knees, had I not halted directly in her path. Where did I find the courage, the effrontery, to take such a bold stand? For a second she did not recognise me, I could see, and when she did she seemed flustered. Could she have forgotten already, or have decided to pretend to forget, the display in the mirror, the embrace in the station wagon? She had no hat and her hair was sprinkled with glittering beads of melted ice. 'Oh,' she said, with a faltering smile, 'look at you, you're frozen.' I suppose I must have been shivering, not from the cold so much as the miserable excitement of encountering her accidentally like this. She wore galoshes and a smoke-coloured transparent plastic coat buttoned all the way up to her throat. No one wears those coats any more, or galoshes either; I wonder why. Her face was blotched from the cold, her chin raw and shiny, and her eyes were tearing. We stood there, buffeted by the wind, help-less in our different ways. A foul gust came to us from the bacon factory out by the river. Beside us the wet stone wall glistened and gave off a smell of damp mortar. I think she would have side-stepped me and walked on had she not seen my look of need and desolate entreaty. She gazed at me for a long moment in surmise, measuring the possibilities, no doubt, calculating the risks, and then at last made up her mind.

'Come along,' she said, and turned, and we walked off together in the direction whence she had come.

It was the week of the Easter holidays, and Mr Gray had taken Billy and his sister to the circus for the afternoon. I thought of them huddled on a wooden bench in the cold with the smell of trodden grass coming up between their knees and the tent flapping thunderously around them and the band blaring and farting, and I felt superior and more grown up than not only Billy and his sister but than their father, too. I was in their home, in their kitchen, sitting at that big square wooden table drinking a mug of milky tea that Mrs Gray had made for me, watchful and wary, it is true, but sheltered, and warm, and quivering like a gun-dog with expectancy. What were acrobats to me, or a dreary troupe of clowns, or even a spangled bareback rider? From where I sat I would have happily heard that the big top had collapsed in the wind and smothered them all, performers and spectators alike. An iron wood-stove in one corner sparked and hissed behind a sooty window, its tall black flue trembling with heat. Behind me the big refrigerator's motor shut itself off with a heave and a grunt and where there had been an unheard hum was suddenly a hollow quiet. Mrs Gray, who had gone off to shed her raincoat and her rubber overshoes, came back chafing her hands. Her face that had been blotched was glowing pink now but her hair was still dark with wet and stood out in spikes. 'You didn't tell me there was a drop on the end of my nose,' she said.

She had an air of faint desperation and at the same time seemed ruefully amused. This was uncharted territory, after all, for her, surely, as much as for me. Had I been a man and not a boy, perhaps she would have known how to proceed, by way of banter, sly smiles, a show of reluctance betokening its opposite—all the usual—but what was she to do with me, squatting there toad-like at her kitchen table with the rain-wet legs of my trousers lightly steaming, my eyes determinedly downcast, my elbows planted on the wood and the mug clutched tight between my hands, struck dumb by shyness and covert lust?

In the event she managed with an ease and briskness that I had not the experience to appreciate properly at the time. In a cramped room off the kitchen there was a top-loading washing machine with a big metal paddle sticking up through its middle, a stone sink, an ironing board standing tensed and spindly as a mantis, and a metal-framed camp bed that could have doubled as an operating table had it not been so low to the ground. But, come to think of it, was it a bed? It might have been a horschair mattress thrown on the floor, for I seem to recall cartoon-convict stripes and rough ticking that tickled my bare knees. Or am I confusing it with the subsequent mattress on the floor at the Cotter house? Anyway, in this place of lying down we lay down together, on our sides at first and facing each other, still in our clothes, and she pressed herself against me full-length and kissed me on the mouth, hard, and for some reason crossly, or so it seemed to me. Casting up a quick glance sideways past her temple towards the ceiling so high above, I had the panicky sensation of lying among sunken things at the bottom of a deep cistern.

Above the bed and halfway up the wall there was a single window of frosted glass, and the rain-light coming through was soft and grey and steady, and that and the laundry smell and the smell of some soap or cream that Mrs Gray had used on her face seemed all to be drifting up out of the far past of my infancy. And indeed I did feel like an impossibly overgrown baby, squirming and mewling on top of this matronly, warm woman. For we had progressed, oh, yes, we had made rapid progress. I suspect she had not intended we should do more than lie there for a certain time chaste enough in our clothes, grinding ourselves against each other's lips and teeth and hip bones, but if so she had not reckoned with a fifteen-year-old boy's violent single-mindedness. When I had writhed and kicked myself free of trousers and underpants the air was so cool and satiny against my naked skin that I seemed to feel myself break out all over in a foolish smile. Did I still have my socks on? Mrs Gray, putting a hand to my chest to stay my impatience, got to her feet and took off her dress and lifted her slip and slithered out of her underthings, and then, still in her shift, lay down again and suffered me to re-fasten my tentacles around her. She was saying *No* over and over in my ear now, *no no no nooo!* though it sounded to me more like low laughter than a plea that I should stop what I was doing.

And what I did turned out to be so easy, like learning without effort how to swim. Frightening, too, of course, above those unplumbed depths, but far stronger than fear was the sense of having achieved, at last and yet so early on, a triumphant climacteric. No sooner had I finished—yes, I am afraid it was all very quick—and rolled off Mrs Gray on to my back to lie teetering on the very rim of the narrow mattress with one leg flexed while she was wedged against the wall than I began to puff up with pride, even as I laboured for breath. I had the urge to run and tell someone—but whom could I tell? Not my best friend, that was certain. I would have to be content to hug my secret close to me and share it with no one. Though I was young I was old enough to know that in this reticence would lie a form of power, over myself as well as over Mrs Gray.

If I was in fear, frantically swimming there, what must she have felt? What if there had indeed been a catastrophe at the circus so that the show had to be stopped and Kitty had come running in to tell how the young man on the flying trapeze had lost his grip and plummeted down through the powdery darkness to break his neck in a cloud of sawdust in the dead centre of the ring, only to find her Mammy engaged in half-naked and incomprehensible acrobatics with her brother's laughable friend? I stand in amazement now before the risks that Mrs Gray took. What was she thinking of, how did she dare? Despite the pride of my accomplishment, I had no sense that it was for the sole sake of me that she was willing, more than willing, to put so much at peril. I should say that I did not imagine myself so treasured, I did not think myself so loved. This was not from diffidence or a lack of a sense of my own significance, no, but the very opposite: engrossed in what I felt for myself, I had no measure against which to match what she might feel for me. That was how it was at the start, and how it went on, to the end. That is how it is, when one discovers oneself through another.

Having had of her what I had most grievously desired I now faced the tricky task of disengaging from her. I do not mean I was not appreciative or that I felt no fondness for her. On the contrary, I was adrift in a daze of tenderness and incredulous gratitude. A grown-up woman of my own mother's age but otherwise as unlike her as could be, a married woman with children, my best pal's ma, had taken off her dress and unhooked her suspenders and stepped out of her drawers—white, ample, sensible—and with one stocking still up and the other sagging to the knee had lain down under me with her arms open and let me spill myself into her, and even now had turned on her side again with a fluttery sigh of contentment and pressed her front to my back, her slip bunched around her waist and the fuzz at her lap wiry and warm against my backside, and was caressing my left temple with the pads of her fingers and crooning in my ear what seemed a softly salacious lullaby. How could I not think myself the town's, the nation's—the world's!—most favoured son and lavishly blest boy?

I still had the taste of her in my mouth. My hands still tingled from a certain cool roughness along her flanks and the outsides of her upper arms. I could still hear her rasping gasps and feel the way that she seemed to be falling and falling out of my arms even as she arched herself violently against me. Yet she was not I, was wholly another, and young though I was and new to all this, I saw at once, with merciless clarity, the delicate task that I had now of thrusting her back into the world among the countless other things that were not myself. Indeed, I was gone from her already, was already sad and lonely for her, though still clasped in her arms with her fluttery breath on the back of my neck. I had once seen a pair of dogs locked together after mating, standing end to end and facing away from each other, the hound casting about in a bored and gloomy fashion, the female hanging her head dejectedly, and God forgive me but this was what I could not keep myself from thinking of now, poised like a spring on the edge of that low bed, yearning to be elsewhere and remembering this lavish, astonishing, impossible quarter of an hour of happy toil in the embrace of a woman-sized woman. So young, Alex, so young, and already such a brute!

At last we got up gropingly and fastened ourselves away into our clothes, bashful now as Adam and Eve in the garden after the apple was eaten. Or no, I was the bashful one. Although I thought I must surely have injured her insides with all my plunging and gouging, she was quite collected, and even seemed preoccupied, thinking perhaps what to make for tea when her family came home from the circus, or, prompted by our surroundings, wondering if my mother would notice telltale stains on my underwear next wash-day. First love, the cynic observes, and afterwards the reckoning.

I too had my distractions, and wanted for instance to know why there should be a bed, or even a bare mattress, if that was what it was, in the laundry room, but feared it would be indelicate to ask—

I never did find out—and perhaps the suspicion crossed my mind that I had not been the first to lie down there with her, though if it did the suspicion was unfounded, I am sure of that, for she was anything but promiscuous, despite all that had just occurred, and all that was yet to occur, between her and me. Also, I was unpleasantly sticky in the region of my groin, and I was hungry, too, as what young chap would not be after such exertions? The rain had stopped a while before but now another shower began to tinkle against the window above the bed, I could see the wind-driven ghostly drops shiver and slide on the greyly misted glass. I thought with what felt like sorrow of the wetted boughs of the cherry trees outside glistening blackly and the bedraggled blossoms falling. Was this what it was to be in love, I asked myself, this sudden plangent gusting in the heart?

Mrs Gray was fastening a suspender, the hem of her dress lifted high, and I pictured myself falling to my knees in front of her and burying my face between the bare and very white tops of her legs plumped up a little and rounded above the tightness of her stockings. She saw me looking and smiled indulgently. 'You're such a nice boy,' she said, straightening, and giving herself a shimmy from shoulder to knee to settle her garments into line, a thing that, I realised with a qualm of dismay, I had often seen my mother do. Then she reached out a hand and touched my face, cupping her palm along my cheek, and her smile turned troubled and became almost a frown. 'What am I going to do with you?' she murmured with a helpless little laugh, as if in amazement at everything. '—You're not even shaving yet!'

I thought her quite old—she was the same age as my mother, after all. I was not sure what to feel about this. Should I be flattered that a woman of such maturity, a respectable wife and mother, had found me, maculate, ill-barbered and far from fragrant though I was, so overpoweringly desirable that there was nothing for it but to take me to bed while her husband and her children all unknowing were splitting their sides at the antics of Coco the clown or gazing up in anxious admiration as petite Roxanne and her blue-jawed brothers cavorted flat-footedly on the high-wire? Or had I been simply a diversion, a plaything of the moment, to be toyed with by a bored housewife in the dull middle of an ordinary afternoon and then unceremoniously sent packing, while she turned back to the business of being who she really was and forgot all about me and the transfigured creatures we had both seemed to be when she was thrashing in my arms and crying out in ecstasy?

By the by, I do not fail to notice how persistently the theme of the circus, with its gaud and glitter, has intruded on proceedings here. I suppose it is an apt background to the hectic spectacle Mrs Gray and I had just put on, although our only audience was a washing-machine, an ironing board and a box of Tide, unless of course the goddess and all her starry fays were present, too, unseen.

I left the house gingerly, drunker than I had been that other time on Billy's father's whiskey, my knees as rickety as an old man's and my face on fire still. The April day that I stepped out into was, of course, transfigured, was all flush and shiver and skimming light, in contrast to the sluggishness of my sated state, and as I moved through it I felt that I was not so much walking as wallowing along, like a big slack balloon. When I got home I avoided my mother, for I was sure the livid marks of a lust so lately, if only temporarily, satisfied would be plainly visible in my burning features, and I went straight to my room and threw myself, fairly threw myself on the bed and lay on my back with a forearm shielding my shut eyes and replayed on an inner screen, frame by frame, in maniacally slow slow-motion, all that had taken place not an hour past on that other bed, gaped upon in awe and astonishment by a gallery of innocent domestic appliances. Down in the drenched garden a blackbird began to rinse its throat with a cascade of song and as I listened to it hot tears welled in my eyes. *'O Mrs Gray!'* I cried out softly, *'O my darling!'* and hugged myself for sweet sorrow, suffering the while from the stabs of a stinging prepuce.

I had no thought that she and I would ever do again what we had done that day. That it had happened once was hard enough to credit, that it should be repeated was inconceivable. It was essential therefore that every detail be fetched up, verified, catalogued and stored in memory's lead-lined cabinet. Here, however, I experienced frustration. Pleasure, it turned out, was as difficult to re-live as pain would have been, this failure part of the price, no doubt, of being shielded from the imagination's re-enactive powers, for had I been allowed to feel again with the same force, every time I thought of it, all that I had felt as I was bouncing up and down on top of Mrs Gray, I think I should have died. Similarly, of Mrs Gray herself I was unable to call up a satisfactorily clear and coherent image. I could remember her, certainly I could, but only as a series of disparate and dispersed parts, as in one of those old paintings of the Crucifixion in which the implements of torture, the nails and hammer, spear and sponge, are laid out in a close-up and lovingly executed display while off to the side Christ is dying on the cross in blurred anonymity—dear God, forgive me, compounding bawdry with blasphemy as I do. I could see her eyes of wet amber, unnervingly reminiscent of Billy's, brimming under half-closed lids that throbbed like a moth's wings; I could see the damp roots of her hair that was drawn back from her forehead, already showing a greying strand or two; I could feel the bulging side of a plump and polished breast lolling against my palm; I could hear her enraptured cries and smell her slightly eggy breath. But the woman herself, the total she, that was what I could not have over again, in my mind. And I, too, even I, there with her, was beyond my own recall, was no more than a pair of clutching arms and spasming legs and a backside frenziedly pumping. This was all a puzzle, and troubled me, for I was not accustomed yet to the chasm that yawns between the doing of a thing and the recollection of what was done, and it would take practice and the resultant familiarity before I could fix her fully in my mind and make her of a piece, in total, and me along with her. But what does it mean when I say in total and of a piece? What was it I retrieved of her but a figment of my own making? This was a greater puzzle, a greater trouble, this enigma of estrangement.

I did not want to face my mother that day, not solely because I thought my guilt must be writ plain all over me. The fact was, I would not look at any woman, even Ma, in quite the same way ever again. Where before there had been girls and mothers, now there was something that was neither, and I hardly knew what to make of it.

• • •

As I was leaving the house that day Mrs Gray had stopped me on the front-door mat and quizzed me as to the state of my soul. She was herself devout in a hazy sort of way and wished to be assured that I was on good terms with Our Lord and, especially, with his Holy Mother, for whom she had a particular reverence. She was anxious that I should go to confession without delay. It was apparent she had given the matter some consideration—had she been thinking it over when we were still grappling on that improvised bed in the laundry room?—and said now that while certainly I must lose no time in confessing the sin I had just committed, there would be no need to reveal with whom I had committed it. She too would confess, of course, without identifying me. While she was saying these things she was briskly straightening my collar and combing my horrent hair with her fingers as best she could—I might have been Billy being seen off to school! Then she put her hands on my shoulders and held me at arms' length and looked me up and down with a carefully critical eye. She smiled, and kissed me on the forehead. 'You're going to be a handsome fellow,' she said, 'do you know that?' For some reason this compliment, although delivered with an ironical cast, straight away set my blood throbbing again, and had I been more practised, and less worried about the imminent return of the rest of the family, I would have hustled her backwards down the stairs to the laundry room and pulled off her clothes and mine and pushed her on to that pallet-bed or mattress and started all over again. She mistook my suddenly louring aspect for a scowl of resentful scepticism, and said she had truly meant it, that I was good-looking, and that I should be pleased. I could think of no reply, and turned from her in a tumult of emotions and stumbled off swollenly into the rain.

I did go to confession. The priest I settled on, after much hot-faced agonising in the church's Saturday-evening gloom, was one I had been to before, many times, a large asthmatic man with stooped shoulders and a doleful air, whose name by happy chance, though perhaps not so happy for him, was Priest, so that he was Father Priest. I worried that he would know me from previous occasions, but the burden I was carrying was such that I felt in need of an ear that I was accustomed to, and that was accustomed to me. Always, when he had slid back the little door behind the grille—I can still hear the abrupt and always startling clack it used to make—he would begin by heaving a heavy sigh of what seemed long-suffering reluctance. This I found reassuring, a token that he was as loath to hear my sins as I was to confess them. I went through the prescribed, singsong list of misdemeanours—lies, bad language, disobedience—before I ventured, my voice sinking to a feathery whisper, on the main, the mortal, matter. The confessional smelled of wax and old varnish and uncleaned serge. Father Priest had listened to my hesitant opening gambit in silence and now let fall another sigh, very mournful-sounding, this time. 'Impure actions,' he said. 'I see. With yourself or with another, my child?'

'With another, Father.'

'A girl, was it, or a boy?' This gave me pause. Impure actions with a boy—what would they consist of? Still, it allowed of what I considered a cunningly evasive answer. 'Not a boy, Father, no,' I said.

Here he fairly pounced. '—Your sister?'

My *sister*, even if I had one? The collar of my shirt had begun to feel chokingly tight. 'No, Father, not my sister.'

'Someone else, then. I see. Was it the bare skin you touched, my child?'

'It was, Father.'

'On the leg?'

'Yes, Father.'

'High up on the leg?'

'Very high up, Father.'

'Ahh.' There was a huge stealthy shifting—I thought of a horse in a horse-box—as he gathered himself close up to the grille. Despite the wooden wall of the confessional that separated us I felt that we were huddled now almost in each other's arms in whispered and sweaty colloquy. 'Go on, my child,' he murmured.

I went on. Who knows what garbled version of the thing I tried to fob him off with, but eventually, after much delicate easing aside of fig leaves, he penetrated to the fact that the person with whom I had committed impure actions was a married woman.

'Did you put yourself inside her?' he asked.

'I did, Father,' I answered, and heard myself swallow.

To be precise, it was she who had done the putting in, since I was so excited and clumsy, but I judged that a scruple I could pass over.

There followed a lengthy, heavy-breathing silence at the end of which Father Priest cleared his throat and huddled closer still. 'My son,' he said warmly, his big head in three-quarters profile filling the dim square of mesh, 'this is a grave sin, a very grave sin.'

He had much else to say, on the sanctity of the marriage bed, and our bodies being temples of the Holy Ghost, and how each sin of the flesh that we commit drives the nails anew into Our Saviour's hands and the spear into his side, but I hardly listened, so thoroughly anointed was I with the cool salve of absolution. When I had promised never to do wrong again and the priest had blessed me I went up and knelt before the high altar to say my penance, head bowed and hands clasped, glowing inside with piety and sweet relief—what a thing it was to be young and freshly shriven!—but presently, to my horror, a tiny scarlet devil came and perched on my left shoulder and began to whisper in my ear a lurid and anatomically exact review of what Mrs Gray and I had done together that day on that low bed. How the red eye of the sanctuary lamp glared at me, how shocked and pained seemed the faces of the plaster saints in their niches all about. I was supposed to know that if I were to die at that moment I would go straight to Hell not only for having done such vile deeds but for entertaining such vile recollections of them in these hallowed surroundings, but the little devil's voice was so insinuating and the things he said so sweet—somehow his account was more detailed and more compelling than any rehearsal I had so far been capable of—that I could not keep myself from attending to him, and in the end I had to break off my prayers and hurry from the place and skulk away in the gathering dusk.

On the following Monday when I came home from school my mother met me in the hall in a state of high agitation. One look at her stark face and her under-lip trembling with anger told me that I was in trouble. Father Priest had called, in person! On a weekday, in the middle of the afternoon, while she was doing the household accounts, there he was, without warning, stooping in the front doorway with his hat in his hand, and there had been no choice but to put him in the back parlour, that even the lodgers were not permitted to enter, and to make tea for him. I knew of course that he had come to talk about me in light of the things I had told him. I was as much scandalised as frightened—what about the much vaunted seal of the confessional?—and tears of outraged injury sprang to my eyes. What, my mother demanded, had I been up to? I shook my head and showed her my innocent palms, while in my mind I saw Mrs Gray, shoeless and her feet bleeding and her hair all shorn, being driven through the streets of the town by a posse of outraged, cudgel-wielding mothers shrieking vengeful abuse.

I was marched into the kitchen, the place where all domestic crises were tackled, and where now it quickly became clear that my mother did not care what it was I had done, and was only angry at me for being the cause of Father Priest's breaking in upon the tranquility of a lodgerless afternoon while she was at her sums. My mother had no time for the clergy, and not much, I suspect, for the God they represented either. She was if anything a pagan, without realising it, and all her devotions were directed towards the lesser figures of the pantheon, St Anthony, for instance, restorer of lost objects, and the gentle St Francis, and, most favoured of all, St Catherine of Siena, virgin, diplomatist and exultant stigmatic whose wounds, unaccountably, were invisible to mortal eyes. 'I couldn't get rid of him,' she said indignantly, 'sitting there at the table slurping his tea and talking about the Christian Brothers.' At first she had been at a loss and could not grasp his import. He had spoken of the wonderful facilities on offer at the Christian Brothers' seminaries, the verdant playing fields and Olympic-standard swimming pools, the hearty and nutritious meals that would build strong bones and bulging muscles, not to mention, of course, the matchless wealth of learning that would be dinned into a lad as quick and receptive as he had no doubt a son of hers was bound to be. At last she had understood, and was outraged.

'A vocation to the Christian Brothers!' she said scornfully. '— Not even the priesthood!'

So I was safe, my sin undisclosed, and never again would I go for confession to Father Priest, or to anyone else, for that day marked the onset of my apostasy.

(*Ancient Light*, 2012)

Playing Parts

STAGE AND RADIO PLAYS

1994–2006

From *The Broken Jug*

CHARACTERS

(as appear in the following scenes)

JUDGE ADAM, town magistrate and 'squireen'
LYNCH, his clerk
SIR WALTER PEEL, Lord Lieutenant's inspector of courts
MARTHA RECK, a widow
EVE, her daughter
WILLIE TEMPLE, a small tenant farmer
ROBERT, his son
BALL, a cockney, Sir Walter's servant

Townsfolk

TIME AND PLACE

The action takes place in Ballybog, a small town in the West of Ireland, in August, 1846.

Act One, Scene Six

JUDGE ADAM'S *chamber. Enter* LYNCH, *leading* MARTHA RECK, EVE, WILLIE TEMPLE *and* ROBERT TEMPLE.

MARTHA (*To* ROBERT)
You'll pay for this, you good-for-nothing cur!

WILLIE Ah, Mrs Reck—

MARTHA Don't Mrs Reck me, you!
If you had took the whip to that one there
(*Pointing to* ROBERT)
While he was still a lad, and biddable,
He wouldn't have ideas above his station,
Thinking he could court that girl of mine.

WILLIE It will be fixed—

MARTHA What? Fixed? You'll fix my jug?

WILLIE We're only simple people, Mrs Reck.

MARTHA *You* may be simple, Willie Temple, yes,
But that lad has his eye on higher things.

ROBERT (*Pointing to* EVE)
If you call *this* thing higher—

MARTHA What! The cheek!

LYNCH Now listen, Missus, and you, Temple, too,
All of you, listen. I brought you this way
In order to avoid that crowd out there.
If you want everyone to know your business,
Then go on, shout, so all the town can hear.

MARTHA All I want is my rights.

ROBERT You'll have them, sure.

WILLIE If you can show it was my boy that broke
The jug then we'll make restitution.

MARTHA What?
Will you make restitution for what's broke?

WILLIE We will replace the jug—

MARTHA Replace it, will you?
You'll mend what's broken, put all back intact?

ROBERT You have a wicked mind, and that's the truth.

MARTHA And you have wicked ways: I've heard the tales
Of you and your fine ways—Oho, I have!
Out drinking half the night and plotting war.

ROBERT That kind of careless talk is dangerous.

MARTHA John Lynch, you hear him, how he threatens me?

WILLIE You know he's off to join the army, ma'am.

MARTHA Oh yes? What army, though, I'd like to know.

WILLIE *glances anxiously at* LYNCH.

WILLIE My lad's no rebel, Mrs Reck.

MARTHA Oh no?

WILLIE I don't know why you've got in such a state.
I've said we'll compensate you for the jug.

MARTHA You'll compensate me, will you? Oh, that's grand.
And how, pray, will you do it? Whose tenant are you?
You think I don't know how things stand with you?
You owe me six months' rent in hanging gale,
And yet you talk to me of compensation?

ROBERT Don't mind her, da; it's not the broken jug
That has her riz, but that I've seen at last
The kind of girl her charming daughter is.
(*To* EVE)
You've had a right lend out of me, you have,
Pretending you were inexperienced.
If you think that I'd marry you, you slut—

MARTHA Oh, holy mother of God, did you hear that—?

EVE Dear Robert—

ROBERT I'm not listening.

EVE Robert, please—
ROBERT You get away from me—
EVE I beg you, please—

MARTHA *grabs* EVE*'s arm.*

MARTHA Don't cheapen yourself talking to him, child.
EVE (*To* ROBERT)
A word in private, love, is all I ask.
ROBERT Away from me, you damned—I won't say what.
LYNCH Here, listen, Temple, mind you watch your tongue.
EVE Next week you go to join your regiment,
And who knows in what place you will end up,
Or that we'll ever see each other more.
ROBERT What are you saying, 'what place I'll end up'?
What's that supposed to mean, I'd like to know?
I'm off to Aldershot, not Timbuktu.
EVE You'll have to go wherever you are sent;
The empire's big, and there are many places
That do need soldiers, worse than Aldershot.
I don't want you to leave with angry feelings.
ROBERT (*Loftily*)
It is not anger that I feel towards you,
But disappointment: that, and bitter rue.
When we first met, I gave you all my heart,
And swore that from your side I'd never part.
You were more dear to me than my own life;
I was determined to make you my wife
And give you all the things a girl dreams of:
A name, a home, and children, and true love—
EVE I'm glad you had my life planned out for me.
ROBERT And even still I wish you happiness,
Good fortune, health, a long life, nothing less.

I'm not the kind of man who holds a grudge;
I am forgiving, to that God's my judge;
But even if I come back from the wars
And live in Ballybog for eighty years,
I won't relent, Eve Reck, of that be sure.
You are a lying and a faithless whore.

MARTHA That's lovely talk! The judge will hear of this.
And you, Eve, come away from him, come here.
I told you he was not the man for you.
That Sergeant Boggan is still soft on you;
Say but a word and he'll produce the ring.
If you so want to marry, go ahead.
We'll have a christening, too, and after that
My funeral as well, for all I care—
So long as first I get to box the ears
Of that young cur who broke my jug last night.

EVE Mother, please, enough about the jug!
I'll go to Dublin, see if I can find
A craftsman who'll repair the thing for you.
If not, then take my savings, buy a new one.
Who'd want, for a mere piece of pottery,
To make such a commotion, such a fuss?

MARTHA Are you that innocent, or just a fool?
Do you know what was in that jug, my girl?
Only your reputation, that was all.
Who'll glue that back for you, I'd like to know?
The magistrate's the craftsman that we need;
Instead of china-clips it's chains that's wanted.
That spalpeen there will go to jail for this,
Or my name isn't Martha Reck, by God!
I will have recompense for what he's done,
And out of Ballybog I'll see he's run!

Act One, Scene Seven

The courtroom. Judge Adam *seated on the bench,* Ball *lounging at the door,* Sir Walter *seated, writing in a notebook; enter* Lynch *with* Martha Reck, Willie Temple, Robert Temple, Eve.

Judge Adam What, Eve?—Miss Reck, I mean. And Mrs Reck!
(*Aside*)
And that young Robert Temple fellow, too.
What does this mean, I wonder? Have they come
To bring a case against me in my court?
If that's their game then I'll give them short shrift.

Eve Please, mother, come away and leave this now;
You know no good will come of it.

Martha Shut up.

Judge Adam *descends from the bench.*

Judge Adam What's going on here, Lynch?

Lynch Oh, I don't know;
Some trifling thing about a broken jug.

Judge Adam A broken jug? Who broke it?

Lynch Don't ask me.

Ball (*Aside to* Lynch)
Who is the bird?

Lynch Her name is Eve.

Ball That so?
I wouldn't mind a bite out of that one's apple.

Judge Adam (*Aside to* Eve)
Dear Eve—

Eve Go 'way!

Judge Adam A word.

Eve I will not listen.

JUDGE ADAM My dearest Eve, please tell me, what's going on?
EVE I've told you, get away from me!
JUDGE ADAM Oh Eve! . . .
(*To* LYNCH)
Here listen, Lynch, I can't take this, I can't;
My head is paining me, and I feel sick.
You take the case, I'm going back to bed.
LYNCH You're what? What's wrong? Have you gone off your head?
JUDGE ADAM Oh Jesus Christ, I think I'm going to spew!
(*Aside to* EVE)
Dear Eve, please tell me, please, why are you here?
EVE You'll soon know why.
JUDGE ADAM That jug, that broken jug,
Is that the real reason?
EVE Yes.
JUDGE ADAM You're sure?
EVE Oh, get away from me, you dirty brute!
JUDGE ADAM Now listen, girl, think twice, then think again.
I've got a paper in my pocket here,
The name on it, writ large, is 'Robert Temple'.
You hear it crackle? In a year from now
I'll let you have it for a mourning band
When news comes that your precious Robert's croaked
In the East Indies from the yellow or
The scarlet fever, take your pick.
EVE For shame!
SIR WALTER Judge Adam, is it common practice here,
To talk to litigants before the hearing?
JUDGE ADAM (*Aside*)
Come on, think, think: was that a crash I heard,
When I was—?
(*To* SIR WALTER)
Pardon, sir? I did not catch—

SIR WALTER I said, Judge Adam, please do not converse
With people in the court before the session;
It is irregular. Here is your seat,
Sit down, and start the questioning at once.

JUDGE ADAM At once, at once!

LYNCH *comes up silently behind* JUDGE ADAM.

LYNCH Did you—?

JUDGE ADAM (*With a start*)
Did I—? Why, no!
(*Distractedly*)
I put the wig down on it, I remember,
But surely I'm not such a clumsy ox . . .

LYNCH What?

JUDGE ADAM What?

LYNCH You're deaf, is what; he's talking to you.

JUDGE ADAM (*Aside*)
Oh, what the hell, it's one way or the other.
If things don't bend they break.
(*To* SIR WALTER)
At once, at once.

SIR WALTER Are you distracted, sir?

JUDGE ADAM Distracted? I?

SIR WALTER Your mind seems elsewhere, judge; what is the matter?

JUDGE ADAM The matter? Well, you see, this . . . guinea hen
A fellow home from the East Indies sold me
Has got the pip.

SIR WALTER (*Incredulous*)
The pip? . . .

JUDGE ADAM That's right, the pip.

BALL *laughs, all turn and stare at him and he falls silent.*

It's prone to pip, you see, the guinea hen,
And cramming is the only cure, they say,
Upon which subject this young woman here
I'm told is expert—

BALL (*Aside*)
Cramming? Yes, I'll say.

JUDGE ADAM So I was asking her advice, that's all.
I have an interest in birds—

BALL (*Aside*)
Oi oi!

JUDGE ADAM And treat my chicks as if they were my children.

SIR WALTER For God's sake, man, stop babbling and sit down.
Let's hear the case, and have it over with.
You, clerk, come, write the depositions down.
(*Aside to* LYNCH)
What is the matter with him?

LYNCH I don't know.
He says he's sick, but I've heard that before.
Some sicknesses come corked up in a bottle.

SIR WALTER Aha . . .

LYNCH Mind you, of course, I have said nothing.

JUDGE ADAM *ascends the bench and takes his seat.*

JUDGE ADAM Tell me, Sir Walter, shall we hear the case
According to our local custom here,
Or must we stick to Dublin rules?

SIR WALTER This is
Your court, Judge Adam, and not mine, so please
Conduct the case as you would normally:
Which I presume is as the law prescribes
For London, Dublin, and for Ballybog.

JUDGE ADAM Quite so, quite so. Clerk Lynch, you're ready, are you?

LYNCH Your honour.

JUDGE ADAM Yes.

(*Aside*)

I'm surely done for now;
I'll be disgraced, and Swisser Swatter here
Will have my hide. Well, that's the way it goes.
Let justice take its course!

(*Aloud*)

First plaintiff, please.

MARTHA That's me.

JUDGE ADAM And who is 'me'? State who you are.

MARTHA State who . . . ?

JUDGE ADAM —You are.

MARTHA Who am I?

JUDGE ADAM Yes! Your name!
Your age, your place of residence, all that.

MARTHA (*To* LYNCH)
He must be joking, is he?

JUDGE ADAM Joking, ma'am?
You would not think it funny if I put
You in the jailhouse for contempt of court.

LYNCH (*Aside to* JUDGE ADAM)
Come down off your high horse, he's not impressed.

MARTHA You peep at me on Sundays through my window
When you are going out to see your farm.
You think I haven't spotted your wall eye
Forever looking out for what's to see?

SIR WALTER You know the woman, do you, judge?

JUDGE ADAM (*Aside to* SIR WALTER)

I do.
She lives just round the corner, past the church.

She is a widow, with a bit of land
That she rents out in rundale.

SIR WALTER — What is that?

JUDGE ADAM (*Settling to the task of explanation*)
Well, rundale, now—

SIR WALTER — All right! Another time.
(*To* LYNCH)
Record this woman's name, and make a note
To the effect, she's well-known to the court.

JUDGE ADAM (*Aside to* LYNCH)
Aha: not such a stickler for the rules
As first we feared.

SIR WALTER — Now ask what's her complaint.

JUDGE ADAM That's simple, sir.

SIR WALTER — It is?

JUDGE ADAM — A jug, that's all,
An ordinary jug. Lynch, write that down:
A broken jug, and well-known to the court.

LYNCH That hardly seems, your honour—

JUDGE ADAM — Write it down!
(*To* MARTHA)
Come, missus, tell us, isn't it the case
That you've come here about a broken jug?

MARTHA That's right—and here it is, in pieces, look.

JUDGE ADAM (*To* SIR WALTER)
You see?

MARTHA — In smithereens.

JUDGE ADAM — Well then, who broke it?

MARTHA (*Pointing to* ROBERT)
That villain there. He broke it, he's the one.

JUDGE ADAM (*Aside*)
A villain brought to book! Begob, that's rich!

(*Aloud*)
Clerk, write that down: 'That villain there, he broke it'-

ROBERT — Your honour, that's a dirty, rotten lie!

JUDGE ADAM — (*Aside*)
Oh is it, now? We'll see about that, boy.
Come, get the bit between your teeth, old Adam!

ROBERT — Don't listen to a word from that old rip—

JUDGE ADAM — Silence in court, by God! or you'll go down
For longer years than you have life. Clerk Lynch,
Write as directed: 'Jug, well-known, etcetera',
And then put down the rascal's name who broke it—

SIR WALTER — Your honour, please! All this is most improper.

JUDGE ADAM — How so?

SIR WALTER — There has not been a formal hearing—

JUDGE ADAM — I thought you didn't like formalities?

SIR WALTER — Judge Adam, if you do not know the way
To run a proper trial, I can't teach you.
If you can do no better, then step down,
And let your clerk preside.

JUDGE ADAM — Forgive me, please;
I did as we do things in Ballybog,
Which is the way you said that I should do.

SIR WALTER — I said—?

JUDGE ADAM — You did.

SIR WALTER — I said that I expected
No difference between the law elsewhere
And here; if that is not the case, say so.

JUDGE ADAM — The fact is, sir, we do things different here.
We have peculiar statutes in these parts
That are not written down, nevertheless
Are tried and true, and come to us direct
From old traditions we in Ballybog

Hold dear. Perhaps in London all is modern,
The old ways all forgot, the past ignored.
We are an ancient civilization, sir;
We had our Brehon Laws when you in England
Still lived in caves and smeared yourselves with woad.
From our old laws I have not here today
Strayed one iota, that you can believe.
I know the other way, the English way,
And if that's what you want that's how I'll go.
The trouble is, when you come over here,
You Englishmen I mean, you do not see
That things are different here to over there,
And try to push your customs down our throats—

SIR WALTER Yes yes, spare me the patriotic speech;
A little English dullness now and then
Perhaps might save a deal of trouble here.
However, let us leave these things aside.
For now, the best thing is to start again.

JUDGE ADAM Agreed. Now, Mrs Martha Reck, stand up
And tell the court what is your grievance, please.

MARTHA My grievance, as you know, concerns this jug.
But let me, please, before I state the case,
Describe how much this jug once meant to me.

JUDGE ADAM The floor is yours.

MARTHA Right. Do you see this jug?

JUDGE ADAM We do, we do.

MARTHA Forgive me, but you don't.
You see the pieces of it, and that's all.
The fairest thing I owned is kicked and smashed.
This jug was in my family for years;
An heirloom, yes, and worth its weight in gold!
A beauteous and historic thing it was,

It told old Ireland's history, all in scenes.
See here, where there's now nothing but a hole,
The Firbolgs and the Tuatha Dé Danann
Were shown in mighty battle on the plain,
And there Cuchulainn swung his hurley stick:
Those are his legs, that's all that's left of him.
There's Brian Boru, at prayer before Clontarf;
You see him kneeling?—That's his backside, see?
Though even that has suffered a hard knock.
There's good Queen Maeve, and Granuaile O'Malley,
And poor Kathleen Ní Houlihan herself;
You see them where they stand, the three of them,
Bawling their eyes out over Ireland's fate?
They're legless now, and Maeve has lost her head,
And Granuaile's two elbows are broke off.
Dermot MacMurrough, look, and Strongbow too,
And Dermot's daughter, what's-her-name, that one.
Strongbow looks like he's going to fall down:
His sword is gone that he was leaning on.
The walls of Limerick, look, the siege of Derry,
The glorious victory at the River Boyne—
Our country's history, broken up in bits!

JUDGE ADAM All that is as it may be, Mrs Reck,
But history lessons won't patch up your jug.
What we're concerned with is the breaking of it.

MARTHA Hold on there, judge, and listen to me now;
I want the court to understand my loss.
This isn't some old pisspot or spittoon;
There's history on it, and within it, too.
My father's father first got hold of it
In Enniscorthy after '98.
A rebel there had stole it from a house,

And granda stove his head in with his sword
And saved the jug, all bloodied from the fight.
My father then inherited the thing,
And drank a toast from it when I was born;
The story's in our family, how he filled—

JUDGE ADAM Now missus, please, keep to the point in hand.

MARTHA —it up with ale and asked the whole town in,
He was so pleased to be a dad at last,
For he was fifty then, my mother forty.
When I was wed I gave it to my Dan—

JUDGE ADAM For God's sake, woman, we'll be here all day!

MARTHA And in the fire of '22 he saved it
By jumping out the window holding it,
And though Dan broke his hip, God bless the mark,
The jug survived the fall without a scratch.
In those days we were living in Cornmarket,
In two rooms over Bunty Ryan's shop—

JUDGE ADAM Now Martha—

MARTHA You are interrupting me!
If I am not to be allowed to speak,
What is the point of coming here, I ask?

SIR WALTER My dear, good woman, you may speak, of course,
But only, please, of matters pertinent.
The jug was dear to you, that much we know;
These other things are all beside the point.

MARTHA Beside the point, you say? Beside the point?
Is it beside the point that I have lost
An heirloom that was in my family
A hundred year?

SIR WALTER Of course not, madam, but—

MARTHA But me no buts, your honour, if you please;
I am an honest woman, God's my judge,

And I demand that I should have my say.

SIR WALTER Yes yes, dear lady, you shall have your say.
The point is, we know all about the jug;
You've told us everything there is to tell
About its history and your love for it.
But you have come to seek a judgement here,
And retribution, if it is deserved.
Just tell us now: who broke the jug, and how.

MARTHA I told you who broke it: that rascal there.

ROBERT That is a lie, your honour!

JUDGE ADAM, *who has nodded off, wakes with a start.*

JUDGE ADAM Silence, you!
Next witness!

LYNCH (*Aside to* JUDGE ADAM)
She's in the middle of her testimony.

JUDGE ADAM Ahem! Yes, quite. The matter now to hand,
The questions of procedure and of law,
Of *nolle prosequi* and *habeas corpus*
Compel me to adjourn the court until—

SIR WALTER Judge Adam!

JUDGE ADAM *looks about him blearily.*

JUDGE ADAM Sorry, lost my concentration.
Well, come on, missus, let us hear the rest;
We haven't got all day—it's nearly noon.

MARTHA Well, it was at eleven o'clock last night—

JUDGE ADAM Eleven at night, you say, you got that, Lynch?

MARTHA I was in bed, about to quench the light,
When from my daughter's room I heard a noise.

BALL (*Aside to* LYNCH)
The busy creak of bedsprings, I don't doubt.

LYNCH Or chamber music, maybe: tinkle tinkle.

JUDGE ADAM What sort of noise?

MARTHA Why, curses, cries and shouts.
I ran downstairs—her room is at the back,
A ground-floor room, above the garden, there.
I found the door burst open on its hinges,
And someone standing shouting, and the jug
In smithereens and scattered on the floor.
'What is it, Eve?' I cries, 'what is it, girl?'
I didn't know but she was being attacked.
Well anyway, I lifted up the candle,
And what, you honour, do you think I saw?
My daughter in her shift, and that lout there
(*Pointing to* ROBERT)
Raging in the middle of the floor!

JUDGE ADAM By heaven!

MARTHA What?

JUDGE ADAM This one, you say?

MARTHA Yes, him!
I challenged him, I said, 'Now listen, you,
What do you think you're doing here like this,
In my house in the middle of the night?'
And he, do you know what he said? The nerve!
It was, he said, another had been there
Before him that had smashed up my poor jug!
The cur proceeded then to heap abuse
Upon me and my daughter, calling her
All sorts of filthy names I won't repeat,
And said she's had a stranger in her bed.

LYNCH Another, eh?

MARTHA That's right, that's what he said.
I turns to Eve and asks her for the truth;
She stands there like a corpse and cannot speak.
'Now Eve,' says I, 'come on and tell me true,
Was there another here, or only him?'
Then she sat down, and swore to me, and said:
'But who else could it have been?'

EVE That's not true!
I didn't swear!

ROBERT (*To* JUDGE ADAM)
See? There you are.

MARTHA (*To* EVE)
You did.

JUDGE ADAM (*To* ROBERT)
You keep your mouth shut, you, unless you want
My fist to shut it for you!

BALL That's the way!
Rough justice from the long arm of the law!

SIR WALTER I don't believe I'm hearing what I hear.
Judge Adam, you—

EVE (*To* MARTHA)
I only said, Who else
Would it have been? You were not listening.

MARTHA I heard you say distinctly—

JUDGE ADAM Listen here
Now, Mrs Reck, you're frightening the girl,
You're getting her confused, and muddled up.
We have to give her time to think things over
And sort out in her mind what was it happened—
(*Looking hard at* EVE)
What happened, mind, and what can happen still,
Unless she says what is required of her.

LYNCH (*Aside*)
'Required', eh? That's very interesting.

JUDGE ADAM Come on now, Eve, let's hear your testimony;
I'm sure you'll say the same as yesternight.

SIR WALTER No no, judge, please, you must not lead the witness!

MARTHA If she now has the gall to swear to me
That yesternight she didn't swear at all,
Well—well, I don't know what! But I tell you,
That even though I can't swear that she *swore*,
Then certainly she *said* he was the one.

EVE (*To* SIR WALTER)
Your honour, I said nothing of the kind.

JUDGE ADAM Remember, Eve, the fourth command of God;
Your mother says you swore that it was him—

SIR WALTER Judge Adam!

JUDGE ADAM Yes, what's wrong, what did I say?
The girl says that she swore, so there's an end.

MARTHA Well: didn't you say, 'Who else was it, then'?

Pause.

EVE I won't deny that that is what I said.

JUDGE ADAM That's it, then.

ROBERT Lying bitch!

JUDGE ADAM Record it, clerk:
The girl said, 'Who else was it, if not him'.

WILLIE Shame on the lot of you, I say!

BALL Cor blimey.
We'll have a faction fight here in a minute.

SIR WALTER Judge Adam, your behaviour baffles me.
I swear, if you had smashed the jug yourself
You could not be more eager, I believe,
To pass suspicion on to this young man.

Clerk Lynch, write down the girl only admits
To what she said, but not to what occurred.
Perhaps, Judge Adam, she should testify?

JUDGE ADAM It's not her turn.

SIR WALTER Her *turn*?

JUDGE ADAM First the accused.
Or am I wrong? Are these things ordered different
In London?

SIR WALTER How ingenious you are!
Yes, question the accused, and get it done.
(*Aside*)
This is the last case you will ever try.

JUDGE ADAM (*Aside to* LYNCH)
What's that he said?

LYNCH I think he thinks
Our ways down here are less than civilised.

JUDGE ADAM A pox on him. Now, Temple, step you up;
(*Aside*)
Let's see you get your neck out of this trap.

ROBERT My name is Robert Temple, of this town;
I am a tenant farmer, with my father,
On land that woman's people stole from us—

MARTHA You dirty lout!—

ROBERT I mean the native Irish;
The Recks were planted on us by King Billy
When Jamesy ran away after the Boyne.

SIR WALTER (*Aside*)
Dear God, more history!

JUDGE ADAM Yes yes, enough!
We know you are descended from high kings,
And all the rest of it, but just for now
Confine yourself to matters more mundane—
This jug you broke, for instance, yesternight.

Will you admit the truth of what Eve says,
That there was no one in her room but you,
Or are you going to try to tell the court
It was the pooka, up to his old tricks?

ROBERT — I won't deny I may have broke the jug—

JUDGE ADAM — Aha!

ROBERT — But what she said is all a lie.

JUDGE ADAM — It is? And can you prove it?

ROBERT — Yes, I can.

JUDGE ADAM — Well go ahead, then, let us hear you do it.
(*To* MARTHA)
Don't worry, Mrs Reck, the truth will out.

SIR WALTER — The devil take it, man, this is outrageous!

Pause, all stare at SIR WALTER.

JUDGE ADAM — Are you all right, Sir Walter? Lynch, a chair—

SIR WALTER — I do not need a chair!
(*Aside*)
Dear Lord, my head!
This godforsaken place will drive me mad.

JUDGE ADAM — Good sir, I really think you should sit down;
Sure, all this talk would dizzy anyone.

SIR WALTER — Clerk, tell me, Mr Lynch, could you conduct
This hearing with a modicum of sense?

LYNCH — (*Simpering*)
Oh but, Sir Walter, please, I would not dream—

JUDGE ADAM — Right, Temple, come now, what have you to say?

ROBERT — I'm trying to—

JUDGE ADAM — Yes yes, man, spit it out!

ROBERT — *If you will let me get a word in!* Now.

ROBERT *strikes an orator's pose.*

It was at ten o'clock last night, about—
It may have been a bit before, or after—
I thought I'd take a ramble into town,
And call on Eve—Miss Reck—that 'lady' there.

Judge Adam — At ten o'clock at night?

Robert — It was as bright
As day, your honour, and the rain had stopped.
And anyway, I was engaged to her.
('Was' is the word.) I said to da, 'Oh, da,
I'm going into town to call on Eve,'
And he said, 'Right, son, but now listen here,
Don't go into the house; you know the town,
And how they talk, and what her ma is like:
She'd have the vicar and the polis on you
Before you could say knife—'

Martha — Well, Willie Temple—!

Robert — 'All right,' says da, and out the door I went.
I did not get to town till half past ten;
I would have been there sooner but the stream
Was flooded after all these weeks of rain.
The gate into the garden was locked up;
Eve shuts it by half ten, if I'm not there—

Judge Adam — You come at that late hour every night?

Robert — Not every night—

Judge Adam — Indecent goings-on.

Sir Walter — Judge Adam!
(*To* Robert)
Well, go on, what happened next?

Robert — I turned away, and set off down the lane,
But then I heard the gate behind me creak.
Eve must be in the garden still, I thought,
And turned back and retraced my steps at once.

Now, as I walked along beside the hedge,
I spied Eve in the garden—with a man!
At first I thought my eyes must be mistaken,
But no, it's Eve, I knew her by her dress.
And there she was, and someone else there with her.

JUDGE ADAM So who was it?

ROBERT That's what I'd like to know.

JUDGE ADAM Aha—you didn't see his face?
(*Aside*)
Thank Christ!

ROBERT That's true, but still I'm sure I know who 'twas.

JUDGE ADAM You do?

ROBERT The cobbler Byrne!

JUDGE ADAM The cobbler who?

ROBERT Joe Byrne, that long streel with the humpty back,
That was declared unfit for soldiering.
The whole town knows that he's been after her
For years. In June I said to her, 'Now Eve,
That fellow's hanging round you much too much;
I seen him in your kitchen, and yourself
Regaling him with spuds and cups of milk.'

EVE (*To* SIR WALTER)
Your honour, this is fantasy; poor Byrne,
He can't get work, he cut his hand last May,
The wound won't heal, he comes to me for food.
(*Pointing to* ROBERT)
He has to think he has a rival for me
In order to puff up his silly pride.
(*To* ROBERT)
But you must be hard up—

BALL (*Aside*)
I'll say he is.

EVE —if poor Joe Byrne is all you can imagine.

ROBERT (*To* JUDGE ADAM, *ignoring* EVE)
I said to her, 'It's him or me, my girl;
The next time that I see him in your house,
That's our engagement off, believe you me.'
I went around next day, and there he was,
Presiding at her table, bold as brass.
Well I can tell you, I soon got him out.
I took him by the scruff and kicked his arse
And fired him out on the street, the scut!

EVE Oh, that was very brave of you, all right,
To set about the likes of that poor cripple.

JUDGE ADAM The name is Byrne, you say? Lynch, write that down:
Accused claims that this hunchback broke the jug.
(*Aside*)
This is a bit of luck—*two* suspects now!
(*To* LYNCH)
You've got all that?

LYNCH Oh, certainly—and more.

JUDGE ADAM (*To* ROBERT, *warmly*)
All right, my boy, let's hear the rest, go on.

ROBERT Where was I?—Yes: I'm at the garden gate,
I see Eve with the cripple on the lawn—

JUDGE ADAM The cripple, yes, go on.

ROBERT They're talking there,
And laughing, like, you know; he's tugging her—

BALL (*Aside*)
He's *whatting* her?

ROBERT They're whispering, and all—

EVE You peeping tom, you! Are you not ashamed,
Admitting how you hid and spied on me?
To think I once thought you a man of honour!

BALL (*Aside*)
A man of honour, or a man on her?

ROBERT So anyway, the cobbler gets her down,
I see her legs up, waving in the air;
By now I'm getting frantic, for she never
Let *me* get that far with her—

MARTHA Oh, you cur!

ROBERT I feel so furious by now, I think
I'm going to have a fit of apoplexy.
I break my way in through the hedge; they're gone;
I spy her window, with a candle in it,
And their two shadows on the window shade,
Still at their two-backed business.

EVE It's a lie!

JUDGE ADAM Now Robert, listen, are you sure of this?
It's quite a charge you're laying here, you know.
(*Aside*)
This fellow certainly is fanciful.

ROBERT I saw them; they were standing up and struggling—

EVE So why then do you think I'd given in?

ROBERT I run up to her door, the garden door,
And thunder on it, and call out her name,
And then with one good kick I kick it in.

JUDGE ADAM (*To* SIR WALTER)
Impetuous fellow, what?

SIR WALTER (*To* ROBERT)
Continue, please.

LYNCH (*To* BALL)
He's getting interested, I can see.

BALL He likes a bit of hot stuff, does the boss.

ROBERT The door flies open—bang!—against the wall,
The jug falls off a shelf, and someone else

	Goes flying out the window like a bat.
JUDGE ADAM	And this was Byrne, you say, the cobbler Byrne?
ROBERT	Who else, your honour—
	(*He jerks his thumb at* EVE)
	—as she said herself.
	She's straightening up her bodice, and so on,
	And tries to stop me following the scut;
	The fellow, though, has got caught on the trellis,
	Some sort of cape he's wearing has got snagged.
	I find I'm holding in my hand the latch—
JUDGE ADAM	The what?
ROBERT	The latch I broke off of the door:
	I have it in my fist, big iron thing;
	I lean out on the sill and bring it down
	With all my force on that usurper's pate.
JUDGE ADAM	A door latch!
ROBERT	What? The latch, that's what I said.
JUDGE ADAM	So that was it.
LYNCH	You thought it was a sword?
JUDGE ADAM	What do you mean, a sword?
LYNCH	It might have been.
	A heavy, short one, with a broken blade.
ROBERT	I hit him with the handle end, the knob.
LYNCH	That could have been the hilt.
ROBERT	That's true, it could.
LYNCH	In any case, a nasty sort of weapon.
	I must say that *I* thought it was a sword.

Pause. LYNCH *and* JUDGE ADAM *look at each other, the former smirking, the latter alarmed.*

SIR WALTER	Perhaps we could continue with the case?
JUDGE ADAM	Yes yes, go on. All that, about the latch,

We do not want all that recorded, clerk.

LYNCH (*Still smirking*)
Just as you say, your honour; all that's struck.

ROBERT So anyway, the fellow struggles up;
He's bleeding from the wallop that I gave him,
And scratched and torn with thorns. I mount the sill,
Ready to leap out and hold him fast,
When suddenly a handful of bonemeal
He scoops up from the roses and lets fly,
It strikes me in the face and blinds my eyes.

JUDGE ADAM *laughs and slaps the desk with his hand; all stare at him, and he turns serious at once.*

JUDGE ADAM The devil! And go on, what happened next?

ROBERT I fall down blinded from the window-sill,
And trip on something and fall on the floor;
She kneels by me, of course, she's all in tears,
It's Robert this, and Oh, poor Robert that.
By God, I tell you, I drew back my foot,
And she can thank her stars I couldn't see,
Or she'd have got a good kick up the—

MARTHA Oh!

ROBERT So anyway, the rest you know.

JUDGE ADAM We do?

ROBERT The old one here comes running, with a lamp,
And shouting bloody murder and all that,
With Nan the maid behind her in her shift,
And neighbours run in, too, to have a look,
And people off the street, and dogs and cats—
'Twas near a riot, with the lot of them,
And Juggins here, of course, half blinded still,
And thinking to himself, what will da say?

The old one wants to know who broke the jug,
And *she* says, as you heard, that it was me.
She's in the right of it, I did break something—
That cobbler's head—but I've a strong suspicion
(*Looking darkly at* EVE)
That something else got broken there as well,
More delicate by far than Joe Byrne's pate.

EVE *tries to speak but* JUDGE ADAM *prevents her.*

JUDGE ADAM Well, Mrs Reck, what have you got to say?
MARTHA What can I say that I've not said already?
That fellow's like the fox gets in at night
And strangles every chicken in the coop;
The coop is truth, and my poor girl's the chick.
If there are any in this court of law
Who care for justice, then they'll get a stick
And whale that dirty prowler of the night!
SIR WALTER But proof, ma'am, what we need to hear is proof!
MARTHA Oh, proof, is it? I'll give you the proof.
(*To* EVE)
Stand up!
Come on, my girl, stand up and speak out now.
JUDGE ADAM Your daughter? Oh no, missus, that won't do.
MARTHA Won't do? Why not?
JUDGE ADAM The Statute Book, you see,
Declares—in section quarto, I believe,
Or is it quinto?—that when jugs are broken,
When jugs, or heads, or anything like that
Get smashed, then daughters cannot testify
In cases where the mother is the plaintiff.
SIR WALTER (*Aside to* JUDGE ADAM)
What nonsense, sir, is this? What Statute Book?

JUDGE ADAM Don't mind me, sir, it's just that they expect
A little bit of Latin now and then,
And talk of statutes, all that sort of thing:
The kind of hocus pocus that they hear
In church—it's how the priests keep hold of them.
The lad, you see, his family are papists,
The widow Reck's a Prod, which will explain—

SIR WALTER I do not want to hear talk of religion!
I've heard of nothing else since I arrived.
(*To the court*)
The girl should make a statement, I believe.

JUDGE ADAM A statement? Well, of course she should, of course—
That's section sexto. Come, clerk, write it down:
The girl will make a statement to the court.

SIR WALTER Come forward, child, come, do not be afraid.

EVE *hesitates, then limps forward with difficulty; for the first time it is seen that she has an iron caliper on her leg.*

EVE All that I have to say is that—

JUDGE ADAM Well well,
Is that the time? I fear we must adjourn.
Sir Walter, there is food, will you partake?
This statement we can hear after the break.

(From *The Broken Jug*, 1994)

Stardust: Three Monologues of the Dead

I Nicolaus Copernicus 1473–1543

Out of dislike of the earth I turned to the sky. Andreas said I walked through life with my eyes averted, looking up. He was right. Poor Andreas, poor brother. He was the elder, but I was the one that shone. Hated me, I think. We never embraced, never once, not even as children. We were not the embracing kind, my family. Mother died too early, and father soon followed her. When Andreas came back from wherever he had been, his face half-eaten away by the pox, I tried to deny him, pretend he was no kin of mine. He hung about the town to spite me, chuckling his contempt as I hurried past. My shadow; my dark other. Now we are all dead, parents, Andreas, my helpmeet Anna Schillings, Tiedemann Giese, Rheticus, me, invisible dust adrift among the stars.

I did not mean to found a revolution. All I wanted was a little order in the world. The Ptolemaic system of the planets was as old as Alexandria, and as corrupt. In theory, the system had a certain beauty, the earth standing still at the centre of eight concentric spheres, the sun and the planets attached one to each of the first seven spheres and the fixed stars to the eighth. What could be more elegant, more classically simple? The devil of it was in the details. The problem is that when we track the orbits of the planets, they do not progress in orderly fashion, but seem to meander, some faltering while their fellows rush forward headlong, playing a kind of leapfrog; on occasion one or other of them will appear to execute a loop, circling back on itself, before hurrying on again. Hardly simple, hardly classical. The reason for these baffling manoeuvres is that we on earth are observing not from the centre of the system, but from within it. Ptolemy solved the difficulty by introducing an elaborate set of epicycles, so complicated that I cannot remember how it was supposed to work. It was a ruse, a sleight of mind, but it saved the phenomena.

Ah, that little phrase: to save the phenomena. You, who have come after, with your terrible instruments to torture the heavens, you claim to pursue the truth of things, the objective reality, *how it is*. That was not the way we worked, we were more humble than that. For us, reality existed only in the mind of God. Our business was to devise systems that would agree with the evidence with which we were presented, those of God's thoughts that he had written out for us, as it were, across the skies. We did not aspire to show the actual, physical reality; it was enough if our hypotheses agreed with, or at least did not entirely contradict, the observable phenomena. Ours was a different kind of science, with Man at the heart of it, and God at the head; we did not even call it science, but *natural philosophy*. When I rejected Ptolemy's system and posited instead a sun-centred universe, I had no intention of displacing humankind from the hub of the world. It was only after I had completed my book *De Revolutionibus* that I saw the likely consequences of what I was proposing. I was afraid, and rightly so. They would burn Giordano Bruno at the stake merely for propounding my heliocentric doctrine. So I got Rheticus to do the dirty work.

He came to Frauenburg, up there on the Baltic . . . when was it, 1540? . . .'39? Georg Joachim von Lauchen, called Rheticus. He was twenty-five, and already professor of mathematics at Wittenberg, when he elbowed his way into my tower, demanding to read *De Revolutionibus*. Such hunger, such ambition. I noted the wild light in his eye, the tremor in his hands. Anna Schillings took against him straight away. Jealous, I suppose. Dear Anna. Rheticus might warm my intellect, but it was Anna who chafed my poor old frozen flesh and put a little life back into it. He expected me to ignore her objections and lodge him with us in the tower. Instead I took him to Löbau, where my friend Tiedemann Giese was bishop. We stayed there at the castle through a pleasant summer and into the autumn, enjoying Giese's generous hospitality. I gave Rheticus my book to read, and when he had read it I suggested—oh, so casually!—that he might write an account of it, from memory, of course, for, as he would understand, I could not contemplate letting the book out of my sight, much less out of my hands. He prevaricated, naturally, but I prevailed. He would be, I said, my John the Baptist. He was not pleased by the comparison.

Thus was conceived the *Narratio Prima de Libris Revolutionum Copernici*, which when Rheticus published it in 1540 caused such a noise in the world. My plan, although needless to say I did not disclose it to John the Baptist, was to destroy the work of which his *Narratio* was a substantial account. Yes, I fully intended to burn *De Revolutionibus*. Better burn the book than face the pyre myself. In the end, on my fevered deathbed—burning, oh, burning!—I relented, and let them take the thing out of my hands and publish it, so that it might join the ranks of the great unread books. I did not care.

Andreas was with me, his ruined face restored. He took me in his arms, and lifted me up, and carried me into the last darkness.

II Johannes Kepler 1571–1630

If you think time a trial, try eternity. Oh, the wretched boredom of it! I was prepared for the fires of Purgatory, or even, God forbid, the other place, but not for this . . . this *beinglessness*. Can this be

Heaven? Surely not; surely in Heaven there would be things to *do*? I was always busy, never at rest. My running about, as she called it, my constant running about, drove Barbara to distraction. What a fury she would get into when I managed to persuade her to test one of my inventions. I was particularly proud of the automatic broom that I devised; it ran on wheels that turned a series of internal paddles, thus setting up a strong air current that would suck the dirt into a bag attached behind. Unfortunately, before I could perfect the mechanism, a wheel came off and one of the paddles struck my wife a painful blow on the ankle, and that was the end of that.

She considered, did Barbara, that my astronomical work was a similar sort of petty tinkering. Even when I was summoned to Prague by the great Tycho Brahe, imperial mathematician to the Emperor Rudolph, she remained sceptical. Prague, January, the year 1600. Lord, it was cold! I did not mind. This was to be, I believed, the greatest moment of my life; perhaps it was. Tycho had read my *Mysterium Cosmographicum* and recognised its worth. Imagine: the great Tycho Brahe had read my book! He was the most famous scientist in the empire, and I was a schoolmaster and 'district mathematician', so-called, in Graz. He wrote to me, inviting me to Bohemia. 'You shall come not as a guest, but as a welcome friend and highly desirable participant in our observations of the heavens.' I believed him—why would I not? In breeding, he was a great lord and I a nothing, but in the science of the heavens we were equals.

He had so much, and I so little. Frederick of Denmark had given him an island, an entire island, and funds to build his fabulous observatory. Now he had come to Prague at the invitation of the Emperor, and was busy building another Uraniborg. Yet when at last we met he spent the first hour complaining of the journey from Hveen to Prague—at a stop along the way his prized pet elk had drunk a dish of beer and fallen down a flight of stairs and died—and the second hour bemoaning his shabby treatment at the hands of Rudolph and his court officials. I did not know what to say. I was not yet accustomed to the ways of the nobility.

In the eighteen months that I spent in his company at Benatky Castle he treated me as little more than a minor assistant. I had expected to be given free access to the mass of planetary data he had assembled in twenty years of observations on Hveen. I was deluded. He guarded the material as jealously as an old man would a beautiful young wife. He set me to work at once on the orbit of Mars—thank you, Tycho—the mysteries of which it would take me nine years to crack. Even the Mars material he doled out in miserly fashion, dropping me bits and scraps of it as if I were a dog under the table and they so many morsels from his piled-up plate. He knew, you see, what I would do with his treasures, what marvels I would make of them. I saw it in his eye when he looked at me that first day, complaining of his dead elk, the recognition of what I was and what I could achieve. He was a technician of genius, the first to understand the necessity for meticulous, long-term planetary observations—that was why the data he had amassed were so precious—but I was the one with the vision, with the quickness and flexibility of intellect, to make the great breakthrough.

Poor Brahe. No imagination. I tried to explain to him one day that the true mark of greatness in a scientist is the ability to take stock of weeks, months—years!—of work and throw it all away and start again. That was what I did, times over. And then I saw what was wrong, that our devotion to the dogma that the planets move in perfect circles was mistaken, that in fact the orbits are elliptical. I could see the beauty of it—ellipses, lovely ellipses!—but he held my discovery a sacrilege. On his deathbed he clutched me fiercely by the wrist and cried, *Let me not have lived in vain!* I did my best for him; I paid him his posthumous due. More than he would have done for me, I suspect. I was fond of him; yes, fond.

III Isaac Newton 1642–1727

It was not the apple, but the plague. Oh, there *was* an apple, or orchardful of apples, but I might not have seen the significance of their fall had not the pestilence at Cambridge sent me for safety to my mother's house at Woolsthorpe. I was—what? If it was 1666 then I was twenty-four. Is that right? I am losing even the power of mensuration; that is what death will do to you.

I did my greatest work that summer, formulated the gravitational laws, cracked the code of the world's working. Years later some fool at court asked me how I had done it. *By thinking upon it continuously*, I said. This answer produced laughter, to my surprise and some annoyance: I was not aware of having made a jest. Courtiers would laugh at your little finger . . . There never was a brain the likes of mine, before or since. Solved the whole mystery, save a few minor odds and ends. Invented single-handed what they now call science; before me it had all been wizardry and sweaty dreams lightened by an occasional instance of brilliant blundering. They were all against me, trying to steal my glory, Leibniz, Robert Hooke the hunchback . . . (*chuckles*) Hooke: well named. *There* was a jest, although the dolts could not catch it. *If I have seen far*, I said, *it was because I stood upon the shoulders of giants*. Hooke was scarce a yard and a half in height. *He* got the joke.

Hypotheses I did not propose. That was where I was different, the new man. Only the factual, only what was provable . . . Science, their science, is such a little thing, though they think it a wonder. I said to Locke, I said, *That which we know is no more than a scrap of what there is to be known*. He said, *Well, yes, of course, but in time it will be known, not by us, perhaps, but by those who come after*. Damned fool, for all his philosophising. Knowledge, mere knowledge, is nothing. Wisdom: wisdom is the thing. It was to the pursuit of wisdom that I devoted the great part of my life. Alchemy they call the dark art, when in truth it is all light. The hours I spent, crouched over the alembic. Hours? Years—decades! That still puzzles them. How could the greatest mathematician the race has ever produced devote the long latter half of his life to magic, to the ancient prophecies, to Apocalyptic speculation? All my secrets, my secrets . . .

The calculus, which I devised and which Leibniz robbed from me—he did, he did, I insist on it!—the calculus operates upon the premise of a closer and closer approach to infinity. Infinity, however, may not be approached. Infinity *is*, and there's an end of it. Yet the calculus works. And my system of the world, it works, too, even though its working depends upon a pair of premises which, strictly speaking, I had no right to allow myself to propose, namely, absolute space, and absolute time. Such absolutes exist in the mind of God, but not in our world, not in this filthy sty into which He has thrown us. Well: thank God for God.

Was that awareness of the hollow at the centre of my system, was that the cause of the . . . the vastation I suffered in my fiftieth year? One day the world darkened, and never came back to full light. That letter I wrote to Locke, accusing him of immorality and seeking to embroil me with women—what a shock it must have been, out of the blue. I picture him pacing the great garden at Oates with my letter in his hands, his eyebrows travelling higher and higher as he goggles at these wild charges. What came over me? It started with that fire in my rooms at Trinity. They tell the story now that my pet dog knocked over a candle and set a pile of papers alight. All nonsense, of course—I never had a dog, abhor the brutes. But there was a conflagration—I may have set it myself—and papers were destroyed. As I stood and stared into that fiery abyss—rain in the window, a choir caterwauling in the distance—I saw what I had not seen before, that it was all . . . nothing.

Just that: nothing. After such insight, what else was there for me to do but turn to deciphering Genesis and burning base metals?

What is left? Ashes; stars and ashes.

(*Stardust: Three Monologues of the Dead*, 2002)

Kepler

I

Sound of iron-shod wheels on a stony road, horse's hoofs, the creaking of a carriage. JOHANNES KEPLER, *his wife* BARBARA, *and Barbara's daughter,* REGINA, *are on their way from Prague to Benatky Castle, in the countryside outside the city.* KEPLER *and* BARBARA *are in their late twenties.* REGINA *is seven.*

BARBARA Johannes! Wake up!

KEPLER What . . . ? What . . . ?

BARBARA You were asleep.

KEPLER Was I?

BARBARA And talking, again.

KEPLER Talking? And what did I say?

BARBARA That number.

KEPLER Which number?

BARBARA The one you're always babbling about. Nought point something something . . . I don't know.

KEPLER Try to remember, my dear.

BARBARA How should I know? You're the mathematician, not I.

REGINA Nought point nought nought four two nine.

KEPLER Why, thank you, Regina. You're a very clever girl. Nought point nought nought four two nine, eh? I wonder what that means? It must mean something, since I keep dreaming of it. (*Pause*) Look, Regina! Barbara, look! There it is, Benatky Castle.

BARBARA Are you sure? It doesn't look much like a castle to me.

KEPLER What do you think, Regina?

REGINA It's very high up.

KEPLER Yes, Herr Brahe wrote that it was set upon an eminence. You can see for miles, miles around. You know, Regina, they call Benatky the Bohemian Venice, for when the river is in spate the land all about becomes flooded.

BARBARA That will be something to look forward to. Listen: what's that noise?

They listen. Sounds in the distance of men at work: pounding of hammers, rasp of saws, the men whistling.

KEPLER Brahe mentioned he was having alterations made.

BARBARA It sounds as if he's having the place rebuilt.

II

The carriage wheels rolling on stone paving, then drawing to a halt. The carriage door is opened, KEPLER *gets out.*

KEPLER Now, Regina—hup!

He lifts REGINA *down.*

BARBARA (*Panting a little as she gets out of the carriage*) Don't mind me, I can get down by myself. Ouf!

Thump of her feet on the paving. JEPPE, *Tycho Brahe's dwarf jester, approaches. He has a piping, ageless voice.*

JEPPE God save you, gentles.

KEPLER Oh . . . Good day to you.

JEPPE I am Jeppe. And you are Sir Mathematicus, I venture?

KEPLER Kepler. Kepler's the name.

JEPPE Welcome to Bohemia. My master expected you before now.

KEPLER We were delayed.

JEPPE All week we have looked for you and your . . . baggage.

Strangled sound of indignation from BARBARA.

KEPLER This is my wife, and her daughter—my daughter, that is; our daughter.

JEPPE And what is your name?

REGINA Regina.

JEPPE Ah, a queenly name. And what age are you?

REGINA Seven.

JEPPE A magic number. As you see, I stopped growing when I was your age.

III

Footsteps on bare floorboards in an echoing room.

JEPPE These are your quarters.

BARBARA (*Panting*) Three flights of stairs . . . ! Oh, I'll never . . .

KEPLER Herr Brahe—is he . . . ?

JEPPE He rises at noon. (*A bell begins to toll*) Ah! The Lord is risen. Excuse me, I must attend him.

Sound of JEPPE*'s rapid, childish walk as he departs.*

REGINA Why did he stop growing when he was seven?

KEPLER He's a dwarf, my dear. It is an affliction. We must be kind to him.

BARBARA walks from empty room to empty room, her footsteps echoing.

BARBARA So these are the grand quarters he promised you. Where is the furniture? (*From farther off*) Look, there is not even a bed in here.

SERVANT enters, panting.

KEPLER Ah, the baggage.

SERVANT Where do you want this stuff?

KEPLER Just . . . just leave it on the floor, will you?

SERVANT unceremoniously drops the bags. A brief silence.

KEPLER Yes ? Oh. (*Sound of him fishing in his purse*) There you are.

SERVANT (*Disgustedly*) Thanks, I'm sure.

SERVANT departs.

BARBARA This won't do. This won't do at all. You'll have to tell him—

KEPLER (*Sighing*) Yes, my dear, yes. Everything will be fixed. Everything will be fine. I shall see to it.

BARBARA Just tell him that—

KEPLER The child will be hungry.

BARBARA The child, the child! Who is the child here, I want to know!

Footsteps enter.

SERVANT TWO Herr Kipper?

KEPLER Yes. Kepler. What is it?

SERVANT TWO The master wants you. Follow me.

SERVANT TWO walking out.

KEPLER (*Nervous and excited*) My dear, I shall . . . I shall return and and and . . .

BARBARA We must have proper quarters. Tell him that.

KEPLER (*Receding*) Yes, of course, I'll . . .

BARBARA Don't forget!

IV

Two pairs of footsteps rapidly descending stone stairs, then on to floorboards. A door is thrust open.

SERVANT TWO Herr Kelper!

TYCHO BRAHE (*From deep in the room*) Ah! Come in! You have arrived at last!

KEPLER Herr Brahe, I hope you will forgive my delay, but—

BRAHE Yes yes. Come, come in.

KEPLER *advances.*

I was about to begin breakfast. You have eaten?

KEPLER Well—

BRAHE Good, good. Sit.

Creak of chair as KEPLER *sits.*

You have dropped your hat.

Sound of KEPLER *shuffling his feet.*

Now you are treading on it.

KEPLER Ah. There. Forgive . . .

BRAHE You had a pleasant journey?

KEPLER Yes. No. There were rats, everywhere we stopped.

BRAHE You stopped?

KEPLER On the way from Graz, yes, of course . . .

BRAHE I meant your journey today, from Prague.

KEPLER Oh, I see. It was—

BRAHE No matter. (*Assumes a formal tone*) You must excuse me, Herr Kepler, that I did not come personally to greet you on your arrival in Bohemia. I rarely go to Prague, myself, unless in answer to a summons from the Emperor. Filthy, unwholesome place. And of course, the coming opposition of Mars and Jupiter, as you will appreciate, encouraged me not to interrupt my work here at Benatky. However, I trust you will understand that I receive you now less as a guest than as a friend and colleague.

KEPLER (*Simpering*) Well, of course, I am deeply—

BRAHE *rings a handbell loudly.*

BRAHE Where is the fellow!

Sound of door opening, footsteps hurrying in.

Where is my coffee!

SERVANT THREE Here, Your Lordship.

BRAHE Ah. It is still hot, I hope?

Sound of coffee being poured.

You will take a cup, Herr Kepler?

KEPLER I don't think I . . . That is, I . . .

BRAHE You do not know this brew? The Turks drink it. I find it sharpens the brain. Here, try it.

KEPLER *hesitantly sips, then exclaims in pain.*

KEPLER It is indeed hot. (*Sips again*) But, yes, very . . . very interesting.

BRAHE *has begun to eat.*

BRAHE (*His mouth full*) An acquired taste.

Pause.

KEPLER Your letter was most kind. Your invitation to Benatky was, well, an answer to our prayers, mine, and my wife's. Speaking of which—my wife, I mean—she urged me to ask if we might—

BRAHE You were a schoolteacher in Graz?

KEPLER Yes. And District Mathematician.

BRAHE Ah?

KEPLER A lofty title, I fear, but a humble post. I was engaged for the most part in drawing up horoscopes for the town and district. Prospects for crops, dangers of plague, so on. I tried for a position at Tübingen, at the university—my alma mater, you know. It seems, however, there are too many lecturers, and too few students. But Graz, Graz was becoming impossible—

BRAHE Impossible?

KEPLER I had many people on my side there, many people, even the Jesuits, but it made no difference, the authorities hounded me without mercy, demanding that I renounce my faith. Ferdinand, the Archduke, is a Catholic, of course, which he uses as an excuse to heap taxes on us Lutherans. I was forced to pay a levy of ten florins for the privilege—the *privilege*!—of burying my infant son and daughter by the Lutheran rites. They closed the Lutheran school where I was earning a pittance, teaching mathematics to the blockhead sons of petty noblemen. Then, not content with robbing me of my livelihood, they ordered all Lutherans to quit the province under pain of death—yes, death! At that time a rumour went about—perhaps you heard it? . . . no, I suppose not—a rumour went about that I had agreed to convert. I! Convert! (*Laughs harshly, a touch hysterically*) I am a Christian, the Lutheran creed was taught me at my mother's knee, I hold fast to it.

I have never mastered the gift of hypocrisy. (*Pause; sound of* Brahe *steadily eating*) So I left, thanks to you. I said to my wife, when your letter came, I said, *Look, Tycho Brahe wants me to work with him—the great Tycho Brahe, Imperial—*

Brahe (*Heavily*) What is your philosophy, sir?

Kepler My . . . ? (*Pause; almost dreamily*) I hold the world to be a manifestation of the possibility of order.

Brahe Hmmph.

Kepler That is . . . that is to say, I espouse the natural philosophy.

Kepler *shuffles his feet.*

Oh, my hat, I've stood on it again . . .

Brahe *rises, begins pacing the floor with heavy tread.*

Brahe When I first came to Bohemia, six months ago, the Emperor lodged my family and me in Prague at the house of one of his court officials, where the infernal ringing of bells from the Capuchin monastery nearby was a torment day and night.

Kepler (*Softly*) Yes. When my children died I—

Brahe I do not even begin . . .

Kepler Infants, both dead within a year of birth, one after the other.

Brahe . . . to speak of Denmark, my troubles there.

Kepler Meningitis.

Brahe One has always to contend with adversity, Herr Kepler.

Kepler Yes. Bells . . . bells would be very troubling.

Brahe Your wife is well? Your child—you have a child?

Kepler My step-daughter. My wife's child. My wife has had two husbands already. (*Laughs, then stifles the laugh*) They died. The husbands.

BRAHE Ah.

Pause.

KEPLER She's well, yes. My wife.

Pause. BRAHE, *his breakfast finished, stands up from the table.*

BRAHE Now I must work.

BRAHE *walks to the door,* KEPLER *hurries after him.*

V

They walk along a stone corridor, their voices echoing.

KEPLER Here, at Benatky, you must be . . . there must be . . . There are no church bells, to disturb you.

BRAHE They call this place a castle—pah!

KEPLER Yes, my wife thought it seemed more like a—

BRAHE *opens a door.*

BRAHE Come, this way.

VI

They step out on to a balcony overlooking the castle yard. From below, sound of workmen as before, so loud that BRAHE *has almost to shout to be heard.*

BRAHE I am making extensive changes, of course, as you can see. I intend to build here a new Uraniborg, even greater than the old.

They step back inside again, BRAHE *shuts the door.*

VII

They set off again along the stone corridor.

BRAHE I had an entire island, you know, granted me by royal charter, yes! Hveen, in the Sound, not far from Copenhagen.

KEPLER Yes, of course, I've heard of—

BRAHE I built a great house in the centre of the island. Uraniborg was the wonder of the world: my observatory, my fabulous instruments, my scores of workers. (*Pause*) One is hampered at every turn. All monarchs are alike. The Emperor is sympathetic to my work, of course, but he cannot attend in person to every detail. The manager of the crown estates, with whom I'm forced to deal, is not so well disposed toward me as I might wish. I think he is a Jew . . .

BRAHE *opens the door.*

VIII

They step into a jakes. Echoing chamber, sound of water dripping. BRAHE *is fumbling with his clothing.*

BRAHE Sometimes I think it was a mistake, after all, to leave Denmark. (*Sound of* BRAHE *passing a copious stream of urine*) The old king was my patron—my friend! When the son succeeded him . . . Christian: a most unsuitable name for that young pup.

KEPLER Patrons. Well, of course—

BRAHE You work the metals, sir?

KEPLER Metals?

BRAHE I mean the alembic and so forth, transmutation, all that. You claimed to be a natural philosopher, did you not?

KEPLER No, no, alchemy is not . . . I am not . . .

BRAHE, *having finished peeing, gives a grunt of satisfaction, fastens his clothing.*

BRAHE But you make horoscopes?

KEPLER Yes, sometimes, when—

BRAHE For payment?

KEPLER Well . . . yes.

BRAHE Come.

Opens the door.

IX

They step out of the jakes, walk along the corridor again.

BRAHE Your writings are of considerable interest. I read your book, the *Mysterium Cosmographicum*, with attention.

KEPLER You're very kind, sir.

BRAHE I do not agree with your methods, of course, but the conclusions you reached are . . . are . . .

He lets his voice drift off.

The fault, may I suggest, was that you based your theories on the system of Copernicus. A great mathematician, but as a theorist . . . I would have thought that something, well, something such as the system I have put forward, would have been more . . . suitable?

They halt.

KEPLER (*Uneasily*) Well, of course, the Tychonic system of the planets is very . . . very . . . interesting.

A terrible pause.

BRAHE (*Icily*) We shall see you at dinner, Herr Kepler.

KEPLER But—

BRAHE *turns and sweeps away.*

BRAHE (*Over his shoulder*) You must meet my other assistants.

KEPLER *scampers to catch up with him.* BRAHE *sweeping along the corridor very fast now,* KEPLER *almost trotting to keep up.*

BRAHE There shall be a redistribution of tasks, now that we are one more. I had thought of setting you the lunar orbit.

KEPLER (*Dismayed*) The lunar . . . ?

BRAHE First, of course, we must consult my man Longberg. You've heard of him? Christian Longberg? My chief assistant. Good man, fine scholar. He has a say in these matters, naturally.

KEPLER But if I might . . .

BRAHE *suddenly halts.*

BRAHE Books.

KEPLER Books?

BRAHE My first book I held back for years.

KEPLER Oh yes?

BRAHE Scribbling, publishing, all that. Hardly a fit occupation for a gentleman.

KEPLER Ah.

BRAHE Well then, good day.

BRAHE *strides away. This time* KEPLER *does not attempt to follow. When* BRAHE*'s footsteps have receded,* KEPLER *heaves a heavy sigh of mingled frustration and resignation.*

X

The Keplers' quarters. BARBARA, *muttering under her breath, is fumbling through their belongings which she has unpacked from their bags.* REGINA *is further off, singing to herself. Door opens,* KEPLER *enters.*

BARBARA (*Expectantly*) Well?

KEPLER Oh, you have unpacked.

BARBARA What happened? What did he say? What did you say?

KEPLER Well, we had breakfast. That is, he had breakfast. See, Regina, I brought you an orange. (*To* BARBARA *again*) And, let me see . . . I had coffee!

BARBARA (*Flat again*) You had coffee.

KEPLER *walks away from her, to the window, where* REGINA *is.*

KEPLER Look out, Regina, look—see those spires, off on the horizon? That's Prague.

BARBARA *lets fall a loud sob, more of anger than sorrow.*

KEPLER (*Faintly*) My dear . . .

BARBARA You did nothing! You settled nothing! You didn't even try!

XI

A door opens. The dining hall. Din of the extensive Brahe household at feed. KEPLER *and* BARBARA *entering.*

BARBARA (*Whispers*) Oh, Johann, I'm frightened!

KEPLER Come on, it's only dinner!

JEPPE *comes scampering forward.*

JEPPE Good evening, gentles.

KEPLER Ah. Yes. Good evening, Jeppe. Is there a place for us?

JEPPE But of course. You are here.

KEPLER But . . . but . . . this is the bottom of the table.

JEPPE But surely soon your star will rise. Come, sit!

KEPLER *and* BARBARA *take their seats.*

XII

BRAHE *can be heard roaring tipsily far off at the head of the long table.*

BARBARA (*Angry whisper*) His assistants, look, are seated higher than us—

SOPHIE BRAHE, *Tycho's sister, comes forward. She is about forty, a brisk and drily humorous bluestocking.*

SOPHIE You are Herr Kippler?

KEPLER Kepler. Yes, yes.

SOPHIE I am Lord Brahe's sister. My name is Sophie. I work with my brother.

KEPLER Of course. I've heard of you. It's an honour. This is my wife, Barbara.

SOPHIE Frau Kepler. Welcome to Benatky. I trust you have found everything to your satisfaction, your rooms, and so on?

BARBARA Well, since you mention—

SOPHIE Excellent. My brother is restless, he tries not to settle anywhere. Any hint of permanence he holds at bay by constantly remodelling his surroundings. (*Loud, brief, horsey laugh*) We suffer for his whims. But he's a great man, Herr Kepler, a great scientist.

KEPLER Yes, yes, of course.

SOPHIE There is great work to be done. We're mapping the skies, nothing less. Has Brahe given you an orbit to work on?

KEPLER No. In fact, I wanted to—

SOPHIE Well, no doubt he soon will. There's no time to waste. *Vita brevis, scientia longa,* eh, Herr Kepler?

XIII

Brahe's workroom. A dozen assistants are at work. BRAHE *showing* KEPLER *out.*

BRAHE This is my main laboratory, Herr Kepler. And those are my assistants. Let me show you some star charts.

He unfolds a large roll of heavy paper.

You see? The record of a full lunar year.

Pause as KEPLER *examines the chart.*

KEPLER (*Awed whisper*) I didn't know . . . I didn't dream . . .

BRAHE System, Herr Kepler, system is everything. Sixty years ago, when Copernicus was alive, a man could be an astronomer simply by calling himself one. No longer. I have seen to that. For twenty years I have been recording the movements of the stars. Here (*turns about to contemplate the room*) is a complete, accurate, continuous picture of planetary motion. This will transform our science, Herr Kepler.

BRAHE *puts the chart away, they walk on.*

KEPLER (*So impressed he is almost speechless*) I must . . . I must start over, start afresh. I . . . everything. (*Pause. Whispers as if to himself*) I shall do wonders. Yes, wonders.

XIV

Kepler's workroom. Kepler *working at his desk.* Regina *happily humming to herself.* Barbara *enters in a fury.* Regina*'s singing stops abruptly.*

Kepler (*Hardly noticing her*) What's that, my dear?

Barbara Regina, go and play outside.

Regina Yes, Mama.

Regina *exits.*

Barbara (*Striding back and forth, muttering*) . . . to be so stuck-up about . . . skivvy's daughter . . . not even married to him . . . concubine, that's all, a concubine! . . . (*Halts*) Am I invisible? Can they see through me? Dear God, what am I come to, in this place, with these . . . these . . . these *pigs*? (*Turns on him*) What's the matter with you?

Kepler Eh?

Barbara Are you in a trance?

Kepler (*Dreamily*) He's giving me Mars.

Barbara What?

Kepler He's giving me the Mars orbit to work on. He's giving it to *me*.

Pause.

Barbara (*Dangerously soft-spoken*) We haven't wood to light a fire, we're put to sit among the servants at table, Brahe's so-called wife won't condescend to speak to me—and you have Mars.

Kepler (*Rising, coming forward*) Now, my dear . . .

Barbara Don't you *now my dear* me!

Kepler I had to wait. I couldn't push him. I had to see what he would allocate to me, which orbit. You do understand? But now, now that I have Mars, I can put all our demands to him.

BARBARA *Today.*

KEPLER Yes, today. Or in a day or two.

BARBARA Today!

KEPLER Yes. Tomorrow, definitely. I'll arrange a meeting. I'll ask his sister—

BARBARA Pah!

KEPLER I'll do it. I promise.

XV

A room in the castle. KEPLER *pacing nervously.*

KEPLER He must listen. He must give me a commitment.

SOPHIE We shall do our best, Herr Kepler. Try to be calm.

KEPLER (*Halts*) Calm? How can I be calm? He has had a month already. I have stated my conditions. I demand the merest consideration, for myself and for my family. He does nothing—nothing!

SOPHIE You must be patient.

KEPLER All I ask is that we should be allocated separate quarters, and a certain quantity of food and firewood. And a salary from the Emperor—

SOPHIE (*Sighs*) The Emperor—ah!

KEPLER —*not* an allowance, *not* an emolument, *not* a bone thrown to a dog, but a *salary*! I ask you, madam, are these unreasonable demands?

SOPHIE Shush. Here he comes now.

BRAHE *and a party approach. They are off to the hunt.*

SOPHIE Brother!

BRAHE (*Not showing his pride*) What is it? I'm going to the hunt.

SOPHIE Herr Kepler wishes to know if you—

BRAHE Not now, woman!

He and his party stride on. SOPHIE *hurries after them.*

SOPHIE Brahe! Wait!

XVI

Kepler's quarters. REGINA *singing to herself.* KEPLER *enters dejectedly.*

KEPLER Where is your Mama, child?

REGINA She's with Madam Brahe.

KEPLER *sits down heavily on a chair.*

KEPLER (*Wearily*) Oh, Regina, Regina. (*Pause. Wistfully, speaking half to the child, half to himself*) You know, Regina, I was born with a vast hunger for great things. My father left home when I was six and never returned. My mother was a simple woman. In school, at university, I drove myself like an ox, training for greatness. At Tübingen I defended the theories of Copernicus, and suffered for it. In Graz my children died, your little step brother and step-sister. My post as a schoolteacher was taken from me, my possessions were confiscated, I was forced into exile. Yet none of that deflected me one degree from my course. I am a dog, I know. I snap and snarl (*snaps and snarls;* REGINA *laughs delightedly*) and bite the hand that would feed me. Yet when I fix my teeth on something (*clenches the teeth*) I do not let go. That is how it is with me. (*Pause; he brightens*) But you, Regina, my queen of the heavens, you are my inspiration (*his voice softens lovingly*), my inspiration and my joy.

A knock at the door. He goes and opens it, JEPPE *enters.*

JEPPE The Lady Sophie sent me to fetch you.

KEPLER (*Eagerly*) Has she news for me? Did she speak to Lord Brahe?

JEPPE She spoke to him. She has news.

KEPLER Oh!—

He rushes out. His footsteps clatter as he disappears down the stairs.

JEPPE (*Murmurs*) But it is not news that you will like . . . (*Gaily, to* REGINA) Well, my lady, would you like another game of Nine Men's Morris?

REGINA Show me again how to make cat's cradles.

XVII

KEPLER *arriving at the bottom of the stairs in a rush.*

KEPLER (*Panting*) My lady, my lady! The dwarf tells me you spoke to your brother . . . ?

SOPHIE I did.

KEPLER And?

SOPHIE I fear Brahe is angry at you, Herr Kepler.

KEPLER But why?

SOPHIE I suspect you know. He claims you said his system of planetary motion is misconceived.

KEPLER I never did! I merely observed, regarding one or two weaknesses I detected in his theory—based, I believe, on a too hasty acceptance of doubtful premises—that a bitch in a hurry will produce blind pups. (SOPHIE*'s stifled splutter of laughter*) Anyway, the truth is, as you well know, madam, the Tychonic system *is* misconceived. He puts the earth at the centre of the world, but makes the five remaining planets circle about the sun! (*Laughs heartily*) Oh, it works, of course, so far as appearances are concerned. You could put any one of the planets at the centre of the system and still save the appearances.

SOPHIE Nevertheless—

KEPLER It's all a trick your brother is playing, aimed at pleasing the pedants without entirely denying Copernicus. The truth is, he expects me to ratify his worthless theories by incorporating them into my work—

SOPHIE (*Firmly*) Herr Kepler! My brother is angry. You have insulted him and his work. The quality or veracity of his theory is neither here nor there. He expects an apology.

KEPLER An apology?!—

SOPHIE In writing. Also, you must swear on oath not to reveal to others any astronomical data he may provide you with in the course of your work. In return—

KEPLER Data? What data? Bits and scraps, that's all he has shown me, worthless stuff, despite promising me the Mars orbit. He's like a miser with his hoard. Like a . . .

SOPHIE In return, I say—

KEPLER Like a dog in the manger!

SOPHIE —he will guarantee lodgings for you and your family, and will press the Emperor to grant you a fixed and guaranteed allowance. These are his terms. What do you say?

Pause.

KEPLER Oh, I accept, of course.

Pause.

SOPHIE (*Astonished*) You accept?

KEPLER What choice have I? Bohemia is my last refuge. There's nowhere else for me to go.

XVIII

A room in the castle.

BRAHE Well, what is it?

SOPHIE Herr Kepler wishes to present the letter that you asked for. Herr Kepler?

KEPLER (*Sullenly*) Here.

BRAHE *unfolds the letter, walks a little way off, reads the text under his breath.*

BRAHE (*Refolding the letter*) Good. (*Inaudible*)

KEPLER (*Sharply*) Pardon?

BRAHE (*Loudly, trying not to laugh, not unfondly*) I said, I knew you would see sense!

XIX

Brahe's workroom. Sounds of many people at work on paper charts, consulting, etc.

SOPHIE I will not give up Jupiter. (*Pause*) Brother, I say I will not give up Jupiter.

CHRISTIAN LONGBERG *is in his thirties. Earnest, diligent, something of a whiner.*

LONGBERG If there is to be a redistribution of work, we must all be prepared to—

SOPHIE Oh be quiet, Longberg, you're not convincing. Are you prepared to give up Mars?

LONGBERG I have worked for eighteen months on the Mars data. My findings have already caused a stir in the world—

KEPLER (*Under his breath*) A stir in the world . . . ha!

SOPHIE (*Sceptical*) Your findings? On the Mars orbit?

LONGBERG That orbit, as every scholar knows, is a mystery, which has defeated the best minds of three millennia. I cannot be blamed if—

BRAHE No one is blaming you.

LONGBERG But you want to take Mars away from me! I have *toiled* over that orbit. It's mine, by right!

BRAHE (*Weary sigh*) There must be a redistribution of tasks, now that Herr Kepler has joined us.

LONGBERG You are going to give Mars to him, isn't that it? (BRAHE *is silent*) I will not tolerate this!

LONGBERG *rises, stalks away.*

SOPHIE He really doesn't bathe often enough, that young man. (*Chuckles*) Well, Herr Kepler, you have made yourself an enemy.

XX

The Keplers' quarters. Night. BARBARA *is bathing in a bath before a crackling fire.* KEPLER *at work at his desk.*

BARBARA Christine says—

KEPLER Who?

BARBARA Christine. Lady Brahe.

KEPLER I thought you didn't like her. I thought she ignored you.

BARBARA We've become friends.

KEPLER You used to say she was no better than a whore.

BARBARA Well, all that's changed. (*Pause*) It's true, he never married her, not properly. (*Portentously, reciting what she has been told*) In Denmark, a woman may live openly with a man without benefit of Church blessing, keeping his keys and sharing his table, and after three winters she is considered to be his wife. (*Normal voice*) Anyway, she's the only one in this place I can talk to.

KEPLER (*Distractedly*) And what does she say?

BARBARA She says the Emperor is setting up a school, for the children of the court, to learn mathematics and . . . and things.

KEPLER *suddenly pays attention.*

KEPLER No.

BARBARA No what? I haven't said—

KEPLER But you were about to. And the answer is no. I will not go back to teaching.

BARBARA But Johann, it would be just a start. The Emperor would notice you, he'd see how clever you are, who knows what might happen. And (*wistfully*) we'd be in Prague—in a city, Kepler, with shops, and people, and and and—and parties! We'd be away from this place.

KEPLER And what about your new friend, Lady Brahe.

BARBARA But think of it, Johann, think of—

He leaps up from his table, strides the floor.

KEPLER NO! I did not come to Bohemia to be a schoolteacher! Don't you understand that? Don't you . . . (*Halts; almost in wonderment*) No, you don't understand, do you. You don't understand anything about me. I don't want cities and shops and and and . . . *parties*! I don't even care about the damned Emperor, unless he can be of use to me.

Barbara But I only want—

Kepler I know what you want, and you will not have it! I will not put on a plumed hat and kiss and curtsy and be a court fop. (*Goes and sits beside her*) Listen to me, madam. Tycho Brahe is sitting on a treasure, a treasure he has been collecting for more than thirty years. Jewels, my dear, jewels from the sky. Never before has anyone kept such precise records of the movements of the planets over such a length of time. (*Laughing incredulously*) I underestimated him, I thought he was little more than an aristocratic dabbler. (*Stands up, paces*) No thought, of course—his theories are worthless. But as a technician, as a *technician* . . . ! A treasure, as I say, and I mean to get my hands on it. With such riches, I can transform astronomy; I can solve the mystery of the world; I can discover, my dear, how God thinks.

Pause.

Barbara But he won't give you this treasure. You said so yourself.

Kepler Then I'll take it. I'll steal it.

Silence, then Kepler *returns to his desk, sits, starts on his papers again. Sound of water sluicing as* Barbara *stands up in her bath.*

Barbara (*Seductive*) Kep—ler.

He does not answer. She walks across the floor, wet feet slapping, embraces him from behind.

Kepler Ow! You're wet! Mind, mind, you'll get bathwater on my papers!

Barbara Who's my clever-clogs, then? Hmm?

Kepler, *despite himself, stands up, embraces her. They kiss.*

KEPLER (*Muttering through kisses*) I can't . . . I have work to . . .

The kisses continue, however.

XXI

The Keplers in bed, after lovemaking. BARBARA *lightly snoring.* KEPLER *gets up.*

KEPLER (*To himself*) Where's that candle . . .

Finds the candle, lights it from the fire. Puts on a robe, goes out, softly shuts the door behind him. He descends the stairs. Suddenly—

BRAHE Put that candle out!

KEPLER *yelps in fright, drops the candle and candle holder.*

This staircase I have always found to be the best vantage point in the castle, I don't know why.

KEPLER *knows about the desire for solitude.*

KEPLER It's out of the way of everybody.

BRAHE Um. (*Pause*) There. Look.

KEPLER My sight is not good.

BRAHE (*Chuckles, not unkindly*) A blind astronomer! It's the conjunction. Jupiter and Mars.

KEPLER Oh.

BRAHE You do not take much interest in the sky, do you. I mean the real, the physical sky. It is the sky inside your head that fascinates you. That's the difference between us. I have stood here, at this window, for three hours, waiting for a clear sky.

And for what? (*Sighs*) To witness the merging of two spots of light. (*Pause*) Enough for tonight. Come.

They descend the stairs together.

BRAHE It was the predictability of astronomical events that always fascinated me, even as a boy. I remember the first eclipse of the sun I ever saw. I was fourteen, already a philosophy student at Copenhagen. The eclipse had been predicted, but I did not believe it, I thought it was just stargazers' hocus-pocus—I didn't yet know the difference between astronomy and astrology. But the day went dark, just at the time the stargazers had said it would. I was amazed. Not the eclipse, you understand, but the fact that the eclipse had been predicted—that was what enchanted me. Never looked back, since that day.

He opens a door, they enter a hall. There is a wood fire crackling.

Drink a mug of wine with me, will you?

KEPLER I have no head for wine, I'm afraid.

BRAHE One won't hurt you. (*Pours the wine*) You worry too much about yourself. But you're strong. You'll outlive me by three decades—I predict it. Here.

Hands him the mug of wine. They drink.

I grew up in a world of horses, luxury and disorder. My Uncle Jørgen stole me from my parents when I was a child—yes, stole me. Jørgen had no son, and my father, being my father, promised him one of his. Then, being my father, he went back on his promise. So Jørgen came and took me away at sword-point. There was almost a war, the King had to intervene. (*Chuckles; pause*) They were always so busy, with their squabbles . . . (*Pause*) I loved the night sky, even as a boy. The stillness there, the silence. Those lights. (*Pause*) Precision: how could one have a passion for mere precision? My Uncle Jørgen used to ask me—we were fond of each other, my uncle and I—*This stargazing,* he would say, *is this a pastime for a Brahe, son of the Governor of Helsingborg, and a future Lord of Knudstrup?* Even if I had been a philosopher, developing theories to stun the schoolmen, my people might have been impressed, might even have understood. But all I wanted to do was record the paths of the planets, accurately, continuously, night after night. Precision, leading to predictability. (*Pause*) What do you think, Kepler? Have I wasted my life?

KEPLER We live as we live. We do what we can.

BRAHE *might not have heard him.*

BRAHE And now I am old.

XXII

The dining hall. The usual Brahe dinner in progress: noisy, drunken, chaotic.

BARBARA (*To* KEPLER, *in an eager undertone*) . . . but then the daughter refused to marry, and Christine said—

JEPPE *pops up between them.*

JEPPE (*Parody of whining servility*) My master would speak with you, sire.

KEPLER What about?

JEPPE The stars, I am sure.

KEPLER Huh.

He rises. He is somewhat unsteady from drink. They walk to the head of the table.

JEPPE Sir Mathematicus, My Lord.

CHRISTINE BRAHE *is middle-aged, fat and slightly breathless.*

CHRISTINE Good evening, Herr Kepler.

KEPLER Good evening, Lady Brahe. (*To* BRAHE) Sir, you summoned me?

BRAHE (*Sullenly drunk*) Did I?

KEPLER (*Sarcastic*) Perhaps you meant to ask how I progress with the problem of the Mars orbit?

BRAHE Hmmph.

KEPLER You set me a difficult task when you gave me that planet—a back-breaking task—and yet you withhold the data without which it is impossible for me to carry out what you ask of me. I call that unreasonable.

BRAHE (*Addressing the table*) *De Tydske Karle ere allesammen halv gale!*

General merriment.

JEPPE (*To* KEPLER) Lord Brahe says . . . let me see . . . 'These German fellows are all half cracked.'

CHRISTINE My father went blind, you know, Herr Kepler, from swilling all his life like a pig. Have another cup of wine, Brahe dear.

LONGBERG (*Smugly*) Having difficulties with the Mars orbit, Herr Kepler?

KEPLER None that I won't solve.

LONGBERG *laughs softly.*

You think I won't? You'll take a wager on it?

LONGBERG I am a poor scholar, sir. I have no money for wagers.

BRAHE I'll back you.

KEPLER Shall we say fifty florins? A hundred?

BRAHE (*To* LONGBERG) Go ahead.

CHRISTINE You'd turn my table into a gambling den?

BRAHE Oh, be quiet, woman.

CHRISTINE Do I not suffer enough humiliation? Bring out the dice, you can cast lots for my garments!

BRAHE (*To* KEPLER) So: a hundred florins says you will fail to solve the problem of the Mars orbit in—shall we say—?

KEPLER Seven days.

BRAHE (*Incredulous laugh*) Seven . . . ?

KEPLER Give me one week free of all other tasks and I'll do it. All this assuming, of course, that I am guaranteed free, unhindered access to the observations, all the records, star charts, not just those for Mars, but for ALL the planets. Everything.

Silence as BRAHE *realises the trap he has fallen into.*

BRAHE (*Growls*) You'll have what you need.

XXIII

Kepler's workroom. KEPLER *is at his desk at work on Mars. Scratching of his pen. He mutters under his breath. He stops.*

KEPLER Regina! Are you still here? Why are you not outside playing? It's summer, look, the sun is shining.

REGINA I like it here, Papa.

KEPLER Ah, Regina. My little queen. My muse.

XXIV

Brahe's workroom. Everyone busy. SOPHIE BRAHE *and* KEPLER *are working side by side.*

SOPHIE (*To herself*) No, that can't be. I must have made some error.

KEPLER Let me look. (*Brief pause*) Yes. There. You see? If the apogee is so, then the perihelion . . . see?

SOPHIE But . . .

KEPLER Two minutes of arc.

SOPHIE (*Laughs*) Of course! Herr Kepler, you are a very clever man. More than clever.

KEPLER (*Bashful*) Oh . . .

SOPHIE How is Mars?

KEPLER I have made some progress, but . . .

SOPHIE Longberg has been complaining. You haven't paid him his wager.

KEPLER *His* wager? It is your brother I am betting against. (*Pause*) There's something wrong. I mean, something . . . fundamental. The orbit . . .

BRAHE *approaches.*

SOPHIE Ah, brother. Herr Kepler has shown me where I was wrong with the apogee of the Jupiter orbit.

BRAHE Let me see. (*He examines the chart*) Why, it's simple. You just add one epicycle and—

SOPHIE Nonsense. We do not use epicycles any more.

BRAHE Nonsense? Copernicus himself incorporated epicycles into his system.

SOPHIE And he was wrong.

BRAHE Ha! Tell that to your friend here, the champion of the Copernican system.

SOPHIE What do you say, Herr Kepler?

KEPLER The epicycle was a useful artifice. But it has no reality. A planet in its orbit cannot play loop-the-loop. The epicycle is a trick.

BRAHE A trick? Are you accusing me of trickery?

KEPLER Excuse me.

He stands, walks away.

BRAHE By God, that fellow . . . !

SOPHIE Look.

She hands him the page KEPLER *was working on.*

BRAHE What this?

SOPHIE His work.

BRAHE *examines Kepler's work.*

BRAHE Hmmph.

SOPHIE He will do great things, brother. Glorious things.

XXV

Creak of carriage, grating of wheels on stone. BRAHE *and* KEPLER *are on their way to see the Emperor.*

BRAHE . . . Thirty years ago I discovered a new star. I was the first. My star. Someone said it wasn't a star, but a comet formed out of the vapours of human sins rising into the sky. Others held there was dust falling from it, causing all sorts of evils—foul weather, plague, Frenchmen. The astronomers were not much better, blind idiots, every one of them. You read my book on it, *De Stella Nova*?

KEPLER (*Bored*) Of course.

BRAHE (*Angrily mimicking him*) Of course. (*Pause*) What about Mars?

KEPLER The orbit is wrong.

BRAHE What do you mean, wrong?

KEPLER It's not circular. It can't be.

BRAHE (*Dismissive laugh*) My dear man, the circular orbit is a dogma of our science.

KEPLER Nevertheless, Mars does not move in a circle. Nor do any of the planets. Not even Earth.

BRAHE What, then? What is the shape of the orbit?

KEPLER I don't know . . . yet.

BRAHE Ha! You're mad, sir. (*Pause*) Here is the castle. (*Pause*) God, how I detest this country. Why did I ever come here?

KEPLER Because . . .

He loses interest.

BRAHE Well? Because I would not bow and scrape to royalty? Because my family ruled at Knudstrup for generations before the House of Denmark got its fat backside on the throne? Because—

KEPLER (*Wearily*) Yes, yes.

BRAHE (*Mimicking him*) Yes, yes. (*His own voice*) What do you know of such things, anyway?

KEPLER I know that a year has passed since you promised to present me to the Emperor. A year.

BRAHE Securing an audience with His Majesty takes time.

KEPLER You kept me from him.

BRAHE I cannot march into the palace with every raw apprentice who comes my way!

KEPLER Raw apprentice?!

BRAHE Bah. (*Pause*) I *am* the Imperial Mathematician, you know.

XXVI

A reception hall in Prague Castle. The EMPEROR RUDOLPH II *is middle-aged, a weary, half-mad hypochondriac.*

RUDOLPH Herr Brahe, it is kind of you to visit us. Men such as you must have so much work to do . . .

BRAHE To see Your Majesty is always a pleasure, and, of course, an encouragement.

RUDOLPH Yes . . .

BRAHE Sire, may I present my colleague, Johannes Kepler.

KEPLER Sire.

RUDOLPH (*Almost laughing*) No no, do not kneel. Get up, please. You are a mathematician, Herr Kepler? (*Almost eagerly*) Do you know, one of our court astrologers has told us a fascinating thing. If the digits of any double number are transposed, and the resulting new number is subtracted from the original, or vice versa, depending on which is greater, the remainder in all instance will be divisible by nine. Is this not a wonderful operation?

KEPLER By nine?

RUDOLPH By nine, always. Of course you, sir, a mathematician of some renown, will doubtless think it not at all remarkable that numbers should behave in what to the rest of us is a strange and marvellous fashion?

KEPLER Your Majesty is too kind. A mathematician I am, but renown . . . Nevertheless . . . (*Thinking hard*) By nines, you say?

BRAHE Perhaps Your Majesty can offer an explanation of this strange phenomenon?

RUDOLPH There is a magic in numbers, beyond rational explanation. You are aware of this, Herr Kepler, in your own work? Perhaps, even, you put this magic to use sometimes . . . ?

KEPLER (*Scoffing*) Oh, no, I would not attempt to prove anything by the so-called magic of numbers. I don't believe it's possible. In fact, I think numerology is all a necromantic monkeyshine, if I may speak frankly, Your Majesty.

RUDOLPH (*Deeply disappointed*) Ah. Pity. I believe in number magic, myself . . . Come, gentlemen, let us walk a little way. (*They walk*) I am going to have these windows blocked off. I am tired looking down upon this city. (*Pause. Softly*) I do not like the world. More and more I desire to transcend the . . . the *mereness* of things. (*Brightening*) I think sometimes I might dress in rags and go among the people, as great kings do in the old stories. I don't see them, you know, the people. I'm told they love me . . . (*Pause*) But then, where would I find rags, here? You see our difficulties. (*Pause*) What was I saying? Yes—these charts that Dr Brahe is drawing up, these maps of the sky—you agree they are a worthwhile venture, Herr Kepler?

KEPLER This work will be the foundation of a new science of the sky, Your Majesty. Herr Brahe is a great and diligent observer. (BRAHE *modestly clearing his throat*) The material he has amassed is a priceless treasure. Those who come after us will bless the name of anyone who had a hand in the venture.

RUDOLPH I see, I see . . .

XXVII

The audience is at an end, BRAHE *and* KEPLER *are leaving.*

BRAHE Good day, Your Majesty. It was as ever a profound pleasure to see you.

RUDOLPH Good day, gentlemen.

BRAHE *and* KEPLER *walk away.*

KEPLER Wait. (*He runs back*) Your Majesty! Your Majesty!

RUDOLPH Yes, Herr Kepler?

KEPLER (*Breathless*) Nines, Your Majesty—nines! You see, it's because of nines, I've just solved it. I mean, it's because we count in tens, that's why the result will always be divisible by nine. If we counted by nines instead of tens, the result would always be divisible by eight. And so on. You see?

RUDOLPH (*Disappointed*) Ah. Is that all? No magic, then.

KEPLER (*With sympathy*) No, Your Majesty. No magic.

XXVIII

Creak of carriage, grinding of wheels. BRAHE *and* KEPLER *are on their way back to Benatky.*

BRAHE (*Furious*) The wrong thing, you said the wrong thing every time! And then explaining about the nines. Why, at times I thought you were *trying* to offend him. (*Pause. Suddenly weary*) Well, it's no matter in the end. Despite your clumsiness, I seem to have convinced him that the work we're engaged on is important. He wants his name attached to the star charts. We are to publish them as the *Tabulae Rudolphinae*. (*Pause*) He's granted you two hundred florins annually—though God knows if you'll ever see it. Well, have you nothing to say?

KEPLER What should I say?

BRAHE 'Thank you.'

KEPLER (*Tonelessly*) Thank you. (*Pause*) He doesn't like the world . . . Did you hear him say that? Strange . . .

BRAHE Kepler, I think you are as mad as he is.

XXIX

The Keplers' bedroom. BARBARA *is asleep.* KEPLER *enters, trying not to make a noise. Barks his shin, exclaims in pain.*

BARBARA Johannes? Is that you?

KEPLER I wish you wouldn't keep moving things around. I think my shin is bleeding.

BARBARA Did you see the Emperor?

KEPLER I saw him. I'm to continue here. The (*sarcastic*) imperial coffers will pay me two hundred florins a year. I'm to go on working with the Dane.

BARBARA *sits up in bed.* KEPLER *is taking off his clothes.*

BARBARA Two hundred florins!

KEPLER It's the best Brahe could squeeze out of the old skinflint.

BARBARA Better than nothing.

KEPLER If it's ever paid.

BARBARA What's he like?

KEPLER Rudolph? Mad. (*Gets into bed*) God, it's cold!

BARBARA Ow! Your feet are like ice!

KEPLER (*Lewdly*) Is this warmer?

BARBARA *giggles.*

XXX

Kepler's workroom. He is at work on Mars. Scratching of pen on paper. He mutters under his breath. REGINA *is with him, singing to herself.*

KEPLER Regina, Regina, the planet Mars is driving me mad. (*Pause*) What are you doing?

REGINA Playing cat's cradles. Jeppe taught me. Look. I can make a circle.

KEPLER Not a circle, exactly.

REGINA What, then?

KEPLER Well, it's more like an ellipse . . . (*Pause; murmurs*) Yes, an ellipse . . . (*Pause; awed tone*) My God . . .

XXXI

Kepler's workroom. Late at night. KEPLER *at work, as usual. He hears a sound outside the door. Tiptoes to the door, pulls it open.*

KEPLER Oh, I thought you might be Longberg, spying on me.

Throughout the scene, BRAHE *maintains a jaded, weary tone. He is old and tired and has acknowledged to himself that* KEPLER *is the greater scientist.*

BRAHE I cannot sleep.

A bell tolls twice in the distance.

KEPLER Bells.

BRAHE *does not get the reference.*

BRAHE Eh?

KEPLER (*Unwillingly*) Will you come in?

BRAHE *enters.*

We must be quiet. My wife is asleep. I was working.

BRAHE You progress?

KEPLER A little, yes. In fact, I have made something of a discovery. I have realised that the orbit of Mars is not a circle.

BRAHE Not a circle.

KEPLER No. It's an ellipse.

BRAHE An ellipse? Don't be ridiculous.

KEPLER But it's true. And not only Mars, but all planetary orbits. Even that of Earth. Each heavenly body moves in an ellipse, with one focus at the Sun. (*Pause; mildly*) I regard this as a law.

Long pause. Then BRAHE *laughs softly.*

BRAHE Moses Mathematicus, giver of laws. (*Pause; as if to himself*) My sister said you would surprise us, one day.

KEPLER I dreamed it. (*Laughs wonderingly*) On the day I first came here, I fell asleep in the carriage and dreamed it. Nought point nought nought four two nine. The value by which the sides of an ellipse . . .

BRAHE You still hold to the Copernican system?

KEPLER Yes. I follow Copernicus, more or less.

BRAHE (*Resignedly*) My system will be forgotten. (*Pause*) Bells . . .

XXXII

A hall in the castle. Noise outside. The door bursts open, BRAHE *enters drunk and roaring.*

BRAHE Out of my way, dwarf, I have to . . .

He strides to the fireplace, opens his clothes, pisses into the flames.

(*In agony*) Christ in heaven, it's like pissing acid!

JEPPE (*In fright*) Master . . . ? (*Groans from* BRAHE) Master!?

With a great cry, BRAHE *collapses. Enter* CHRISTINE BRAHE *at a run.*

CHRISTINE What is that foul smell—Brahe! My God, what has happened?

She kneels by him.

JEPPE He . . . he fell down.

CHRISTINE (*Hysterical*) Go, get someone! Go! Oh, Brahe, Brahe, Brahe . . . !

XXXIII

Brahe's bedroom. BRAHE *in bed.* KEPLER *enters.*

KEPLER (*Sleepily*) What do you want?

BRAHE I'm ill.

KEPLER And I'm tired. It's six o'clock in the morning.

BRAHE I'm ill, I tell you! Something's burst in my gut. Look in that basin. I pissed that in the night.

KEPLER Looks like Rhenish wine.

BRAHE Blood! I was at Hoffmann's for dinner. My bladder was full for three hours, I couldn't leave the table.

KEPLER Why not?

BRAHE (*Shouts*) A gentleman does not leave his host's table while dinner is in progress!

KEPLER A martyr to etiquette, that's you.

BRAHE I'm dying, Kepler.

KEPLER (*Impatient sigh*) Oh, for God's sake . . .

BRAHE Be careful of my family, they'll try to thwart you. Longberg, too. Protect my poor fool. (*Pause*) Remember me, and all I have done for you.

Pause. KEPLER *is wondering if* BRAHE *might really be dying. He knows a way to test the Dane.*

KEPLER What about the observations, the star charts, the tables?

BRAHE I've given you—

KEPLER Pah. You've given me nothing. You've held on to the vital data. I need my breakfast.

KEPLER *exits.*

BRAHE (*Roars*) Come back here, Kepler! (*Groans in agony*) Oh, dear God . . . !

XXXIV

The Keplers' quarters. KEPLER *enters.*

KEPLER (*Muttering*) Damn the man . . .

BARBARA How is he?

KEPLER Says he's dying. He drank too much, now he's passing blood.

BARBARA (*Whispers*) Sweet Jesus . . .

KEPLER Don't you start!

BARBARA Have you thought, have you, what's to become of us when he's gone?

KEPLER Oh, for heaven's sake! He drank too much at dinner, he was too lazy to leave his chair and go to the jakes, and thereby strained his bladder. He'll be over it by nightfall.

BARBARA You see nothing! Are you alive at all, with your stars and your precious theories and your laws of this and that? (*Begins to sniffle*) Rotting away in this hole, no friends, no one to talk to . . .

KEPLER (*Under his breath*) Oh, Lord . . .

XXXV

KEPLER *walking along a corridor. Footsteps approach behind him.*

SOPHIE Herr Kepler.

KEPLER Yes, Madam Sophie?

SOPHIE My brother asked me to give you this.

KEPLER What is it?

SOPHIE It is the key to his treasures.

KEPLER The observations, the star charts?

SOPHIE He urges you to take them, without delay, before . . . before the others can get their hands on them.

Pause.

KEPLER Thank you.

SOPHIE My brother wishes you to understand that he is doing this not for you.

KEPLER For what, then?

SOPHIE For science. Go now. Do it.

KEPLER *hurries away.*

XXXVI

Brahe's bedroom. Murmur of a number of people gathered about his bed. KEPLER *enters.*

BRAHE (*Weakly*) Kepler!

KEPLER I am here.

BRAHE Lean closer. (*Whispers*) Have you done it? Have you secured my treasure hoard?

KEPLER Yes.

BRAHE Good. (*Pause; a weak laugh*) Ah, Kepler, you have killed me. (*Pause*) Remember me. (*Pause*) Do not let me seem to have lived in vain.

LONGBERG *enters at a rush.*

LONGBERG Lord Brahe! That man has—that man has stolen your observations, the charts, the tables—everything!

CHRISTINE What? Brahe—what is this?

BRAHE I gave them to him.

CHRISTINE You . . . ?!

JEPPE (*Cries out*) He is going!

All crowd around the bed.

CHRISTINE Brahe! Don't leave me!

JEPPE (*Weeping*) Master!

BRAHE*'s death rattle.*

XXXVII

KEPLER *walking rapidly along a corridor,* LONGBERG *behind him.*

LONGBERG Kepler! I want a word with you.

KEPLER *opens a door, hurries out into the courtyard. Horse's hoofs coming to a stop. The rider dismounts.*

MESSENGER You are Johannes Kepler?

KEPLER (*Grimly, to himself*) Someone has at last got my name right. (*To the* MESSENGER) Yes, I am Kepler.

MESSENGER *unfolds a parchment.*

MESSENGER (*Reads*) Be informed that His Gracious Majesty, the Emperor Rudolph, anointed of God, of his special favour and grace has decreed, and now by this open letter does announce, that Johannes Kepler, his man and Servant, shall succeed the beloved Tycho Brahe, Otto's son, of Knudstrup, in the kingdom of Denmark, in the post of Imperial Mathematician to the court of Prague and to the Empire. Given this day by the hand of his serene highness Rudolph II, at Prague, the 6th day of November, sixteen hundred and one, *anno domini*.

KEPLER (*In triumph*) Yes, Longberg, you were saying . . . ?

(*Kepler*, 2004)

A World Too Wide

Look at this face. I'm sixty and might be a hundred. I take off the make-up and put on forty years. Perhaps I should wear it all day long, like poor dear Micheál. I'd look a sight, strutting about the streets with the slap dripping off my dewlaps. Oh, that would make her notice me, I'm sure. I can just see her, laughing behind her hand as she does when old Adam's stammer comes on. *Why wo-wo-wo-wo-would you be so fo-fond to overcome The bo-bonny pu-pu-pu-prizer of the humorous D-d-d-d-d-d-duke?* The groundlings think he does it deliberately, he gets the only laughs in the show. Have to admire him, all the same. Imagine having a stammer like that and going for the stage. What was his mammy thinking of, all those centuries ago, when he was young and starting out?

[sings] *Don't put your daughter on the stage, Mrs Worthington . . .*

A poor crowd tonight, what there was of it, very poor, sitting there like cardboard cut outs. Not that I blame them. This is not the most polished production I've ever been in. Orlando is so camp he's under canvas, and dainty Celia is built like a brick *cabinet d'aisances*. But it's not all our fault. Here's a blasphemy, I whisper it: the piece itself is no bloody good. Wait. No, no bolt of lightning to strike me down. Emboldened, I say it outright: as far as *As You Like It* is concerned, I don't—like it, I mean: the opening is weak, the end is laughable, though not, God wot, in a funny way, and the middle, truth be told, is no great shakes either. Ha! I did a pun! *No great shakes!*

I mean to make more than a quibble on a title. The trouble with his comedies, as everybody knows but no one says, is that they're not comic. All that banter, that so-called wit, but honestly, where's the humour? And of course, I'm the one who's supposed to have them rolling in the aisles, but look at the material I'm given to work with. *The more pity that fools may not speak wisely what wisemen do foolishly*, or *I had rather bear with you than bear you; yet I should bear no cross if I did bear you, for I think you have no money in your purse.* I ask you. Touchstone is about as comic a character as old King Lear.

I wonder if she'll come for a drink with us again one of these nights? She came to the Swan after the first preview, but since then she hasn't graced our wild midnight revels with her presence. The curtain is barely down and she's off. Some man, I suppose. Probably he collects her at the stage door. I keep picturing him, this Johnny, it's become a bit of an obsession with me. For some reason I see him as fair, with a blond lock falling over one eye. A big bloke, certainly, since she's a good five-ten herself. Rugger type I'm sure he is, leather jacket, trailing scarf. Extraordinary how clearly he appears in my mind, the swine, while probably he's not like that at all. And yet, there he is, before my glowering green eye, as large as life. He puts his big arm around her shoulders and they stroll off into the night, murmuring, head to head, while I sit like a sad old toad before the mirror here in my dressing room, eating my heart out, thinking of them. He's not the husband. When I asked her if she was married she only looked at me and said, *Hardly*. What was that supposed to mean, I wonder?

I watched her in the Swan that night. She bites her nails. When she's listening to someone she looks in their face and keeps giving little nods and going *Um, um*. Nod, nod, *Um, um*. Wonderful profile, that Greek nose. Might be Greek, in fact, or from some southern clime, anyway, with that dark skin and hair like pouring oil. Galway girl, the Spanish blood. Funny thing is, she's not my type, what used to be my type. I always liked them trim and shapely, not rangy like her. No bust to speak of, and a bum like a boy's. Am I turning queer, after all these years? I might as well, since everyone assumes I am already. I sidled up to her in the Swan and offered to buy her a drink, oh so casual. She said no, she had to be going. That quick smile, like a hand brushing carelessly against my heart.

O Rosalind!

• • •

Another night's hard labour done with. I used to love this moment, just after coming off, feeling nicely weary, the adrenalin draining away, the smell of my own sweat drying, the cosiness in the dressing room. Never cared what kind of a kip I was in, next door to the lavatory or whatever. My things laid out: rabbit's paw, the musical steel ball someone bought for me in Arles, the tattered Arden edition with my scribbled notes. Three times I've played Touchstone, still hate the part. I'm surprised they cast me this time, at my age. I'll be playing Adam, next, or Sir Oliver Martext, with his three lines. The years are edging me off the stage, one of these days I'll find myself tumbling arse-over-tip into the pit.

And here I am, in love, like a swooning boy. In the pit of love. I'm blushing, look, I can see it in the glass. What a farce.

I wonder if I'm any good as an actor. A fine stage of my so-called career I'm at to be asking myself that. Another pun, there—*stage of my career*, get it?—I must be catching it from the Bard himself. Impossible to judge your own talent, of course. The critics—the critics!—are no help. I got one mention this run, one solitary mention. Where is it, I have it here somewhere. Yes: *A somewhat lethargic Touchstone declaimed his lines with old-fashioned resonance*—old-fashioned resonance? what's that when it's at home? —*but nevertheless managed to throw away most of his comic lines.*

Thanks very much. What comic lines, I'd like to know. Do I declaim? I was trained in the old school, I can't help that. [sings] *Hey, fiddle-de-dee, an actor's life for me . . .* Love the work, though, maybe too much. It's my home, this little round; my life. Pathetic.

Yet I've played Hamlet, must remember that. I was an upcoming lad, an ascendant star. Yes, I too was once adored. Wonder what happened.

Recently I thought I'd start wearing a hat again and took down my old black Borsalino. It was a bit mildewed around the brim but brushed up nicely. Bought it in my impetuous youth but hadn't worn it in thirty years. When I put it on I had a sense straight away of something wrong. It took me a while to realise what was the matter. The hat was the same as it always was, but the face underneath it was not the face I had expected to see there. What the hat required was the face I had when I was thirty; this new one, I mean this old one, didn't fit at all. Shaken and—what's the word?—abashed, yes, I put the titfer back in its box and quietly returned it to the top of the wardrobe to gather another three decades' deposit of dust.

Shaken and Abashed: a comedy in two acts, thirty years apart.

Unsettling how sometimes, when you've been looking in the mirror for a long while, all at once you seem to yourself to be a stranger. Or not a stranger, exactly. Someone familiar and yet at the same time completely unknown. That expression, look at it now: insinuating, mocking, malignantly amused. It unnerves me. It's myself, plainly, and yet it seems to know something that I don't; something . . . shameful.

I remember in the old Paradiso Restaurant, with the mirrors on the walls, there was a place at a particular table that when you sat there you found yourself looking into a corner where the mirrors met and by some fluke you saw your reflection not reversed as usual in a looking-glass but the right way round, the way other people see you. Now, there was a fright. Like my evil twin smirking at me from across the room and about to stand up and denounce me for a fraud and an impostor.

She's one of those actors who don't meet your eye. On stage, that is. Or she does, rather, but doesn't see you. She's looking into herself, watching herself. Not a natural, that's obvious. I can feel the tension, can almost see it, it comes off her in waves. That night when she snagged her heel in the hem of her costume and stumbled and I caught her wrist it was like catching hold of an electric cable, the fizz in it, the fire. She wasn't a bit pleased that I was the one to save her from going down, gave me a slithery sort of glance and said something under her breath. Doesn't like to be touched, or not by me, anyway, my old paw on her young arm. I should recite Adam's line to her, *Though I look old, yet I am strong and lusty,* that would give her a laugh. *I'll do the service of a younger man In all your business and necessities.* In fact, she's not in the first bloom herself. Thirty-five, if she's a day. That still makes me the older of the two of us by a quarter of a century.

If the scorn of your bright eyne
Have power to raise such love in mine,
Alack, in me, what strange effect
Would they work in mild aspect?

That last line's not right, doesn't scan, unless you pronounce it ass-*pect*. Maybe that's how it was pronounced in his day? My granny used to say *tay* for *tea*, that's Elizabethan. Some things change, others stay the same.

Why did I never marry?

Good God, where did that come from?

Marry, sir, why should I marry? I haven't done badly, in my time. When I was young I had girls, could have had more, they were mine for the asking. There was never one I wanted to stay with, though. I used them up too quickly, that's the fact of it. There are two kinds of people in the world, the users-up and the used. Selfish I always was, I know it. And also, I think, I grew accustomed to myself too quickly. Hang on, what do I mean by that? I suppose, that I decided too early who and what I was, and accepted it, and therefore didn't need a wife to help me find myself, to identify myself, I mean properly. Hmm. I must say, that does sound like a lot of horse shit. Probably it was absent-mindedness and nothing more that kept me single. I don't notice other people very much, I mean not with sufficient attention. That's why noticing her—and, oh, what noticing—has been such a shock for me.

It wasn't love at first sight. She's been about for years, after all. I saw her play Pegeen Mike, and Hedda, I think—or was it Nora in *A Doll's House*?—and the madwoman in that awful thing by what's-his-name, and I was never particularly struck. Being in the same show with her, that's what did it, that's what worked this misfortunate magic on me. Seeing her striding about there in front of the scenery, vivid and real in the midst of so much mere flummery, the flashing eyes and dashing wit—even if the wit is not her own—mistress of the action, and sometimes master, too—dear Lord, but she looks a treat in trousers!—I fell for her. And fell is the word.

A few years ago I took a bad tumble in the street myself, purely accidentally. Don't know what came over me, I wasn't drunk, or sick, but down I went like a bag of bricks and banged my forehead on the pavement. Talk about collapse of stout party! What stayed in my memory afterwards was not the injury, the duck-egg on my forehead, the grazed hands and knees, all that, and not even the humiliation of making a spectacle of myself in public—after all, that's what I do for a living—but the feeling itself of falling, the dreamy slowness of it, the almost . . . the almost voluptuous, swooning way that I pitched forward, as if the air around me had become lighter and at the same time more dense than air, something like the atmosphere on the moon. Yes, the moon. It was the same with her, when I watched her from the wings walking on that first night, making her entrance, that same sense of helpless, slow-motion toppling. *Dear Celia, I show more mirth than I am mistress of, and would you yet I were merrier?* I had heard her say those same lines I don't know how many times, in the read-through, in rehearsal, in previews, but somehow it was only then that I *heard* her, only then that I *saw* her, and I was . . . overwhelmed.

First night. I say it, and how the words mock me. There will be no first night, with her, for me, ever. That's the awful thing about getting old, the certain knowledge that some things simply will not be.

• • •

I feel mortified. What a fool I am, what a fond old fool. I don't know how it happened. I'm not even sure what it was that happened, or even that it did happen, for it's possible I imagined it all, though I don't think so, the smart is too sharp, the blush too burning. It started so well. We all have them, those nights, rare and fine, when everything seems to flow, wonderfully, when the stuff comes out like silk, like a long trail of silk out of your mouth, every line a polished thread. I couldn't put a foot wrong, a word wrong, at first, anyway. Act One, Scene Two, our first exchange. She's there, Celia's there, I enter. Usually I trudge on, being the dullard fool so that my wit will shine the brighter, at least that's the director's intention—His Nibs, don't get me started on him—but tonight, without any new thought, I fairly leapt into the middle of the action. I, to Celia: *Mistress, you must come away to your father.* Celia: *Were you made the messenger?* I: *No by mine honour, but* and so on. Then she, fair Rosalind: *Where learned you that oath, fool?* Then I go into my shtick, *Of a certain knight, that swore by his honour* blah blah blah.

But wait, let me paint the scene more sharply, so I might understand it better, or just understand it. There I am, all swagger and glide doing that thing with my hand, that elegant flourish that I invented for myself and that His Nibs hates—*an ill-favoured thing, sir, but mine own*—and she's downstage right, posed in the way she does, a hand on her hip, left foot forward, head thrown back, hair flowing on her shoulders, my magnificent maid. Big fat Celia is centre stage somewhere, stumping about, we ignore her, practically. It's Rosalind and me, all eyes on us, I'm sure of it. Even when Le Beau enters no one takes much notice. I do the line *Or as the Destinies decrees*, and Celia, quickly, *Well said! That was laid on with a trowel*, to which I: *Nay, if I keep not my rank*— And then . . .

And then I'm not sure what happened. Still with hand on hip, that lovely knee and slender foot thrust out, she throws her head back farther still, until I can see the blacks of her nostrils, and looks at me down the length of that noble nose of hers and fairly spits it out: *Thou losest thy old smell*. Such contempt, especially on the word *smell*! Yet it wasn't the words, it was the tone. Le Beau twitched, like a startled rabbit, and Celia gaped from her to me and to her again, her little mouth open in shock. The audience, the majority of whom, I know, hadn't the foggiest what the exchange was supposed to be about, gave a great laugh, a roar such as we haven't heard yet and, I hope, won't hear again, but even in that laughter there was a hesitation, an uncertainty, as if I had taken a pratfall so convincing that there were those amongst them wondering if I mightn't be acting at all but having a real heart attack.

What provoked her to such a bitter tone, so contemptuous a look? Did she think I was trying to upstage her? Or was she doing some variation of her own part, as I was doing of mine, and not paying attention to me at all? At any rate, the rest of the night for me passed in a haze of shame and bafflement. The lines that had been silk now fell from my trembling lips like strips of lead piping. I couldn't wait for the thing to end, then scuttled in here and shut the door with a hand that shook, sweating, my heart shrivelled to the size of a nut.

What am I to think? What am I to tell myself? How am I to account for such a violent blow, what compress can I apply to the bruise?

Can't say what a dolt I think myself. Really, what a dolt.

The show closes at the end of the week, so we heard tonight. No one surprised. No one very regretful, either. No one except me, that is. I'll never get so close to her again, if you can call this close.

• • •

When I sit here like this for long enough my mind wanders and I drift into a sort of trance. It's like that state before going to sleep at night, or in the morning between sleeping and waking up. The strangest thoughts occur to me, I don't know if they can even be called thoughts. Fantasies, more like, amazing, some of them. All sorts of people appear, people I've never seen before, doing inexplicable things. That must be something like the way he worked, in a trance all day, his head full of places and events, characters striding up and down, making speeches, and squabbling with each other, and falling in love. Who was it said the plays were *all fighting and fucking tarts*? Sums the whole thing up, really, when you come down to it.

How could I have been so stupid, not to see, not to realise? *We that are true lovers run into strange capers.*

We've had our final night, our last curtain. They've all gone off to the Swan, her included. I said I'd come along later but I won't. Too ashamed to show my face.

How could I not have *realised*?

I was right about the lover, anyway: tall, fair-haired, handsome, even has a leather jacket. Hardly a rugby player, though. Hardly.

The Fool: *Are you married?*

The Heroine: *Hardly.*

I think it was the smell of her that went to my head. She was on the way down to the dressing rooms and had stopped at the turn of the steps when I came up behind and almost bumped into her. She was standing with a hand on the rail, leaning down and doing something to her shoe. It wasn't the smell of greasepaint or sweat, but of her, herself, her, I don't know, her *essence*. I suppose even an old bird like me is still programmed to pick up the—what do you call it?—the pheromones? She sensed me behind her and turned. I was probably giving off a sound, as she was giving off a smell, the rusty old dynamo inside me humming and clanking. She looked startled, even a bit alarmed. Well, I was very close to her, looming over her, there on the steps. We both said something at the same time, and laughed, and stopped for a second. I could hear her breathing, she was still a bit breathless from running in after the final bow. I caught the smell of her again: milk and vinegar. Then I made a grab at her. Oh, God.

How many actions most ridiculous
Hast thou been drawn to by thy fantasy?

I didn't mean it to be a grab. I tried to do it in such a way that at the last moment, the very last instant, I could if necessary turn it into what was no more than a polite offer of an arm to lean on. The human hand, however, especially the male variety, has a mind of its own.

Women's flesh is always much harder to the touch than one expects, or than I expect, anyway. Not harder, that's not it. More . . . resistant. It's not even the flesh itself, I suppose, but the things they wear, the armour-plating they put on. Brittle!—that's the word I want. I still remember the first time I got to put my hand on a girl's leg, in the back row of the Palace picture-house one Christmastime when I was fifteen or so. I expected something soft and giving, what I got was the raspiness of nylon. Exciting, and yet a let-down.

When I grabbed her, there on the steps, it was not her I felt but the stuff of her dress, brittle, again, almost metallic. She looked at me for a second in amazement, then laughed. Yes, laughed. A scream I could have put up with, a slap in the face, even a knee in the crotch. But a laugh . . .

Her lover's name is Lucy. Big and butch. She introduced her to everyone, except me. Not that she was angry at me, after the grapple on the steps, only she had a look that told me she'd laugh again if she met my eye.

Extraordinary quiet. Nothing so silent as an empty theatre. I could be alone in the world, a world too wide for my shrunk shank.

[sings, softly]
Heigh-ho, sing heigh-ho, unto the green holly,
Most friendship is feigning, most loving mere folly.
Then heigh-ho the holly,
This life is most jolly.

(*A World Too Wide*, 2005)

Conversation in the Mountains

I

Interior. Freiburg University. Night.

PAUL CELAN *(aged forty-seven) is giving a reading of his poetry in an auditorium packed with a thousand-strong audience. His delivery is calm and measured, which gives extra force to the lines. He is reading the final stanzas of his most famous poem,* 'Todesfuge' ('Deathfugue').

CELAN *. . . Black milk of daybreak we drink you at night*
we drink you at midday Death is a master aus Deutschland
we drink you at evening and morning we drink and we drink
this Death is ein Meister aus Deutschland his eye it is blue
he shoots you with shot made of lead shoots you level and true
a man lives in the house your goldenes Haar Margarete
he looses his hounds on us grants us a grave in the air
he plays with his vipers and daydreams der Tod ist ein
Meister aus Deutschland

dein goldenes Haar Margarete
dein aschenes Haar Sulamith

There is a brief pause and then a storm of applause. The organiser of the event, GERHART BAUMANN, *addresses the audience.*

BAUMANN Thank you, ladies and gentlemen. I know that I am right in saying that in times to come we shall tell our children how on this day, the 24th of July 1967, in Freiburg in the old heart of Germany, we saw and heard the greatest poet of the age, Paul Celan . . .

His voice fades.

II

Interior. Freiburg University. Later that night.
A reception after the reading. Many voices conversing amid the clink of wine glasses. BAUMANN *is talking to* CELAN.

BAUMANN A momentous evening, Herr Celan. The student body here at the university would wish me to offer you their profound thanks and appreciation for your beautiful reading.
CELAN Thank you, Professor.
BAUMANN We know what it is for you to come here to Freiburg—what it is for you to be among us Germans.
CELAN Your language is my mother tongue, Professor. Literally—my mother was a German-speaker.
BAUMANN There's someone who wishes to meet you.
CELAN Oh, yes?
BAUMANN Will you come this way?

Sound of them moving through the crowd. MARTIN HEIDEGGER *is a vigorous seventy-eight-year-old.*

Herr Celan, Doctor Martin Heidegger. Doctor—Paul Celan.
HEIDEGGER A great honour, Herr Celan.
CELAN Likewise, Herr Doctor.
HEIDEGGER I know your poetry very well, of course. It is of great interest to me. I once wrote that all of my work was no

more than an effort to say philosophically what Rilke had already said poetically. I might add your name to his in that formulation.

CELAN You flatter me, Doctor.

HEIDEGGER No, no, I mean no flattery, only—But ah, it seems the photographer wishes to take our portrait together. Shall we . . . ?

CELAN (*Sharply*) No. (*Softens his tone*) No, please. I . . . I have an aversion to being photographed.

A moment of awkward silence. HEIDEGGER *realises* CELAN *is deliberately refusing to be photographed with him.*

HEIDEGGER Ahem. Yes, of course, I understand . . . (*Pause*) And your health has improved, yes? We had heard that you were in hospital.

CELAN I was in a Swiss clinic. I suffer from depression. And other things. (*Brief laugh*) I have bad dreams. Bad memories.

HEIDEGGER You should come to the mountains. In such pure air up there the mind finds a higher clarity.

BAUMANN You'll have heard of Doctor Heidegger's famous 'hut' at Todtnauberg, of course?

CELAN Of course.

HEIDEGGER It would be an honour for me to welcome you to Todtnauberg for a visit. Perhaps, if you have time, tomorrow . . . ?

CELAN I think not. I must return to Paris.

BAUMANN If you wish to stay a little longer we can make the arrangements, of course.

HEIDEGGER Todtnauberg is where I wrote the bulk of *Being and Time*. It would mean much to me if the greatest German poet of our time should visit that birthplace.

CELAN I'm not German, Herr Doctor.

HEIDEGGER But you write in the German language. That is our common homeland, yours and mine.

BAUMANN I'd be happy to drive you up to Todtnauberg in the morning, Herr Celan, if you wish . . . ?

III

Interior. Motor car. Day.

BAUMANN *is driving* CELAN *into the mountains.*

BAUMANN We're almost there. Another kilometre or two. (*Pause*) I confess, Herr Celan, I was a little surprised that you agreed to come up here

CELAN (*Faint laugh*) So was I. (*Pause*) I know, of course, why he's so eager for me to visit him in his mountain fastness. It's just like with the photographer last night—he wants to be seen with me: *The Jew poet Celan, survivor of the camps, embraces Heidegger the former Nazi.*

BAUMANN Then why . . . ?

CELAN Oh, I don't know. Because despite everything he's a great philosopher? His concerns echo mine—we're both dwellers in the house of language. (*Pause*) And because I'm curious to hear if he'll offer an account of himself.

BAUMANN He has never spoken in public about his Nazi past—not a word.

CELAN But perhaps, to me, he'll utter that word. We shall see.

The car tyres crunch on a mountain track, the car stops.

BAUMANN So. Here we are. And there he is, waiting for you.

Car doors open, CELAN *and* BAUMANN *get out,* HEIDEGGER *comes forward.*

HEIDEGGER Welcome, Herr Celan. Here it is, my famous 'hut'. Not very prepossessing, I'm afraid.

CELAN I envy you such a place. In my apartment where I live in Paris I frequently feel I'm suffocating.

HEIDEGGER (*To* BAUMANN) Professor, you'll stay a while?

BAUMANN No, thank you, Doctor. I must get back. Herr Celan, I'll return this evening. At six, shall we say?

CELAN Six will be fine.

BAUMANN Enjoy your visit. (*To* HEIDEGGER) Herr Doctor.

HEIDEGGER Thank you, Baumann.

BAUMANN *gets into the car, drives away.*

Well. Let me show you my little kingdom. I bought the plot of land here in 1922—or was it '21?—so I've been a presence in this clearing for forty-five years. (*To himself*) Lord, so long! (*To* CELAN) My wife oversaw all of the building—she's immensely practical, something I am not.

CELAN It's all very beautiful, very beautiful and simple.

HEIDEGGER When I secured the professorship at Marburg I knew I'd need a place to escape to. The work was so intense. I was inventing a new way of philosophising, returning to basics and throwing out two and a half millennia of metaphysical dross . . .

Cut to:

HANNAH ARENDT (*Voice-over as a nineteen-year-old student; passionately*) *In you, thinking has come alive again. And in you I, too, am alive, as never before.*

Cut to:

HEIDEGGER I'm sorry, what was I . . . ?

CELAN You were speaking of Marburg, your early days there.

HEIDEGGER Yes, yes. Often now the past seems more real to me than the present. (*Brief laugh*) It's the way with all old men. (*They walk forward*) Those trees are mine, on the slope. And this is my well, you see, with the wooden star above it. Now. (*He unlocks the door*) Please. (*They enter the cabin. Pause*) History will remember this day, Herr Celan.

CELAN And what will history's judgement be, I wonder?

Pause. HEIDEGGER *clears his throat.*

HEIDEGGER What will you take? There's coffee, and I think somewhere there's even a bottle of schnapps.

CELAN A glass of water from the well, perhaps.

HEIDEGGER I'll fetch it.

HEIDEGGER *goes out.*

CELAN (*Murmurs*)

Streak in the eye:
so as to guard
a sign dragged through the dark . . .

HEIDEGGER *returns. Sound of water being poured from a can into a glass.*

Thank you. (*Drinks*) Ah!

HEIDEGGER It tastes of the mountains, yes?

CELAN And of the deeps. (*Pause*) I wanted to send you one of my poems when I wrote it. I thought of it again when I saw the wooden star over the well.

Soul-stridden threads,
glass trace
rolled backward
and now
filmed white
by the Eyes' Thou on a steady
star above you.

HEIDEGGER I would have been honoured, to have had a poem straight from your hand. (*Pause*) Do sit. Sit here, by the window, where we can see the mountains. Later, perhaps, we might take a walk, up on the moorland.

They sit. There is an awkward pause.

CELAN There are so many things we may not talk about it's impossible to know where not to begin.

HEIDEGGER (*Polite laugh*) You are, as ever, a master of the forceful negative.

A Nothing
we were, are now, and ever
shall be, blooming:
the Nothing-, the
No-One's-Rose.

Very beautiful, very moving. (*Pause*) But tell me, what things are they that we may not mention?

CELAN (*Dreamily, as if to himself*) When they built the camp at Buchenwald the SS were careful to preserve Goethe's famous, favourite oak tree on the site. You have a great feeling for culture, you Germans.

HEIDEGGER *rises, goes and pours a glass of water for himself, drinks.*

HEIDEGGER Yes, you're right: the water tastes of the deeps. (*Pause*) I was never an anti-Semite, you know. I defy anyone to find a single word anywhere in my writings to indicate otherwise. I see you're sceptical. You're thinking, *A man may harbour in his heart things he will never allow himself to say*. But we're men of the word, you and I. We know the importance of what's said and not said, and the distinction between the two.

CELAN (*Lightly*) Are you a man of your word, Herr Doctor?

Cut to:

ARENDT (*Voice-over, in her early twenties; angrily*) *I know, I know, you never said you would, but I trusted you, and hoped in secret.*

Cut to:

HEIDEGGER If you mean, have I lied, I'll answer you what Nietzsche said: *There are no facts, only interpretations.*

CELAN Six million is a fact. Six million facts. Are they to be denied?

IV

Interior. Marburg University. Day.

It is February 1924. Professor Heidegger's office.

SECRETARY There is a young lady to see you, Herr Professor. Hannah Arendt.

HEIDEGGER Ah, yes. Show her in.

HANNAH ARENDT *enters.*

Fräulein Arendt. Sit, please.

ARENDT Thank you.

HEIDEGGER You wished to see me?

ARENDT I'd like to take your philosophy course.

HEIDEGGER I see. I've looked at your qualifications. I'm impressed. You already have a sound knowledge of Kant, it seems. You've read Kierkegaard, you've read my colleagues Professor Husserl and Karl Jaspers. You're fluent in Greek and Latin. I see no impediment to your becoming my student.

ARENDT I spoke to your colleague Professor Bultmann. I wanted to attend his seminar on the New Testament. I informed him that I am Jewish and said that if I were to take up his classes there must be no anti-Semitic remarks, from anyone, or I would walk out immediately.

HEIDEGGER (*Amused, but impressed*) Did you, now?

ARENDT The Professor was very understanding. (*Pause*) My friend Günther Stern told me of his encounter with your wife.

HEIDEGGER Oh? What encounter was that?

ARENDT It was at your place in the mountains, at . . . ?

HEIDEGGER Todtnauberg.

ARENDT Yes. There was a party, perhaps a house-warming. Everything was friendly and gay, my friend said, until Frau Heidegger asked him if he would like to join the Nazi youth group here in Marburg. When he told her he was a Jew she turned away and would not speak to him again.

HEIDEGGER (*Sighs*) My wife is a very fine woman, but like all of us she has her blind spots. (*Pause*) Where are you living?

ARENDT I have an attic room in Höhe Straße.

HEIDEGGER You live alone?

ARENDT There's a mouse who has befriended me. We keep each other company.

HEIDEGGER Is he your only friend, this mouse?

ARENDT There are some people here at the university I know from my days at home in Königsberg. Otherwise . . .

HEIDEGGER You are a solitary, I think. That's good. (*Pause*) We have a great deal of work ahead of us, my dear Fräulein Arendt. The crisis in German philosophy is acute. On the one hand there are the materialists, the positivists, the empiricists, on the other the neo-Kantians, who are particularly well entrenched here at Marburg. I intend to flush them out, all of them. Our 'third way' will be a return to essentials. Professor Husserl put it succinctly in his injunction: *Back to the things themselves!* We must give up fruitless metaphysical questing and concentrate on the phenomena as they are present to the mind. I'm engaged on a long work aimed at revealing the things that will stand when the deadwood of metaphysics has been cleared away. What's needed above all is a new mode of thought, a passionate thinking.

ARENDT That's the rumour that attracted so many of us here to Marburg, the rumour of a teacher in whom thinking has come alive again.

HEIDEGGER As I say, a great task lies before us. Man has left the house of Being and become lost; we must find the way back inside again. The Greeks, as always, will set us on the right road. I welcome you as a traveller along that road.

ARENDT (*Greatly moved*) Thank you, Herr Professor. I shall try my best to keep pace with you.

V

Interior. Todtnauberg. Day.

On the gramophone the pianist Edwin Fischer is playing the closing bars of a Bach piece. The last note fades into a silence.

HEIDEGGER Edwin Fischer. A very great pianist, a great artist. Do you play, Herr Celan?

CELAN No. A little.

HEIDEGGER But you know your music. Your great poem, 'Deathfugue', is a masterpiece of musical concentration and intensity.

CELAN It has been criticised for those very qualities.

HEIDEGGER Oh?

CELAN I mean for its artistry. People say you can't make art out of the Holocaust, that it's a thing beyond art.

HEIDEGGER Pah!—that's Adorno. What was it he said: *To write poetry after Auschwitz is barbaric*. Typical Bolshevist thinking. You have refuted him.

CELAN Have I? I wonder. I almost met him once, Adorno. It was eight, nine years ago. I was in Sils-Maria with my wife and my little son. Adorno was to be there, but we left and returned to Paris before he arrived. (*To himself*) It wasn't an accident that I left. Why did I avoid him? I don't know.

HEIDEGGER He branded my philosophy as fascist. I don't know which is worse, the characterisation itself, or the shallowness of the mind that formulated it. He attacks me specifically in that book of his that's just come out—what does he call it?

CELAN *The Jargon of Authenticity*.

HEIDEGGER That's it. A total misunderstanding of my thinking and my position. Jargon! Ha! He should know, he and his fellow-travellers in the so-called Frankfurt School.

CELAN And yet in his strictures on modern-day technology he can sound remarkably like you.

HEIDEGGER Nonsense! Adorno is a fool and a coward who sold himself to the Americans, like his pal Herbert Marcuse, my one-time pupil. Don't talk to me of Adorno. His real name is Wiesengrund, did you know that? Why did he change it?

CELAN He took his mother's maiden name.

HEIDEGGER Yes, but why? What was it in the sound of Wiesengrund that he disliked?

CELAN He never denied his Jewish origins.

HEIDEGGER A charlatan! (*Pause*) Forgive me. I'm overwrought. You'll understand, I hope, something of the causes of my bitterness.

Pause.

CELAN I'm not sure, Herr Doctor, why I agreed to come here

today. I suppose, foolishly no doubt, I'd hoped for a word of explanation from you, even, maybe, a word of apology.

HEIDEGGER I've given an interview to *Der Spiegel*, to be published after my death. The interviewer too spoke of an apology. I said to him, *I would be prepared to apologise for my dealings with the Nazis only if Hitler could be brought back from the dead to apologise to me!* Ha!

HEIDEGGER *laughs delightedly.*

CELAN Let me ask you this, then: when did you realise how wrong you had been? You joined the Nazi Party in—what, 1933, at the very beginning?—and I've read that you were still paying your party dues as late as 1945. In your inaugural address as Rector at Freiburg in that fateful year 1933 you praised Hitler and the National Socialists. You introduced Nazi slogans and salutes into university classes—you even gave classes yourself dressed in full Nazi regalia. You removed Husserl's name from the dedication page of *Being and Time* because he was a Jew, and banned him from entering the university—

HEIDEGGER A lie! I never closed the door against him.

CELAN But you let him go adrift, into obscurity and isolation. You made no attempt to contact him, who had been your mentor and your friend. It broke his heart. Do you feel no guilt for these things?

HEIDEGGER Guilt! Guilt! Don't talk to me of guilt. Guilt is the self-abuse of a liberal and degenerate democracy. (*Controls himself*) Listen, let me try to explain to you how it was. I saw in the revolution that the National Socialists brought about in 1933 a chance at last to break out of the mechanisation and soullessness of the modern German state and find again the sustenance of our ancient roots lying deep in the German soil.

CELAN (*Mutters*) Oh, for God's sake—!

HEIDEGGER No, wait. Indulge me in my rhetoric. I'm trying not to exonerate myself but to explain, so that you might understand. This is how I thought, this was the essence of my philosophy. Yes, I recognised the failings of many of the leaders, but I resolved that it was a matter of holding out for long enough, and salvation would come. But the liberals, the educated gentlemen surrounding me, the tenured professors who were content to churn out the same old centuries-old sweaty metaphysics and call it philosophy, they held themselves aloof, above the struggle, until it was too late. If those gentlemen had not been too refined to get involved everything would have been different. But instead, I was entirely alone. And where were the likes of Herr Wiesengrund Adorno? In America, that pigsty, swilling with the Yanks.

Pause.

CELAN (*Mildly*) You know, I too changed my name. My family was called Antschel.

HEIDEGGER Why—why did you give yourself a new name?

CELAN (*Brief laugh*) Do you know, I can't remember.

VI

Interior. Antschel home, Czernowitz. Day.
June 1941. Fritzi Antschel, Paul's MOTHER, *is calling urgently.*

MOTHER Paul! Paul!

PAUL (*Aged twenty-two*) What is it, Mother?

MOTHER Your friends are here.

PAUL (*Sceptical*) What friends?

MOTHER They want you to go with them.

PAUL's footsteps descending stairs.

PAUL Who is it?

MOTHER The Lackner girl, and Immanuel What's-his-name. They want you to come out with them.

PAUL You know I won't go, Mother.

MOTHER What good will it do, your staying home? (*Calls loudly*) Leo! Leo! Come and talk some sense into your son! (*To* PAUL *again, urgently*) Go, Paul. Go with your friends . . .

Her voice fades, replaced with CELAN*'s voice reciting.*

CELAN (*Voice-over, in the university auditorium*)
It's falling, Mother, snow in the Ukraine:
The Saviour's crown a thousand grains of grief . . .

VII

Interior. Todtnauberg. Day.

CELAN June 27th, 1942. A Saturday. In the end I gave in to my mother's urgings, and went with my friends Ruth Lackner and Immanuel Weissglas to Immanuel's house, and stayed there overnight. There was a curfew. Ruth said I would be shot if I tried to go home. In the end Immanuel had to hold me back by force. At least, that's what Immanuel and Ruth and I let ourselves believe. In reality, I was afraid to go, afraid of the curfew, afraid of the dark. I was twenty-two. In the morning when I arrived home it was no longer home: the house was deserted, the front door was sealed, and my mother and father were gone. (*Takes a drink of water from the glass*) It wasn't until years later that I learned what had become of them. They were taken in a transport east to Transnistria, another of those joke countries that have disappeared, like the Bukovina, lost land of my birth. Five days in the heat of high summer, packed in cattle trucks, across the Dniester into the Ukraine. They were put to work at road mending, in gravel pits. My father died from typhus in the autumn of that year, and in the winter my mother was shot, being no longer fit for work.

Cut to:

CELAN (*Voice-over in the university auditorium*)

'. . . Oh for a cloth, child,
to wrap myself when it's flashing with helmets,
when the rosy floe bursts, when snowdrift sifts your father's bones, hooves crushing
the Song of the Cedar . . .
A shawl, just a thin little shawl, so I keep
by my side, now you're learning to weep, this anguish,
this world that will never turn green, my child, for your child!'

Autumn bled all away, Mother, snow burned me through:
I sought out my heart so it might weep, I found—
oh the summer's breath,
it was like you.
Then came my tears. I wove the shawl.

Cut to:

On the gramophone again, very softly, Fischer playing Bach.

HEIDEGGER And you? How did you survive?

CELAN I was drafted into a work battalion organised by the Jewish Council and sent to a labour camp run by the Romanian army and the Germans.

HEIDEGGER What was the work you did there?

CELAN (*Drily*) Shovelling.

HEIDEGGER And?

CELAN And I survived. The Red Army was driving westwards, and in their wake I got back to Czernowitz, God knows how, I remember so little of that time. What I do recall is a dream that I had, over and over—I have it still, sometimes. I'm standing outside one of the camps. It's afternoon, the light is pearl-grey. I can see the lines of workers in the distance, the guards with their guns and their clubs, I can see the smoke from the chimneys. I'm at the perimeter wire, and my father is on the other side. I put my fingers through the wire, and my father clutches them. He's smiling, tenderly, and nodding, not saying anything. I have the bitter sense of being forgiven, I'm not sure for what, exactly, except that it's something great and terrible. Then suddenly there's a guard there, I can see his face, young and fresh. Without warning the guard bites my hand, like a dog, hard, in the flesh, here, at the side, and I pull it back quickly and let go. I let Papi's hand go, and I run away.

Five seconds or so of the piano music.

HEIDEGGER Your people have suffered too much, too much.

CELAN (*Mildly*) 'My' people? Could they not be yours, too?

HEIDEGGER I've said it already, I was never an anti-Semite.

CELAN Being not against is not the same thing as being for.

HEIDEGGER I did what I could. There were students I helped, colleagues I protected.

CELAN You abandoned Husserl. You offered no helping hand to Jaspers.

HEIDEGGER What, like you, as in your dream, you mean? I withdrew my hand and ran away?

VIII

Interior. Heidelberg. Day. 1922.
HEIDEGGER *has arrived for a visit to the home of his fellow philosopher* KARL JASPERS. *Sound of* HEIDEGGER*'s footsteps approaching the Jaspers' house.*

HEIDEGGER (*Voice-over*) *I met him first in—what?—oh, 1922, I think. He invited me to stay at his home in Heidelberg. Those eight summer days we spent together were some of the most important days of my life. I remember Jaspers saying,* We don't know yet ourselves what it is we want—we're both carried along by a knowledge that doesn't yet explicitly exist. *We were making everything over.*

Cut to:

JASPERS Heidegger, my dear fellow! Give me your hand. You're welcome to Heidelberg.

HEIDEGGER Herr Professor.

JASPERS Oh, please, call me Jaspers! By the end of your stay, who knows, you may be calling me Karl. Unless, of course, we should fall to quarrelling!

HEIDEGGER I'm sure we shall not.

JASPERS But come in, come in. Let me take your bag.

They walk inside, JASPERS *shuts the door.*

I hope you'll be comfortable here. I could have put you up at a hotel, but . . .

HEIDEGGER I'm honoured to be invited to your home.

They climb a staircase, walk along a corridor.

Cut to:

HEIDEGGER (*Voice-over*) *I was in the beginning stages of* Being and Time. *Jaspers had already published his* Psychology of Ideologies, *which caused such a stir in the philosophical dovecotes, and which I had reviewed, voluminously, I'm afraid.*

Cut to:

JASPERS I thought it would be good if we could be together a few days, and test and consolidate our comradeship-in-arms.

JASPERS *opens a bedroom door.*

I've put you in here, with a view over the valley.

HEIDEGGER Splendid.

JASPERS My wife is away, so we shall be all to ourselves, apart from the cook and the maid. We've much to talk about.

HEIDEGGER (*With emotion*) We have. The time has come to speak out in face of the professional philosophers, those metaphysical time-servers.

JASPERS Exactly. We won't rant, but discussion will be ruthless!

They both chuckle.

IX

Interior. Jaspers' house, Heidelberg. Night.
JASPERS *and* HEIDEGGER *at dinner.*

HEIDEGGER (*Voice-over*) *What was marvellous was that each of us knew what the other was talking about, even if we didn't yet ourselves understand exactly what it was we were saying.*

Cut to:

. . . For me, the subject of the philosophical question is human existence, which I call *Dasein*—the question, that is, is the question of the character of Being.

JASPERS Have some more wine.

Sound of wine pouring.

(*Tentatively*) When you speak of Being, my dear Martin, I am troubled by the largeness you give to the word. It has, if you'll forgive me, a religious overtone.

HEIDEGGER No doubt it has. Don't forget, I spent a year with the Jesuits, studying for the priesthood, before I realised my true way was the way of philosophy. But God has never ceased to goad me.

JASPERS Then Being, like God, may have an autonomous existence?

HEIDEGGER Certainly. There can be Being without beings. (*Pause*) Or not, as the case may be.

Pause, then HEIDEGGER *suddenly bursts into laughter, in which* JASPERS, *somewhat uncertainly, joins.*

HEIDEGGER (*Voice-over*) *Forgive me, Karl. These things are so new, so difficult. Sometimes it seems to me I'm speaking Chinese. One of the key concepts of the work I'm engaged in is the concept of Care, which the other day I found myself defining as* Ahead-of-itself-already-being-in *bracket* a-world *bracket* as-Being-alongside *bracket* entities-encountered-within-the-world *end bracket, all hyphenated. Of course, the complexity of the language mirrors the complexity of the everyday world in which we find ourselves thrown, which is my subject, but all the same—what must my students make of me?*

Cut to:

X

Interior. Arendt's room, Marburg. Day. 1924.

Beginning of a soft knock on a door, cut off as the door is flung open impetuously.

HEIDEGGER Hannah—

ARENDT Don't speak! Kiss me.

They kiss.

HEIDEGGER Oh, my darling girl—

ARENDT Where were you? You were so long in coming!

HEIDEGGER Elfride wanted me to—to do something, what does it matter. Sometimes I think she suspects.

ARENDT Come, sit with me on the bed.

They sit.

You mustn't worry so. I'll protect you, I'll keep you safe. Your wife will never know, I promise.

HEIDEGGER How can you promise such a thing? Marburg is so small. It's a hothouse in which everyone watches everyone else.

ARENDT Don't you love me?

HEIDEGGER Of course, of course! Of course I love you. But Hannah my darling, I'm twice your age, I'm a married man with two small sons. And you're my student. If the authorities should come to hear that you and I are . . . are . . .

ARENDT *Lovers*, Martin. 'Lovers' is the word you can't bring yourself to say.

HEIDEGGER (*Abject*) Forgive me.

ARENDT *Why do you give me your hand*
Shyly?

HEIDEGGER What?

ARENDT It's a poem I wrote for you.

Why do you give me your hand
Shyly, as if it were a secret?
Are you from such a distant land
That you do not know our wine?

HEIDEGGER Oh, my sweet child, how beautiful, and how sad. (*Pause*) You're wearing your green dress. That's what your fellow students call you, you know: *The Green One*. They're all in love with you. And I am, too. Hopelessly.

ARENDT (*More sadly than bitterly*) Hopelessly, yes.

Pause.

HEIDEGGER Where's your friendly mouse today?

ARENDT I've already fed him. He particularly likes black bread. I call him Heraclitus—

She breaks off and begins to weep.

I'm sorry. I promised myself I wouldn't cry.

HEIDEGGER Come, my green one. Come to my arms.

XI

Interior. Todtnauberg. Day.

HEIDEGGER I sent Hannah Arendt to Jaspers, at Heidelberg, to be his pupil. Years afterwards she said to me how fortunate she was, to have studied with Germany's two greatest philosophers. By then, of course, after the war, he had become Swiss. (*Bitterly sarcastic*) Karl Jaspers, 'the Magician of Basel'! Whereas I was the sorcerer's disgraced apprentice.

CELAN When did you break with him?

Heidegger rises agitatedly from his chair.

Heidegger Come, let's walk. The weather won't last, the sky is darkening.

XII

Exterior. Todtnauberg. Day.

Heidegger and Celan walking along a mountain path.

Heidegger . . . I never broke with him, nor he with me. We drifted asunder.

Celan What happened?

Heidegger It was always difficult. He had been dismissed from his post and prohibited from publishing—he was married to a Jew, you see. He wrote to me, *My soul has fallen silent . . .* By then, a couple of years before the war, I was long out of favour myself with the powers-that-be—(*Laughs bitterly*)—no longer a useful idiot, I suppose. (*Pause*) What is that?

Celan walks back to him from some paces away.

Celan Arnica. Good for bruises. And here's eyebright, *Scrophulariaceae*, a cure for the eyes. (*Soft laugh*) Mother Nature's pharmacopeia.

Heidegger You even know the Latin names—I'm impressed.

Celan *How with this rage shall beauty hold a plea,*
Whose action is no stronger than a flower?
Shakespeare. The Sonnets. Hard to get into German.

They walk on.

Heidegger There was always an edge of rivalry between Jaspers and me, for all the depth of our early friendship.

In 1930 I was offered a professorship at Berlin that he had coveted. It was salt in the wound that I felt secure enough to turn it down and stay in Freiburg instead. In a letter at the time he wrote to me, rather touchingly, that the news of the Berlin offer, which he had read of in the newspaper, had caused him *a gentle pain, but it is of the slightest, now that you have this invitation.*

CELAN Did you see him, after you joined the Party?

HEIDEGGER We corresponded, infrequently. My stance puzzled him. He couldn't grasp the potential there was in the National Socialist revolution. (*Pause*) He wasn't a real philosopher, you see. He came to philosophy through psychiatry, that mumbo-jumbo. He couldn't grasp the purity of my stand, couldn't see, as I did, the chance there was for a true, a radical new beginning. For me, at that time, the only worthwhile philosophy was a philosophy that was of its time, a philosophy, I mean, that was *in control* of its time.

CELAN Do you still think that?

HEIDEGGER No, no. The moment of opportunity was past before people realised. Then came the great betrayal, and the inevitable debacle. Hitler and his toadies, they were unworthy of us. Now everything is lost and the great evil is spreading wider and wider around us, to the east and to the west, and the Moloch of technology is devouring us. Only a god could save us now.

CELAN You tried appealing to a god and he betrayed you, as you say.

HEIDEGGER He was a false god.

A rumble of thunder in the distance.

CELAN Or an idol?

HEIDEGGER There's a storm coming, we should go back.

They turn and walk away along the mountain track.

Cut to:

XIII

Interior. Hotel. Day. Mid-1920s.

A hotel in an anonymous German town. Sound of thunder and heavy rain. HEIDEGGER *enters, walks to the reception desk.*

HEIDEGGER (*Uncomfortably*) Has Frau Schmidt arrived?

RECEPTIONIST Yes, sir, she arrived an hour ago. Number 11, first floor.

HEIDEGGER Thank you.

He walks away.

RECEPTIONIST (*Insinuatingly*) Will you be requiring anything, sir? Drinks, perhaps?

HEIDEGGER (*Brusquely*) No, thank you.

He climbs the stairs, walks along a corridor, knocks softly.

(*A loud whisper*) Hannah? It's me.

The door opens, he enters, shuts the door behind him.

What's wrong?

ARENDT (*Dully*) Nothing is wrong. You're late again.

HEIDEGGER Yes, I'm sorry. The rain . . . my car . . .

ARENDT Oh, please, no more excuses.

HEIDEGGER You're angry with me. (*He embraces her*) Come, my green girl, don't be angry.

ARENDT I can't continue like this, meeting in secret, in seedy hotels in anonymous towns. It's killing me.

HEIDEGGER What can I do? Elfride—

ARENDT Stop, don't speak that name. I've asked you before.

HEIDEGGER I'm sorry. (*Pause*) I can't abandon her. I never—

ARENDT (*Voice-over as in Scene III*) *I know, I know, you never said you would, but I trusted you, and hoped in secret.*

Pause. HEIDEGGER *silent.* ARENDT *sighs, strikes a match to light a cigarette.*

Well? How goes the great work?

HEIDEGGER I've finished the first part. It's to be published soon. The title is *Being and Time*.

ARENDT You'll have a great success.

Pause.

HEIDEGGER You've been my muse, Hannah. I couldn't have done it without you.

ARENDT Will you put my name in it?

HEIDEGGER I've dedicated it to Husserl, 'in friendship and admiration'.

ARENDT So: the muse must remain silent. Silent and hidden.

XIV

Exterior/interior. Todtnauberg. Day.

Thunder and sound of rain. HEIDEGGER *and* CELAN *returning from their walk, running into the house.*

HEIDEGGER Ach! Look at us, we're soaked.

CELAN It's nothing.

HEIDEGGER Now I really must find that schnapps.

He opens various cupboard doors.

Aha! Here we are.

Sound of glasses being produced, of the schnapps being poured.

There. Drink. It'll warm you.

CELAN Thank you.

They drink.

HEIDEGGER So: what have you salvaged from the storm?

CELAN There's wild orchid, and Turk's cap, eyebright, some pinks—*Dianthus superbus*—and arnica.

HEIDEGGER For your bruises.

CELAN I'll take them back with me, to Paris.

HEIDEGGER Won't they wither?

CELAN Yes. But that's all right. (*Pause*) My wife and I, we lost our first-born within days of his birth. François, he was called. Coincidence: it was the feast day of St Francis, the day he died. We went to Assisi, on a sort of pilgrimage, I suppose, the Jew and his Catholic wife and the ghost of their dead son. A strange town. Tourist stalls selling weapons and implements of torture made from plastic—crossbows, maces, thumbscrews—very lifelike. A kind of collective joke, do you think, a mocking riposte to the legend of the gentle saint?

CELAN (*Voice-over, in university auditorium*)

Brightness that sheds no comfort, brightness.
The dead—they still go begging, Francis.

XV

Interior. Todtnauberg. Day.
A little later. HEIDEGGER *is standing in the open doorway.*
Sound of rain abating, and a last, distant roll of thunder.

HEIDEGGER It's over. It'll be fine again for your drive back down to the valley.

CELAN I must get ready. Professor Baumann will be here, and I need to pack for the train.

HEIDEGGER I tried to see him, Jaspers, afterwards. It was 1950, and he was making his triumphant way down the Rhine to lecture in his old place in Heidelberg. I said I would come to the railway station as his train was passing through, if only that we might shake hands through the window.

Cut to:

XVI

Exterior. Railway station. Day.
Sounds of a busy station. In the foreground, HEIDEGGER*'s footsteps as he slowly paces the platform.*

HEIDEGGER (*Voice-over*) *He'd already taken his revenge on me, although I didn't know it at the time. In December 1945, when everything was terrible, I wrote asking him for his intervention in my attempt to be reinstated in the Faculty of Philosophy at Freiburg. He intervened, all right, with a long letter to one of the members of the commission the Faculty had set up to examine my case, in which among other pretty things he called me an 'earnest nihilist' and a 'mystagogue-cum-sorcerer'.*

During the following, a train pulls slowly into the station, coming nearer and nearer, more and more loudly.

JASPERS (*Voice-over*) *Heidegger's mode of thinking, which seems to me to be fundamentally unfree, dictatorial and uncommunicative, would have a very damaging effect on students at the present time. And the mode of thinking itself I believe is more important than the actual content of political judgements, whose aggressiveness can easily be channelled in other directions. Until such time as a genuine rebirth takes place within him, and is seen to be at work in him, I think it would be quite wrong to turn such a teacher loose on the young people of today, who are psychologically extremely vulnerable. First of all the young must be taught to think for themselves.*

The train halts with a long, agonised screech of brakes. HEIDEGGER*'s footsteps approach, as he walks along by the windows looking for Jaspers.*

HEIDEGGER (*To* PORTER) This is the Basel train, yes?

PORTER Yes, sir.

HEIDEGGER You're sure?

PORTER It's the Basel train, all right.

HEIDEGGER*'s heavy, slow footsteps as he walks away.*

HEIDEGGER (*Voice-over*) *He recommended I be given a pension, but not a teaching post.* (*Pause*) *He quoted Max Weber:* Children who stick their fingers into the wheel of world history are going to get them broken.

XVII

Interior. Todtnauberg. Day.

CELAN You could have gone to him. Surely he wouldn't have refused to see you.

HEIDEGGER I couldn't. I wrote to him, I said the reason I had not set foot in his house again after 1933 was that I was simply too ashamed. (*Suddenly angry*) There, is that enough for you? I was ashamed!

CELAN Shame is not guilt. One can be ashamed of an action and still believe it to have been a right action.

HEIDEGGER You're relentless, Celan.

CELAN It's a quality we have, we Jews.

HEIDEGGER I could declare my guilt, I could apologise to the world, and I would be accepted back with open arms into the brotherhood of man—but it would be a lie. I joined the National Socialist Party because I believed it was going to save us. I quickly saw my mistake—I resigned as Rector at Freiburg after only a year in the post—but it was the leaders and not the politics that were wrong. How can I feel guilt for taking what I thought was the right course? A mistake is not something one feels guilt for. Shame, perhaps, but not guilt.

CELAN You supped with the devil. It was a bitter feast.

XVIII

Interior. Hotel. Day. Freiburg, 1950.

HANNAH ARENDT, *now living in America, is paying her first visit to post-war Germany. She is in the hotel dining room.*

WAITER Frau Arendt? There is a gentleman to see you.

ARENDT Yes. Show him here to the table, please.

HEIDEGGER *approaches.*

HEIDEGGER (*With deep emotion*) My dear Hannah.

ARENDT Martin. Thank you for coming.

HEIDEGGER How would I not? When I got your note, saying you were here . . .

ARENDT Sit, please. Will you take something? A coffee?

HEIDEGGER No, nothing, thank you. Hannah, I . . .

Pause.

ARENDT How strange, meeting like this. It's seventeen years and a world war since we saw each other last.

HEIDEGGER You've been travelling?

ARENDT Yes. I wanted to see Germany for myself, the devastation. I'm shocked.

HEIDEGGER Yes, we're in a sorry state.

ARENDT No, Martin—what shocks me is the attitude of the people, their self-pity, their refusal to confront honestly what has happened to them, and the reasons for it. Everywhere I encounter either apathy or a ridiculous devotion to hard work—as if you can work yourselves out of your crimes. The intellectuals are as bad as the common people. The same tired notions, a clinging to old, worn-out ideas. You've lost yourselves, Martin. You've given up your soul. Mephistopheles has claimed his side of the bargain.

HEIDEGGER You don't know what it was like, Hannah. You weren't here.

Pause.

ARENDT So: you too.

HEIDEGGER I?

ARENDT Self-pitying, self-justifying—oh, yes, I can see it in your eye, in your hangdog look.

HEIDEGGER I apologise for the way I treated you. You were a girl, and I betrayed your trust.

ARENDT For God's sake, Martin, I don't care about any of that. It's twenty-five years ago. What matters is what you did afterwards, the beasts you threw in your lot with. How could you?

HEIDEGGER You believed as strongly as I did that there must be a change, that the rot must be cleared away and a new beginning made. We needed saving.

ARENDT And you thought Hitler would be Germany's saviour. (*Cold laugh*) I tell people who attack you, *Oh, he was not a Nazi, he was too primitive for that, he lived in his own, primordial world of thought.* But I'm not sure I believe it, even as I'm saying it.

HEIDEGGER I'm touched, that you defend me.

ARENDT I can think of no one more in need of defending.

XIX

Exterior. Freiburg. Day.

ARENDT *and* HEIDEGGER *are walking in a park. Birdsong, sounds of children at play.*

ARENDT I went to Basel.

HEIDEGGER You saw Jaspers?

ARENDT Yes. I saw him, and Gertrud. Oh, Martin, how could you have abandoned him as you did? Your treatment of Husserl, vile as it was, I can at least partly understand—he was your mentor, and I know how you hate having to acknowledge anyone's help or influence. But Jaspers—Jaspers loved you.

HEIDEGGER I've written to him.

ARENDT Yes, he showed me your letters. Don't scowl, so, Martin. We were two friends talking of a third.

HEIDEGGER I wrote, greeting him in the name of Being.

ARENDT (*Sardonic*) Yes, you were your usual grand and elevated self.

HEIDEGGER I wrote as I saw fit. He replied with nothing but circumspection.

ARENDT (*Laughs*) What did you expect? The Nazis drove him out of the academy, into poverty and invisibility. He and Gertrud expected daily to be taken. They carried cyanide capsules with them at all times. And you offered him not a word of comfort or support. Not a word.

HEIDEGGER That's what everyone asks of me, demands of me—a word. I will not speak it.

Pause.

ARENDT Jaspers and I were in his study, and he said to me, *Poor Heidegger, we sit here now, the two best friends he has, and see right through him.*

XX

Exterior. Freiburg. Day.
A little later, still in the park.

ARENDT I've finished my book. It owes everything to those earliest days in Marburg, to you, and what you were then. I wanted to dedicate it to you, but how could I?

HEIDEGGER Of course, I understand. I'm touched.

ARENDT I was faithful to you and unfaithful, and both were aspects of the love I bore you.

HEIDEGGER (*Emotional*) Hannah . . .

Pause.

ARENDT (*Briskly*) Anyway, I'll send you a copy. You probably won't read it—

HEIDEGGER Of course I will! Why would I not?

ARENDT You probably won't read it, so I'll tell you. I don't espouse your philosophy. There are many echoes of you in the book, but there are denials as well.

HEIDEGGER Such as?

ARENDT Yours is a philosophy of the individual, mine of plurality.

HEIDEGGER I see. Your years in America have had their effect.

ARENDT Yes, they have. I believe it's not the authenticity of the individual but the virtuosity of acting together with others that brings into the world the openness that you've always sought.

HEIDEGGER So, you've thrown your lot in with the They, in whose world everyone is the Other, and no one is himself.

ARENDT The Greeks, your Greeks, knew that the world we have in common is necessarily viewed from an infinity of standpoints, and they learned to understand it in that way. You've turned your back on them.

HEIDEGGER This is the chatter of the poor deluded ones in Plato's cave.

ARENDT The world becomes inhuman without the continual talk in it of humans. That's what you never understood, Martin. And it's your tragedy.

Pause.

HEIDEGGER I told my wife about you.

ARENDT (*Astonished*) You did?

HEIDEGGER When I got your note today, asking me to come to the hotel, I told her. I said you had been the passion of my life.

ARENDT Was that wise?

HEIDEGGER About some things I have to be honest.

ARENDT But there are things more important to admit to.

HEIDEGGER There aren't, not for me.

ARENDT Poor woman, to hear such a thing at this late stage of her life. (*Pause*) You know I always despised her. I saw your marriage as an alliance between the mob and the elite.

HEIDEGGER She supported me, cared for me, stood by me. And now I've wounded her, down to the bone

XXI

Interior. Todtnauberg. Day.

HEIDEGGER *and* CELAN *in the hut.*

HEIDEGGER I asked her to come to the house. I wanted her to meet Elfride again, under the new dispensation, the new openness.

CELAN And did she come?

HEIDEGGER Yes. Frightful scene. Rancour, bitterness, anti-Semitic taunts. My wife, poor woman, was insane with jealousy, and hating herself for it. Yet when Hannah was leaving they embraced. (*Pause*) The subject of all my philosophising is the strangeness of human existence. You know that wonderful line of Grabbe's, *Only once in the world, and of all things as a plumber in Detmold!* The great systematisers, the Kants and the Hegels, tried to unstrange this strangeness by hiding it inside their cavernous and empty systems, which is why I despise them. The life of ordinary men in their ordinary days, that's what I sought to illuminate and know, and to give this illumination and this knowledge back to men so they might begin to live again in light and truth. We're thrown into the world naked, under a pitiless sky. Only by seizing our fate, and acting in the full acceptance of our predicament, can we be said to live authentically.

CELAN But why the Nazis? Why their system?

HEIDEGGER Because of their tragic affirmation of death! Death is the salient fact of human existence. Death stands beside the midwife and takes the infant from her hands, saying, *Come with me, for I am the giver of life.* Everything we are and do takes its savour from the knowledge of death. That's our tragedy, and our glory. Existence—*Dasein—being there*—is a process, and that process is Time, and Time for each one of us has an end. Death leads us into the wilderness of the future, our only guide.

Cut to:

The university auditorium, CELAN *reading.*

CELAN ... *der Tod ist ein Meister aus Deutschland* ...

Cut to:

Sound of a motor car drawing to a stop outside the hut.

HEIDEGGER It's Baumann. Our time is up, Herr Celan. The prison visit is at an end.

CELAN The key to the cell door is in your own hand.

The car horn sounds outside. They rise, CELAN *prepares to leave.*

HEIDEGGER Will you sign my visitors' book?

CELAN Of course.

Sound of the book opening, of CELAN *writing, closing the book.*

Goodbye, Herr Doctor. I shall remember this day.

HEIDEGGER As will I.

The door opens. CELAN *exits.*

(*From the doorway*) Safe journey! (*He shuts the door, opens the visitors' book*) What did he write? *Into the hut-book, looking towards the well-star, with hope for a coming word in the heart. On July 25th, 1967. Paul Celan.*

Cut to:

CELAN, *alone, reading aloud.*

CELAN *Arnica, Eyebright, the*
drink from the well with the
star-die on top,

in the
hut,

into the book
—whose name did it take in
before mine?—
the line written into
this book about
a hope, today,
for a thinker's
(un-
delayed coming)
word
in the heart . . .

Fischer playing Bach. Fade.

(*Conversation in the Mountains*, 2006)

A Blest World

ESSAYS, LECTURES AND REVIEWS

1990–2010

Survivors of Joyce

I begin with a quotation from Nietzsche:

> Every great phenomenon is succeeded by degeneration, especially in the domain of art. The example of greatness incites all vainer natures to extreme imitation or attempts to outdo; in addition to which, all great talents have the fatal property of suppressing many weaker shoots and forces, and as it were laying nature waste all around them. The most fortunate thing that can happen in the evolution of an art is that several geniuses appear together and keep one another in bounds; in the course of this struggle the weaker and tenderer natures too will usually be granted light and air.

The figure of Joyce towers behind us, a great looming Easter Island effigy of the Father. In the old days it was considered fitting that children should honour the parent, and I could, indeed, spend the next fifteen or twenty minutes paying tribute to that stone Nobodaddy at my shoulder. But when I think of Joyce I am split in two. To one side there falls the reader, kneeling speechless in filial admiration, and love; to the other side, however, the writer stands, gnawing his knuckles, not a son, but a survivor.

There are artists whom one can use, from whom one can learn one's trade. I am thinking of, let us say, Catullus, Piero della Francesca, Beethoven, Henry James; they are the strugglers, the self-conscious ones, the *sentimental*, in Schiller's sense of the word.

Their work is to some extent exoskeletal, in that one can see, or at least glimpse here and there on the surface, the processes by which the work was produced. Such glimpses are invaluable for the apprentice. This is how we learn—and not the least part of the lesson is the manner by which the struggle, the visible labour, is welded into the work, to become another *aspect* of the work, so that form is constantly *trans*formed into content. This generative and transfiguring process is a large part of the greatness of the *Carmine Catulli*, of Piero's frescoes, of the String Quartet Opus 131, of *The Golden Bowl*.

And then, there are the artists who are of no use to the tyro, from whom one learns nothing. Let us pick another four at random: Virgil, Vermeer, Mozart, James Joyce. In the work of artists such as these, the methods of production are well-nigh invisible, buried so deeply inside the work that we cannot get at them without dismantling the parts, as a schoolboy with a Swiss watch. The greatness, or part of the greatness, of an *Aeneid*, of a *View of Delft*, of a *Don Giovanni*, of a *Ulysses*, rests in the fact that they are, in an essential way, *closed*. By this I do not mean to say that these works of art are difficult, or obscure—what could be more limpid than the light that hovers over Delft?—but that they are *mysterious at their core*. There is something uncanny about such art. It does not seem to have been produced by human hands, but to have created itself out of nothing by some secret, unknowable means. And so the work stands before us, light and lightsome, glossy as an apple, full of chat—and utterly impenetrable. Such art is not to be known except in its surface—but of course, as we know, the surface of a work of art can be as deep as the deepest depths.

I think, myself, that the truly great works of art, the ones before which we fall silent, and simply stand and gape, all have this quality of reticence, of being somehow turned away from us, gazing off, like nature itself, into another sphere of things, another reality. I want to emphasise this. For the most part we think the 'best', the most 'successful' art is that which is most accommodating to us, which exists on the same scale as ours, which *gives* itself to us: 'Shatter me, Music!' Rilke cries, but Music hears him not, Music is too busy singing to itself. The gaze which great art gives us back is utterly vacant; the sirens are silent.

I am conscious that, to many, Joyce will seem more aptly set among my first quartet of masters than my second. Who, you will say, could have been more self-conscious, more one of Schiller's sentimentalists, than he? And it will be no good my pointing out that Joyce himself held that the artist should stand disengaged from his art, off in the background somewhere, paring his nails—no one pays much attention any more to *that* piece of piety. And further, you will say, where in literature can the *process* have been more a part of the work itself than in *Portrait*, or *Ulysses*, or *Finnegans Wake*?

For the most part, of course, I must bow to these objections. Nothing is simple. But I would invite you to consider the evidence. What is it in *Ulysses*, in *Finnegans Wake* (I leave aside the problematical *Portrait*) that compels our awed attention? Is it, in the former, the sense of 'real life' that is conveyed through Bloom and Stephen and Molly and the myriad other characters, so that we seem to look at ourselves, as it were, through the wrong end of a telescope, dainty, loveable, and wonderfully clear—is this what brings us back, over and over, to *Ulysses*? Permit me, once again, to quote Nietzsche, at somewhat more length this time:

> *Created people*.—When we say the dramatist (and the artist in general) actually *creates* characters, this is a nice piece of deception and exaggeration in the existence and dissemination of which art celebrates one of its unintentional and as it were superfluous triumphs. In reality we understand

very little of an actual living person and generalise very superficially when we attribute to him this or that character: well, the poet adopts the same *very imperfect* posture towards man as we do, in that his sketches of men are just as *superficial* as is our knowledge of men. There is much illusion involved in these created characters of the artists; they are in no way living products of nature, but, like painted people, a little too thin, they cannot endure inspection from close to. And if one should even venture to say that the character of the ordinary living man is often self-contradictory and that created by the dramatist the ideal that hovered dimly before the eye of nature, this would be quite wrong. An actual human being is something altogether *necessary* (even in those so-called contradictions), but we do not always recognise this necessity. The invented human being, the phantasm, desires to signify something necessary, but only in the eyes of those who comprehend even an actual human being only in a crude, unnatural simplification: so that a couple of striking, often repeated characteristics, with a great deal of light on them and a great deal of shadow and twilight around them, suffice to meet all their demands. They are thus quite ready to treat phantasms as actual, necessary human beings because they are accustomed when dealing with actual human beings to take a phantasm, a silhouette, an arbitrary abridgment for the whole.—That the painter and the sculptor, of all people, give expression to the 'idea' of the human being is mere fantasising and sense-deception: one is being tyrannised over by the eye when one says such a thing, since this sees even of the human body only the surface, the skin; the inner body, however, is just as much part of the idea. Plastic art wants to make characters visible on the outside;

> the art of speech employs the word to the same end, it delineates the character in sounds. Art begins from the natural *ignorance* of mankind as too his interior (both bodily and as regards character): it does not exist for physicists or philosophers.

So much for the people in *Ulysses*.

• • •

In *Finnegans Wake*, is it the element of the crossword puzzle that attracts us? Much has been made of the mephistophelian pact between Joyce's work and academe, and it is true that without the attentions of the academics, much in Joyce would have gone unexplained. (The corollary of this is that without the surety of an academic posterity, Joyce might have done things differently; but that is another lecture). What the burners of midnight oil glean from the *Wake*, however, are mere *facts*. They are *interesting* facts, they are sometimes *beautiful* facts, but still, they are only facts. Edmund Wilson shrewdly pointed out that, in the case of *The Waste Land*, the more widely we read in other works, the more references we spot, and the more references we spot, the more *The Waste Land* diminishes. Something the same is true of *Finnegans Wake*. The more of it we decipher, the more we 'use it up'. Of course, it is not serious diminishment; but anyone who has ever completed a crossword knows that curious, ashen sense of futility, of nausea, almost, that comes along with the 'solution'.

I hasten to add that I am not suggesting that understanding of a work of art makes one feel sick: I do believe, however, that what we come to know about a work is simply that: *a knowing about*, a peripheral knowledge. Knowing a thing, however intimately, however deeply, is not always the same as *understanding* it. We are back to the boy with the dismantled Swiss watch.

We are asking: what is it fascinates us about *Ulysses* and *Finnegans Wake*?—what quality is it in such works that prompts us to set them up as canonical? Wallace Stevens believed, or professed to believe, that in our post-religious age, poetry could be the supreme, sustaining fiction without which Man would perish. Works such as *The Waste Land* and *Ulysses* have taken on, or have been conferred with, a biblical quality: they have become the Psalms, they have become the Book. Why? What constitutes the quality of the numinous in them? What is that speaks to our need for texts, for Holy Writ?

I believe it is the quality of *closure*.

• • •

To repeat: great art, I am convinced, does not 'reveal' itself to us, does not open outward to our needs; on the contrary, it is great precisely because it is closed against us. This, I realise, is not a comfortable formulation. Art, as I have said, is supposed to be accommodating, 'all-embracing', as one might say. It is supposed to let us know things—morals, psychology, the world of nature, ourselves. I don't believe this is so—or, I should say, I believe the matter is more complicated, more circuitous than we ordinarily imagine. Far from allowing us to know things with any immediacy, art, I believe, *makes things strange*. This it does by illuminating things, literally: the making of art is a process in which the artist concentrates on the object with such force, with such ferocity of attention, that the object takes on an unearthly—no, an *earthly* glow. As Rilke has it:

> Perhaps we are *here* only to say: house, bridge, fountain, gate, jug, fruit-tree, window—at most: column, tower . . . but to *say*, that is, oh, to say them *more* intensely than the things themselves ever dreamed of existing.

And later, in the same Elegy:

> And these things, that live by perishing, know you are praising them; fleeting, they look to us for deliverance: us, the most fleeting of all. They want us to change them, utterly, in our invisible heart, within—oh, endlessly—within us. Whoever we may be at last.
>
> Earth, isn't this what you want: to arise within us, *invisible*? Is it not your dream to be wholly invisible someday?—O Earth, invisible!

This is not such a mystical, not such a high-falutin process as it may seem, this interiorisation of things, this taking into us of the world, of all that stuff out there which is not ourselves. It happens all the time, continuously, in art. And its result is a different order of understanding, which *allows* the thing its thereness, its outsideness, its absolute otherness. Such understanding is wholly individualistic, yet profoundly democratic. Every thing has its own place, its own space, which it inhabits utterly.

This process of incorporation, I hold, is a process of *style*. Has North America ever existed so intensely—if a great deal more economically—as it does in the pages of *Lolita*? Has the light of day ever fallen on a patch of wall with such heartbreaking tenderness as it does in certain pictures by Vermeer? Has Dublin ever *spoken* so vividly as it does in *Ulysses*, in the *Wake*? And yet, from such works, what do we *know*, that we have not always known? Nothing, except style. Here is Henry James:

> In literature we move through a blest world in which we know nothing except by style, but in which also everything is saved by it.

Style. Does Joyce *have* a style?—does he have *a* style, as distinct from styles, in the plural? Eliot thought not (and Eliot was always good when it came to Joyce, mainly, I think, because the poet did not quite trust the novelist, and was definitely not in awe of him, as so many of us are). Certainly there *had been* a style, or the makings of one, in *Dubliners* and *Portrait* and the first forty or fifty pages of *Ulysses*. It was a curious, ambiguous style—how, for instance, are we to take the closing pages of *Portrait*, which read like the gushing of a poetic adolescent: is it irony, or not? It was a style which Joyce thought better of—or worse, depending on your opinion of the rest of *Ulysses*, and the *Wake*. It is one of the great mysteries of Modernism, this transformation of a Nineties aesthete into the Rabelaisian author of *Ulysses* and the *Wake*. I speak, of course, not of the transformation of a soul, but of a style. The movement is, surprisingly, a movement not from impurity to purity, but vice versa; it is a movement from Flaubert to Balzac, contrasted here by Proust:

> In Flaubert's style, every aspect of reality is converted into a similar substance, a vast surface glistening monotonously. No impurities remain. Every surface has become reflective. Everything is depicted there, but by a process of reflection, without altering its homogeneous nature. All that was different has been converted and absorbed. In Balzac, on the other hand, exist side by side all the undigested, as yet unconverted elements of a future style which is not yet in existence.

'. . . a future style which is not yet in existence': could there be a better characterisation of the methods of the *Wake*?

• • •

It is, I believe, the absence of, or the concealment of, a unified, recognisable style, that gives to Joyce's work its peculiar, impregnable, *frightening* authority. He is one of those writers . . . or should I say, *he is a writer* (for he is probably unique) whose work is utterly free of solecisms, of errors of judgement, of mistakes: for such things, should they seem to appear, are immediately transformed, by a sort of continuous chain reaction, into *inventions*. I happen to think that a formulation such as 'The heaventree of stars hung with humid nightblue fruit' is pretty ghastly, yet when one comes across it in its context, the surprise of it, the possible-humour of it, the *ambiguity* of it, leaves one breathless.

Joyce was never silent, but he was certainly cunning. He was the supreme escape-artist, a Houdini of the word, who used every possible rhetorical device in order to bury himself—the living, breathing self—so deep inside the work that when we knock we get back only the faintest response, and even that may be, for all we know, merely an echo of our knuckles on the wood. Under the guise of an all-accepting humanism, Joyce created an impenetrable fortress, an edifice like that in which Maggie Verver finds herself immured in *The Golden Bowl*:

> . . . it had reared itself there like some strange, tall tower of ivory, or perhaps rather some wonderful, beautiful, but outlandish pagoda, a structure plated with hard, bright porcelain, coloured and figured and adorned, at the overhanging eaves, with silver bells that tinkled, ever so charmingly, when stirred by chance airs.

One might pause over the ever so charming silver bells, but the hard, bright porcelain, that's the stuff, all right.

Do not mistake me; I am not criticising. I believe the trick that Joyce pulled in creating at least two great, closed works of art out of an aesthetic that *seemed* to descend from the ethereal to the earthly, is the true mark of his genius. As a reader, I can only applaud. As a writer, I feel, to paraphrase Simon Dedalus, that I have been left where Jesus left the Jews. Nor is *this* a criticism: it's no business of Joyce to haul the rest of us on to the raft, nor even to give us a peek inside the pagoda. It's just that it is cold out here, and, half the time, it feels like drowning.

('Survivors of Joyce', 1990)

The Personae of Summer

I do not think I am a novelist. As a writer I have little or no interest in character, plot, motivation, manners, politics, morality, social issues. The word *psychology* when it is applied to art makes me want to reach for my revolver. To those of you who at this point are about to stop reading, let me hasten to say that this is not an anti-humanist attitude I am striking, nor even, really, a postmodernist one. I do believe that the art of fiction does deal with the world, that world which in our arrogance we call 'ordinary', but that it deals with it in very special and specialised ways. I am enough of a deconstructionist to acknowledge that the novelist's intentions for his novel may in the end not count for as much as he imagined or desired that they would. Frequently it happens that a novel will live on into posterity—a rare phenomenon, I grant—because of qualities which for the author were secondary, or of which at the time of writing perhaps he was not even aware. In saying this, however, I do not mean to agree with those critics—and they are by no means only the most advanced ones: read the fiction reviews in the Sunday supplements—who look on the novelist as a dead hand which performs a kind of automatic writing. Novelists themselves contribute to this misconception of what they do and how they do it. When I hear a writer talking earnestly of how the characters in his latest book 'took over the action' I am inclined to laugh (or, if I am in a good mood, acknowledge a colleague doing his best to get through yet another interview). Fictional characters are made of words, not flesh; they do not have free will, they do not exercise volition. They are easily born, and as easily killed off. They have their flickering lives, and die on cue, for us, giving up their little paragraph of pathos. They are at once less and more than what they seem.

The writers I most admire are the ones who have abandoned the pretence of realism, who have ceased to try to speak about things in favour of speaking the things themselves, such as Beckett, or Thomas Bernhard, or those who took the old forms and worked a revolution from within, such as Henry James, or, well, Henry James. The wrought and polished object itself, an astonishment standing in the world—a jar in Tennessee!—that is what interests me. The world and being in it are such a mystery that the artist stands before it in a trance of bafflement, like an idiot at High Mass. In confrontation with the total enigma, all that the artist can do, it seems to me, is set up analogues, parallel microcosms, tiny models of the huge original with which the mind may play in earnest. I am speaking of a pictured world, not a world anatomised. Nietzsche was the first to recognise that the true depth of a thing is in its surface. Art is shallow, and therein lie its deeps. The face is all, and, in front of the face, the mask.

By what means, then, does fiction *get at* the world? Not by engagement, I am convinced, but precisely by disengagement, by adopting a posture of bland innocence, standing back with empty palms on show. Listen, the writer says, listen—here is the music of things as they are, changed upon the blue guitar. The subject matter hardly matters. Flaubert is wondered at and excoriated in equal measure for his stated wish to write a book that would be *about nothing*, but he was merely acknowledging the fact, unpalatable to many, that all art aspires to the condition of pure style. 'In literature,' says Henry James, 'we move through a blest world in which we know nothing except by style, but in which also everything is saved by it.' And here is Theodor Adorno, certainly no proponent of the doctrine of art for art's sake:

> The unresolved antagonisms of reality reappear in art in the guise of immanent problems of artistic form. This, and not the deliberate injection of objective moments or social content, defines art's relation to society.

I believe, with Hermann Broch, that art is, or should be, a mode of objective knowledge of the world, not an expression of the subjective world. As Kafka momentously said, the artist is the man who has nothing to say.

• • •

First comes, for me, the shape. Before I put down even a note for a novel, there exists in my mind, or just outside it somewhere, a figure, not geometrical, exactly, not like something out of Euclid, more a sort of self-sustaining tension in space, tangible yet wholly imaginary, which represents, which in some sense *is*, the completed thing. The task is to bring this figure out of the space of the potential and into the world, where it will be manifest yet hidden, like the skeleton beneath the skin.

At an essential level, therefore, the work of art is for me no more and no less than the solution—partial, always, of course—to a technical problem. The problem is that of placing certain figures on a certain ground so that they shall seem to move, and breathe, and have their lives. How is it to be done? Will it seem paradoxical, in the light of what I have said so far, if I now insist that the only way to portray life in art is to be as lifelike as possible? All that the writer has to work with is human being, his own and that of the mysterious others, what little he can know of it, of them. Even the most abstract art is grounded in the mundane, composed, like us, of Eros and of dust. Life will keep breaking in. However, 'life' here means life in its *appearance*, that is, both in the way it looks, and in the way it makes itself manifest in the world. The phenomenological breath that wafts from that sentence makes me think that the word I should be using in this context is not *life*, but *being*, or even—I whisper it—Being.

The novel, since it is an organic growth, generates, or should, its own rules, which will govern every smallest ramification of its form and content. The novel grows by a process of genetic building, filling itself out, matching itself to its vision of itself, as a tree grows, becoming a tree by becoming a tree. To break the rules of generation is to break the book. Of course, the novelist can make mistakes, and will, since he is human. Randall Jarrell defined the novel as an extended work of prose fiction which has something wrong with it. There are critics who contend that the being wrong—that is, being defective in form, loose in content, ragged in style—is a large part of the novel's strength, that its imperfections make it sturdy and vigorous and lifelike. As Frank Kermode has pointed out, we seek in art a completedness, a 'sense of an ending', not available to us in life (who remembers his own birth, who will know his own death?—all we have is the drifting moment), and, yes, I suppose the truest art will be that which refuses us the neatness of the finished thing. But there is wrong and wrong (there is true and true, also, but that is another matter). Human endeavour can always be counted on for inbuilt flaws, for infelicities of tone and clumsiness of execution. It is when the rules, the deep grammar, of the work of art are bent or broken that the internal structure crumbles. In the novel, such transgressions are more easily detected, I think, than in other forms of art, precisely because the novel is the most lifelike form there is.

Is it not a curious thing, this true-to-lifeness that fiction manages? Albert Einstein was always fascinated, and made not a little uneasy, by the weird way in which physical reality conforms so neatly to the manmade discipline of mathematics. It is hardly less strange that a progression of dark marks on a light surface should cause an eerily persuasive version of the quotidian world to blossom in the brain of the reader sitting under the lamplight with his book, forgetful of himself and of his surroundings. What magic is it that makes us think we are sailing on the Pequod, that we are a little in love with Isabel Archer, that we see the streets of Dublin on a summer day in 1904 through the eyes of Leopold Bloom? How is it that a made-up story should seem to utter that which Wallace Stevens's Large Red Man reads aloud out of the purple tabulae, 'The outlines of being and its expressings, the syllables of its law'? Fiction is a kind of infinitesimal calculus, approaching nearer and ever nearer to life itself and yet never really having anything of real life in it at all, except the fictionist's obsessive and doomed determination to *get it right* (if that really is a human desideratum). Or am I giving too much weight to the merely real?

This is Wallace Stevens again:

from 'Credences of Summer'

The personae of summer play the characters
Of an inhuman author, who meditates
With the gold bugs, in blue meadows, late at night.
He does not hear his characters talk. He sees
Them mottled, in the moodiest costumes,

Of blue and yellow, sky and sun, belted
And knotted, sashed and seamed, half pales of red,
Half pales of green, appropriate habit for
The huge decorum, the manner of the time,
Part of the mottled mood of summer's whole,

In which the characters speak because they want
To speak, the fat, the roseate characters,
Free, for a moment, from malice and sudden cry,

Complete in a completed scene, speaking
Their parts as in a youthful happiness.

As always with Stevens, I am not sure that I know what it is he is talking about here, but I find the passage strangely affecting, and hear in it a description of sorts of what it is I do when I come to write fiction. The fat, the roseate characters move as in a moving scene, in this little glass untouchable theatre of the mind. If they are lifelike it is because so much of life is missing from them and their doings, the dross which is true life itself thrown out in obedience to the laws of a necessary economy. Fledgling novelists are forever worrying about the furniture (how will I get these characters into bed?—how, for God's sake, will I even get them up the stairs and through the bedroom door?); it takes a long time for the apprentice to realise that action in a novel is not a matter of stage management but of artistic concentration. Under the artist's humid scrutiny the object grows warm, it stirs and shies, giving off the blush of verisimilitude; the flash of his relentless gaze strikes them and the little monsters rise and walk, their bandages unfurling. The world they inhabit is a world of words, and yet, as with Josefine the mouse singer's piping song, 'something of our poor brief childhood is in it, something of a lost happiness that can never be found again, but it also has something of our busy life here and now, of that little admixture of unfathomable gaiety which persists and cannot be extinguished'. I do not know how it is done. Is it magic or mere sleight of hand? (Mere?)

('The Personae of Summer', 1993)

Thou Shalt Not Kill

Works of art have humble beginnings. They grow, like everything else, from a seed. Sitting at my desk recently, unable to work, I found myself thumbing through an old notebook, the one that I kept during the writing of my novel *The Book of Evidence*. The first page is dated 7 April, 1986. Here are the first few notes:

> Notice in a cemetery (true): 'Planting and cultivation restricted to dwarfs.'
>
> Browning's 'tender murderer'?
>
> 'There are no moral phenomena at all, only a moral interpretation of phenomena'
>
> —Nietzsche, *Beyond Good and Evil*
>
> (A small ad, clipped from a newspaper and pasted to the page:) 'Premature Baby Incubator, Vickers 59 for sale, as new. Offers, Box 402, Baby.'
>
> The living being is only a species of the dead, and a very rare species'
>
> —Nietzsche, *Fröliche Wissenschaft*
>
> *Is it wrong to kill people?* (underlined twice)

I do not think those cemetery dwarfs featured in the book, nor did the baby in its 'as new' incubator make an appearance, though they probably did lend the tale their own particular, subliminal touches of the macabre. Nietzsche is there in the pages, certainly, sometimes quoted directly, without acknowledgement—but not the two aphorisms that I have quoted from my notebook. Of course, the real origin of the book, the real gleam in the progenitor's eye, was that simple-seeming question: *Is it wrong to kill people?*

I am not a philosopher, not a psychologist, not a theologian, not a jurist. I address the subject of murder—or at least, the Mosaic injunction against murder—because I have written a series of three novels which together form an artistic meditation on the subject of a killing and its aftermath. The three volumes are *The Book of Evidence*, *Ghosts* and *Athena*. I did not set out to write a trilogy. Nor did I set out to write 'about' a murder (the work of art is never about something, though it may be about everything). I did, I suppose, have identifiable themes and ideas, which however loose and vague as artistic themes and ideas always are, could perhaps be grouped under the general heading, *The Search for Authenticity*.

The question of the authentic, of how to work authentically in a medium—art, that is—which at a certain level is necessarily fake, is one that obsesses the artist, consciously or otherwise. You take a square of stretched canvas and with infinite pains and manic concentration apply to it a series of multi-coloured daubs to make a pattern according to rigid but unknown laws: you arrange a series of sounds for voices or instruments or both combined, sounds which you may never hear outside your head (Schubert did not hear the bulk of his work performed), but which yet make a medleyed web in which an ineffable something is caught: you assemble a group of characters you have never known and will never encounter and make them dance their slow, intricate way through a story which is nothing like life—no novel is ever anything like life, though it may, as Henry James has it, *make* life—but which yet engages the reader as do those troubling dreams that come to us once in a while like succubi, drawing us into and out of ourselves, troubling our days—years, even—with the sensation of a reality more real than that which we experience in lived life itself. Where, is authentic; the territorial song of the oriole is authentic. But what of the sky painted from pigments? What of the imagined stone over which an imagined character trips as he hurries down the road to meet the love of his life? What of the stylised re-presentation of the bird's song in a piano piece by Messiaen?

You may think these matters only of significance, or interest, to the painter, the composer, the novelist, but you only have to ponder for a moment to realise that the problem of authenticity is at the very centre of the human predicament, and perhaps never more centrally located than in our, now closing, century.

So I set out, in *The Book of Evidence*, to invent an emblematic figure who in his actions and meditations would swing between the poles of the authentic and the inauthentic. I did not attempt to create what book reviewers would call an 'original' character—there are, as we all know, no original characters. This one had a particularly luxuriant family tree, with many an odd bird squawking among its branches. Dostoevsky's Underground Man is perched there, of course, sometimes in his own words (he figures darkly in that notebook of mine; 'Can a thinking man have any self-respect whatever?' he asks, and what thinking man can give an unequivocal answer?). The narrator of Sartre's *La Nausée* flexes a blue-black wing, and Camus's Meursault is heard every so often to sound a weary note. Nabokov's Humbert Humbert flashes like a firebird. Oh, there is a whole aviary here: Goethe's Werther, Büchner's Woyzeck, Kleist's Judge Adam, Wilde's Dorian Gray, Musil's brutish killer Moosbrugger ('if society could dream collectively,' says Musil, 'it would dream Moosbrugger'), and many, many more. Out of such bits and borrowings are characters made.

I gave him a name, at once ponderous and preposterous;

Frederick Charles St John Vanderveld Montgomery. Usually a novelist—my kind of novelist, that is—will infuse a character's name with as much resonance as it will bear: Godkin, Lawless, Grainger, Gabriel Swan, are some that I have employed. In this case I needed a name that would fall on the page with false resonance, or no resonance at all: Frederick Montgomery, *l'homme armée*, scion of a 'good' family, waywardly brilliant, self-regarding, dandyish, deceitful, feckless, vicious, murderous.

Freddie claims to have been in the far past, some kind of scientist, a mathematician, apparently. I am not sure that I believe him about this (I am not sure that I believe him about anything). In California, ten years before the time of the main events of the book, something occurs—or perhaps nothing occurs—and his life goes into crisis. Under this nameless affliction he is like Philip, Lord Chandos, in Hugo von Hofmannsthal's *The Chandos Letter*, who writes to his friend Francis Bacon: 'My case, in short, is this: that I have utterly lost the ability to think or speak coherently about anything at all.' My Freddie Montgomery can think, yes, and he can speak—by golly, how he can speak—but what is gone is coherence. Meaning has fallen out of his life like the bottom falling out of a bucket. Here he is, addressing the trial judge in particular and the rest of us in general, describing a pause on his way home from the Spanish island where he has been aimlessly footling away his life for years: the paragraph occurs early on in the book, but constitutes, nevertheless, a central moment:

> A washed-blue dawn was breaking in Madrid. I stopped outside the station and watched a flock of birds wheeling and tumbling at an immense height, and, the strangest thing, a gust of euphoria, or something like euphoria, swept through me, making me tremble, and bringing tears to my eyes. It was from lack of sleep, I suppose, and the effect of the high,

> thin air. Why, I wonder, do I remember so clearly standing there, the colour of the sky, those birds, that shiver of fevered optimism? I was at a turning point, you will tell me, just there the future forked for me, and I took the wrong path without noticing—that's what you'll tell me, isn't it, you, who must have meaning in everything, who lust after meaning, your palms sticky and your faces on fire! But calm, Frederick, calm. Forgive me this outburst, your honour. It is just that I do not believe such moments mean anything—or any other moments, for that matter. They have significance, apparently. They may even have value of some sort. But they do not mean anything.
>
> There now, I have declared my faith.

Freddie is obsessed with how thick is the texture of things that yet seem lacking in all substance. The world is solid as stone yet constantly quaking and shifting and sinking under him. He regards this world with the anguished fearfulness of a lover constantly in danger of losing the beloved. In this passage he is returning by ship to Ireland:

> It was evening. The sea was calm, an oiled, taut meniscus, mauve-tinted and curiously high and curved. From the forward lounge where I sat the prow seemed to rise and rise, as if the whole ship were straining to take to the air. The sky before us was a smear of crimson on the palest of pale blue and silvery green. I held my face up to the calm sea-light, entranced, expectant, grinning like a loon. I confess I was not entirely sober, I had already broken into my allowance of duty-free booze, and the skin at my temples and around my eyes was tightening alarmingly. It was not just the drink, though, that was making me happy, but the tenderness of

> things, the simple goodness of the world. This sunset, for instance, how lavishly it was laid on, the clouds, the light on the sea, that heartbreaking, blue-green distance, laid on, all of it, as if to console some lost, suffering wayfarer. I have never really got used to being on this earth. Sometimes I think our presence here is due to a cosmic blunder, that we were meant for another planet altogether, with other arrangements, and other laws, and other, grimmer skies. I try to imagine it, our true place, off on the far side of the galaxy, whirling and whirling. And the ones who were meant for here, are they out there, baffled and homesick, like us? No, they would have become extinct long ago. How could they survive, these gentle earthlings, in a world that was made to contain *us*?

If Freddie Montgomery is obsessed by the world, half in love with its tenderness and beauty, and half in terror of its inexplicable insubstantiality, he hardly notices the people surrounding him. He compares them to mirrors into which he peers anxiously, searching for his own, hardly existent reflection (Count Dracula is another of his forebears). He comes upon a painting, and, in a passage to which he brings all his linguistic and imaginative skills, conjures a life for the long-dead woman who is its subject. Yet when, in the process of stealing the painting, he is confronted by a real, living woman, he bashes her head in, swats her out of his way as if she were no more substantial than a cobweb. *The Book of Evidence* is just what the title says it is; a presentation of the facts, not in any effort by Freddie Montgomery to prove his innocence or to excuse his murderous deeds, but as a kind of appalled act of witness. Look, he says to us, look, here is what happened! I can no more make sense of it than you can. When at the end of the book, after his capture, the police ask him why he killed the woman, he can only reply: 'I killed her because I could, what more can I say?'

As Freddie comes to realise, his *crime* was murder, but his *sin* was a radical failure of the imagination. We make others real only by imagining them: both the lover and the murderer know this. Yet where the lover and the murderer are different is that what the lover conjures into existence out of the white-hot furnace of his imaginings is a stylised image, a kind of magically detailed hologram of the beloved, while on the contrary, the murderer *makes the other real*. Here is Freddie dealing the first blow:

> I turned to her. I had the hammer in my hand. I looked at it, startled. The silence rose around us like water. Don't, she said. She was crouched as before, with her arms bent and her back pressed into the corner. I could not speak, I was filled with a kind of wonder. I had never felt another's presence so immediately and with such raw force. I saw her now, really saw her, for the first time, her mousy hair and bad skin, that bruised look around her eyes. She was quite ordinary, and yet, somehow, I don't know—somehow radiant.

This immediacy, this radiance, are what the subject of the murder and the subject of the painting have in common. Although none of the critics has remarked it, this seems to me the real scandal at the heart of *The Book of Evidence*. The living, though soon to be dead, woman is no more real to Freddie—and to us—than the painted woman: less so, in fact. The border between art and life has become blurred and not just for Freddie. We too are somehow implicated in this crime.

Freddie Montgomery, under other guises, and other names, meditates on this failure of imagination, through *Ghosts*, which is an account of his time in Purgatory; and *Athena*, his attempt to set a new life in place of the one that he took. For all the passionate *looking* that takes place in *Athena* ('looking' being for Freddie a far more important act than that other act with which it indecently rhymes), the failure remains as it must. The dead cannot be made to live again, and art cannot be put in the place of life. Even so, he is determined that something will be salvaged from the disaster he has wrought—and wrought is the most suitable word here. At the end of *Athena*, when he has been abandoned by his love, and after he has discovered that although he looked and looked and *looked* at her, he did not succeed in seeing her, he is granted a final, fleeting vision.

> I saw her yesterday, I don't know how, but I did. It was the strangest thing. I have not got over it yet. I was in that pub on Gabriel Street that she liked so much. The place is fake, of course, with false wood panelling and plated brass and a wooden fan the size of an aeroplane propeller in the ceiling that does nothing except swirl the drifting cigarette smoke in lazy arabesques. I go there for the obvious reason. I was in the back bar, nursing a drink and my sore heart, sitting at that big window—I always think of windows like that as startled, somehow, like wide-open eyes—that looks down at the city along the broad sweep of Ormond Street. The street was crowded, as it always is. The sun was shining, in its half-hearted way—yes, spring has come, despite my best efforts. Suddenly I saw her—or no, not suddenly, there was no suddenness or surprise in it. She was just there, in her black coat and her black stilettos, hurrying along the crowded pavement in that watery light at that unmistakable, stiff-kneed half-run, a hand to her breast and her head down. Where was she going, with such haste, so eagerly? The city lay all before her, awash with April and evening. I say *her*, but of course I know it was not her, not really. And yet it was. How can I express it? There is the she who is gone, who is in some southern somewhere, lost to me forever, and then there is this other, who

steps out of my head and goes hurrying off along the sunlit pavements to do I don't know what. To live. If I can call it living; and I shall.

• • •

The most terrifying discovery in life is that we are free. Constrained, yes, but free. I sometimes feel, in my darker moments, that the only truly interesting achievement of the human species—the most dangerous, the most terrible, species the world has ever known—is not the development of philosophy or religion, the application of science, the invention of romantic love, but the success with which we have ameliorated the horror we experience in face of our state of freedom. What stratagems we have devised to blind ourselves to the abyss that gapes always at our feet. What somersaults of logic we have performed, even on the lip of the precipice.

How are we to cope with that profoundly horrifying dictum of Nietzsche's I quoted at the outset, to the effect that 'there are no moral phenomena at all, only a moral interpretation of phenomena'? In the absence of a moral imperative, is it wrong to kill people? Religion is not much help, being itself steeped in the blood of saviours and martyrs and Philistines. Nor will art come to the rescue, as Freddie Montgomery can attest. Where, in Emerson's famous and characteristically ambiguous formulation, where do we find ourselves? As I have said, I am not a philosopher, theologian, jurist. I have no pronouncements on the problem of evil, of the just war, abortion, euthanasia, capital punishment. All that an artist can do is present the evidence. *Here is what happened, this is how it felt, this is how the light fell, how the characters spoke: it is all made up, yet strangely real.* When I think of Freddie Montgomery and his dogged search for authenticity through the three novels that are, we may say, his creation, I return again and again to a brief little passage that occurs at the end of *Ghosts*:

> I think of a picture at the end of a long gallery, a sudden presence come upon unexpectedly, at first sight a soft confusion of greens and gilts in the calm, speechless air. Look at this foliage, these clouds, the texture of this gown. A stricken figure stares out at something that is being lost. There is an impression of music, tiny, exact and gay. This is the end of a world. Birds unseen are fluting in the trees, the sun shines somewhere, the distances of the sea are vague and palely blue, the galliot awaits. The figures move, if they move, as in a moving scene, one that they define, by being there, its arbiters. Without them only the wilderness, green riot, tumult of wind and the crazy sun. They formulate the tale and people it and give it substance. They are the human moment.

It is one of the chief ironies of the trilogy that it is in those passages when Freddie contemplates the literally inhuman—the figures in paintings, or the figments of his own imagination—that he most closely approaches that state of full feeling humanness which is his one, consistent aim. Being a murderer, he must now, as he says at the end of *The Book of Evidence*, live for two. I am, he declares, 'big with possibilities'. He is pregnant with his own incipient humanity. He has learned to use his imagination, and, as Wallace Stevens has it, 'God and the imagination are one'. It is not the God of Moses, that merciless slaughterer, but the god in our own heads that injuncts us: it is the imagination that commands. Thou shalt not kill.

('Thou Shalt Not Kill', 1997)

'Speaks True Who Speaks Shadow'

Selected Poems and Prose of Paul Celan translated by John Felstiner (W. W. Norton);

Fathomsuns and Benighted by Paul Celan, translated by Ian Fairley (Carcanet Press)

Paul Celan was born Paul Antschel, in Czernowitz, former capital of Bukovina, in 1920. At the time of his birth, Bukovina was a province of Romania. In 1940, it was occupied by Soviet troops, then by German and Romanian forces, and in 1944 was seized by the Soviet Union and annexed to the Ukraine. And we in Ireland think we have a troubled history.

Celan—the name is an anagram of Ancel, the Romanian spelling of Antschel—at first studied medicine, and it was as a medical student that he went to Paris in 1938. The following, fateful, year he returned to Czernowitz, and when the war broke out he was studying Romance languages and literature. Somehow the Antschels, German-speaking Jews, remained free until 1942. Then, on the night of June 27th that year, when Paul was staying with friends in order not to be caught breaking the curfew, his parents were rounded up by the Gestapo and deported to a labour camp in Transnistria in the Ukraine.

John Felstiner, who has written a fine biographical study of Celan, remarks that the poet 'could never readily give an account of this event', an event which was to mark him for life, and probably contributed to his death. It seems that he had urged his parents to go into hiding, but they had refused, preferring to face their fate—not knowing, of course, how terrible it would be—and that after an argument with his father he had stormed out of the house. When he returned in the morning, the house was empty, the front door sealed.

After an earlier round-up of Jews, Felstiner tells us, an acquaintance of Celan's had gone to the station and succeeded in getting her parents off the deportation train. 'Celan,' says Felstiner, 'remained conscious of not having done as much.' His father was to die of typhus in the labour camp, and later his mother was shot when she could no longer work. A month after the deportation of his parents, Paul himself was sent to a Romanian-run labour camp in Wallachia, and may have served time in a number of other camps as well, returning to Soviet-occupied Czernowitz in March 1944.

How he escaped from the camps is not clear; one published account by a fellow poet, which Felstiner says contains 'implausible elements', claims that Celan survived an SS 'selection' by slipping from the line headed for the gas chambers and into the line of those about to be released, so that another man died in his place. Celan himself never spoke directly of the details of that time. In a biographical note of 1949 he wrote, with remarkable terseness: 'What the life of a Jew was during the war years, I need not mention,' while in a letter sent in July 1944 to a boyhood friend he said: 'I've experienced only humiliations and emptiness, endless emptiness.' Whatever the fact of those terrible years may be, it is certain that the loss of his parents, his own sufferings, and the Holocaust in general—which he always referred to simply as 'that which happened'—formed him not only as a man but as a poet. Indeed, it might be said that he had only one subject—'that which happened'.

After the war he moved first to Bucharest, and in 1948 to

Paris, where he lived until his death. He married the artist Gisèle de Lestrange, taught German literature at the École normale supérieure, worked as a translator, and, despite increasingly severe bouts of depression, wrote in total some eight hundred poems collected in seven volumes, all the time resisting, like his fellow exile Samuel Beckett, the siren-song of silence 'which was a not-able-to-speak and thus believed itself an ought-not-to-speak'.

• • •

Celan's work is a standing rejoinder to Theodor Adorno's declaration that after Auschwitz, to write poetry is a scandal. Yet it would be wise to keep in mind the fact that art cannot be validated by suffering. Pain may ennoble the soul, but it will not advance your poetry one whit. Celan's experience in the European catastrophe, the loss of his parents, even his suicide, should not lead us to imagine that his voice has more authority or authenticity than that of a poet—Philip Larkin, say—who experienced none of these horrors.

In 1958 Celan was awarded the Bremen Literature Prize, and in 1960 the Georg Büchner Prize, the highest German literary award. The speeches he made at the two prize-givings, which are translated in Felstiner's superb *Selected Poems and Prose*, constitute Celan's most extended meditations on the art of poetry in general and on his own work in particular; however, anyone hoping to find in these speeches illumination and guidance for an encounter with some of the most difficult poetry written in the twentieth century will likely be disappointed. 'The Meridian', Celan's celebrated response to the Büchner Prize, is, in its rhythmical, ecstatic denseness, worthy of Heidegger at his most gnomic: 'Homage here is to the Majesty of the Absurd, testifying to human presence. And that, ladies and gentlemen, has no fixed name once and for all time, yet it is, I believe . . . poetry.' Well, quite.

Celan's depressions grew steadily deeper and more frequent

during the 1960s, and one night in April 1970 he drowned himself in the Seine, taking with him into those midnight waters what Felstiner calls his 'incurable wounds'. Celan might have said of himself what another great writer in German, Heinrich von Kleist, wrote in a letter shortly before he, too, committed suicide: 'There is no help for me on this earth.'

It would be misleading, and a disservice to Celan, to pretend that his poetry is anything other than difficult. Many critics have questioned Celan's 'torsions'—the word Seamus Heaney in his Nobel acceptance speech applied to Celan's work—criticising his 'insistent minimalism' and his 'unwillingness to commit himself to accessibility', charges which are hard to rebut. Here is Felstiner's attempt:

> Celan's writing may baffle the reader unready to give it that 'attentiveness' he considered 'the natural prayer of the soul'. To grow attentive . . . is to activate these poems. Their truth, after all, may consist in obscurity or ambiguity, as also in occasional radiance.

This is well put, but not of much comfort to the baffled reader, no matter how patient or sympathetic. Ian Fairley's new translation of the late collection *Fadensonnen* (1968), is a brave and frequently inspired attempt to make over into English some of Celan's most oblique and intricate poetry. Fairley's introduction, though in places almost as obscure as the poems themselves, is full of insights, particularly in the comparisons he makes with the work of other poets, especially Rilke. But *Fadensonnen* is hard going, as are the eleven 'abandoned' pieces in *Eingedunkelt*, translated by Fairley as *Benighted*.

Celan's poems, even the very early ones, are furled tight as rosebuds; we may admire their appalling beauty, but it will take the light of only the strongest attentiveness to make them burst into full blossom. It is worth the effort. There *is* radiance here, even in the midst of obscurities. John Felstiner's translations communicate a real sense of Celan's peculiar musicality and tragic resonance. They are an advance on the work of the late Michael Hamburger, who did so much to bring Celan to the attention of the English-speaking world, as Felstiner generously acknowledges.

Nevertheless, like many poets, Celan wrote too much, and at times he is, despite that 'insistent minimalism', positively garrulous. His most famous, or infamous, poem, 'Todesfugue' ('Deathfugue'), which some, mainly Jewish, critics have condemned for making a beautiful object out of the horrors of the Holocaust ('Death is a master from Germany'), is wonderfully translated by Felstiner, who in a stroke of translator's genius lets the German original gradually seep back into the English version, like the 'black milk' the doomed dancers of the poem must drink; thus the 'master from Germany' reverts to 'ein Meister aus Deutschland', and the two women, Gentile and Jew, who are repeatedly invoked throughout the poem, at the close are addressed in their *Muttersprache*: 'dein Goldenes Haar Margarete / dein aschenes Haar Sulamith'.

'Todesfugue', though certainly impressive, is not among Celan's greatest poems. For that sombre, transcendent beauty which is the mark of his profoundest work, go to quieter pieces such as 'Tenebrae', or 'Psalm', or that exquisite, heartbreaking early lament, 'Black Flakes', in which the poet imagines his dead mother begging him from her place of captivity for a shawl 'to wrap myself when it's flashing with helmets':

> Autumn bled all away, Mother, snow burned me through:
> I sought out my heart so it might weep, I found—
>   oh the summer's breath,
> it was like you.
> Then came my tears. I wove the shawl.

Paul Celan is the poet who most directly, most valiantly, and, for all his negativeness—his is the anti-poem, the '*Genicht*', the 'noem'—most triumphantly faces, perhaps even at times faces down, the horrors into which the world allowed itself to blunder in the middle of the twentieth century. He was, in the religious no less than the artistic sense, a true witness. He insisted that his poems could and should be understood, declaring that his work is '*ganz und gar nicht hermetisch*' ('absolutely not hermetic'), yet for him, as for Beckett, the darkness could never be denied. As one of Celan's early poems declares: 'Speaks true who speaks shadow.'

('Speaks True Who Speaks Shadow', 2001)

Fiction and the Dream

A man wakes up in the morning. He gets out of bed, feeling light-headed, even somewhat dazed. Standing in the curtained gloom in his pyjamas, blinking, he feels that somehow he is not his real, vital, fully conscious self. It is as if that other, alert version of him is still in bed, and that what has got up is a sort of shadow-self, tremulous, two-dimensional. What is the matter? He was not drinking last night, he does not have a hangover. Is he 'coming down with something'? He does seem a little feverish. But no, he decides, what is afflicting him is no physical malady. There is, rather, something the matter with his mind. His brain feels heavy, and as if it were a size too large for his skull. Then, suddenly, in a rush, he remembers the dream.

It was one of those dreams that seem to take the entire night to be dreamt. All of him was involved in it, his unconscious, his subconscious, his memory, his imagination; even his physical self seemed thrown into the effort. The details of the dream flood back, uncanny, absurd, terrifying, and all freighted with a mysterious weight—such a weight as is carried by only the most profound experiences of life, of waking life, that is. And indeed, all of his life, all of the essentials of his life, were somehow there, in the dream, folded tight, like the petals of a rosebud. Some great truth has been revealed to him, in a code he knows he will not be able to crack. But cracking the code is not important, is not necessary; in fact, as in a work of art, the code itself is the meaning.

He puts on his dressing gown and his slippers and goes

downstairs. His wife is at the stove, making scrambled eggs and toast and fried tomatoes with olive oil and a sprinkling of pepper—his favourite breakfast. He sits down at the table and she serves him—this is an old-fashioned household—piling his plate with the delicate, aromatic food. That mingled smell—coffee-eggs-toast-tomatoes-oil—was that in the dream, or is it just the intensity of it now that is echoing the dreamt intensities? He gazes at the gleam of morning light on the cheek of the coffee pot, a tiny galaxy, streaming out its grainy radiance in all directions. Everything looks strange. Has his wife's eyes developed overnight that slight imbalance, the right one a fraction lower than the left, or is it something he has never noticed before? The cat in its corner watches him out of an eerie stillness. Sounds enter from the street, familiar and at the same time mysterious, inexplicable: the postman's whistle, the neighbour's dog barking, a car engine revving. He closes his eyes a moment. The dream is infecting his waking world. Nothing will ever be quite the same again. The infection is low-grade, hardly detectable, and in time it will fade, and he will become used to the myriad tiny changes it has wrought in the things around him, and he will negotiate his way amidst the furniture of his world with the old ease, the old, unnoticing, ease.

He begins to tell his wife about the dream, feeling a little bashful, curbing his eagerness. He knows how silly the dreamed events will sound. He remembers when as a little boy he tried to tell a girl in his class at school about the facts of life, a jumbled version of which he had lately discovered in an article in the *Reader's Digest*. The circumstances of human reproduction seemed just as wildly improbable then as the things the people got up to in his dream last night. His wife listens to his account of the dream, nodding distractedly. He tries to give his words something of the weight that there was in the dream. He is coming to the crux of the thing, the moment when his dreaming self woke in the midst of the dark wood, among the murmuring voices. Suddenly his wife opens her mouth wide—is she going to beg him to stop, is she going to cry out that she finds what he is telling her too terrifying—is she going to scream? What she does is, she yawns, mightily, with little inward gasps, the hinges of her jaws cracking, and finishes with a long, shivery sigh, and asks if he would like to finish what is left of the scrambled egg.

The dreamer droops, dejected. He has offered something precious and it has been spurned. How can she not feel the significance of the things he has been describing to her? How can she not see the bare trees and the darkened air, the memory of which is darkening the very air around them now—how can she not hear the murmurous voices, as he heard them? He pushes his plate aside, the scraps of uneaten food congealing, and trudges back upstairs to get himself ready for another, ordinary, day. The momentous revelations of the night begin to recede. It was just a dream, after all.

But what if, instead of accepting the simple fact that our most chaotic, our most exciting, our most significant dreams are nothing but boring to others, even our significant others—what if he said to his wife, *All right, I'll show you, I'll do more than show you, I'll sit down and write out the dream in such an intense and ravishing formulation that when you read it you, too, will have the dream; you, too, will find yourself wandering in the wild wood at nightfall; you, too, will hear the dream voices telling you your own most secret secrets.*

I can think of no better analogy than this for the process of writing a novel. The novelist's aim is to make the reader *have the dream*—not just to read about it, but actually to experience it; to have the dream, to write the novel.

Now, these are dangerous assertions. In this post-religious age—and the fundamentalists, Christian, Muslim and other, only attest to the fact that ours is an age after religion—people are looking about in some desperation for a new priesthood. *Signs are taken for wonders*, T. S. Eliot writes, *'we would see a sign'*. And there is something about the artist in general and the writer in particular which seems priest-like: the unceasing commitment to an ethereal faith, the mixture of arrogance and humility, the daily devotions, the confessional readiness to attend the foibles and fears of the laity. The writer goes into a room, the inviolable domestic holy of holies—the *study*—and remains there alone for hour after hour in eerie silence. With what deities does he commune, in there, what rituals does he enact? Surely he knows something that others, the uninitiates, do not; surely he is privy to a wisdom far beyond theirs.

These are delusions, of course. The artist, the writer, knows no more about the great matters of life and the spirit than anyone else—indeed, he probably knows less. I have a friend whose emotional life is somehow constantly in turmoil and who turns to me and says, *Please, tell me how to handle these things, these crises, you who write and know so much about the inner organisation of human affairs.* And I tell her, *Ah, my dear, you've come to exactly the wrong person, for I know nothing about life, only about art.* She protests: *But you write so perceptively, so incisively, about people, their motives and their fears, their joys, their dark desires.* And I answer: *Yes, I write about them, but why does that make you think I know about them?* This is the paradox. As Henry James has it—and Franz Kafka would have agreed—we work in the dark, we do what we can, the rest is the madness of art.

So the writer is not a priest, not a shaman, not a holy dreamer. Yet his work is dragged up out of that darksome well where the essential self cowers, in fear of the light.

I should emphasise here that I have no grand psychological theory of the creative process to offer you. I am not a Freudian, although I admire Freud as a great literary fabulator. And I am certainly not a Jungian. (Fiction is the presentation of hard evidence—but that's another day's lecture.) I do not pretend to know how the mind, consciously or otherwise, processes the base metal of quotidian life into the gold of art. Even if I could find out, I would not want to. Certain things should not be investigated.

When I began to write I was a convinced rationalist, if a decidedly ecstatic one. I believed, and fiercely and indignantly defended my belief, that I, the writer, was in control of what I wrote. When I began a book, I knew where I was going. Before I wrote down the first line I had the last line planned. I would, for instance, divide the parts of a book according to the rule of golden section. Hearing that Bach had composed the crucifixion scene in one of his Passions so that the notes would form the shape of a crucifix in the score—in the score, mind: the effect is wholly undetectable to the ear—and that Bartók frequently worked like a medieval numerologist, counting the number of notes in this or that piece so as to make a mystic code of it, I became obsessed with proportion in my own work. My novel on the life of the astronomer Nicolaus Copernicus employs musical figures—fugue, theme and variation, rondo, and so on—as its hidden structure, in an attempt to mimic the unheard music of the spheres. When I took Johannes Kepler as the protagonist of a subsequent novel, I devised a fiendishly complicated and, for me, exhausting system based on Kepler's theory of the five perfect solids; Kepler believed God had founded the universe on a system whereby inside each of the spaces between the then-unknown six planets there could be inscribed one of the five perfect geometric solids—and there are only five, from the cube up to the dodecahedron. So I divided my book into five, ellipse-shaped sections—Kepler was the first to realise that planets move not in circles but ellipses—and divided each section into the number of sides of each of the perfect solids . . . Let me say, that if you find this scheme hard to follow, imagine what it felt like to write a book based on it.

The point is, I saw myself as the scientist-like manipulator of my material, the 'devised deviser devising it all', as Beckett beautifully writes of one of his fictional alter egos. But then, around the middle of the 1980s, something happened, I am not sure what it was, or what caused it, whatever *it* may have been. Both my parents had died within a few years of each other, and perhaps I was in a state of sublimated grief. Certainly there was a great deal of pain and sorrow in the novel I wrote in that time. The book, *Mefisto*, is a sort of demented dream. It was dreamlike not only in its content and the mode of its narration, but in the manner in which it was written. For the first time, out of whatever extreme of distress it was that I was in, I began to let things happen on the page which my conscious, my waking, mind could not account for. And this was, I realised, a new way of working. I do not say it was a freer way, or even that it was a more productive way, but certainly it was different.

The dream world is a strange place. Everything there is at once real and unreal. The most trivial or ridiculous things can seem to carry a tremendous significance, a significance which—and here I do agree with Freud—the waking mind would never dare to suggest or acknowledge. In dreams the mind speaks its truths through the medium of a fabulous nonsense. So, I think, does the novel.

Sometimes, and usually for no good or at least plausible reason that I can think of, I incorporate my dreams into my fiction. A case in point is a dream related in the early pages of my novel *The Sea*. One of the strong themes of the book is the way in which the far past can seem far more present to us than the present itself, especially as one begins to get old. One night I dreamt a dream of myself as a boy, embarked on a mysterious journey, which affected me profoundly, and haunted my days for long afterwards, and which even still I recall with a prescient shiver. So strong and so mysteriously meaningful did it seem that I could not resist putting it into the book. At the risk of making you yawn and reach for the scrambled eggs, here it is. The narrator of the novel, whose wife has recently died after a lengthy illness, has returned to the seaside village where he spent his summers as a child, and is lodging in the house where in that far past there came to stay one year a family, the Graces, with whose lives he became, for a brief but intense, calamitous, period, intimately entangled.

> A dream it was that drew me here. In it, I was walking along a country road, that was all. It was in winter, at dusk, or else it was a strange sort of dimly radiant night, the sort of night that there is only in dreams, and a wet snow was falling. I was determinedly on my way somewhere, going home, it seemed, although I did not know what or where exactly home might be. There was open land to my right, flat and undistinguished with not a house or hovel in sight, and to my left a deep line of darkly louring trees bordering the road. The branches were not bare despite the season, and the thick, almost black leaves drooped in masses, laden with snow that had turned to soft, translucent ice. Something had broken down, a car, no, a bicycle, a boy's bicycle, for as well as being the age I am now I was a boy as well, a big awkward boy, yes, and on my way home, it must have been home, or somewhere that had been home, once, and that I would recognise again, when I got there. I had hours of walking to do but I did not mind that, for this was a journey of surpassing but inexplicable importance, one that I must make and was bound to complete. I was calm in myself, quite calm, and confident, too, despite not knowing rightly

> where I was going except that I was going home. I was alone on the road. The snow which had been slowly drifting down all day was unmarked by tracks of any kind, tyre, boot or hoof, for no one had passed this way and no one would. There was something the matter with my foot, the left one, I must have injured it, but long ago, for it was not painful, though at every step I had to throw it out awkwardly in a sort of half-circle, and this hindered me, not seriously but seriously enough. I felt compassion for myself, that is to say the dreamer that I was felt compassion for the self being dreamed, this poor lummox going along dauntlessly in the snow at fall of day with only the road ahead of him and no promise of homecoming.

I have no idea what this dream was about, either when I had dreamed it, or when I put it into the book; nor can I say what its function in the narrative might be. It just felt right to incorporate it into the action, such as it was, at that point. Strangely, or perhaps not strangely, a number of readers have told me how deeply they were affected by that particular passage. Why? What encoded meaning or message did it carry out of my subconscious into the inhospitable medium of cold print? When I think of the dream, or when I read this novelised description of it, I am struck by something plangent, grief-stricken, almost, in that word *home*—'I was calm in myself, quite calm, and confident, too, despite not knowing rightly where I was going except that I was going home'—yet I cannot say what *home* means here, or why this simple, this *homely*, word, in this context, 'pierces me', as Wallace Stevens writes of 'life's nonsense', why it 'pierces me with strange relation'. But it does. And knowing, without knowing why, is, in this instance, enough.

The writing of fiction is far more than the telling of stories. It is an ancient, an elemental, urge which springs, like the dream, from a desperate imperative to encode and preserve things that are buried in us deep beyond words. This is its significance, its danger and its glory.

('Fiction and the Dream', 2005)

Beckett's Last Words

One night in the early 1980s Samuel Beckett was having dinner with his long-time English publisher, John Calder, probably at the Îles Marquises in Montparnasse, Beckett's favourite restaurant at the time, or the beautifully named bistro the Closerie des Lilas. During the course of the evening Beckett diffidently announced to Calder that he had something for him, and drew out of his shoulder bag a plastic folder containing the typescript of *Ill Seen Ill Said*, the English version of the short text—though long by Beckett's standards—originally written in French and entitled *Mal vu mal dit*.

Calder was of course greatly excited at the prospect of a new Beckett work, following closely as it did on *Company*, 'the fable of one with you in the dark', a startlingly autobiographical work, first written, unusually, in English rather than French, which the author had completed at the very end of the 1970s. Calder put the typescript on the seat beside him and the two men went on with their meal, finishing, no doubt, with a glass or two of *marc*. When, some time later, Calder got back to his hotel he realised to his horror that he did not have the typescript. In panic he telephoned the restaurant, but the folder was not to be found. Could it have been thrown out? He hurried back to the restaurant, which by now was closing, and persuaded the staff to let him look through the night's garbage. After a long and unpleasant search in bags of potato peelings and sodden bread and mussel shells he at last found the folder, smeared with food stains but with the typescript safe inside it—'Thank God,' Calder said, 'that the folder was made of plastic!'

Beckett was amused by the story, when Calder found the courage to tell it to him. How apt, after all, that a work by this connoisseur of detritus should have found its way accidentally into the rubbish bin. Yet when, some years after Beckett's death, I heard of the near-catastrophe a shiver ran down my spine—Beckett was notoriously lax in keeping copies of his work—at the thought of the typescript going into the garbage truck, for *Ill Seen Ill Said*, short though it be, is one of the glories of late twentieth-century literature, or, indeed, of world literature of any period.

Beckett's artistic venture, from his first, exuberant volume of stories, *More Pricks than Kicks*, published in 1934, to his last published writing, the poem 'what is the word'—which first appeared, I might add, in the books pages of *The Irish Times*—was unequalled in its dedicated single-mindedness and unrelenting ideological rigour. That venture was always and only a struggle with and against language; as the narrator says in the wonderful fragment, *From an Abandoned Work*: 'I love the word, words have been my only loves, not many.' After the great trilogy of *Molloy*, *Malone Dies* and *The Unnamable*, and the last full-length work, the novel *How It Is*, which appeared in English in 1964, the texts became shorter and shorter as the author pared down his material, until he achieved a kind of 'white-out' in such pieces as *Imagination Dead Imagine* and *All Strange Away*.

The effort, the concentration, the risk involved in this continuing throwing-out of literary ballast provides a rare and exemplary instance of artistic good faith. Throughout the 1960s and the 1970s Beckett's readers greeted each of the author's successively shorter and bleaker texts with a mixture of awe and apprehensiveness; it was like watching a great mathematician wielding an infinitesimal calculus, his equations approaching nearer and still nearer to the null point. Surely after *this*, we would say, the only possible advance will be into total silence at last. In those decades, however, the danger was not that he would go mute—Beckett's is a clamorous silence—but that the work would wither into sterility. Yet somehow he always found an escape route, no matter how strait the tunnel or how dim the light at the end of it.

Beckett was first and last a prose writer, and regarded his plays as little more than footnotes to the novels—as late as 1966 he was still referring to the novel trilogy as '*toute mon oeuvre*'. However, in the 1960s and the 1970s, Beckett turned repeatedly to the theatre, 'in search for a respite from the wasteland of prose', as he put it. To his surprise and shy pleasure, it brought him somewhat out of himself, especially after the success of *Waiting for Godot*, which thrust him to world fame in the 1950s, and later when he made a number of genuine and lasting friendships among actors and directors. As the 1980s approached, however, he began to feel in earnest the fleeting of time, and yearned again for the solitude and concentration in which in the years after the war he had produced the trilogy—he spoke of that enterprise as 'the siege in the room'—and went off frequently to his modest country cottage at Ussy-sur-Marne to work on what would become the final masterpieces, *Company*, *Ill Seen Ill Said*, *Worstward Ho* and *Stirrings Still*.

Because of the lateness and comparative brevity of these pieces they are often regarded as mere shavings from the workbench, the ageing master's final whittlings as he prepared to succumb at last to that silence which throughout his writing life had sung to him as the siren sang to Odysseus's sailors. This view is entirely mistaken. In his last decade Beckett found a new access of inspiration—'Imagination at wit's end spreads its sad wings,' as the voice in *Ill Seen Ill Said* has it—a final efflorescence which in these late texts would produce one of the most beautiful, profound, and moving of literary testaments.

In Paris in the late 1920s and throughout the 1930s the young Beckett was much under the influence of James Joyce, for whom he did some secretarial work, and whose writings he championed, notably in his essay on what was to become *Finnegans Wake*, 'Dante . . . Bruno . Vico . . Joyce', in which he made the by now famous distinction: '[Joyce's] writing is not *about* something; *it is that something itself*', a formulation that may apply more comfortably to Beckett's own work than to the encyclopaedic fabulations of Joyce. Later, Beckett sought artistically to strike the father dead (as all artists must do), speaking of Joyce's tendency towards 'omnipotence and omniscience', while he himself worked with 'impotence, ignorance'. This did not mean, he insisted, that in his own, new kind of art there would be no form, but only that there would be a new form, 'and this form will be of such a type that it admits the chaos and does not try to say that the chaos is really something else . . .'

In an early essay on Proust, Beckett had insisted that the only progression possible for the modern artist is a *progression in depth*; the vast effort of inclusiveness of Balzac or Proust, or, indeed, of Joyce, must be abjured. In the first of three dialogues with the editor of *transition*, Georges Duthuit, published in 1949, Beckett speaks of 'an art . . . weary of puny exploits, weary of pretending to be able, of being able, of doing a little better the same old thing, of going a little further along a dreary road'. But what, the interviewer asked, is the alternative? Beckett's answer was simple, uncompromising and mordantly witty: 'The expression that there is nothing to express, nothing with which to express, nothing from which to express, no power to express, no desire to express, together with the obligation to express.'

Beckett had a deep love for the art of painting—indeed, he could have been a great art critic, as his biographer James Knowlson has shown us—and his views on painters, expressed especially in early letters to his friend Thomas MacGreevy, who was later to become director of the National Gallery of Ireland, are revealing of his own general aesthetic. He loved in particular Poussin and the Dutch masters of the Golden Age, and of course Caspar David Friedrich, whose little painting *Two Figures Contemplating the Moon* was, he said, one of the inspirations for *Waiting for Godot*. However, at times Beckett the artistic iconoclast and innovator displayed a violent impatience with the assurance and poise of painters for whom he had a high regard. In 1934, after looking at the Cézannes in the Tate collection he wrote to MacGreevy: 'What a relief the Mont Ste. Victoire after all the anthropomorphised landscape—van Goyen, Avercamp, the Ruysdaels, Hobbema, even Claude . . .' against whose work Cézanne's is 'alive the way a lap or a *fist* is alive'.

Beckett at this time, the early 1930s, was seeking desperately for a way out of the artistic impasse in which he was trapped, and which he would not begin to escape from until the famous revelation, on Dun Laoghaire pier one stormy night at the end of the war, half described in *Krapp's Last Tape*—in fact, as Beckett insisted Knowlson make clear in the biography, it was not at Dun Laoghaire but in his mother's room that he experienced his 'revelation'—when he at last began 'to write the things I feel'.

> I realised that Joyce had gone as far as one could in the direction of knowing more, in control of one's material. He was always *adding* to it; you only have to look at his proofs to see that. I realised that my own way was in impoverishment, in lack of knowledge and in taking away, in subtracting rather than adding.

As Knowlson shrewdly points out, 'in defining what he saw as Cézanne's recognition that landscape had nothing to do with man, that man was quite separate from and alien to it, [Cézanne] was defining a view that was excitingly close to his own . . .' In another letter to MacGreevy Beckett wrote:

> What I feel in Cézanne is precisely the absence of a rapport that was all right for Rosa or Ruysdael for whom the animising mode was valid, but would have been fake for him, because he had the sense of his incommensurability not only with life of such a different order as landscape, but even with life of his own order, even with the life . . . operative in himself.

The fact of this general 'incommensurability', of man's predicament as a figure in a landscape—a mere figure in a hostile or at least an indifferent landscape—was what, as he discovered that night on the stormy pier or the afternoon in his mother's room, he must find a way of affirming in his work, in full acknowledgement of the bitter irony implied by such an effort of affirmation.

Beckett was a philosopher who hated philosophy, if we accept the conventional notions of what philosophy is. Despite his deep admiration for Cartesian rigour and rationality, he regarded with suspicion, if not outright contempt, all efforts to systematise reality and answer the great questions which have pestered man since first he crawled out of the cave. His own efforts, that is, the efforts of all the Murphys, Molloys and Malones, to tackle the fundamentals of life—and what fun he would have had with such a phrase—spur him to thrilling extremes of disgust and mockery. Here is Molloy:

> I was speaking then was I not of my little pastimes and I think about to say that I ought to content myself with them, instead of launching forth on all this ballsaching poppycock about life and death, if that is what it is all about, and I suppose it is, for nothing was ever about anything else to the best of my recollection. But what it is all about exactly I could no more say, at the present moment, than take up my bed and

> walk. It's vague, life and death. I must have had my little private idea on the subject when I began, otherwise I would not have begun, I would have held my peace, I would have gone on peacefully being bored to howls, having my little fun and games with the cones and cylinders, the millet grains beloved of birds and other panics, until someone was kind enough to come and coffin me. But it is gone clean out of my head, my little private idea.

There are many readers still who find even the postwar trilogy of novels too daunting to attempt. Yet Beckett for all his seeming bleakness is a thoroughly entertaining writer. At one level, as we see for instance in the passage just quoted, the trilogy is a comic masterpiece, sparkling with wit and humour, and containing some splendid, blackly funny set-pieces. And the prose, of course, is never less than beautiful. Consider this passage from *Malone Dies*, in which the young Malone—if any of Beckett's characters can be said ever to have been young—lies in bed listening to the sounds of the night:

> There was nothing, not even the sand on the paths, that did not utter its cry. The still nights too, still as the grave as the saying is, were nights of storm for me, clamorous with countless pantings. These I amused myself with identifying, as I lay there. Yes, I got great amusement, when young, from their so-called silence. The sound I liked best had nothing noble about it. It was the barking of the dogs, at night, in the clusters of hovels up in the hills, where the stone-cutters lived, like generations of stone-cutters before them. It came down to me where I lay, in the house in the plain, wild and soft, at the limit of earshot, soon weary. The dogs of the valley replied with their gross bay all fangs and jaws and foam.

> From the hills another joy came down, I mean the brief scattered lights that sprang up on their slopes at nightfall, merging in blurs scarcely brighter than the sky, less bright than the stars, and which the palest moon extinguished. They were things that scarcely were, on the confines of silence and dark, and soon ceased. So I reason now, at my ease. Standing before my high window I gave myself to them, waiting for them to end, for my joy to end, straining towards the joy of ended joy.

Beckett's style is classical, poised, incantatory, yet one that will 'admit the chaos'. His models are the great masters of plain yet sonorous prose, such as Swift, Sir Thomas Browne, the English divines of the seventeenth and eighteenth centuries, and, above all, the translators of the King James Bible. The last century's other master of English, James Joyce, was essentially a Catholic writer; his work bristles with imagery from the Catholic liturgy, and many of the effects it seeks for depend on typographical presentation: these texts—even *Finnegans Wake*, for all its vaunted musicality—were written to be *seen on the page*. On this level Beckett is very much an Anglo-Irish Protestant, his language resonating—'like a verse of Isaiah, or of Jeremiah,' as Molloy says—as if delivered from the pulpit of a bare, three-quarters-empty church.

It will perhaps seem paradoxical to suggest that Beckett even in his late work is in many ways a traditional novelist, but I believe that he is. His characters, though few in type, are strongly drawn, and certainly memorable, and his plots are interesting (consider in the novel *Molloy* Moran's vain pursuit of its eponymous protagonist, or the drama of the nameless narrator's agonised journey through the mud in *How It Is*); his fictions, even the briefest of them, have beginnings, middles, and ends; and practically all of them have a 'twist in the tail'—Beckett, after all, was an avid reader of American and French thrillers. In *Molloy*, Moran begins his narrative thus: 'It is midnight. The rain is beating on the windows.' At the very end, after much journeying and many vicissitudes, he tells how he returned home to find himself mysteriously estranged from all that he once knew as familiar: 'Then I went back into the house and wrote, It is midnight. The rain is beating on the windows. It was not midnight. It was not raining.' And with that, the entire book collapses like a house of cards.

Beckett's themes are simple, and universal; as the critic S. E. Gontarski puts it: 'Childhood memories, adolescent unhappiness, fears of mortality, wasted opportunities, familial and cultural alienation, memories of suicidal sweethearts: these are the elements Beckett's art needs and needs to undo as he struggles to make universal art out of personal neurosis.' In other words, what he is dealing with is no less or more than life, the commonplace thing itself, in all its disorder, hilarity, ecstasy and pain.

But if the content of Beckett's work is conventional, its methods are not. His fictions advance by a kind of reverse progression, denying and consuming themselves as they go; as Wolfgang Iser has it: 'The Beckett reader is continually being confronted by statements that are no longer valid. But as the negated statements remain present in his mind, so the indeterminacy of the text increases, thus increasing the pressure on the reader to find out what is being withheld from him.' This is what Gontarski calls 'the intent of undoing'.

Of course, Beckett is not the first artist to 'affirm by negation'. Some of the greatest writers of the twentieth century, from Rilke and Hofmannsthal to Celan and Thomas Bernhard, have produced work that derives its power and pathos from the negative, from all that is absent from it. Negation is not nihilism. The statement of an absence implies a presence elsewhere. (Oh yes, Kafka remarked to his friend Max Brod, there is hope, plenty of hope—but not for us.) This is not to claim Beckett as a covert champion of an outmoded humanism, yet neither is he a harbinger of The End, as posthumanist commentators such as Theodor Adorno have all too often and too fiercely affirmed him to be. The essence of art is that like a river in spate it flows around obstacles and finds new ways of progressing. One of Beckett's favourite lines from Shakespeare is the observation by Edgar in *King Lear* that 'the worst is not/ So long as we can say "This is the worst".' And *The Unnamable*'s last words are, famously: 'I can't go on. I'll go on.' Even *Worstward Ho*, the most uncompromising of the late texts, ends thus:

> Nohow less. Nohow worse. Nohow naught. Nohow on.
>
> Said nohow on.

The point being, in my reading of it, that to have *said* nohow on is already to have found a way forward.

It is meaningless to describe Beckett, as he is often described, as a pessimist. His work is neither pessimistic nor optimistic; like all true art, it simply *is*. By its very existence it affirms—but affirmation is not always and not necessarily positive. A story is told of Beckett walking with friends to Lords cricket ground in London one fine summer morning and remarking on the splendours of the day. One of the friends agrees, and suggests that on such a day it is good to be alive, to which Beckett replies: 'Well, I wouldn't go so far as that!' Yet Beckett's narrators, even in their worst extremes of anguish, profess a deep fondness for the world. 'Great love in my heart too for all things still and rooted,' says the voice in *From an Abandoned Work*, and goes on:

> Oh I know I too shall cease and be as when I was not yet, only all over instead of in store, that makes me happy, often

> now my murmur falters and dies and I weep for happiness as I go along and for love of this old earth that has carried me so long and whose uncomplainingness will soon be mine. Just under the surface I shall be, all together at first, then separate and drift, through all the earth and perhaps in the end through a cliff into the sea, something of me.

When we consider these and countless other such tender passages in the work of his middle period, we realise that the fictions of the 1980s represent no real change of direction but merely an intensification of concerns that were always present but repressed in favour of the ferocity of Beckett's sensibility in the immediate postwar period.

'A voice comes to one in the dark. Imagine.' Thus begins *Company*. It is, I feel, the least successful of the four final works. The conjunction is uneasy between the solitary hearer lying in blackness and the bright images called up for him from childhood; the 'intent of undoing' is too apparent. Also, Beckett comes perilously close here to sentimentality. The images of the little boy holding his mother's hand, or sitting with his father in the summerhouse, or trying to make a pet of a hedgehog, have a touch almost of the Enid Blytonesque about them. Yet *Company* contains some of late Beckett's sparest and most supple prose, and in the end the old, harsh honesty is there, as this 'devised deviser devising it all for company' comes clean at last:

> You now on your back in the dark shall not rise to your arse again to clasp your legs in your arms and bow down your head till it can bow down no further. But with face upturned for good labour in vain at your fable. Till finally you hear how words are coming to an end. With every inane word a little nearer to the last. And how the fable too. The fable of one

> with you in the dark. The fable of one fabling of one with you in the dark. And how better in the end labour lost and silence. And you as you always were.
>
> Alone.

While *Company* and *Worstward Ho* may be described as autobiographical in the broadest sense, *Ill Seen Ill Said*, the finest of these late works, is narrated in the third person and has as its central figure a dying old woman, alone amid the snows at lambing time and watched over by a mysterious Twelve who ring the clearing where her cabin stands. It is profound and moving, an extended poetic meditation on eschatology; these last things shake the heart:

> Winter evening in the pastures. The snow has ceased. Her steps so light they barely leave a trace. Have barely left having ceased. Just enough to be still visible. Adrift the snow. Whither in her head while her feet stray thus? Hither and thither too? Or unswerving to the mirage? And where when she halts? The eye discerns afar a kind of stain. Finally the steep roof whence part of the fresh fall has slid. Under the low lowering sky the north is lost. Obliterated by the snow the twelve are there

Though all the movement of the work is towards death, the end is strangely joyful: 'One moment more. One last. Grace to breathe that void. Know happiness.' Lawrence Graver has remarked, somewhat menacingly, that 'speculation about the biographical significance' of the piece cannot go far 'until scholarly studies tell us a good deal more than we now know about the fiery relationship of May Beckett and her son,' yet he does declare 'how extraordinary it is that the mother-haunted *Ill Seen Ill Said* should be—for all its provisionality and anguish—arguably the most conclusive and serene of the old master's works'. Certainly it is the most tender. Beckett here seems to hover over the old woman who is his creation with all of a benign creator's care and helpless sorrow. Once even he lets himself appear directly in the text: 'She shows herself only to her own. But she has no own. Yes yes she has one. And who has her.'

Serene is not a word one would apply to *Worstward Ho*. This is a difficult, spiky work, built up arduously out of short, percussive sentences, as if the bearer of some terrible news had come stumbling to a halt before us and begun to stammer out his message: 'On. Say on. Be said on. Somehow on. Till nohow on. Said nohow on.' The entire piece is contained *in ovo* in this opening. Over the following couple of dozen pages the breathless speaker strives, mostly in vain, to unravel the sense of things. It is a frightful task. 'Less worse then? Enough. A pox on void. Unmoreable unlessable unworseable evermost almost void.' And yet despite the difficulties there are pleasures to be derived. The piece is strangely bracing in its energy and pace, and we are gripped by a sense that all this that is going on—whatever it may be—does *matter*. 'The words . . . How almost true they sometimes almost ring!' As always in Beckett, there is consolation to be had from the right articulation of even the deepest sorrow. The void is not void but 'almost void'.

What do they *mean*, these strange, fraught, desperate fictions? Are we to take any meaning from them? Are they 'about' something, or are they that something itself? There are many explicitly religious references, especially in *Ill Seen Ill Said*, which speaks of one of the old woman's gestures being 'full of grace', and of a nail in the wall 'All set to serve again. Like unto its glorious ancestors. At the place of the skull. One April afternoon. Deposition done.' Where such references are concerned, however, it would be well to remember Beckett's remarks about his use in *Waiting for Godot* of the anecdote of the two thieves crucified with Christ, one of whom was saved and the other damned: it was not the theological aspect that interested him, he said—he merely *liked the shape of the idea*.

I believe that all of Beckett's work, from the fumblings of the hapless Belacqua in *More Pricks than Kicks* to the final, benighted groping for speech in the poem 'what is the word', is first and foremost a critique of language, of the deceptiveness of words, and of our illusions about what we can express and the value of expression, and that it was his genius to produce out of such an enterprise these moving, disconsolate, and scrupulously crafted works. Writing in *The New York Review of Books* on the occasion of the centenary of Beckett's birth, Colm Tóibín quoted Beckett writing to his German translator in the 1930s and insisting: 'Grammar and Style. To me they seem to have become as irrelevant as a Victorian bathing suit or the imperturbability of a true gentleman. A mask.' 'And yet,' Tóibín went on,

> as we know from his work . . . he was half in love with grammar and style. He knew the power of a sharp sentence and a well-placed comma. He was constantly prevented from putting his own agenda into operation. His higher goal constantly eluded him. This battle between austerity, distance, a refusal to play games, and the distraction of wit and the sound of words gave his work its power and its unpredictability. . . . [T]he gap between Oscar Wilde's wit and eloquence and Joyce's embrace of the world was one that he sought not to fill at all, but to leave empty and stark. He sought to enter that dark space with all his damaged talent, his mixture of arrogance and humility. He was determined to leave the void empty and to fill it with echoes, all at the same time.

Beckett is an exemplary figure. He presents for the writers who came after him a model of probity and tenacity which is a source of encouragement and strength in an age when literature itself seems under threat. He refused to take part in the cult of personality, maintaining an admirable reticence in the face of a gossip-obsessed world. He lived, he wrote; the rest, in the wise words of Henry James, is the madness of art. When I think of him I always recall his description in *Malone Dies* of young Sapo watching the flight of the hawk, 'fascinated by such extremes of need, of pride, of patience and solitude.'

('Beckett's Last Words', 2006)

Living Ghosts

Human Chain by Seamus Heaney (Farrar, Straus and Giroux)

Poetry has always been half in love with easeful death. There must have been a time, as Thomas Hardy in his great poem 'Before Life and After' assures us there was, when death constituted nothing more than the end of life, a time when 'if something ceased, no tongue bewailed'; a far-off time, that is, before the poets discovered their calling as elegists. It was a discovery they made early on. The Epic of Gilgamesh, one of the oldest surviving works of literature, is obsessed with the mystery of mortality, Homer too lingers often among the shades, and Shakespeare and Milton are ever mindful that the very notion of cadence implies a lapsing, a falling away. Death, Wittgenstein assures us, is not an experience in life, but the poet knows otherwise, and seeks to catch us in the web of words as we fall.

The mourning bell tolls throughout *Human Chain*, Seamus Heaney's new collection of poems, his twelfth, but the sound it makes is a sonorous call to life and continuity: 'The dead here are borne/Towards the future.' In these marvellous poems Heaney displays all that sweetness and ease of gesture, that colloquial accommodation, that are the unmissable traits of his art; but the thinking in these lines evinces new 'torsions'—a word Heaney used tellingly in his Nobel acceptance speech—that Donne and Dowland would have recognised and approved:

Too late, alas, now for the apt quotation
About a love that's proved by steady gazing
Not at each other but in the same direction.

Yet if this is metaphysical poetry, it is without the yawning tomb, the death's-head rictus, the bracelet of bright hair about the bone. Heaney's dead are vibrantly alive, fleshed out by the force of memory and through the power of poetry, even if the flesh here often has the 'webby weight' of his dying father's underarm in the poem 'Album.' *Human Chain* marks many deaths but all the markings are a celebration of what was lived:

As between clear blue and cloud,
Between haystack and sunset sky,
Between oak tree and slated roof,

I had my existence. I was there.
Me in place and the place in me.

Baudelaire somewhere remarks that literary genius—the word 'genius' used here in the Latin sense of begetting or making—consists in an ability to summon up childhood at will. Seamus Heaney's power of recall, especially of his earliest years, is a phenomenon that has awed critics from the time of his first collection, *Death of a Naturalist*, in 1966—the title poem of which remembers in exact and gloriously turbid detail the flax-dam near his childhood home where 'Bubbles gargled delicately, bluebottles/Wove a strong gauze of sound around the smell,' and frogspawn 'grew like clotted water.' One of this poet's great gifts is to have found a way of making a music that sounds like the rough music of the past itself, a music that is guttural, consonantal, as he has said himself, yet wonderfully delicate, too, as in 'Song,' a poem from *Field Work* (1979), that opens with the ash tree called a rowan, which has red berries:

A rowan like a lipsticked girl.
Between the by-road and the main road
Alder trees at a wet and dripping distance
Stand off among the rushes.

There are the mud-flowers of dialect
And the immortelles of perfect pitch
And that moment when the bird sings very close
To the music of what happens.

• • •

As many of his readers will know by now, Seamus Heaney was born in 1939 on a small farm, Mossbawn—a wonderfully Heaneyesque name, soft and allusive—near the village of Castledawson, County Derry, in Northern Ireland, the first of nine children. In *Stepping Stones* (2008), a book of interviews with Seamus Heaney by Dennis O'Driscoll, the poet describes the 'one-storey, longish, lowish, thatched and whitewashed house' consisting of three rooms attached to a stable. Here, as he said in his Nobel acceptance address, the family

> lived a kind of den-life which was more or less emotionally and intellectually proofed against the outside world . . . We took in everything that was going on, of course—rain in the trees, mice on the ceiling, a steam train rumbling along the railway line one field back from the house—but we took it in as if we were in the doze of hibernation. Ahistorical, pre-sexual, in suspension between the archaic and the modern . . .

The family later moved to a larger farm a few miles away, called The Wood, and built a new, modern, featureless house. By then Heaney was fifteen, and although he speaks of summer days there that 'were among the most idyllic of my life,' and despite the fact that a number of later poems are set in The Wood, it is probably fair to say that Mossbawn is Heaney's true treasure-house of memory. The poem 'Mossbawn,' consisting of two parts and dedicated to the poet's mother, conjures and celebrates a childhood world:

And here is love
like a tinsmith's scoop
sunk past its gleam
in the meal-bin.

'Mossbawn' appeared in *North*, Heaney's most politically *engagé* and most politically troubled collection, published in 1975, when the Northern Ireland conflict was in one of its most savage phases; yet even here, amid these tense and often tormented poems, it is plain that the prelapsarian world of childhood is the poet's abiding inspiration. And if childhood is for Heaney, as it is for all of us, a recent antiquity, he found in the more ancient past of northern Denmark as depicted in the archaeologist P. V. Glob's book *The Bog People* a landscape that was to him politically and poetically familiar.

When *North* was published Heaney came in for criticism, especially in southern Ireland, for what seemed to some a too easy and even dangerous comparison between the ritual Iron Age slayings that Glob described and the sectarian slaughter being carried out almost daily among Catholics and Protestants in the North. Already, however, in 'The Tollund Man,' an early 'bog poem' from his 1972 collection *Wintering Out*, he had declared that 'Some day I will go to Aarhus' to see the body of this sacrificial victim preserved by peat-acids:

Out there in Jutland
In the old man-killing parishes

I will feel lost,
Unhappy and at home.

And in *District and Circle*, published in 2006, the collection that preceded *Human Chain*, he imagined 'The Tollund Man in Springtime':

. . . neither god nor ghost,
Not at odds or at one, but simply lost
To you and yours, out under seeding grass
And trickles of kesh water, sphagnum moss,
Dead bracken on the spreadfield, red as rust.

In *Human Chain* the deaths are more prosaic and more recent, and the poet's relation to them is more intimate, more pained, and more urgent, for now he is feeling the pinch of his own mortality and confronting the dismaying and immediate fact that one day perhaps not very far off he will be numbered among these shades that he is invoking. In the very beautiful title poem he combines the appalling present of foreign wars and catastrophes with a characteristic memory from his own past and an intimation of an inevitable future. Here is the poem in full:

Seeing the bags of meal passed hand to hand
In close-up by the aid workers, and soldiers
Firing over the mob, I was braced again

With a grip on two sack corners,
Two packed wads of grain I'd worked to lugs
To give me purchase, ready for the heave—

The eye-to-eye, one-two, one-two upswing
On to the trailer, then the stoop and drag and drain
Of the next lift. Nothing surpassed

That quick unburdening, backbreak's truest payback,
A letting go which will not come again.
Or it will, once. And for all.

• • •

It is always difficult to know whether to take a poetry collection as an intended whole and read it through from first poem to last, or pick one's way about in it as one might in a summer meadow, fixing on this blossom and then on that, haphazardly, happily. *Human Chain*, however, is unmistakably of a piece, for as its title suggests it is a series of links stretching in a great arc from an opening moment of airy epiphany to a final loosening and lightening as a kite breaks free of its string and 'takes off, itself alone, a windfall.' 'Had I Not Been Awake,' the initial poem—and it does stand at the head of the collection like the compact but elaborate first letter of a medieval codex—crackles with the force of a presentiment that seems as dangerous as it is exciting, as the poet awakes to hear

A wind that rose and whirled until the roof
Pattered with quick leaves off the sycamore

And got me up, the whole of me a-patter,
Alive and ticking like an electric fence . . .

After this opening gust we are at once transported to the land of the dead, although the second poem, 'Album,' also starts off with a whoosh and a whop as 'the oil-fired heating boiler comes to life/Abruptly, drowsily, like the timed collapse/Of a sawn-down tree . . .' The image of the felled tree sets the poet to imagining his parents in a time before he knew them even though he was somehow present with them:

It's winter at the seaside where they've gone
For the wedding meal. And I am at the table,
Uninvited, ineluctable.

The poem centres on the poet's father, and a thrice-enacted embrace between him and the son, the first one that might have taken place but did not 'on the riverbank/That summer before college,' the second when the father was drunk and needed help, and the third when he is dying and the son is helping him to the bathroom, 'my right arm/Taking the webby weight of his underarm,' an Aeneas, as it might be, about to sling Anchises up onto his back. Heaney has always been a Virgilian, and this poem finds an echo much later in the collection, in 'The Riverbank Field,' a lovely reimagining of passages from *Aeneid* VI in which the poet declares that he will

confound the Lethe in Moyola

By coming through Back Park down from Grove Hill
Across Long Rigs on to the riverbank—

That poem is followed by a masterly twelve-part sequence, 'Route 110,' which opens with the poet as a young man buying a second-hand copy of *Aeneid* VI, and where again we find ourselves on the banks of the Lethe watching the dead being transported to their final destination, as the poet 'hurried on, shortcutting to the buses,/Parrying the crush with my bagged Virgil' and in a market passes by

racks of suits and overcoats that swayed
When one was tugged from its overcrowded frame
Like their owners' shades close-packed on Charon's barge.

The true beauty of 'Route 110,' however, is revealed only at the end, when we find that we are not in the land of the dead at all, or at least not all of us are, but in the place of the living, in a lying-in room where there is not death, but the birth of a grandchild:

So now, as a thank-offering for one
Whose long wait on the shaded bank has ended,
I arrive with my bunch of stalks and silvered heads

Like tapers that won't dim
As her earthlight breaks and we gather round
Talking baby talk.

• • •

A few years ago Seamus Heaney suffered a serious stroke, from which he recovered fully, though it is plain that he still can feel the place where death laid its chill hand on his brow. Deaths crowd upon these pages, the past deaths of others and the poet's own death that is to come, but, Heaney being Heaney, both the remembrance and the expectation are spurs to a meditation upon what it is to be alive, both as an individual in one's own life and as a survivor standing in the shadow of those who have, in that gentle old phrase, gone before. Ghosts abound in this volume, not only the ghosts of family and friends, but of previous work, too. Heaney's early and, in all senses of the word, signature poem, 'Digging,' from his first collection, *Death of a Naturalist*, opens with a recollection of his father plying a spade and ends with the poet's famous declaration of intent:

Between my finger and my thumb
The squat pen rests.
I'll dig with it.

In *Human Chain* he picks up that pen again, and this time it is a specific model, a Conway Stewart with a fourteen-carat nib, three gold bands in the screw-top, and a pump-action lever that the shopkeeper demonstrates, treating the pen 'to its first deep snorkel/In a newly opened ink-bottle,' and allowing the poet and his parents

> time
> To look together and away
> From our parting, due that evening,
>
> To my longhand
> 'Dear'
> to them, next day

Another revenant is the final, thrilling poem in this collection, 'A Kite for Aibhín,' naming Heaney's granddaughter in a version of Giovanni Pascoli's '*L'Aquilone*,' which ends with that splendidly consoling image of death already quoted, as the kite breaks free of its earthly tether and 'takes off, itself alone, a windfall.' The poem brings us back to another kite poem, from the 1984 collection *Station Island*, 'A Kite for Michael and Christopher,' in which the poet urges his two sons to take the kite-string 'in your two hands, boys, and feel/the strumming, rooted, long-tailed pull of grief.'

In *Human Chain* grief is not debilitating, does not stop the poet in his tracks or blind his sight with tears; rather, it is a token of sensibility, of fellow feeling and loving-kindness, a proof of being alive and capable of treasuring others, and the memory of others, the lost ones. This kind of grieving is touched with a Virgilian nobility, and although it is a strong link between the poems in *Human Chain* it pervades all of Heaney's work. Reading of the dying father being helped to the lavatory in 'Album' we recall a similar ministration in the poem 'Home Help' in *District and Circle*, where the poet tells of himself and another carrying a dying aunt upstairs every night in her wooden chair—'carefully manhandled'—and thinking 'of her warm brow we might have once/Bent to and kissed before we kissed it cold.'

• • •

That last is an example of the kind of heart-stopping ending that Heaney is such a master of, and in *Human Chain* such instances of sudden lift and illumination carry us again and again to that riverbank where the shades are crowded together, twittering as they wait for Charon to come and bear them away. In two of the poems, 'Chanson d'Aventure' and 'Miracle,' it is the poet himself who is being transported, 'strapped on, wheeled out, forklifted, locked/In position for the drive,' not to the land of Pluto but to a more mundane but no less frightening destination, the hospital where this stroke victim's life will be saved. The third section of 'Chanson d'Aventure' is a resplendent evocation of the ancient statue of the charioteer in the museum at Delphi, who

> holds his own,
> His six horses and chariot gone,
> His left hand lopped
>
> From a wrist protruding like an open spout,
> Bronze reins astream in his right, his gaze ahead
> Empty as the space where the team should be,
>
> His eyes-front, straight-backed posture like my own
> Doing physio in the corridor, holding up
> As if once more I'd found myself in step
>
> Between two shafts, another's hand on mine,
> Each slither of the share, each stone it hit
> Registered like a pulse in the timbered grips.

In 'Miracle' the place of the bronze charioteer is taken by the paralysed man saved by Christ in the New Testament, a passing glimpse of whom we are given in the phrase 'the one who takes up his bed and walks,' and just as the paralytic, summoned back to health and vigour, finds himself at first dazed and bewildered, so the poet stretches out an infirm hand to steady himself, as in the ambulance he and his wife 'careered at speed through Dungloe, / Glendoan, our gaze ecstatic and bisected / By a hooked-up drip-feed to the cannula.' Here, now, the old certainties are gone—'Where can it be found again, / An elsewhere world, beyond / Maps and atlases . . . ?'—but out of the new uncertainty a marvellous poetry springs.

And what poetry it is. Heaney writes with such easy assurance that one tends not to remark the technical mastery with which he achieves his effects. In this volume he has found a new fluidity of line, and his rhythms have a lightly skipping quality that belies the sombre themes he addresses. At times this lightness produces the quality of a Japanese print, or of William Carlos Williams at his most limpid—

The full of a white
Enamel bucket
Of little pears.

Still life
On the red tiles
Of that floor.

—or, describing the look of a coal fire banked up with slack and burning itself out from within, the wit of one of the Elizabethans:

The cindery skull
Formed when its tarry
Coral cooled.

Perhaps one might ask for a harsher note now and then, a drop of acid to bring a bit of bitterness to all this lush and celebratory remembering—something of Lowell's lordly rancour, say, or even of Eliot's calculated reprehensions—but surely it would be churlish to spurn anything of the rich late gift that is so generously offered to us in these poems. In his Nobel address, acknowledging the awe we rightly feel before the 'torsions in the poetry of Paul Celan' and the 'suspiring voice in Samuel Beckett,' he quoted lines from Yeats's great poem 'Meditations in Time of Civil War' in which the poet invokes images of blood and terror and yet tenderly invites the honeybees to come and build in an empty bird's nest at his window—lines that, Heaney insists, satisfy

> the contradictory needs which consciousness experiences at times of extreme crisis, the need on the one hand for a truth telling that will be hard and retributive, and on the other hand, the need not to harden the mind to a point where it denies its own yearnings for sweetness and trust.

In *Human Chain* the poet faces death squarely, and faces it down. Who else in our time but Seamus Heaney could have taken up his bed and walked with such fortitude, such insouciance, and such tenderness? What he has found is nothing less than

> A way for all to see a way to heaven,
> The same as when a pinholed *Camera*
> *Obscura* unblinds the sun eclipsed.

('Living Ghosts', 2010)

Fidgets of Remembrance

MEMOIR

1989, 2003

Lupins and moth-laden nights in Rosslare

Lupins are for me what the *madeleine* was to Proust. When I glimpse a clump of these ungainly flowers, and catch their faintly rancid scent, time falls away and I am a child again. Distinctly I hear the sound of the sea, feel the sting of salt on sunburned skin, taste banana sandwiches, and smell that mingled smell of crushed grass, seaweed, nightsoil and cows, that wafts across the years to me from Duggan's Field in Rosslare Strand.

Rosslare was always 'our' seaside place. We lived in Wexford town, and some of my earliest memories are of standing with my bucket and spade on the platform of the South Station while the tracks, and I, trembled in anticipation of the arrival of the enormous black steam-train that would take us the fourteen miles or so to The Strand.

Those were day trips; later on, when I was seven or eight, we began to spend most of July and August there each year, staying in Duggan's Field in one of the wooden chalets collectively known, with touching unpretentiousness, as 'the huts'. The hut that we rented in the early years was a wooden railway carriage from which the wheels had been removed: I can hear still the mysteriously satisfying *clunk* that the doors made when we swung them shut on the moth-laden night and gathered round the table for card games by the light of an oil lamp.

I was very fond of that railway carriage. I held it up repeatedly, clad in cowboy hat and fringed chaps and brandishing a pearl-handled six-shooter. Then one day someone—a girl, probably—

asked with a curled lip if I belonged to that family who couldn't afford to rent a *real* hut and had to make do with that awful old train thing. I think it was my first taste of social ignominy.

Hut-life was rudimentary. In the early days my mother cooked on a Primus stove, though later there came the Kosangas hob. We drew water from a communal pump, lugged it across the field in twin enamelled buckets from which somehow, always, a splash would fall into our sandals, first the left one, then the right. Lavatory facilities hardly bear discussion: the name 'Elsan' still strikes dread into my heart. The rickety door, the bolt I did not trust, the squadron of flies unable to believe their good fortune, and, of course, the *stink*. Oh, and don't forget the fortnightly foray at dead of night into the lupins, where a hole had been dug in which we buried *it* . . . No wonder those flowers thrived.

There were pleasanter chores. I liked to go down the lane first thing to fetch a can of milk from Cormie Duggan's farm. Cormie was as shy as we were, a decent, gentle man. How white and cool the dairyroom was: a hen would come and stand on one leg in the doorway, with a look in its beady eye at once tentative and bold. The milk had a warm thick smell.

• • •

We lived outdoors for the most part. When the weather was good we even ate outside. (Butter melting in a cheap glass dish . . .) And we played. Rounders was the favourite game, but there was a whole season, I remember, devoted to Scotch. Scotch was not exactly complicated: we threw a ball at each other, and if we caught it we got a turn to throw it back, but if we didn't catch it we were 'out'.

I played it so much that year that I developed a pain in my arm and was rushed to the doctor (polio was still a great fear) who pronounced me the first recorded case of Scotch Elbow; my brother, who had been forced to spend a fine afternoon sitting with me in the surgery, was not amused.

There was also a game called Hunt, a sort of elaborate hide-and-seek. Hunt had a vague but palpable tang of sex to it: something to do with stalking a warm quarry through long grass and ferns (the lupins, that might harbour a freshly filled-in hole, we avoided). Hunt, yes, Hunt definitely reared its ugly head. But there was always the sea in which to cool off.

We were almost sea creatures (in fact, one boy who came to stay in the field had webbed toes). We knew the water in all its summer moods, from blue and brisk to stormy green and back again to dove-grey, dreamy stillness. It strikes me now, though it did not then, what a strange thing is the ocean. It is like nothing else on earth. Rocks, trees, mountains, seem homely compared to it.

Even the sky is not as strange as the sea. How did we manage to get used to it, how could we frolic and wrestle with it, shrieking, as if we were playing with a large, friendly pet? Well, we just did. It was there, and so were we. It is only time, constantly manufacturing the past, that makes us see the oddness of things.

I was never a good swimmer, but I had tenacity. Girls were impressed by the great distances I could go, doggedly churning along; I cannot think they were impressed by what came out of the water at the end of these marathons, a shrivelled, grey, shivering creature with blue lips and red eyes. I was good at swimming underwater, and could stay down for long stretches. And then, going along like that, blear-eyed and with bursting lungs, there was no telling whom one might bump into, whose legs one's own might become entangled with.

• • •

Girls again. Yes, in Rosslare I lived *à l'ombre des jeunes filles en fleurs*. With what a piercing sense of sweetness I fell in love, repeatedly. I can hardly remember their names, but I can see, as if they had turned away from me just this moment, their sun-bleached hair, their shoulders like ill-folded wings, the achingly vulnerable pale backs of their knees, the heart-shapes of suntan printed on their insteps through the cut-out uppers of their Clark's sandals.

Extraordinary, the weight of passion a mere kiss could carry in those days.

My early teens were the best of my times in Rosslare. In those years my brother and sister and I shared a hut with two first cousins. I was the youngest, and so I could feel grown-up and cosmopolitan. Strangely, perhaps, I recall most clearly the bad-weather days of this period. We played endless games of cards, progressing, as the years went on, from Snap to Forty-Five, to Rummy, to Sevens, and even, in the end, to Canasta. We cooked chips on the Kosangas stove, and drank Brazil Orange, and my cousin Mary made desserts with ice cream and fruit cocktail (remember fruit cocktail?—not a hint of a kiwi fruit) and hundreds-and-thousands.

We went to the pictures in the afternoons, to a corrugated-iron cinema where the projectionist had to change the reels twice, plunging the place into breathless, throbbing darkness for minutes on end (girls, again . . .). I remember coming out of that cinema one 'lonely rain-ceased midsummer evening' (Philip Larkin) and seeing, with an inexplicable pang, of happiness or sorrow, I was not sure which, a boat with a red sail, far out on the sea, turning slowly into the sunlight.

September. One last day on the beach, listening to 'the small hushed waves' repeated fresh collapse' (Larkin again), while the season's end hovered in the air, out over the water, like an approaching cloud. Then home, with its startlingly familiar smell, and the town, shabbier than ever, and the scratchy feel of a school uniform, and everything grey and dull and awful, and probably she won't write, though she promised she would.

Then something, impossible to say what—the memory of a chestnut's oiled smoothness, perhaps, or the thought of Hallowe'en parties—rises like a little melody, impossible to resist, and you turn, and walk away, whistling, with your hands in your pockets, and you know for a moment, beyond all doubt, that she *will* write, that the party will be great, that Rosslare will still be there next summer, and that you'll never, never die.

('Lupins and moth-laden nights in Rosslare', 1989)

‘It was winter the first time I saw Prague’

It was winter the first time I saw Prague, the city blanketed with snow and glistening in the sunlight of an unseasonably bright late January. Perhaps it is the snow that intensifies the silence of the city in these, my earliest memories of it. Prague’s silence is more a presence than an absence. The sounds of the traffic, the voices in the streets, the tolling of bells and the chiming of innumerable public clocks, all resonate against the background hush as if against a high, clear pane of glass. There is too in my recollections a sense somehow of incipient flight, of everything in that sparkling scene being poised to slip its tethers and rise up into the dome of brilliant blue: poised, but never to break free. At that time, in the early 1980s, the Cold War was going through one of its decidedly warmer phases, although it was, did we but know it, already beginning to end. I had come to Czechoslovakia in the expectation that all my received ideas of what life was like in Eastern Europe would be overturned. I was to be disappointed—most of the clichés about communist rule would prove dispiritingly accurate—but also strangely exhilarated. Elsewhere is always a surprise.

We had agreed to meet up, J. and G. and I, in Trieste, that melancholy, pearl-grey port where the two women were spending a couple of waterlogged days—Prague’s snow was Trieste’s slush. The women were eager to get away, and we left on the evening of my arrival, taking the Budapest train and changing at midnight in Ljubljana to the sleeper for Prague. That word, ‘sleeper’, proved to be a misnomer, for in our carriage of couchettes no one slept, except a large fat man in a shiny pinstriped suit, who snored. At every unpronounceable station along the way the train had to stop and catch its breath, standing in the dark and wheezing like a sick horse. Did we pass through Vienna or did I dream it in a doze? At the Czech border two greatcoated guards with automatic rifles got on board and examined our passports with sceptical frowns, thumbing doggedly back and forth through the pages, searching for something they seemed aggrieved not to find. Their guns looked altogether too square and stubby and ill-designed to be effective, and might have been made of cardboard, but still were frightening. The fat man was hard to wake; at last he sat up blearily and began patting his pockets; producing his papers, he muttered something that made the waiting guards glance at each other briefly and laugh. I rubbed a clear patch on the window and looked out on a bleak expanse of no man's land the size of a football pitch, with ghostly patches of glittering ice, and a watchtower on stilts, starkly lit, and lamps glowing in the frozen mist like giant dandelion heads, and dim, bundled figures moving spectrally over the countless criss-crossing lines of dully gleaming rail. As I was turning from the window I noticed that someone had blown his nose on the tied-back oatmeal-coloured curtain beside me. The guard who had been inspecting my passport handed it back and in a guttural accent straight out of an old war movie bade me welcome to Czechoslovakia.

Our hotel, the name of which refuses to be recalled, was a large, gaunt cube of concrete and dusty glass on a nondescript street which in subsequent sojourns in the city I have been consistently unable to re-find. It was somewhere not far from Wenceslas Square. The hotel was one of a not extensive list of such establishments officially approved to accommodate tourists from the West, all of whom, we had been warned, were regarded by the authorities as part-time spies, by illegal money-changers as a costive but surely inexhaustible source of precious dollars, and by the young as spoilt playboys and playgirls who, despite their fabulous and ostentatious wealth, might be persuaded to take their jeans off in the street and sell them for handfuls of next to worthless Czech koruny. And indeed, we had hardly stepped into the hotel lobby when we were approached by a broadly smiling young man, hands jauntily hitched in the high pockets of his tight leather jacket, who in a curious, crooning English offered to convert our money at what he assured us would be 'top-dollar rates, the highest in town'. In demonstration of the weight of this offer he quickly flashed a brick-sized block of koruny—because of that currency's unsayable abbreviation, *ǩcs*, we were to give it the nickname *kecks*—and as quickly palmed it again into his pocket. He was the first of many of his kind that we were to encounter, not dangerous, not seriously criminal, even, just would-be entrepreneurs, immediately recognisable by that professional smile, meant to display innocence and winning candour, behind which there lurked a beseeching something that the smile itself could not keep from admitting had small hope of being assuaged. And, to his unsurprised regret, we did decline his services, and passed on with vague apology, feeling uneasily that we might have failed to answer the first distress call directed at us by this bludgeoned, impoverished city. In an alcove, sitting over cold coffee cups at a table under a plastic palm, two achingly beautiful girls in poor imitations of last year's Paris or New York fashions, slim-wristed, pale, with bruise-brown shadows under huge eyes, looked me up and down, flaring their nostrils. Another offer, another regretful no.

For me, bad traveller that I am, there is always a moment of mild panic that comes immediately after the hotel porter has set down my bags, accepted his tip and softly exited from what is suddenly, dismayingly, *my room*. This is the enigma of arrival. How resentful of one's presence this unhumanly neat box seems, the bed hermetically sealed under its mighty bedspread, the chair that no one has ever sat in at the writing table where no one has ever written, that room service menu in its plastic-covered folder, slightly and appetite-killingly tacky to the touch. And how shabby one's poor old suitcase looks, how shamefaced, standing there on the no-colour carpet. Light-headed after that sleepless train journey and buzzing still with travel fever I clambered on to the bed and lay with hands folded on my breast, staring up desperately at the dim ceiling with its sprinkler vents and its miniature, fake chandelier. There was what looked like a wad of chewing gum stuck up there, the legacy of what must have been a prodigiously powerful spitter. Now would be a suitable moment to contemplate a brief history of Prague. Instead, I get up and go down the corridor to talk to J. and G.

Because they are two, they have been allotted a bigger room than mine, a room so vast, indeed, that a thin, chill mist seems to hang in the farther reaches of it. Intimidated by the scale and mortuary stillness of the place, they have not yet unpacked, and J. has not even taken off her coat. We speculate on the possibility of breakfast. The women recount with a shudder an experience at an early-morning buffet in the Gellert in Budapest, when they lifted the lid of a nickel receptacle, unencouragingly suggestive of a kidney-dish, and were confronted with a bloated, grey, semi-circular sausage floating in an inch of warm, greasy water. We wonder if we might go out and look for a café. We are thinking of somewhere small and cosy, as unlike this terrible room as possible, a local place, where locals go, with fogged windows and a copper coffee machine and newspapers on sticks, the kind of place, we know very well, that is never to be found in the vicinity of a hotel such as this one. We have hours to kill before noon, when the Professor is to come and meet us. Despite their hunger pangs the women decide on sleep. I fetch my guidebook and go in search of the river.

I had something more than a visitor's curiosity. Some years previously I had written a novel partly set in Prague at the turn of the seventeenth century. When I was working on the book I did not regard the inventing of a city I had never seen as any more of a challenge than, for example, having to re-create the early 1600s—all fiction is invention, and all novels are historical novels—but I was interested to know what level of verisimilitude, or at least of convincingness, I had achieved. Many readers had complimented me on the accuracy with which my book had 'caught the period', to which I was too grateful and too polite to respond by asking how they could possibly know; I understood that what they were praising was the imaginative feat they felt I had performed in persuading them that this was just how it had been then. But fancy does sometimes summon up the concrete, as anyone who has had a prophetic dream will know. There have been a number of eerie instances when this or that character or happening that I thought entirely my invention subsequently turned out to be historically real. In another novel, set long ago in what is now Poland, I had fashioned—forged, perhaps, would be the better word—a minor character, a soldier, whose presence the plot had demanded, but whose real existence I learned of when, after the book had been published, I received a biographical sketch of him from a helpful Polish historian. The making of fiction is a funny business.

The Charles Bridge was deserted that morning, a thing the latter-day visitor will find hard to credit, since that statued stone span must now be one of the world's most densely peopled spaces, all day long, and throughout most of the night. Frost glittered in the air over the river, just as it had that morning in sixteen-hundred-and-something when my protagonist, the astronomer Johannes Kepler, arrived here from Ulm on a barge, to present the first printed copies of the *Tabulae Rudolphinae* to the Emperor after whom he had so hopefully named his almanac. There, looming above me now as it had loomed above my disembarking astronomer, was the great, blank fortress of Hradčany, and over there was Malá Strana, the Little Quarter, where Kepler would live when he took up his appointment as Rudolph's imperial mathematician. Yes, I had got it right, to a startling degree. Why was I not pleased? In part because, standing there surveying my handiwork, I was struck yet again by the essential fraudulence of fiction. Conjure a winter morning, a river and a castle and a traveller disembarking with a book under his arm, and for the space of a page or two an implied world comes to creaky life. It is all a sleight of the imagination, a vast synecdoche. And yet one goes on doing it, spinning yarns, trying to emulate blind Fate herself.

Much has been written on the beauty of Prague, but I am not sure that beauty is the right word to apply to this mysterious, jumbled, fantastical, absurd city on the Vltava, one of Europe's three capitals of magic—the other two being Turin and Lyon. There is loveliness here, of course, but a loveliness that is excitingly tainted. In his book *Magica Praha*, that ecstatic paean of *amor urbi*, Angelo Maria Ripellino figures the city as a temptress, a wanton, a she-devil. 'The antiquary coquetry with which she pretends to be nothing more than a still life, a silent succession of glories long since past, a dead landscape in a glass ball, only increases her sorcery. She slyly works her way into the soul with spells and enigmas to which she alone holds the key.' Ripellino's Prague is not that miraculously preserved museum piece of noble prospects and Biedermeier frontages which in the Seventies and Eighties of the last century earned some desperately needed hard currency as a backdrop for Hollywood movies set in the never-never time of Mozart and Salieri; his is the city of 'surreptitious passages and infernal alleys . . . still smelling of the Middle Ages,' of cafés and *Kaffeehäuser*—'in our time,' Kafka writes, 'the catacombs of the Jews'—low dives such as The Poison Inn, The Old Lady, The Three Little Stars, although he does sometimes escape the 'sinister narrowness of those lanes, the stranglehold of those baleful alleys' by fleeing to 'the green islands, the efflorescent districts, the parks, belvederes and gardens that surround Prague on all sides.' This is the old Prague, wistful, secretive, tormented, which survived the communist takeover of 1948, and even the Russian invasion twenty years later, but which, irony of ironies, finally succumbed to the blow delivered to it by a velvet fist in a velvet glove in the revolution of 1989. Now the dollar is everywhere, the young have all the blue jeans they could desire, and there is a McDonald's just off the Charles Bridge. Well, why not. Praguers have the same right to vulgar consumerism as the rest of us. Freedom is freedom to eat cheap hamburgers as much as it is to publish subversive poetry. Yet one cannot help but wonder what Ripellino, who lectured in Czech literature at the University of Rome and died in 1978, and who tells us how in the dark years he would often go to Germany and gaze longingly eastward, a heartsick lover pining for *die ferne Geliebte*, toward the 'serrated mountain ranges of Bohemia', would have made of the tourist hive that his beloved temptress has turned into. Yet he was a great democrat, loving Prague for her promiscuity as well as for her secretiveness, delightedly citing the grotesque image in Vilém Mrštík's 1893 novel, *Santa Lucia*, of the city reminding the book's protagonist with 'shrill cries that trains were approaching her body and ever new crowds, ever new victims, were disappearing into her infinite womb.'

Ripellino's vast effort of recuperation is an attempt not so much to express the city as to ingest it, to make that metamorphosis of world into self that Rilke tells us is our task on earth. It is analogous to the effort every serious visitor must make. One will not know a city merely by promenading before its sites and sights, *Blue Guide* in hand. Yet how can one know an entity as amorphously elusive as Prague, or any other capital, for that matter? What *is* Prague?

Does its essence inhere in the pretty Old Town Square, with its cafés and its famous clock, or, on the far contrary, in the smouldering concrete suburbs, where the majority of Praguers live their decidedly unbohemian lives? Time lays down its layers like strata of rock, the porous limestone of the present over the granite of the communists over the ashes-and-diamonds of the Habsburgs over the basalt of the Přemyslids . . . Where, in what era, may one station oneself to find the best, the truest, view? When I was young I thought that to know a place authentically, to take it to one's heart, one must fall in love there. How many cities have seemed to spread themselves out before me in the very contours of the beloved's limbs. Solipsism. There are as many Pragues as there are eyes to look upon it—more: an infinity of Pragues. Confused and suddenly glum I make my way back toward the hotel. The frost has turned my face to glass.

While we wait, the three of us, in the women's bedroom for the Professor to arrive, we are aware of a faint but definite sense of nervousness, or perhaps it is only an intensity of anticipation. We have come to Prague with a mission. G. has an acquaintance, a young Czech *émigré* recently arrived in New York, I shall call him Miloš. Miloš hopes to study architecture at Columbia, but as yet he has not been able to find a job to support himself while going through college. His father believes he has found a way to help him, by sending him some art works which he will be able to sell for a lot of money. The difficulty is in getting these valuables out of Czechoslovakia. We have volunteered to do it—to smuggle them out. When J. and G. and I were discussing this plan over the international phone lines between Dublin and California it had seemed a bold adventure, but here in the winter light behind the Iron Curtain the inevitable misgivings had begun to assail us. In those days travellers' tales were rife of Western tourists being seized for the most trifling contraband offences and detained for months, for years, even, beyond the help of consular entreaty or ministerial bargaining. While I had often entertained the idle fancy that a jail cell might be the ideal place in which to write, I did not relish the prospect of mouldering for an indefinite period in an Eastern Bloc prison. There rose before me again the image of that Gellert sausage described by J. and G., or a distant relative of it, anyway, all mottled and shrunken with age, and floating not in a nickel dish but plonked down on a rusty tin plate beside a hunk of grey bread . . . Too late to back out now, however, for here was the Professor's hushed tapping at the door.

He was a tall, spare man with pale, short hair brushed neatly across a narrow forehead, a Nordic type unexpected this far to the south and east. Impossible to tell his age; at first sight he might have been anywhere between thirty and sixty. He was handsome, with that unblemished surface and Scandinavian features, yet curiously self-effacing, somehow. Even as he stood before me I found it hard to get him properly into focus, as if a flaw had suddenly developed in the part of my consciousness that has the task of imprinting images upon the memory. I think it was that he had spent so many years trying not to be noticed—by the authorities, by the police, by spies and informers—that a layer of his surface reality had worn away. He had something of the blurred aspect of an actor who has just scrubbed off his make-up. He shook hands with each of us in turn in that grave, elaborate, central European way that makes it seem one is being not greeted for the first time but already being bade farewell. Such a melancholy smile. His English was precise, with only the faintest accent. He welcomed us to Prague in a mild but calmly seigneurial tone, as if it were not Prague we had arrived in but his own private domain. We were to catch this proprietorial note repeatedly here, especially in intellectual circles; so many things that were precious had been taken from the lives of these artists, critics, scholars that they clung to the idea of their city, its history, its shabby magnificence, its unyielding mysteriousness, with the passion of exiles. I had brought a litre of duty-free Irish whiskey as a gift. 'Ah, Jameson!' the Professor said, in the tone of one acknowledging a precious gift from what had seemed a mythic place, silk from Cathay, spices from Samarkand. He took the bottle from my hands delicately, almost tactfully, with a finely judged degree of gratitude. Courtly: that was the word. It struck me I had never met anyone to whom the term could be so aptly applied.

He had advanced no more than a pace or two into the room, and when I moved to shut the door I seemed to detect behind the rimless spectacles that he wore a flicker of unease, of alarm, even. Still holding the whiskey bottle, he stood with his elbows pressed into his sides, his grey raincoat buttoned to the throat. When G. began to speak of the mission that had brought the three of us to Prague he silenced her at once by putting a finger to his lips and pointing to the dusty light fixture in the middle of the ceiling. It was another Prague gesture, always accompanied by a hapless apologetic smile, with which we were to become depressedly familiar. There were, there really were, hidden microphones everywhere.

We went down to the lobby, where the Professor judged that it was safe for us to talk, albeit in guarded murmurs. The two beautiful, black-eyed girls had gone, though their empty coffee cups, the rims printed with smeary lipstick kisses, remained on the table under the plastic palm. There were some twenty pictures, the Professor said, that he wished us to take to his son—not paintings, as I had thought, but photographs, highly valuable original contact prints by a Czech master whose name was unknown to me. The Professor was anxious to assure us that if we had any doubts about taking them out of the country we should say so and he would find another means of getting them to New York. It was perfectly apparent, however, that we were his only hope. No no, we protested stoutly, we were determined to help him. Again that pained, melancholy smile, and he cleared his throat and carefully pressed the tip of a middle finger to the frail gold bridge of his spectacles. In that case, would we do him the honour of coming to dinner that evening at his apartment, where we could not only view the photographs but meet his wife?

[• • •]

The Professor's wife was short, dark, handsome and intense. Her name was, let us say, Marta. The clothes she wore were too young for her, a tight black jumper and a black leather skirt, far too short, and black stockings. The outfit, at once severe—all that black—and slightly tartish, was I think a form of protest, a gesture of defiance against what she saw as the meanness and enforced conformity of her life. Of all the people I met in Prague that first time, no matter how oppressed or angry or despairing, she was the one who seemed to me truly a prisoner. There was a manic quality to her desperation, a sense of pent-up hysteria, as if she had passed the day, and so many other days, pacing the floor, from door to window, window to door, one hand plunged in her hair and the other clutching a shaking cigarette. She would have been frightening, in her violent discontent, had it not been for her humour. In the midst of a tirade against the State, against her family—she seemed to have a great many relatives, all of whom she professed to despise—she would suddenly stop and turn her face aside and give a snuffly cackle of laughter, and shake her head, and click her tongue, as if she had caught sight of a younger, happier, more cheerfully sceptical version of herself smiling at her and wagging a finger in rueful admonishment. I think that in her heart she simply could not credit her predicament, and lived in the angry conviction that a life so absurd and grotesque must be at any moment about to change. I liked her at once, the menacing black outfit, the scarlet fingernails, the frankly dyed hair, the flashing look that she gave me as, with a flamenco dancer's flourish of the shoulders, she handed me a bilious-green glass tumbler three-quarters full of vodka.

We were in a small, neat, bright room with a lot of blond, fake-Scandinavian furniture. Everywhere, on every available flat surface, Marta's collection of Bohemian glass vied for space with the Professor's books. Through an archway there was a galley kitchen where saucepans were seething and steaming. J. and G. and I sat crowded hip to hip on a narrow sofa, our knees pressed against the edge of a low coffee table. The Professor sat opposite us in what was obviously 'his' chair, an old wooden rocker draped with a faded, tasselled rug; when he grew animated, or when Marta was provoking him with one of her tirades, he would propel himself back and forth with steadily increasing speed until, just when it seemed the madly rearing chair would tip him forward on to the floor, he would grasp the armrests and pitch himself stiffly back against the headrest and go suddenly still, queasily smiling, like Dr Strangelove in his wheelchair, pinioned by a gravitational force all of his own. I made the first gaffe of the evening by asking how many rooms there were in the apartment. The Professor winced, and Marta in the galley turned from her steaming pots and gave a bitter snort of laughter; this room, it seemed, along with a tiny bathroom down the hall, was the extent of their living quarters. 'Our bed!' Marta said, pointing with a wooden spoon at the sofa where we were sitting. 'It unfolds,' the Professor corroborated helpfully, showing how with a graceful gesture of his hands. I am sure I was blushing.

[• • •]

After dinner Marta plied us with a sweet liqueur, a local speciality, the name of which I have forgotten—was it green, or was it just the glasses that were green?—and the Professor took from a drawer in his desk a music-case, exactly like, I saw with a start, the satchel that my sister had when we were children and she took piano lessons, an old leather one with a silver metal clasp like an attenuated dumbbell. He put the case on the coffee table and opened it flat. Inside was a sheaf of some thirty photographs, carefully wrapped in tissue paper. Perhaps it was the effect of the wine at dinner, and now the liqueur, but there seemed to me a vaguely religious, vaguely sacramental, tenor to the moment. And why not? True works of art are a real presence, after all.

The photographs were by Josef Sudek. They were in black-and-white, mostly views of Prague streetscapes, with a few interior studies, including 'Labyrinth in My Studio', two oneiric still-lifes from the 'Remembrance' series of the late 1960s, and the ravishing 'Nude', the one seated sideways with her hair partly hiding her face, from the early 1950s. I had not seen Sudek's work before; in fact, I had not heard of him before coming on this mission to Prague. He is, I believe, a great artist, in a league, or almost, with that other visual celebrant of a great city, the Parisian Eugène Atget, with whom he shares significant artistic traits. But these sober evaluations came later.

It is strange, that sense of familiarity one has on even a first encounter with an artist's work. As I looked at those photographs one by one I was convinced that I had seen them before, many times, and knew them well—that, indeed, there had never been a time when I did not already know them. Plato's by now trite notion must be true, that somewhere in the unconscious there is a myriad of ideal forms, the transcendent templates, as it were, against which is fitted and measured each new object that one encounters in the world. But there was a more immediate, less lofty, cause of the soft shock of recognition, a sort of shivery drizzle down the back of the mind, that I experienced as I took in these reticent yet ravishing, dreamy yet precise and always particular images. It was, simply, that in them I discovered Prague. Art, Henry James insisted in a famous letter of rebuke to the philistine H. G. Wells, art '*makes* life, makes interest, makes importance', by which he may be understood to mean that the work of art singles out, 'beautifully', as H. J. himself would have it, the essential matters, the essential moments, in the disordered flux that is actual, lived life, while ever acknowledging the unconsidered but sustaining dross left behind, the Derridean *rien* that is supposedly *de hors-texte*. All day I had been walking about the city without seeing it, and suddenly now Sudek's photographs, even the private, interior studies, showed it to me, in all its stony, luminous solidity and peculiar, wan, absent-minded beauty. Here, with this sheaf of pictures on my knees, I had finally arrived.

[• • •]

When I think back to those days, and nights, in Prague, I am not sure whether what I am summoning up are images from my memory, or from the photographs of Josef Sudek, so thoroughly has his work become for me an emblem of the place. I try to recall our leavetaking of the Professor and his wife; they lived in an anonymous apartment block on an unremarkable street to the west of Wenceslas Square, yet what I see is a scene straight out of one of Sudek's nocturnes, something like the view of Prašný Bridge on a snowy evening, or that lamp-lit cobbled square on Kampa Island, with the winter tree, and the Charles Bridge behind, and the city farther off, the light of the street lamp in the foreground all blurred and gauzy, as if seen through tears. At the door, Marta clutched G.'s hand in hers and bade her 'Say hello for me to California,' a greeting that sounded to our ears more like a farewell to an impossible dream. I do not think that Marta made it to America, in the end, although it is not impossible that she did. A couple of years ago we heard that the Professor had died. How quickly the past becomes the past! That night we walked in silence, the three of us, through the empty, frostbound streets back to our hotel. G. carried the photographs, rolled up tightly and concealed in a cardboard tube supposedly containing nothing more than a reproduction of a poster from the 1930s for an exhibition of formalist Czech art. Next morning, under a shower of sleet, we left the city by train. At the Austrian border we were held up for an hour while crossing guards went through the carriages with implements like giant versions of dentist's mirrors, searching under the seats and on the luggage racks for anyone who might have hidden there in an attempt to flee the country. My palms were damp: what if G. were to be made to open the cardboard tube and show its contents? But the guards were not interested in art. When we crossed to the Austrian side the first thing I saw was a hoarding of a half-naked woman advertising some degenerate Western luxury—Dior fashions or Mercedes motor cars—and something in me revelled instinctively, irresistibly, in the sight of what seemed such happy, hopeful, life-affirming colours, and I thought of the Professor, and Marta, and felt ashamed.

(*Prague Pictures: Portraits of a City*, 2003)

Firstlings

EARLY FICTION

1966–1971

The Party

I knew from the very start the party wouldn't be any good. I just had that feeling, you know? But since I don't often get invited to parties I had to go to this one, just in case. Anyhow, when one of the fellows in the office came up to me just as I was closing up the books for the night and asked me if I'd like to go to a 'do,' as he called it, out in Rathmines, I was so surprised that I said 'yes' straight off. I suppose I didn't really think about it then, but later on, when I went home, I asked myself, what's the use? But as I say, I had to go, just in case.

So I washed my hair—it gets very greasy—and I put on my best suit, and a clean shirt. When I was ready I found that I still had some time to go before I set out. I couldn't think of anything to do. Just sitting down and doing nothing wasn't much use, I soon got bored, and anyhow the creases in my trousers would only get ruined that way. I walked around my digs for a while, but since I have only one room, and a small one at that, I got fed up very quickly. I began to tell myself that I shouldn't have bothered with all this fuss, but should have sat down in my old clothes and read a book until it was time to go to bed. That's how I spend most of my evenings, and I'm always quite happy that way. I don't go out very often. I haven't got many friends—I don't need them really, I'm quite self-sufficient—and anyhow, with three pounds ten a week for digs, and laundry money besides, I don't have much left out of my pay packet. I really don't know how these fellows I hear talking about the great times they have can manage it on pay like ours. Sometimes it doesn't seem fair, them having such a good time, and me not—though mind you, as I say, I'm always quite happy to spend a quiet evening at home. I'm contented. I have to be, for it's not much fun if you want to go out with women and all, and can't afford it. Anyhow, the girls don't really go for me, I don't know why. I'm small, I know, with hair that's beginning to thin already, though I'm only twenty-two, and a long, thin nose that's always red, no matter what the weather. No, I'm not good-looking, but then I'm not really ugly either. And I have a nice manner, if I do say so myself. I'm always polite, and if I'm in female company I'm always careful to keep my language clean, and I never make any smutty remarks, as some people do. Talk like that only makes girls embarrassed, you can see that a mile off. But girls are strange too, they always seem to go for the fellows who talk smutty to them, and use double-meaning phrases. Girls are easily led, I suppose, and they don't know any better.

Anyhow, I was standing there in the middle of the room, wondering if I should get back into my old clothes, and not bother going to this party after all. But then I decided that it wouldn't do any harm to go out and have a look. I suppose I was hoping I'd have a good time: you know what they say about hope springing eternal, etcetera.

When I came out into the street I was pleasantly surprised to find that it was a nice night, for October, anyhow. The sky was full of stars, and a big, round moon lay down low, among wisps of black, silver-edged cloud, on the horizon of the dim rooftops. The air was soft and still, without a breath of wind to stir it. Seeing the weather so good, and since the party wouldn't be starting for a long while yet, I decided to walk out to Rathmines, though it was a good four miles. I'm used to walking, though, for bus fares mount up, and you can save a good few pence by using your own two feet to get wherever you want to go. So off I went, striding along at a good pace with that strong walk of mine which I've often thought must look well to anyone watching.

But by the time I reached Rathmines I must admit I was feeling a bit tired out. Also, I was getting a bit worried about my left shoe, for the sole of it wasn't too good—I'd meant to get it mended, but decided that it would hold for another while: shoe repairs cost money. But it would be terrible, I felt, to go to a party with your toes sticking out of your shoes. But it held okay, I'm glad to say.

It was easy to find the road I was looking for, but the house was a bit more difficult. Finally, however, I found it, number fifty-two, a big, square building, standing far back from the road among dark trees. I pushed open the gate, hoping, silly though it may seem, that the hinges wouldn't squeak. I've always had a thing about going into other people's gardens. I always get the feeling that the people in the house are looking out at me and telling each other that I'm coming, as sometimes they do. There were no lights in the front windows, and I began to wonder, as I walked up the path, if it was the right house after all. I was just going to press the doorbell when an awful thought struck me: perhaps the fellow who invited me was only playing a joke on me? They did that once before in the office, gave me an address and told me there was a party on there, and wouldn't I come? When I went to the house an old lady answered the door. I'd said I'd come to the party and she threatened to call the police. If that was their idea of a joke then I don't think it was very funny. Why they did it, of course, was because they knew I hardly ever got invited to parties, and they knew I'd jump at the chance. Why do people pick on people?

Anyhow, I decided to chance it, and pressed the bell. But, though I waited a long time, nobody came. I was turning away to go home, having decided that the whole thing had indeed been a joke, when I noticed that the door was ajar. Should I go straight in?

I wasn't very fond of the idea, I'll admit, but since I'd gone to the trouble of coming out I wasn't going to give up now. I can be stubborn when I want to be, you know.

So anyhow, I pushed open the door and went into the dark hall. For a moment I just stood there, but then I heard, as though coming from above me somewhere, the sound of music. My eyes had got used to the dark by now, and I noticed a stairs on my left leading up from the hall. I went quietly up the stairs, still a bit afraid, of what I don't know. I suppose I'm just nervous by nature. When I reached the landing above I saw a crack of light under one of the doors before me. The music was coming from behind it, and I could hear people talking and laughing too. So there really was a party. That was a bit of a relief for me. I then tapped lightly on the door, but, as before, nobody came. This time I told myself not to be such a fool, and taking my courage into my hands I went into the room.

At first the only sensation I had was of light, coloured light moving before me in a haze. My eyes are not too good, things are usually a bit blurred. I blinked my eyelids a few times and shut the door behind me. I stood where I was and didn't move, for I must confess I was feeling a bit awkward with all these people I didn't know. When the glare of the light had worn off my eyes I looked around me. The room was bare of furniture save for a bed which stood, draped with a crimson blanket in one corner. A few couples were already lying on it, kissing and giggling. I looked away from them with a grimace. Some people have no shame. The room seemed crowded, though there weren't as many people there as I'd thought at first. There must have been only seven or eight couples in all, but they were enough to fill the place, which wasn't all that big.

I was still standing there when the fellow from the office who had invited me caught sight of me as he was dancing by. He grinned and started to come over, but I could see he wasn't that pleased to see me. Made me feel a bit like the poor relation at a wedding the way he looked around to see if any of his friends had noticed me. Why did he invite me? I suddenly thought. It hadn't struck me before, that. Maybe he took pity on me—but I certainly don't need his pity, or anyone's for that matter. But he came up to me, his arm still around the waist of the girl he'd been dancing with. 'How'ya, Charlie,' he said. That's my name—Charles, really, but everybody calls me Charlie. 'How'ya, Charlie,' he said, 'you made it anyway?' 'Yes,' I said back to him, very polite as usual, but at the same time I was just thinking that if he wasn't going to introduce me to his girl he could at least have taken his arm from around her waist. Of course, he may have been afraid that I'd steal her away from him, or something like that. I took a look at her. She wasn't much, long and gawky, with wispy yellow hair and big teeth—you know the sort. But when I looked at her I suddenly had the idea I'd seen her somewhere before, that I'd met her sometime. Maybe I had, I don't know. It's strange, isn't it, how you meet people, so many people, you talk to them for a minute, and then they're gone out of your life forever, and even if you do meet them again you don't remember them.

He saw me looking at her then, and he coughed and said 'Did you bring anything to drink at all?' 'I don't drink,' I said, cold like. 'Oh yes, yes I forgot that,' he said, and stopped smiling. 'Well . . .' he punched me playfully on the arm, 'you want to get yourself a woman now, or something . . .' He grinned again, and with a wave of his hand him and the girl went back to where the others were dancing. As I watched him disappear into the mob I realised that I'd never really liked him. He's a bit of a smart aleck.

I didn't feel much like dancing or anything—anyhow there didn't seem to be anyone to dance with—so I moved a little to one side and sat down on the floor with my back to the wall. Somebody opened the door just then, and the corner of it nearly hit me.

But I didn't move, I liked to be near the door. I looked around me. I saw to my dismay that everyone here was with a partner, except me, of course. I was the odd man out. But I was still hoping that something would make it a good night for me. You never can tell with a party.

But a few hours later I had lost all hope altogether. They had turned out all the lights now, and were playing no fast records, only slow ones—'romantic,' I suppose you'd call them. But by that time I wasn't feeling very romantic. I hadn't moved, but was still sitting in the same place, on the floor. My back was sore from leaning against the wall, and of course other parts of me were sore too. I had nothing to do really, sitting there on the floor with my arms around my knees, except look at the window. For some reason the window, which was high and wide, and set in a sort of little alcove, looked nice to me. The moonlight was coming in through it, and splashing on the floor and falling silvery on the dancers as they moved slowly about like some kind of ghosts. Thin lace curtains hung before the alcove, moving with tiny little rippling movements in the little wind which came in through the open window. I don't know. I can't explain it. It just looked, well, nice. Then I noticed that there was a girl standing behind the curtains, looking out the window. I wondered for a minute or two what she was doing there, but then I forgot about her. I was getting sleepy, but still I wouldn't go home. Something will surely happen. I kept saying that to myself, but it was only words, all the hope was gone.

Once someone flicked on the light, and I had to avert my eyes from all the hands that were dropped from beneath dresses, and all the bloated, twisted faces that looked up suddenly, guiltily, in the glare of the naked bulb. I have always been a little disgusted by sex. It seems to make animals of people. But then I suppose you don't think about that at the time. I don't suppose my mother and father thought about it in the big double bed with the brass legs on the other side of the room I had to share with them when I was a little boy. If they had thought about it, would they have done it while I was there, listening to them?

But everything was alright when they turned out the lights again. You could hear little moans and that, but it wasn't so bad. And the window was beautiful, really lovely. I suppose it's silly to say that something like a window was beautiful, but there in that hot, smoky room, with the smell of bodies all around me, that window seemed to be the only thing that was clean, something that no-one or nothing could dirty. Silly, I suppose.

Then I began to notice the girl again, the one behind the curtains. She was still standing there. Like me, she hadn't moved either. She was so still, like a statue. I wondered if I might go and, well, talk to her. I spent a while working up the courage, but finally I stood up and went over to her. When I reached her, though, I didn't know what to say. I stood there for a while, behind her where she couldn't see me, and she didn't turn around. Then I put my face in around the curtain and said, 'Peep'. Immediately I felt silly, and sorry I'd said it. But she didn't laugh or anything, just turned around and looked at me, and then back out the window. I pushed back the curtain and went into the alcove. I remember hearing, above the noise of the party, the slithery sound of the lace rubbing against the back of my coat as the curtain swung to behind me. I didn't want to look at her, so I too looked out the window.

I still couldn't think of anything to say. She wasn't very helpful either, the way she just stood there, as if she'd forgotten about me. I suppose she thought I was trying to get off with her or something. I would have liked to be able to tell her that that wasn't the reason I came over, but I didn't say anything. I took a look at her out of the corner of my eye. In the moonlight her face was dead pale. Her eyes were two little points of light close-set on either side of a nose that looked like a bit of squashed-up putty. She was tall and fat, her body was all the wrong shape. She looked a bit like—like a fish, that's it. 'Did you come on your own?' I asked, casual like. 'No,' she said, and shook her head. 'Oh,' I said 'and where's the boyfriend gone?' She didn't answer for a minute, and I began to regret that I'd asked. Then she said, 'Oh, he had to go off—on business or something.' Business this hour of the night? I thought. But of course I didn't say anything. All this time she hadn't looked at me once and I was beginning to think she didn't want me there. But for some reason I didn't move. 'Not much of a party, is it?' I said. She clicked her tongue and said 'No'. 'I like the quiet life more, myself,' I remarked, but she didn't say anything to that.

When I looked at her again I noticed her dress was too long. It came down below her knees. And when I saw it I suddenly felt sorry for her, I don't know why. It looked so—so pathetic, that dress. I knew then that the fellow she'd come with hadn't really gone off on business, but had got fed up with her and left her there. She didn't want to admit it of course. I know how she felt. I looked away from her, out the window. I didn't want to pity her. We shouldn't have to pity anybody, not anybody. It's not right, and it's not fair.

Down below the garden was dark and deep in shadow, the masses of the trees black and silent. Beyond the gate the smooth road gleamed in the cold, silver light from the street-lamps. The scene didn't strike me as beautiful, as I suppose it should, with the moonlight and all. It just looked sad to me out there, just sad. And looking out, the garden seemed to pass some of that sadness on to me, so that I too became sad. It was very strange. 'Sort of—of sad, like, isn't it?' I said. 'What?' she asked. 'The—the garden and all,' I said, suddenly confused. 'Yes,' she said, just yes, like that.

And then suddenly I felt there was something I had to tell her. I didn't even know what it was, but I knew that it was something important. 'It—it's lonely, sometimes, isn't it? At a party, like, you know,' I said, stumbling over my words. When she didn't answer I went on quickly, 'But I suppose you get used to it . . .' I could feel my face going red with the confusion I felt, and the shame of the things I was saying that she probably thought stupid. My mind was in a whirl. I felt sad, and sorry for her, and tired, and there were so many feelings inside me that I didn't know what was what. She didn't say anything, or look at me, just went staring out the window. She was thinking about something, and it didn't seem as if she'd heard anything I had been saying. But she heard me all right.

I stood there a little while longer, and then I moved quietly away. She didn't turn or anything, or say goodbye. Maybe she didn't even hear me go. She just kept looking out, as though she were hypnotised or something. But I don't think she really saw anything out there, except maybe the dark.

I left the party a little while after that. The night outside was still, and cool and silent. I didn't mind walking home, even, it was so nice. But I still felt a bit sad. It was like one of those feelings you get, and know you'll never lose. I began to think about the girl by the window, but I couldn't even remember her face. As I say, it's strange how you meet people, and then suddenly they're gone forever, and you never see them again.

('The Party', 1966)

Wild Wood

A fine rain began to fall, it drifted soundlessly through the tangled branches and settled on the carpet of dead leaves on the ground. The boy turned up the collar of his jacket and crouched by the fire. He was cold. About him the wood was silent, yet beneath the silence there were movements and strange sounds, strange stirrings and rustlings in the trees. He shivered, and blew into his cupped hands. A burning branch fell in a shower of sparks from the fire and rolled near his feet, hissing in the wet leaves. In the hazel grove behind him a tuneless whistle rose, punctuated by the dull cracks of an axe wounding wood. He stood up and went into the trees.

—Is the fire all right? Horse asked, turning with the axe held above his shoulder.

—Yes, said the boy.

—You didn't put any of them green branches on it?

—I only used the dry wood like you said.

He made another chop at the branch before him and muttered:

—They'd see the smoke.

Horse was sixteen, a great hulking boy whose clothes never fitted because he outgrew them while they were still new. He had a raw bony face and huge hands, and a mop of carroty red hair sprouted up from his skull like the stalks of a root vegetable. Horse knew the wood from which the best bows could be made, and he had a secret method of hammering nails flat for arrowheads. He could build a fire in the worst conditions, and he knew how to skin and cook a rabbit. Such gifts made him the natural leader of the gang, but he never acknowledged this leadership, and seemed unaware of the unspoken honour. A strange wild creature who rarely spoke and never smiled, his own secret lonely ways took all his concentration.

The boy sat down on the rotten stump of a tree and looked at his hands.

—Horse, he said. Are you going to school tomorrow?

Horse said nothing, but went on chopping at the branch as if he had not heard. The boy went on:

—I think I better go in tomorrow. If I mitch again they might send someone home to my aunt to see what's wrong. Then they'd find out and I'd be in trouble.

—Here, said Horse, peel that.

He threw the long branch like a spear and it plunged into the ground at the boy's feet, then he turned back and attacked another part of the tree. The boy pulled the branch from the ground and with his penknife began to peel away the bark in long green strips.

—Well you won't be going in tomorrow then, Horse?

For a while there was no reply, then Horse said violently:

—Not going back anymore. Never.

—But what will you do?

—I'll build a hut here and live in it.

—But they'll come and take you away, Horse. You heard Harkins what he said, that he'd send you to Artane.

—Too old, Horse grunted.

The boy looked at the knife in his hand, shaping silent words on his lips, testing them. He said:

—They might put you in prison.

Horse turned, the axe held loosely by his side. His pale blue eyes were wide, his mouth worked uncertainly.

—They won't put me away anywhere, he muttered. They come for me here, I'll show them.

He whirled about and with a grunt brought the axe down savagely into the fork where two long branches met. They split apart with a crack, one fell on either side, torn and dead. He moved on into the tree, the axe flashing as he swung it again and again, white chunks of wood flying about him.

The boy watched the wood falling and flying, the axe flashing, and Horse's mouth moving mutely, and thought he heard, far away in the wood, other sounds of destruction echoing these about him. At last Horse's axe embedded itself in the trunk of the tree, and he grew calm as he worked it loose.

After a long time the boy said quietly:

—I saw someone in the wood.

The wind rattled the leaves above them.

—In the trees out by the fire, he said. I thought someone was moving around and watching me.

Horse stared at him with his mouth open, then he turned and crashed away through the trees towards the clearing where the fire burned. Alone now, the boy looked at the branch in his hands, bare of its bark and gleaming like a moist bone. He raised his eyes and looked fearfully into the shadows gathering about him, and listened to the stirrings and rustlings. He stood up and went out to the fire. Horse was sitting on his heels among the leaves, carefully feeding the flames with pieces of dry wood. The boy sat down beside him.

—Did you see anyone?

Horse shook his head absently. His eyes were vague, as though his mind were moving in some private landscape. They sat silent, listening to the small voice of the fire singing. The rain stopped, and in its place the night began to fall. The boy said:

—Maybe I only imagined there was someone.

Horse was biting his knuckles and gazing pensively into the fire. The red flames flashed in his eyes.

—How could you live here, Horse, in the cold and wet? the boy asked. And you know they'd come and get you. They'd come for you and then they'd say you were mad and put you away. What would you do then?

Horse pushed another stick into the flames.

—They wouldn't get me. I'd be gone before they came. Run away.

The boy sighed and rubbed his forehead.

—All right, Horse. But maybe we should go home just for tonight. Just until you have everything fixed up here.

—I'm not going home.

He began to rock slowly on his heels. A long tongue of flame leaped in the fire. The boy shivered as the damp ground sent a chill along his spine. Horse said:

—I had a white rabbit one time. She had pink eyes and a pink snout. She was a nice rabbit. I kept her in a hutch I made with chicken wire and all. Something got in at her one night and killed her. Ripped her throat like that—slash. Like that.

He paused, and turned his great pale eyes on the boy.

—They won't find me.

And then, as though his challenge had been heard, there came to them the sounds of something moving through the wood. Horse got to his feet and stood with the axe held in his fist. The boy looked up at his face, searching for a sign. The noises came nearer, and then a figure left the trees and came slowly toward the light.

Horse raised the axe, and the flames flashed along the wicked cutting edge. He took a step forward, and another, and the figure before him halted in uncertainty. All was still. Far off in the wood something cried out, and the strange voice called to them over the tops of the dark trees.

—What's up, Horse? said the figure in the shadows. It's me.

Horse gave a grunt of surprise, and the boy jumped to his feet.

—Rice, he cried. You gave us a fright, boy you really did.

Startled at the loudness of his own voice, he lowered his head and looked at his hands in confusion. Rice advanced, and Horse lowered the axe but did not move from where he stood. Rice passed him by, laughing nervously.

—You gave me a bigger fright, he said. Your man there with the hatchet, I thought he was going to take my head off.

He laughed again, and stood by the fire with his hands on his hips. Horse came and sat by them without a word. Rice looked from one of them to the other and asked:

—What's up here?

—Nothing, said the boy. Why?

—You're very pale, the two of you. Who did you think I was, anyway?

—Why did you come out here? Horse asked quietly.

—Do you not like my company, Mr Big Shot?

Horse shrugged his shoulders and looked away. Rice turned and grinned at the boy, and winked. Rice was a fat little boy with a plump round face and straw-coloured hair. He had short thick fingers with broken nails, and he was always short of breath. He turned to Horse again and said:

—You're getting dangerous with that hatchet. Some day you'll go rightly off your nut and brain somebody.

He gave a little wheezing laugh. Rice was the only one of the gang who was not awed by Horse. Now he said:

—Hey Horse.

—What?

—I have a message for you. I came out with it specially.

—What message?

—Ah let it wait a while, Rice said slyly.

He slipped his hand into his pocket and drew out a sticky pink sweet and popped it into his mouth. Sucking noisily, he gazed into the fire.

—Funny thing, he said, I met a fellow out on the road.

They looked up at him, waiting, but he seemed to have forgotten about them. He brooded, his cheeks working slowly on the sweet, and then the boy prompted:

—Well? What about it?

Rice looked down at him, startled.

—What about what?

—The fellow you met.

—O yes. Yes.

He sat down between them, taking great care that his bottom was covered by the tail of his raincoat.

—Well, he said. I was coming up the hill on the bike and it was getting dark. There was this fellow sitting in the ditch at the top. Well, I wasn't afraid of him or anything, but as I said it was getting dark, like. Anyway, when I was going past him he calls me over and tells me about this murder.

He paused, and the silence about them seemed to grow more intense. After a moment Rice went on:

—He said there was a woman killed in town last night. Her head was battered in.

—What woman? Horse asked, without raising his head.

—That Mrs Hanlon that had the shop in the lane down by the picture house. You know her. We used to get the sweets from her when the matinees were on. Her.

—I know her, the boy said. I remember her.

—This fellow, anyway, he said that she wasn't found until this evening. She was on the floor behind the counter and the shop was shut. She was on the floor and her head battered in and blood everyplace.

—Who did it? the boy asked.

Rice ignored him. He was staring into the fire with a perplexed look.

—He was a funny guy, he murmured.

—Who?

—This fellow that said about her getting murdered. Funny-looking.

—But who did the murder, Rice?

—What? O I don't know. He said that no one knew. The guards are looking for a man but he says they won't find him. He says anyone who'd do a thing like that would be smart enough not to get caught. He was a queer guy.

Horse moved a little away from them, and with his axe began to cut a notch in a thick green branch. Rice and the boy stared into the fire.

—Nothing was took, Rice said.

—What do you mean?

—He said there was nothing took out of the shop. No money or anything. Nothing at all. That's queer, isn't it?

—Queer all right.

The boy looked at the wood that encircled them. It was fully dark now, and the firelight threw long shadows that pranced and leaped against the trees. He shivered, and turned to Horse. But Horse was gone.

—Horse, he called softly, but no answer came.

Rice stood up and looked about him.

—Where's that mad eejit gone to now. I never heard him make a move.

They stood side by side and peered into the darkness that lay between the trees. They looked at each other uneasily. The boy crossed the clearing to where Horse had been sitting. No trace was left of him but the branch he had been whittling, it lay there in the firelight with a deep wound in its side, bleeding a trickle of sap.

—Hey, Rice softly called to him. Look at this.

The boy went and stood beside him and looked where he pointed. Horse's axe lay at their feet, a wicked weapon among the leaves. They turned and walked slowly together about the perimeter of the clearing. They searched the shadows, and even stepped among the trees, but would go no deeper than where the firelight reached. They called to him, and called, and nothing answered but the wild wood's echo.

('Wild Wood', *Long Lankin*, 1970)

On *Nightspawn*

My wife's American grandmother always held that when pancakes were being made, the first one, being a test-run, should be thrown away. I am sure most novelists, with notable exceptions such as Thomas Mann and Joseph Heller, see the wisdom of this piece of advice when they take a cringing peek between the covers of their first effort. Writers in other genres do not seem to have such queasy feelings about their firstlings; the novel, however, is remarkably intolerant of youth and inexperience.

I have not read *Nightspawn* since I corrected the proofs more than twenty years ago. When I started to write it I already had another book—*Long Lankin*, a collection of stories and a novella—being prepared for publication, and at the age of twenty-five I had no doubt that I was about to transform the novel as we knew it.

I suppose my strongest feeling in those days, one which I have never entirely lost, was a deep distrust of the novel form. The novelists I admired—Nabokov, Waugh, Lawrence Durrell—were master artificers whose primary interests were language and form. I remember a reviewer of *Nightspawn* gently suggesting that I had been reading the wrong people; at the time I was outraged, but now I think perhaps he was right. Not that I think the writers I have named, and the others I read in adolescence, are less good than I thought they were then; but perhaps they were not the best models for an ambitious tyro to adopt.

I set *Nightspawn* in Greece—on the island of Mykonos, to be exact—because I wanted to get as far away from Ireland as my limited experience of the world would allow. The novel, and the stories and novella before it, were concerned with the question of freedom: how to achieve it, and what to do with it when it had been achieved. The Greek setting was meant as a declaration that whatever my characters achieved, certainly I had freed myself. However, by the time *Nightspawn* appeared I had moved back to Ireland, where I have stayed. Freedom is not a matter of geography.

• • •

I have no doubt that *Nightspawn* was the most difficult of my books. In the space of a year, in a small upstairs room on a damp and dreamy street in Fulham, I wrote eight versions of it, all in the third person; then one afternoon—I remember the moment with piercing vividness—I realised that what the poor thing had been crying out for was a first-person narrator. After that, it took me about a month to write the finished version.

Do not mistake me: the book holds a dear place in my heart. Whatever its faults, it contains the best of what I could do. It is incandescent, crotchety, posturing, absurdly pretentious, yet in my memory it crackles with frantic, antic energy; there are sentences in it that I still quote to myself with secret and slightly shame-faced pleasure. I love the first paragraph*, the first of my first paragraphs, that place of engagement where the new reader is taught anew how to read. There sounds in it too, I think, however faintly, that

* I am a sick man, I am a spiteful man. I think my life is diseased. Only a flood of spleen now could cauterize my wounds. This is it. Hear the slap and slither of the black tide rising. The year has blundered through another cycle, and another summer has arrived, bringing the dog rose to the hedge, the clematis swooning to the door. The beasts are happily ravening in the sweltering fields of June. How should I begin? Should I say that the end is inherent in every beginning? My hyacinth is dead, and will never bloom again, but I keep the pot, like Isabella, and water with my tears in vain the thorn and withered roots. What else is there for me to do? They took everything from me. Everything. (*Nightspawn*, 1971)

tragic note which is the mark of all true works of art, great and small.

It catches, I believe, something of the harsh thereness of the Greek landscape. I remember the moment when the idea for the book—not characters, not plot, not any of that, but the idea—came to me. I was on a boat rounding a headland off the island of Delos. The light of the October afternoon was dense as bullion, the sea was, well, wine-dark, the meltemi was blowing; suddenly from behind the rocks there appeared a sloop with a sail the colour of old blood angled sharply to the world, and I knew I had it in me.

('On *Nightspawn*', 1994)

Begettings

IN PROGRESS / IN RETROSPECT

2006 / 2009

Amphitryon

— ~~"a novelette"~~ —

Quisque suos patimur manes (the spirits who haunt us are ourselves)

Virgil Aeneid IV 743

A man is a god in ruins.

Emerson

11. i. 2006

Of the things we gave them that they might be comforted
dawn is the one that works. When darkness sifts from the
air like [soft] soot and [light spreads thinly from the east
that soft effulgence spreads from the east [as if] as if
something tremendous were being brought slowly to memory
even the most wretched of humankind rally. It is a
spectacle [the pathos] we enjoy, this little daily resurrection [of
the spirit], often we will gather at the ramparts of the
clouds and gaze down upon them, our little ones, [as
they] [the early risers among them,] as they greet the [days
[morning-] new morn. Most of them sleep on, of course, oblivious of Aurora's benefaction. [What a silence falls upon
us then, the sad silence [of envy.] of the envious.] But there
are always the [lovelorn, tossing on their beds] insomniacs,
the restless sick, or just the early risers, the busy ones.

Of the things we gave them that they might be comforted, dawn is the one that works. When darkness sifts from the air like [soft] soot and [light spreads dimly from the east] that soft effulgence spreads from the east [as if] as if something tremendous were being brought slowly to memory even the most wretched of humankind rally. It is a spectacle [the pathos] we enjoy, this little daily resurrection [of the spirits], often we will gather at the ramparts of the clouds and gaze down upon them, our little ones, [as they] [the early risers among them,] as they greet the [day] [morning -] new morn. Most of them sleep on, of course, oblivious of Aurora's benefaction. [What a silence falls upon us then, the sad silence [of envy.] of the envious.] but there are always the [lovelorn, tossing on their beds] insomniacs, the restless sick, or just the early risers, the busy ones, with their stretches and knee-bends and cold showers. Yes, all greet the dawn with joy, more or less, except of course the condemned man, for whom first light will be the last.

Here is one, [condemned not to death, not yet, but to a life in which he does not feel at home] standing by the window in his father's house, watching day's first glimmer touch the sky above the trees beyond the railway line. He is condemned not to death, not yet, but to a life in which he feels he does not fit. He is reminded of how when he was a child here his mother would insist on dressing him up for special occasions, Christmas, or his birthday, or some Church festival, and how he would feel exposed, worse than naked, in those awful tweed suits with short trousers that she bought for him, the white shirts with starched collars and, worst of all, the [tartan] dickey-bows which [when] it afforded him a vain, [pleasure] vindictive [pleasure] satisfaction to [pull out on its elastic and let it snap] snap on its elastic [during] when someone was making a speech, or singing a song, or the priest was holding up the communion wafer like, he always thought, the [Irish] Sweepstakes nurse holding up the winning ticket.

with their stretches and knee-bends and cold showers. Yes, all greet the dawn with joy, more or less, except of course the condemned man, for whom first light will be the last.

Here is one, [condemned not to death, not yet, but to a life in which he does not feel at home.] standing by the window in his father's house, watching day's first glimmer touch the sky above the trees beyond the railway line. He is condemned not to death, not yet, but to a life in which he feels he does not fit. He is reminded of how when he was a child here his mother would insist on dressing him up for special occasions, Christmas, or his birthday, or some Church festival, and how he would feel exposed, worse than naked, in those awful tweed suits with short trousers that she bought for him, the white shirts with starched collars and, worst of all, the [tartan] dickey-bows which [when] it afforded him a warm, [pleasure] vindictive [pleasure] satisfaction to [pull out on its elastic and let it snap] snap on its elastic [during] when someone was making a speech, or singing a song, or the priest was holding up the communion wafer like, he always thought, the [Irish] Sweepstakes nurse holding up the winning ticket.

That is how it is. [This] life fits him ill, [and scratches him] tight-buttoned life, scratching him, making him aware of himself and his littleness.

[His name is Adam] He is called Adam. No special significance attaches to the name. He is thirty, the young son of an ancient father, the product, he once heard that father say with a phlegmy chuckle, "of my second coming."

[He does not like to be up at this hour. There is something inhuman, it seems to him.]

He is wearing pyjamas his mother found for him, pale blue with a bluer stripe, washed-to-softness cotton. whose are they, were they? [His father's perhaps] Unlikely they were his father's not grand enough for [that dandy] his dandified tastes. Could they have been his own? [They are too small for him, and [certainly he feels childish in them, and they pinch at the armpits and the crotch.] They are too small for him, they pinch at the armpits and the crotch, but that is how everything is here, everything pinches and scratches and makes him feel he is a child again.

His father is dying. That is why he is here, in these too-small pyjamas, watching the dawn break over the trees. Idly he admires the dense blue of the shadows under the boughs. A faint smoke hovers [over the] above the grass.

That is how it is, [his] life fits him ill, [and scratches him] tight-buttoned life, scratching him, making him aware of himself and his littleness.

[His name is Adam] He is called Adam. No special significance attaches to the name. He is thirty, the young son of an ancient father, "the product," he once heard that father say with a phlegmy chuckle, "of my second coming."

[He does not like to be up at this hour. There is something inhuman, it seems to him,]
He is wearing pyjamas his mother found for him, pale blue with a bluer stripe, washed-to-softness cotton—whose are they, were they? [His father's perhaps] Unlikely they were his father's not grand enough for [that dandy] his dandified tastes. Could they have been his own? [They are too small for him, and] [Certainly he feels childish in them, and they pinch at the armpits and the crotch.] They are too small for him, they pinch at the armpits and the crotch, but that is how everything is here, everything pinches and scratches and makes him feel he is a child again.

His father is dying. That is why he is here, in these too-small pyjamas, watching the dawn break over the trees. Idly he admires the dense blue of the shadows under the boughs. A faint smoke hovers [over the] above the grass.

An early crow flies across of a slant lazily from somewhere to somewhere else, and he thinks of the early worm. He becomes aware of something [happening], a general tremor, as if the air itself were quaking. Alarmed, he takes a soft step backwards, into the dimness of the room. He can feel his heart beating with large, sluggish thuds. A part of his mind knows what is happening but it is not the part that thinks. Now something behind him sets up an urgent, silvery tinkling. Then out of the trees the thing appears, huge and blunt and gaping, and draws to a shuddering halt. The lights are still on in the carriages, they make the dawn draw back a little. Bent heads in the windows, like the heads of seals — are they all asleep? — and the conductor walking [down] along an aisle, hand over hand along the seat backs. The engine gives a steamy snort, seeming to paw the earth. Why it stops at just this spot every morning no one knows, or will say. His mother has complained to the authorities, has even written to the Minister for Transport. There is not another house along the line for miles, so why just here? 'I wouldn't mind,' his mother says, 'what noise it made going past after all, your father in his wisdom insisted on [buying] setting up home beside the railway line — it's the stopping that disturbs me.'

Instinctively now he listens for the sound of her step above him. Though large, the house is mainly made of wood,

An early crow flies across / at a slant lazily from somewhere to somewhere else, and he thinks of the early worm. He becomes aware of something [happening], a general tremor, as if the air itself were quaking. Alarmed, he takes a soft step backwards, into the dimness of the room. He can feel his heart beating with large, sluggish thuds. A part of his mind knows what is happening but it is not the part that thinks. Now something behind him sets up an urgent, silvery tinkling. Then out of the trees the thing appears, huge and blunt and gasping, and draws to a shuddering halt. The lights are still on in the carriages, they make the dawn draw back a little. Bent heads in the windows, like the heads of seals—are they all asleep?—and the conductor walking [down] along an aisle, hand over hand along the seat backs. The engine gives a steamy snort, seeming to paw the earth. Why it stops at just this spot every morning no one knows, or will say. His mother has complained to the authorities, has even written to the Minister for Transport. There is not another house along the line for miles, so why just here? "I wouldn't mind," his mother says, "what noise it makes going past—after all, your father in his wisdom insisted on us [buying] setting up home beside the railway line—it's the stopping that disturbs me."

Instinctively now he listens for the sound of her step above him. Though large, the house is mainly made of wood, and sounds travel far. He does not want to have to deal with his mother, just now. In fact, as he admits to himself, there is no occasion when he deals with her willingly. [She] [This] It is not [because] that he dislikes her; he does not feel towards her that troubled mixture of love and hate which [grown sons are supposed] is supposed to [[be the dominant] [mark] grown sons are supposed to] be what grown sons feel towards their mothers; he does not feel that she is like a mother at all. She is absurdly young, hardly twenty years older than he is, and seems every year a little younger, or at least not any older, so that he has the [alarming] worrying sensation of catching up with her. She too, his mother, seems aware of this phenomenon, as if it were perfectly natural. Indeed, since he was old enough to register how young she was, he has detected now and then, or imagined he has detected, a certain tight-lipped briskness in her manner towards him, as if she were impatient for him to attain an impossible majority [at which moment they would be equals] so that, [equals at last] equals at last, they could turn arm in arm and set out together into a future that would be... what? Fatherless, for him, he suddenly realises, and husbandless for her.

Are we both, then, just waiting for the old man to die?

and sounds travel far. He does not want to have to deal with his mother, just now. In fact, as he admits to himself, there is no occasion when he deals with her willingly. [She] [This] It is not [because] that he dislikes her; he does not feel towards her that troubled mixture of love and hate which [grown sons are supposed] is supposed to [[be the dominant] [mark] grown sons are supposed to] be what grown sons feel towards their mothers; he does not feel that she is like a mother at all. She is absurdly young, hardly twenty years older than he is, and seems every year a little younger, or at least not any older, so that he has the [alarming] worrying sensation of catching up with her. She too, his mother, seems aware of this phenomenon, as if it were perfectly natural. Indeed, since he was old enough to register how young she was, he has detected now and then, or imagined he has detected, a certain tight-lipped briskness in her manner towards him, as if she were impatient for him to attain an impossible majority [at which moment they would be equal] so that, [equals at last] coevals at last, they could turn arm in arm and set out together into a future that would be . . . what? Fatherless, for him, he suddenly realises, and husbandless for her.

Are we both, then, just waiting for the old man to die?

Shaken, turns his attention to the train again. One of those seat-heads has turned and he finds himself regarded across the expanse of sward by a small boy's pale pinched face. How intently he stares, how hungry his scrutiny. What is it he is so seeking, what knowledge, what [secret] revelation? Adam is convinced the child can see him, skulking there in the shadows, yet how can he, for the window surely is a black blank or else even ablaze [with] already with [the] sunlight. Apart from those burning eyes the boy's features are nondescript, or seem so from what of them can be made out at this distance. He might be a Ganymede, for all one might know. [Adam thinks: the eye makes the horizon. It is one of his father's sayings, cribbed from someone else.] What does he want to stare so? Now the engine bethinks itself and gives itself a sort of shake, and a repeated clank runs from [carriage to carriage] along the coupling of the carriages, and with a groan the thing sets off, and as it moves the sun [runs from window] strikes through each carriage window in turn, having its revenge on the still-burning bulbs, [and] putting them to shame with its irresistible harsh [shafts] fire. The boy, craning, watches him to the last.

He is cold, and [his bare feet are half stuck to the floor] the soles of his bare feet are [half-glued to the floor.]

Shaken, turn[ed]s his attention to the train again. One of those seal-heads [have] has turned and he finds himself regarded across the expanse of sward by a small boy's pale pinched face. How intensely he stares, how hungry his scrutiny. What is it he is st seeking, what knowledge, what [secret] revelation? Adam is convinced the child can see him, skulking there in the shadows, yet how can he, for the window surely is a black blank or else even ablaze [with] already with [the] sunlight. Apart from those burning eyes the boy's features are nondescript, or seem so from what of him can be made out at this distance. He might be a Ganymede, for all one might know. [Adam thinks: the eye makes the horizon. It is one of his father's sayings, cribbed from someone else.] What does he want to stare so? Now the engine bethinks itself and gives itself a sort of shake, and a repeated clank f runs from [carriage to carriage] coupling to coupling of the carriages, and with a groan the thing sets off, and as it moves the sun [runs from window] strikes through each carriage window in turn, having its revenge on the still-burning bulbs, [and] putting them to shame with its irresistible harsh [shafts.] fire. The boy, craning, watches him to the last.

He is cold, and [his bare feet are half stuck to the floor] the soles of his bare feet are [half-glued to the floor.]

clammily [stuck] sticking to the floor. He knows he is not fully
awake but in that state between sleep and waking when
everything [takes on a] seems unreally real. When he turns
from the window the furniture looks as if it had [stopped
that instant] been moving/circling stealthily and had stopped
that instant. [From the depths of the shadows the [blank] glass
face of the clock regards him with blank hostility] [In the
shadows the glass front of a clock on the mantelpiece [cover of
a clock] face of a clock] [round glass face] convex glass face]
cover of a clock] [The convex glass cover of a clock, catching
the light from the window, stares at him with blank hostility
out of the shadows. [Out of the [shimmers] depths of the room
the convex glass cover of a clock eyes him with blank
hostility. He thinks again of the child in the train and is
struck as so often by the mystery of otherness. Yet the child
was only other to him, as he was other to the child, which
is [why they think it mysterious] the source of the mystery.
To us, for whom everything is present everywhere at every
instant, their world is uniform. They do not know how
lucky they are, these blithe solipsists. But I shall give
my Adam an inkling: he thinks, the eye makes the
horizon. The child was my horizon as he was the child's.
Pleased with this insight he paddled across the floor—[the
[staring eye of the clock followed him] clock gave [at his passing

clammily [stuck] sticking to the floor. He knows he is not fully awake but in that state between sleep and waking when everything [takes on a] seems unreally real. When he turns from the window the furniture looks as if it had [stopped that instant] been moving/circling stealthily and had stopped that instant. [From the depths of the shadows the [blank] glass face of the clock regards him with blank hostility] [In the shadows the glass [front of a clock on the mantelpiece] [cover of [a clock] face of a clock] [round glass face] convex glass [face] cover of a clock] [The convex glass cover of a clock, catching the light from the window, stares at him with blank hostility out of the shadows.] Out of the [dimness] depths of the room the convex glass cover of a clock eyes him with blank hostility. He thinks again of the child in the train and is struck as so often by the mystery of otherness. Yet the child was only other to him, as he was other to the child, which is [why they think it mysterious.] the source of the mystery. To us, for whom everything is present everywhere at every instant, their world is uniform. They do not know how lucky they are, these blithe solipsists. But I shall give my Adam an inkling: he thinks, the eye makes the horizon. The child was my horizon as he was the child's. Pleased with this insight, he padded across the floor—[the [staring eye of the clock followed him] clock gave] at his passing for God's sake!

the clock on the mantel gave a single, soft, admonitory tinkle — and opens a door into the hall and stops short with a stifled cry of fright.

He quickly sees that it is only his sister. She is squatting by [the low door of one of [doors of the cupboard under the stairs.] many cupboard doors in the white panelling under the stairs] a low door in the white wood painted panelling under the stairs. He thinks for some reason of Alice] Vaguely he is reminded of Alice grown huge in the ?? house, but cannot think why. [Since his sister is the opposite of huge] so his sister is certainly not huge. 'What are you doing?'

She turns up to him quickly her little white face and once again he sees the child's face at the train window.

'Mice,' she says, and goes back to rummaging in the cupboard.

He sighs. He can tell by [the tightness of] her voice that she is in one of her states.

'For God's sake,' he says again, wearily this time.

He leans back against the wall, watching her. It is he realises the same pose he has been adopting with her since she was a child. Not that, at nineteen nearly twenty, she is much more than a child. He asks how she knows there are mice in the cupboard and she snorts, not turning, and says a muffled something.

'What?'

'In my room, you fool!' she snarls, the neck bent back of her head — another fool! — [shaking] ashake with disgusted contempt.

sudden access of happiness in midnight — childhood again? / Her p.j.s — Pols

"For God's sake!"

the clock on the mantel gave a single, soft, [admonitory tinkle—and opens a door into the hall and stops short with a stifled cry of fright.

He quickly sees that it is only his sister. She is squatting by [the low door of one of [doors of the cupboard under the stairs.] many cupboard doors in the white panelling under the stairs] a low door in the white wood painted panelling under the stairs. [He thinks for some reason of Alice] Vaguely he is reminded of Alice grown huge in the —? house, but cannot think why, [since his sister is the opposite of huge] for his sister is certainly not huge. "What are you doing?"

She turns up to him quickly her little white face and once again he sees the child's face at the train window.

"Mice," she says, and goes back to rummaging in the cupboard.

He sighs. He can tell by [the tightness of] her voice that she is in one of her states.

"For God's sake," he says again, wearily this time.

He leans back against the wall, watching her. It is he realises the same pose he has been adopting with her since she was a child. Not that, at nineteen nearly twenty, she is much more than a child. He asks how she knows there are mice in the cupboard and she snorts, not turning, and says a muffled something.

"What?"

"In my room, you fool!" she snarls, the sleek dark back of her head—another seal!—[shaking] ashake with disgusted contempt.

(She [stands up]) bounces to her feet, light and lithe, and wipes her hands on her flanks. She does not meet his eye; she does not meet anyone's eye, if she can help it.

"What are you wearing?" he says in forced dismay.

"They're Pa's."

[Something in blue silk that hangs on her meagre frame, the straps and sleeves and legs comically too long.]

"Oh, Pete."

Her name is Petra, called by the family Pete, for a reason no one now remembers. She is tiny with a heart-shaped face and tiny thin pink rodent hands. [There are] The mice know one of their own, he spitefully thinks.

"How do you know?" he asks.

"How do I know what" — a petulant whine.

"The mice?"

"I see them. They run around the floor in the dark."

"And you see them, in the dark."

She blinks, as if she might be about to cry, but it is only a tic, he knows.

"Leave me alone," she mutters.

When she was little she sleepwalked, appearing at the head of the stairs, eyes rolled into her head and her miniature fists clenched at her sides. His loony sister, hearing voices, seeing things — one of ours, that is, one of our special ones, our beloved.

She [stands up] bounces to her feet, light and lithe, and wipes her hands on her flanks. She does not meet his eye; she does not meet anyone's eye, if she can help it.

"What are you wearing?" he says in forced dismay.

"They're Pa's."

Something in blue silk that hangs on her meagre frame, the [arms and] sleeves and legs comically too long.

"Oh, Pete."

Her name is Petra, called by the family Pete, for a reason no one now remembers. She is tiny with a heart-shaped face and tiny thin pink rodent *hands. [There are] The mice know one of their own, he spitefully thinks.*

"How do you know?" he asks.

"How do I know what"—a petulant whine.

"The mice?"

"I see them. They run around the floor in the dark."

"And you see them, in the dark."

She blinks, as if she might be about to cry, but it is only a tic, he knows.

"Leave me alone," she mutters.

When she was little she sleepwalked, appearing at the head of the stairs, eyes rolled into her head and her miniature fists clenched at her sides. His loving sister, hearing voices, seeing things—one of ours, that is, one of our special ones, our beloved.

With a cocked leg too he pushes shut the cupboard door. She makes a gesture, jerking her right arm out from her side and letting it fall again.

'I thought there were traps,' she says. 'There used to be.'

He catches a whiff of her, she has a faint, greyish smell, like the smell of an invalid. She does not bathe enough. 'I despair [of her],' their mother says of her, 'really, I do.' As if they had not all done that, long ago.

The light here in the hall is murky but the sun is already shining in the panes of gaudy stained-glass of the front door. ~~Booty~~ Plunder brought back by Pa from one of his marauding jaunts to Venice — as if, Adam glumly reflects, he and his sister had been locked indoors while a party was going on outside. They stand in silence, at a loss, each thinking [and yet not thinking] while trying not to think of what it is that constrains them so, their dying father, whose sleeplessly sleeping presence fills the house like a fog, inhabiting, inhibiting. No one in these days dares to speak above a murmur, though the doctor insists that Pa can hear nothing — how do they know, how can they say, Adam would like to know, what is the ground for their assurance. His father is in another kingdom now, but [who can] who is to say that news of the old

With a cocked big toe he pushes shut the cupboard door. She makes a gesture, jerking her right arm out from her side and letting it fall again.

"I thought there were traps," she says. "There used to be."

He catches a whiff of her, she has a faint, greyish smell, like the smell of an invalid. She does not bathe enough. "I despair [of her]," their mother says of her, "really, I do." As if they had not all done that, long ago.

The light here in the hall is murky but the sun is already shining in the panes of gaudy stained-glass of the front door, booty plunder brought back by Pa from one of his marauding jaunts to Venice—as if, Adam glumly reflects, he and his sister had been 'locked' indoors while a party was going on outside. They stand in silence, at a loss, each thinking [and yet not thinking] while trying not to think of what it is that constrains them so, their dying father, whose sleeplessly sleeping presence fills the house like a fog, inhabiting, inhibiting. No one in these days dares to speak above a murmur, though the doctor insists that Pa can hear nothing—how do they know, how can they say, Adam would like to know, what is the ground for their assurance. His father is in another kingdom now, but [who can] who is to say that news of the old realm does not reach him still?

"Why are you up so early?" Pete asks, accusingly. "You're never up this early."

"These short nights," Adam answered. "I can never sleep."

This answer she accepts in a resentful silence. It is she, he knows, who is supposed to be the wakeful one. Often he hears her in her room, behind its balefully locked door, watching the night as it ticks slowly by. Or no, not hears. Hears is the wrong word, for she makes not a sound. Rather, her wakefulness, like their father's dying, is a [nothing something] swollen tension in the house, like the air inside a balloon.

[He thinks: I cannot breathe, they will suffocate me.]

"Is the Dead Horse coming down today?" he asks.

"He says he will. I don't know."

This leaves nothing more to be said on the subject. He unfolds his arms and lets them fall limp by his sides. He has that feeling of vague desperation that his sister never fails to inspire in him. She [has a [way of standing, expectant and yet cowering] pose, expectant and yet cowering, as if] stands as she always does, half expectant and half cowering, as if hoping [she [might be embraced and yet knowing she will not]] for or to be embraced and yet dreading the possibility. When she was little she had no ticklers and would squirm away with a scowl but *realm does not reach him still?*

"Why are you up so early?" Pete asks, accusingly. "You're never up this early."

"These short nights," Adam answered, "I can never sleep."

This answer she accepts in a resentful silence. It is she, he knows, who is supposed to be the wakeful one. Often he hears her in her room, behind its balefully locked door, watching the night as it ticks slowly by. Or no, not hears, hears is the wrong word, for she makes not a sound. Rather, her wakefulness, like their father's dying, is as [something something] swollen tension in the house, like the air inside a balloon.

[He thinks: I cannot breathe, they will suffocate me.]

"Is the Dead Horse coming down today?" he asks.

"He says he will. I don't know."

This leaves nothing more to be said on the subject. He unfolds his arms and lets them fall limp by his sides. He has that feeling of vague desperation that his sister never fails to inspire in him. She [has a [way of standing, expectant and yet cowering] pose, expectant and yet cowering, as if] stands as she always does, half expectant and half cowering, as if hoping [she [might be embraced and yet knowing she will not] [for an] to be embraced and yet dreading the possibility. When she was little she had no tickles and would squirm away with a scowl but then would [come back again] be drawn back again, [against her / sorer will) droopingly, her [little] slim bony shoulders indrawn, resisting another teasing attempt to make her squeal.

"There's nothing wrong with her, you know," their mother would say, "not in the clinical sense."

He feels [as if] light-headed; it is as if he were suspended [an inch or two] a millimetre [above the] off the floor. He wishes he could help his sister, could somehow assuage her so many itches. Yet he resents her, too, has always resented her, since before she was born, even, his usurper. Pete is right, he is not used to being up at this hour, when the earth seems [another planet] a [cunningly fashioned] imitation of itself, cunningly [but not quite convincingly] fashioned yet not [quite convincing] sufficiently convincing. Oh, she'll see to you, Granny Godkin would say — you'll think your arse is haunted.

He thinks of his wife [asleep upstairs] in the sky room, teeming blade of light through the curtains smiting the foot of the bed.] his princess in her tower. She is real, surely, the thing itself.

"Come on," he says, "come on and we'll have our breakfast."

And sister and brother shuffle off into the shadows.

then would [lean back again] be drawn back again [even against her will] droopingly, her [little short] bony shoulders indrawn, inviting another teasing attempt to make her squeal.

"There's nothing wrong with her, you know," their mother would say, "not in the clinical sense."

He feels [as if] light-headed; it is as if he were suspended [an inch or two] a millimetre [above the] off the floor. He wishes he could help his sister, could somehow assuage her so many itches. Yet he resents her, too, has always resented her, since before she was born, even, his usurper. Pete is right, he is not used to being up at this hour, when the earth seems [another planet] an [cunningly fashioned] imitation of itself, cunningly [but not quite convincingly] fashioned yet not [quite convincing] sufficiently convincing. Oh, she'll see to you, Granny Godley would say—you'll think your arse is haunted!

He thinks of his wife asleep up[stairs] in the sky room, [a teeming block of light through the curtains smiting the foot of the bed.] his princess in her tower. She is real, surely, the thing itself.

"Come on," he says, "come on and we'll have our breakfast."

And sister and brother shuffle off into the shadows.

First Light

Of the things we fashioned for them that they might be comforted, dawn is the one that works. When darkness sifts from the air like fine soft soot and light spreads slowly out of the east then all but the most wretched of humankind rally. It is a spectacle we immortals enjoy, this minor daily resurrection, often we will gather at the ramparts of the clouds and gaze down upon them, our little ones, as they bestir themselves to welcome the new day. What a silence falls upon us then, the sad silence of our envy. Many of them sleep on, of course, careless of our cousin Aurora's charming matutinal trick, but there are always the insomniacs, the restless ill, the lovelorn tossing on their solitary beds, or just the early-risers, the busy ones, with their knee-bends and their cold showers and their fussy little cups of black ambrosia. Yes, all who witness it greet the dawn with joy, more or less, except of course the condemned man, for whom first light will be the last, on earth.

Here is one, standing at a window in his father's house, watching the day's early glow suffuse the sky above the massed trees beyond the railway line. He is condemned not to death, not yet, but to a life into which he feels he does not properly fit. He is barefoot, and wearing pyjamas that his mother on his arrival last night found for him somewhere in the house, threadbare cotton, pale blue with a bluer stripe—whose are they, whose were they? Could they be his, from long ago? If so, it is from very long ago, for he is big now and they are far too small, and pinch him at the armpits and the fork. But that is the way with everything in this house, everything pinches and chafes and makes him feel as if he were a child again. He is reminded of how when he was a little boy here his grandmother would dress him up for Christmas, or his birthday, or some other festival, tugging him this way and that and spitting on a finger to plaster down a stubborn curl, and how he would feel exposed, worse than naked, in those already outmoded scratchy short-trousered tweed suits the colour of porridge that the old woman made him wear, and the white shirts with starched collars and, worst of all, the tartan dicky bows that it afforded him a wan, vindictive pleasure to pull out to the limit of their elastic and let snap back with a pleasingly loud smack when someone was making a speech or singing a song or the priest was holding up the communion wafer like, he always thought, the nurse on the Hospital Sweepstakes tickets brandishing aloft the winning number. That is how it is: life, tight-buttoned life, fits him ill, making him too much aware of himself and what he glumly takes to be his unalterable littleness of spirit.

He hears from somewhere unseen the faint, muffled clopping of small hoofs; it will be the early postman on his pony, in Thurn und Taxis livery, with his tricorn cap and his post-horn looped on his shoulder.

The man at the window is called Adam. He is not yet thirty, the young son of an elderly father, 'product', as he once overheard that twice-married father say with a sardonic laugh, 'of my second coming.' Idly he admires the dense, mud-purple shadows under the trees. A kind of smoke hovers ankle-deep on the grey-seeming grass. Everything is different at this hour. An early blackbird flies across at a slant swiftly from somewhere to somewhere else, its lacquered wing catching an angled glint of sunlight, and he cannot but think with a pang of the early worm. He fancies he can hear faintly the fleet-winged creature's piping panic note.

Gradually now he is becoming aware of something he cannot

identify, a tremor that is all around, as if the air itself were quaking. It grows more intense. Alarmed, he takes a soft step backwards into the protective dimness of the room. Clearly he can hear the sluggish thudding of his heart. A part of his mind knows what is happening but it is not the part that thinks. Everything is atremble now. Some small mechanism behind him in the room—he does not look, but it must be a clock—sets up in its innards an urgent, silvery tinkling. The floorboards creak in trepidation. Then from the left the thing appears, huge, blunt-headed, nudging its way blindly forward, and rolls to a shuddering halt and stands there in front of the trees, gasping clouds of steam. The lights are still on in the carriages; they make the dawn draw back a little. There are bent heads in the long windows, like the heads of seals—are they all asleep?—and the conductor with his ticket thing is going up an aisle, clambering along hand over hand from seat-back to seat-back as if he were scaling a steep incline. The silence round about is large and somehow aggrieved. The engine gives a testy snort, seeming to paw the earth. Why it should stop at this spot every morning no one in the house can say. There is not another dwelling for miles, the line is clear in both directions, yet just here is where it halts. His mother has complained repeatedly to the railway company, and once even was moved to write to someone in the government, but got no reply, for all the renown of her husband's name. 'I would not mind,' she will say in a tone of mild sorrow, 'what noise it made going past—after all, your father in his wisdom insisted on us setting up home practically on the railway line—but the stopping is what wakes me.'

A dream that he dreamt in the night returns to him, a fragment of it. He was dashing through the dust of immemorial battle bearing something in his arms, large but not heavy, a precious but burdensome cargo—what was it?—and all about him were the mass of warriors bellowing and the ringing clash of swords and spears, the swish of arrows, the creak and crunch of chariot wheels. A venerable site, an antique war.

Thinking of his mother, he listens for her step above him, for he knows she is awake. Though the house is large and rambling the floors are mostly of polished bare boards and sounds travel easily and far. He does not want to deal with his mother, just now. Indeed, he finds it always awkward to deal with her. It is not that he hates or even resents her, as so many mortal sons are said to resent and hate their mothers—they should try dealing with our frenzied and vindictive dams, up here on misty Mount Olympus—only he does not think she is like a mother at all. She is absurdly young, hardly twenty years older than he is, and seems all the time to be getting younger, or at least not older, so that he has the worrying sensation of steadily catching up on her. She too appears to be aware of this phenomenon, and to find it not at all strange. In fact, since he was old enough to notice how young she is he has detected now and then, or imagines he has detected, a certain tight-lipped briskness in her manner towards him, as if she were impatient for him to attain some impossible majority so that, coevals at last, they might turn arm in arm and set out together into a future that would be—what? Fatherless, now, for him, and, for her, husbandless. For his father is dying. That is why he is here, foolish in these too-small pyjamas, watching the dawn break on this midsummer day.

Shaken by thoughts of death and dying he forces himself to fix his attention on the train again. One of the seal-heads has turned and he is being regarded across the smoky expanse of lawn by a small boy with a pale, pinched face and enormous eyes. How intensely the child is staring at the house, how hungry his scrutiny—what is it he is seeking, what secret knowledge, what revelation? The young man is convinced the young boy can see him, standing here, yet surely it cannot be—surely the window from outside is a black blank or, the other extreme, blindingly aflame with the white-gold glare of the sun that seemed to take such a long time to rise but now is swarming strongly up the eastern sky. Apart from those avidly questing eyes the boy's features are unremarkable, or at least are so from what of them can be made out at this distance. But what is it he is looking for, to make him stare so? Now the engine bethinks itself and gives a sort of shake, and a repeated loud metallic clank runs along the carriages from coupling to coupling, and with a groan the brutish thing begins to move off, and as it moves the risen sun strikes through each set of carriage windows in turn, taking its revenge on the still-burning light bulbs, putting them to shame with its irresistible harsh fire. The boy, craning, stares to the last.

Adam is cold, and the soles of his bare feet are sticking unpleasantly to the chill, tacky floorboards. He is not yet fully awake but in a state between sleep and waking in which everything appears unreally real. When he turns from the window he sees the early light falling in unaccustomed corners, at odd angles, and a bookshelf edge is sharp as the blade of a guillotine. From the depths of the room the convex glass cover of the clock on the mantelpiece, reflecting the window's light, regards him with a monocular, blank glare. He thinks again of the child on the train and is struck as so often by the mystery of otherness. How can he be a self and others others since the others too are selves, to themselves? He knows, of course, that it is no mystery but a matter merely of perspective. The eye, he tells himself, the eye makes the horizon. It is a thing he has often heard his father say, cribbed from someone else, he supposes. The child on the train was a sort of horizon to him and he a sort of horizon to the child only because each considered himself to be at the centre of something—to be, indeed, that centre itself—and that is the simple solution to the so-called mystery. And yet.

He pads across the floor—at his passing that busy clock on the mantel gives a single soft admonitory chime—and opens the door into the hall and stops short with a grunt of fright, his heart setting up again its slurred clamour, like an excited dog pawing to be let out.

He quickly sees that the figure in the hall is only his sister. She is squatting on her haunches at one of the little slanted doors in the white-painted panelling that closes off the space under the stairs. 'For God's sake!' he says. 'What are you doing?'

She turns up to him her miniature white face and yet again he sees in his mind the child's face at the train window. 'Mice,' she says.

He sighs. She is in one of her states. 'For God's sake,' he repeats, wearily this time.

She goes back to rummaging in the cupboard and he folds his arms and leans one shoulder against the wall and watches her, shaking his head. She is nineteen and so much younger than her years, and yet possessed too of an awful ancientness—'That one,' Granny Godley used to say of her darkly, 'that one has been here before.' He asks how she knows there are mice in the cupboard and she laughs dismissively. 'Not the cupboard, you fool,' she says, the sleek dark back of her head—another seal!—aquiver with contempt. 'In my room.'

She rises, wiping her hands on her skinny flanks. She does not meet his eye but bites her lip and frowns off to the side; she does not meet anyone's eye, if she can help it.

'What is that you're wearing?' he asks.

It is another pair of ill-fitting pyjamas, these in faded blue silk, hanging limp on her meagre frame, the sleeves and legs absurdly too long; hers are too long, his too short, as if to mark something sadly comical about them both. 'They're Pa's,' she says sulkily.

He sighs again. 'Oh, Pete.' Yet who is he to talk?—whose cast-offs is he wearing?

His sister's name is Petra, he calls her Pete. She is tiny and thin with a heart-shaped face and haunted eyes. For a long time she had her head shaved bare but now the hair is beginning to grow back, a bulrush-brown nap that covers her skull evenly all over. Her hands are the scrabbly pink claws of a rodent. The mice, her brother thinks, must recognise one of their own.

'How do you know?' he asks.

'How do I know what?'—a petulant whine.

'About the mice.'

'I see them. They run around the floor in the dark.'

'In the dark. And you see them.'

She blinks slowly and swallows, as if she might be about to cry, but it is only a tic, one among the many that afflict her. 'Leave me alone,' she mutters.

He is so much larger than she is.

As a child she used to sleepwalk, appearing at the top of the stairs with her eyes rolled up into her head and her mouse-claws lifted in front of her chest. At the memory the small hairs stir at the back of Adam's neck. His loony sister, hearing voices, seeing things.

With a cocked big toe he pushes shut the cupboard door. She makes a gesture towards it, her left arm jerking out stiffly from her side and a finger childishly pointing and then the arm falling weakly back. 'I thought there were traps,' she says. 'There used to be traps kept in there.'

When she did that with her arm he caught a whiff of her, a musty, greyish smell, like the smell in the bedroom of an invalid. She does not bathe enough. Her mother says she despairs of her. As if they had not all done that, long ago, except for Pa, of course, who claims she is his inspiration, his muse made flesh, the invariable quantity in all his equations. But Pa claims many things. Or claimed: for Pa is in the past tense, now.

The light here in the hall is still dim but the sun is burning gaudily in the front door's stained-glass panes as if, Adam thinks, he and his sister were confined indoors while outside a gay party is in full swing. In their clownishly ill-fitting pairs of pyjamas they stand before each other in silence, the large young man and the diminutive girl, at a loss, each thinking and yet not thinking of what it is that constrains them so: the fact of their dying father, whose sleeplessly sleeping presence fills the house like a fog. In these latter days no one in the house dares speak above a murmur, though the doctors blandly insist that nothing any longer passes beyond the portals of Pa's hearing—but how can they be so certain, Adam would like to know, where do they get such assurance? His father is in another kingdom now, far off to be sure, but may it not be that news from the old realm reaches him still?

'Why are you up so early?' Petra asks accusingly. 'You never get up this early.'

'The time of year,' Adam says, 'these short nights—I can't sleep.'

This answer she receives in silence, sullenly. It is she who is supposed to be the sleepless one. Her unsleepingness, like their father's gradual dying, is a pervasive pressure that makes the atmosphere in the house feel as dense as the air inside a balloon.

'Is the Dead Horse coming down today?' he asks her.

She gives a shrug that is more a twitch. 'He said he would. I suppose he will.'

They can get no more from this topic and are silent again. He has that feeling of helpless exasperation his sister so often provokes in him. She stands as she always does, half turned away, at once expectant and cowering, as if longing to be embraced and at the same time in dread of it. When she was little she had no tickles and would squirm away from him with a scowl but then would lean back again, droopingly, unable to help herself, her sharp, narrow shoulders indrawn like folded wings and her head held to one side, seeming miserably to invite him to try again to make her squeal. How thin she had been, how thin and bony, like a sack half filled with sticks, and still is. Now she lifts a hand and scratches her scalp vigorously, making a sandpapery sound.

Adam feels light-headed, weightless, seeming to float an inch above the floor. He supposes it is to do with the supply of oxygen to the brain, or lack of it. His sister is right, he is not used to being up at this hour—*everything is different*—when the world looks like an imitation of itself, cunningly crafted yet discrepant in small but essential details. He thinks of Helen his wife asleep up in the room that used to be his when he was a boy. Stretched beside her rigid and wakeful in the pre-dawn dusk he had wanted to rouse her but had not had the heart, so soundly was she sleeping. He might go up now and lie down again on the too-narrow bed and close her to him, but something that is a sort of shyness, a sort of fear, even, holds him back.

Good thing, by the way, that this young husband does not know what my doughty Dad, the godhead himself, was doing to his darling wife up in that bedroom not an hour since in what she will imagine is a dream.

On the subject of fathers: Adam has not seen his yet. When they arrived last night he pleaded his and Helen's weariness after the journey and said they would go straight to bed. He thought that to visit the old man then would have been gruesome; he would have felt like a body-snatcher measuring up a fresh specimen, or a vampire-hunter breaking into a crypt. Although he has not told her so he thinks his mother should not have insisted on taking Pa out of the hospital. Bringing him home to die is a throwback, something Granny Godley would have approved. Yet this morning he is sorry that he did not go at once and at least look at him, his fallen father, for with each hour that passes it will be so much the harder to force himself up those stairs and into that sickroom. He does not know how he will behave at the side of what everyone, without saying so, has acknowledged is his father's deathbed. He has never been at a death before and hopes not to have to be present for this one.

Petra is still scratching, but with decreasing momentum, absently, like a cat slowly losing interest in its itch. He wishes he could help her, could assuage even one of her sore, inflamed spots. Yet he resents her, too, has always resented her, since before she was born, even, his usurper. He has a sudden clear memory of her as a baby in her cot, wrapped tight in a blanket, like a mummified yet all too living infanta. 'Oho, my bucko, she'll make you hop,' Granny Godley would say with a cackle, '—you'll think your arse is haunted!'

'Come on,' he says now brusquely to the girl, 'come on, and we'll have our breakfast.'

And sister and brother, these waifs, shuffle off into the shadows.

• • •

It is shadowed too up in the Sky Room where Adam Godley at the centre of a vast stillness is going about his dying. Yes, he too is Adam, like his son. By the way, apropos names and the like, I suppose I should before going further give some small account of myself, this voice speaking out of the void. Men have made me variously keeper of the dawn, of twilight and the wind, have called me Argeiphontes, he who makes clear the sky, and Logios, the sweet-tongued one, have dubbed me trickster, the patron of gamblers and all manner of mountebanks, have appointed me the guardian of crossroads, protector of travellers, have conferred on me the grave title Psychopompos, usher of the freed souls of men to Pluto's netherworld. For I am Hermes, son of old Zeus and Maia the cavewoman.

You don't say, you say.

I understand your scepticism. Why in such times as these would the gods come back to be among men? But the fact is we never left—you only stopped entertaining us. For how should we leave, we who cannot but be everywhere? We merely made it seem that we had withdrawn, for a decent interval, as if to say we know when we are not wanted. All the same, we cannot resist revealing ourselves to you once in a while, out of our incurable boredom, or love of mischief, or that lingering nostalgia we harbour for this rough world of our making—I mean this particular one, for of course there is an infinity of others just like it that we made and must keep ever vigilantly in our care. When on a summer's day a sudden gale tears through the treetops, or when out of the blue a soft rain falls like the fall of grace upon a painted saint, there one of us is passing by; when the earth buckles and opens its maw to eat cities whole, when the sea rises up and swallows an entire archipelago with its palms and straw huts and a myriad ululating natives, be assured that one of our number is seriously annoyed.

But what attention we lavished on the making of this poor place! The lengths we went to, the pains we took, that it should be plausible in every detail—planting in the rocks the fossils of outlandish creatures that never existed, distributing fake dark matter throughout the universe, even setting up in the cosmos the faintest of faint hums to mimic the reverberations of the initiating shot that is supposed to have set the whole shooting-match going. And to what end was all this craft, this labour, this scrupulous dissembling—to what end? So that the mud men that Prometheus and Athene between them made might think themselves the lords of creation. We have been good to you, giving you what you thought you wanted—yes, and look what you have done with it.

All this, of course, I cast in the language of human-kind, necessarily. Were I to speak in my own voice, that is, the voice of a divinity, you would be baffled at the sound—in fact, you would not be able to hear me at all, so rarefied is our heavenly speech, compared to your barely articulate gruntings. Why, the music of the spheres has nothing on us. And these names—Zeus, Prometheus, grey-eyed Athene, Hermes, even—these are your constructions. We address each other, as it were, only as air, as light, as something like the quality of that deep, transparent blue you see when you peer into the highest vault of the empyrean. And Heaven—what is that? For us, the deathless ones, there is no Heaven, or Hell, either, no up, no down, only the infinite here, which is a kind of not-here. Think of that.

This moment past, in the blinking of your eye, I girdled the earth's full compass thrice. Why these aerial acrobatics? For diversion, and to cool my heels. And because I could and you cannot. Oh, yes, we too are petty and vindictive, just like you, when we are put to it.

Adam, this Adam, has suffered a stroke. By the way, I pause to remark how oddly innocuous, even pretty, a term this is for something so unpleasant and, in this case, surely final—as if one of us had absent-mindedly laid a too-heavy hand upon his brow. Which is perfectly possible, since we are notorious for not knowing our own strength. Anyway, for some time prior to this stroke that he suffered old Adam had been subject, all unbeknownst, to a steady softening of the brain due to a gradual extravasation of blood in the area of the parietal lobe—yes, yes, I have also some expertise in matters medical, to meliorate the more obstreperous of my attributes—which means in other words he was already a goner before that catastrophic moment when, enthroned at morning within the necessary place—to put it as delicately as I may—he crouched too low and strained too strenuously in the effort of extruding a stool as hard as mahogany, and felt, actually felt, a blood vessel bursting in his brain, and toppled forward on to the floor, his face to the tiles and his scrawny bare bum in the air, and passed at once, with what in happier circumstances would have been a delicious smoothness, into death's vast and vaulted antechamber, where still he bides, in a state of conscious but incommunicate ataraxia, poised upon the point of oblivion.

He is not alone—as one of your most darkly glowing luminants has observed, the living being is only a species of the dead, and a rare species at that. He senses the multitude of his fellows all about, uneasy and murmurous in their state of life-in-death. And I am here as well, of course. When our time comes we shall go together, he and I, into what is next, which I may not speak of.

His wife has entered the room, making hardly a sound, as is increasingly her wont these days. She feels she is becoming more and more a wraith, as if Adam in his last illness were siphoning something vital from her, drop by glistening drop. She closes the bedroom door softly behind her and stands motionless a moment, letting her eyes adjust to the dimness. A teeming sword of early sunlight is falling through a parting in the heavy curtains of the middle window, breaking its blade across the foot of the bed. The Sky Room is a most capricious touch added on to the house by the man who built it, the famously eccentric St John Blount, a timber eyrie set into the north-west—or is it south-east?—corner of the main edifice, glazed on three sides and surmounted by a conical roof with a metal weathervane in the shape of a fleeting, short-cloaked figure, wearing a pudding hat with a circular brim and bearing a staff, who can only be—well, me, I suppose. How disconcerting. I did not expect to encounter myself here, in such surroundings, at this elevation, especially in the form of a two-dimensional tin representation of a godling. My staff must double as a lightning rod—that is something, I suppose, flash and fire and the reek of brimstone; that will liven things up.

Ursula with a qualm acknowledges to herself how restful she

finds it being here. There is a dense, intent quality to the silence in the sickroom; it is like the silence that reigns deep down inside her and soothes her heart, even in the midst of so much inward tumult. She can make out his form now, supine in the big bed, but although she listens breathlessly she cannot hear him breathing. Perhaps—? At the unthought thought something stirs in her, a yearning something that she tries to deny but cannot. Yet why should she reprove herself? Everyone says the end will be a blessèd release. Those are the words they use, *a blessèd release*. Yes, she reflects bitterly, a release—but for whom? All except, perhaps, the one being released. For who can know but that Adam in some part of his mind might not be awake in a way and experiencing wonders? People who are deeply asleep seem unconscious but still may be dreaming the most fantastic things. Anyway, even if she cannot hear him she knows he has not gone. The elastic link between them has not been broken yet: she can feel still the old twanging tug. She is sure he is thinking, thinking away, she is sure of it.

She closes the chink in the curtains and at once the dark seems total, as if the world had been suddenly switched off. Feeling her way through the black and therefore somehow heavier air she advances to the bed soundlessly on slippered feet. In their early days together he used to call her his geisha girl for her pattering, rapidly stepping gait. She recalls the antique kimono he brought back for her from one of his trips—'A kimono from Kyoto for my geisha!'—cut from heavy, jade-green silk, a garment so exquisite she could not bring herself to wear it but folded it away in tissue paper in a drawer, from where subsequently it somehow disappeared. He had threatened to take the thing back—perhaps he did?— and give it to one of his girls, all those girls he said he was well aware she imagined that he had, hidden away. Then he looked at her, with his head back, fiercely smiling and showing his teeth, daring her to call his bluff. For it was a bluff, about the girls, about there not being any, she knew it, and he knew she knew it. That was a way of lying that amused him, saying a version of the truth in tones of high, mocking irony so that to challenge him would be to seem a hapless dolt.

Her eyes are growing used to the blinded dimness. She can see more than she wants to see. Uncanny, to enter this room each morning and find him just as she left him the night before, the blanket moulded smoothly to his form, the sheet uncreased, the cockscomb of silky hair—still black!—rising unruffled above the high, white dome of his forehead. His beard too is dark still, the spade-shaped, pointed beard that gives him the look of a faintly diabolical saint. She has always loved his skin, the moist cool translucent paleness of it that the years have not sullied. She hates, knowing how he would hate them, the plastic tubes that are threaded into his nostrils and held in place with strips of clear sticking-plaster. There are other tubes, farther down, hidden from sight by the bedclothes. What a trouble there was settling him here, Dr Fortune fidgeting and the nurses cross. But she insisted, and so determinedly it surprised everyone, herself included. 'He must be at home,' she kept on saying, ignoring all their objections. 'If he is to die he must die here.' She hated the cottage hospital he had been rushed to, a caricature off the lid of a chocolate box, grotesquely pretty with ivy and rambling roses and a glassed-in porch; imagine if Adam died there and along with her grief she had to put up with all that flummery. Old Fortune, who looks like Albert Schweitzer and has been the family's physician since Granny Godley's day, squeezed her hand and mumbled a mollifying word through the yellowed fringes of his moustache, but the two young nurses narrowed their eyes at her and stalked off, their backsides wagging professional disapproval.

By now her ears have become accustomed to the acoustics of the sickroom and she can hear her husband breathing, the faint rustle of air in the passages of his throat and chest. At the end of each indrawn breath comes a tiny flutter, like an impatient twiddling of fingers. She realises what it is that is familiar about this sound. It is just how he used to sigh when she did something that exasperated him, with just that same little fluttering flourish. She misses him, as though he were already gone. She feels a pain such as she thought only those who are still young can feel, new and sharply surprising, enough to take her breath away.

Something brushes past her in the air, less than a draught, more than a thought. She has sensed it before, in recent days. Whatever it is she is convinced it is not benign; she has the impression of haughtiness and a bridling resentment, as if something were bent on jostling her out of position. There are other strange phenomena too, other haunting effects. She has glimpses of figures that cease to be there when she tries to look at them directly, like floaters in the eye. She wakes in the night with a start, her heart pounding, as if there had been a tremendous noise, an explosion or a clap of thunder, which shook her out of sleep but of which there is not even an echo remaining. When she speaks to people on the telephone she is convinced there is a third party on the line, listening intently. She wonders fancifully if perhaps this angry revenant might not be the ghost of Adam's first wife, or of his long-dead mother, Granny Godley the old hag, come back to claim her son and carry him off with her to the land of the shades. You see?—they think it is the dead that haunt them, while the simple fact is, as her husband could tell her and has often tried to, they live amidst interpenetrant worlds and are themselves the sprites that throng the commingling air. For all she knows it might be one of her countless selves that she is meeting, drifting from another plane into this one all unawares.

Or perhaps it is merely my ever-attentive presence that she senses, the whirring of dainty wings on my hat and at my heels that she almost hears. But I ask—am I haughty? Do I bridle? A little, I suppose. A little.

She dislikes her name. Adam was able to tell her of St Ursula of Dumnonia, martyred at Cologne along with her eleven thousand virgins—'What a day that must have been, eh,' he said teasingly, lifting an eyebrow, *'im alten Köln?'*—although this Ursula was recently removed from the calendar of saints, in a fit of anti-German pique, by one of the more reform-minded English pontiffs. When the children were small they called her La, and still do. Adam is Pa and she is La. She wonders if there is ill-intent in their keeping on with these pet-names. She fears she has not been a good mother. She did her best with Adam but poor Petra was too much for her. Having Petra was the start of all her troubles. For nine months she was sick, vomiting all day and not able to keep anything down, until in the end she could not swallow even her own spit; with a shudder she recalls the nurse taking the glinting nickel dish of slime and floating froth out of her trembling hands and emptying it into the washbasin. Then at last the pallid little fish that was her daughter slithered out of her and lay gasping on her breast, so wearied already that no one expected she would live. But live she did, and was called Petra, another stone dropped into Ursula's already heavy heart.

She touches her husband's hand where it lies on the blanket. It has an unsettling feel, the skin brittle as greaseproof paper and the flesh pulpy underneath; it is like a package of scrap meat from the butcher's, chill and sinewy; it is not the hand that she remembers, so delicate and fine. That invisible presence barges past her again, or through her, rather, and she feels it is she that is without substance, as if she and not this other were the ghost. Her husband's eyelids spring open and his eyes after a moment of agitated searching find her face. She smiles with an effort and speaks his name softly. It is hard to make out his features in the dimness but she is loath to switch on the light. Dr Fortune assures her that it is her loving care that is keeping her husband alive and nothing else—why then does he look at her now with such seeming fury?

Her head is very bad today, very bad, she must take something soon to soothe it.

• • •

In the well of the kitchen the morning light has a sharply metallic sheen and the square of sunlit garden in the window behind the sink is garish and implausible, like a primitive painting of a jungle scene. Adam and his sister are seated at one end of the long deal table, hunched over cereal bowls. When their mother appears at the top of the three wooden steps that lead up to or down from the rest of the house they sense rather than hear her—Rex the elderly labrador, lying on his blanket in the corner, gives a few listless thumps of his tail but makes no effort to get up—and they stop eating and lift their faces and look at her. She sees again with a faint start how alike they are, despite Adam's great size and Petra's diminutiveness, each with the same broad brow and little sharp chin and ash-blue eyes so pale they are almost colourless. Perhaps because she had no siblings herself she finds family resemblance always a little eerie, even in her own offspring. Both of them take after her, for it was from her they inherited the wide forehead and sharp chin and azury eyes.

'How is he, today?' her son asks. His skin is mottled from the sun and he has a scorched, raw look. For some reason just now she finds well-nigh intolerable his palely candid gaze. 'Much the same,' she says, answering him, and Petra laughs, who knows why, making a nasty sound. Yes, sometimes she thinks her children dislike and resent her, as if she were not their mother at all but a person brought in to be in intimate charge of them, a heartless guardian, say, or a bitterly resented stepmother. But surely she is mistaken. These are the creatures she carried inside her and gave birth to and fed from her own breast, phoenix-like. She recalls Adam just now glaring at her with that vengeful fire in his eyes. 'He seems peaceful,' she says.

Her son considers her as she hovers on the stair at the far end of the long, high-ceilinged room. He seems unable to focus on her properly. She has a new quality, of being not entirely present, of seeming to hesitate on an invisible threshold that is there under her feet wherever she steps. She has become blurred, as if under a fine layer of dust. This must be the effect on her of the catastrophe that has befallen old Adam; she has lost the sense of herself. She is wearing a cotton dress like a smock and a baggy grey cardigan the hem of which sags below the level of her hips. Her hair, the colour of a knife-blade, is pulled back in two flattened wings and pinned at the nape of her neck. She descends the steps and comes forward and stands by the table, absently kneading the worn wood with the fingertips of one hand, as if to test its solidity. 'You're up early,' she says to both of them. 'Did the train wake you?'

Neither will answer. 'Roddy will be here later,' Petra says, looking aside frowningly. Her tone is truculent, as if to forestall disparaging comment. Roddy Wagstaff, dubbed the Dead Horse by her brother, is Petra's young man, or so convention has it, although everybody knows it is not she but her famous father that Roddy comes to visit.

'Oh,' her mother murmurs, and a pained frown passes over her already frowning face, 'then there'll have to be lunch!' Since Adam fell ill the household has been content to shift for itself, but a visitor must be fed a proper, sit-down meal; Adam would insist on it, for in such small matters he is a strict observer of the conventions.

'We could take him into town,' her son says, without conviction. 'Doesn't that place what's-it-called serve lunches?'

'Oh, yes,' Petra says archly, with a sneer, 'let us all go into town and have a lovely time—we can bring Pa and prop him up at the head of the table and feed him soup through his tubes.'

She glares at her cereal bowl. Under the table her left leg is going like a sewing-machine. Adam and his mother exchange an expressionless look. Her father's collapse has been for Petra a great excitement, being at last a calamity commensurate with the calamitous state of her mind. The question of lunch is let hang. In the corner Rex the dog gives a contented, shivery sigh. He can see me plainly, lolling at my ease in mid-air, with folded arms, in the midst of these sad souls, but it is nothing to him, whose world is already rife with harmless spectres.

Petra has her subject now and will not let go of it. In a thick, tense voice, goitrous with sarcasm, she embroiders upon the notion of a family lunch in town to which her father would be brought—'in a hammock maybe or a sling slung between us or one of those things with two poles that red indians drag the wounded along behind them in'—and at which they would all celebrate his achievements and make speeches and raise toasts to him as man, as father and as savant. When she gets going like this she has a way of speaking not directly to the others in the room but to the air beside her, as if there were present an invisible twin version of herself off whom she is bouncing her taunts and who will give to them, thus relayed, an added extension of sarcasm. Adam and her mother say nothing, for they know there will be no stopping her until she has exhausted herself. The dog, lying with his muzzle between his paws, eyes her with wary speculation. The table-top vibrates rapidly along with the girl's bobbing knee. Adam tries to eat his cereal, which has gone gluey; he sees himself yet again as a boy, sitting at this table, listening to his father talking, in that coolly vehement, uninterruptible way that he did, and recalls how he would feel his throat thicken and his eyes scald with inexplicable tears he dare not shed, shaming tears, heavy and unmanageable like big drops of mercury. He glances sidelong at his sister now and sees the dab of sallow light shaking in the spoon-shaped hollow above her clavicle as she tries not to choke on the torrent of words that wells up out of her unstaunchably.

Their mother, standing by the table, regards her son and daughter with a troubled gaze. They seem to her still so young, hardly more than children, really, even Adam—especially Adam—with that babyishly fat overlip that trembles so when he is excited or upset. She notices the bowls the two of them have been eating from. Why does it irritate her that they are unmatched? Latterly so many things irritate her. She tries not to feel resentful of her son for so far not having set foot in the room where his father lies dying. She supposes it is simply the fear of death, its awful presence, that prevents him. But after all he is not a child, however he may seem. She crosses to the sink and looks out through the big, many-paned window above it at the sunlit day, a hand lifted vaguely to her face.

She thinks of Adam growing up in the humid conspiracy that was his Granny Godley. The old woman had seized on him early, a hostage against all the slights she imagined herself the victim of. Then Petra was born and her brother was at once usurped. A blundering, blond fellow he was, with a huge, round head, baffled at being so unceremoniously thrust aside in favour of this tiny, watchful creature clasped jealously in his grandmother's bony embrace. For the coming of Petra had brought on a grisly transformation in the old woman: she turned tender and clumsily solicitous, reminding Ursula of those shaggy clambering rust-coloured primates in the zoo, all hooped arms and peeled-back lips and baleful starings, that her husband was so fascinated by and would make her come with him to see on Sunday afternoons when Adam was a baby. Granny Godley was dying of a damaged heart and grimly turned over each new day like a playing card from a steadily diminishing deck, anticipating of each one that it would be the ace of spades, while what had come instead was this solemn-eyed coat card, this miniature queen of diamonds, swaddled and uncannily still and always looking at something off to the side that only she it seemed could see, clutching in her white-knuckled fist the wilting flower of the future.

'And and and,' Petra is saying now, her voice ashake on the sliding crest of its arc, 'and and and *and*—'

—And I it is who have contrived these things: this house, the train, the boy at the train window, that slanting blackbird, the dawn itself, and this mother musing on love and her losses, and her troubled daughter at the table gabbling out her woe, and the wife asleep in her husband's boyhood bed, and her husband, young Adam here, who presently will make up his mind and rise reluctantly from the table and ascend those three short steps and be borne upwards on my invisible wings into the presence of his earthly father.

(*The Infinities*, 2009)

Acknowledgements

My greatest debt of gratitude is to this *Reader*'s first reader, Janet Dunham, for her sustaining goodwill throughout the book's long gestation. I am likewise grateful to Robin Robertson.

For diverse acts of kindness and assistance, my thanks go to Paul Baggaley, Kris Doyle, Wilf Dickie, Nicholas Blake and Jonathan Pelham at Picador, to Ed Victor and his team in Bedford Square; to Cormac Kinsella at Repforce Publicity; to David Adamson at Macmillan; and to Ciarán ÓGaora at Zero-G.

For permissions in respect of previously published material, grateful acknowledgement is made to Jean and Peter Fallon at Gallery Press, publishers of Banville's 'firstlings' (*Long Lankin* and *Nightspawn*), his stage and radio plays (*The Broken Jug, God's Gift, Love in the Wars* and *Conversation in the Mountains*), and *The Ark*; to sundry permissions managers at Penguin, Bloomsbury, Granta, Ryan Publishing, Colin Smythe, New Island and Joe McCann; to the respective editors of the *Irish University Review, The New York Review of Books*, the Associação Editorial Humanitas in São Paulo, *The Irish Times* and *The Independent*; and to John Felstiner.

Various librarians and broadcasting personnel showed great courtesy and tolerance whenever I troubled them for more fugitive material, and I should like to acknowledge those anonymous helping hands which steadied my own when fumbling about the National Library of Ireland, RTÉ and the BBC.

I would like to record my particular gratitude to Bernard Meehan, Keeper of Manuscripts at Trinity College, Dublin, whose staff facilitated my requests with such promptness and prowess. Without them, 'Begettings' could not have been begotten.

To Ralph Fiennes, I offer a warm handshake in thought and thanks.

For their indefatigable support, I am especially grateful to my family: to my parents, Brian and Imelda, to whom this volume is dedicated; and to my siblings, Brian, Alison and David.

• • •

Finally and foremost, *Possessed of a Past* is my salute to the progenitor of its parts, John Banville. It is made in friendship and admiration, and with thanks for such long-lasting enrichment. May this *Reader* be to others what the greater canon has been to me.

Sources

Revelations

FICTION, 1973–2012

'Summer at Birchwood', *Birchwood* (Secker & Warburg, 1973, first published by Picador in 1999), pp. 22–26; pp. 59–62; pp. 68–72 • 'Rheticus', *Doctor Copernicus* (Secker & Warburg, 1976, first published by Picador in 1999), pp. 174–181 • 'The Harmony of the Spheres', *Kepler* (Secker & Warburg, 1981, first published by Picador in 1999), pp. 19–27 • 'Fern House', *The Newton Letter* (Secker & Warburg, 1982, first published by Picador in 1999), pp. 11–20 • 'Gabriel Swan', *Mefisto* (Secker & Warburg, 1986, first published by Picador in 1999), pp. 8–19 • 'Possessed of a Past': I 'The painting is called', *The Book of Evidence* (Secker & Warburg, 1989, first published by Picador in 1998), pp. 104–119; II 'I am always fascinated', *Ghosts* (Secker & Warburg, 1993, first published by Picador in 1998), pp. 171–187; III 'When she urged me to beat her', *Athena* (Secker & Warburg, 1995, first published by Picador in 1998), pp. 171–185 • 'The Golden World', previously published under the title 'Life and Art' in *Granta 41* (Granta, Autumn 1992), pp. 219–231 • 'Taking Possession', *The Untouchable* (Picador, 1997), pp. 31–44 • 'The Lost Ones': I 'The telephone began to shrill, giving me a fright', *Eclipse* (Picador, 2000), pp. 40–50; pp. 71–76; II 'So this, she saw, was where it would end', *Shroud* (Picador, 2002), pp. 381–387; III 'A charming spot it was Cass chose to die in', *Eclipse* (Picador, 2000), pp. 202–209; IV 'We had a dreadful night', *Ancient Light* (Penguin, 2012), pp. 18–23 • 'Lady Laura and the Dowager Duchess', *Shroud* (Picador, 2002), pp. 262–279 • 'Only Dying, After All', *The Sea* (Picador, 2005), pp. 13–23 • 'O Lost,

Raw World!', *The Infinities* (Picador, 2009), pp. 62–71 • 'Blest Boy', *Ancient Light* (Penguin, 2012), pp. 38–52

Apart from *Ancient Light* (Penguin), the above fiction titles are currently available in paperback from Picador in editions whose pagination corresponds almost entirely with that of their first publications. They differ only as follows: 'Summer at Birchwood', *Birchwood* (Picador, 1999), pp. 30–33; pp. 64–67; pp. 73–77; 'Fern House', *The Newton Letter* (Picador, 1999), pp. 13–23.

Playing Parts

STAGE AND RADIO PLAYS, 1994–2006

'From *The Broken Jug*', *The Broken Jug: After Heinrich von Kleist* (Gallery Press, 1994), pp. 32–55; first produced in the Peacock Theatre, Dublin, on 1 June 1994 • *Stardust: Three Monologues of the Dead*, broadcast by BBC Radio 3's *The Verb* on 11 May 2002; previously unpublished • *Kepler*, broadcast by BBC Radio 4 in October 2004; previously unpublished • *A World Too Wide* first published in the *Irish University Review*'s special issue on John Banville, guest-edited by Derek Hand (*Irish University Review*, Spring/Summer 2006), pp. 1–8; broadcast by RTÉ on 8 February 2005 as part of their series, 'Shakespeare's Seven Ages of Man', this being the sixth age, that of 'the lean and slipper'd pantaloon' • *Conversation in the Mountains* (Gallery Press, 2008); broadcast (as *Todtnauberg*) by BBC Radio 4 on 20 January 2006; excerpts from 'Deathfugue', 'Streak', 'Psalm', '[Winter]', 'Black Flakes', 'Assisi' and 'Todtnauberg' translated by John Felstiner, the complete versions of which may be found in *Selected Poems and Prose of Paul Celan*, W. W. Norton, NY 2001.

A Blest World

ESSAYS, LECTURES AND REVIEWS, 1990–2010

'Survivors of Joyce', *James Joyce: The Artist and the Labyrinth*, edited by Augustine Martin (Ryan Publishing, 1990), pp. 73–81 • 'The Personae of Summer', *Irish Writers and Their Creative Process: Irish Literary Studies 48*, edited by Jacqueline Genet and Wynne Hellegouarc'h (Colin Smythe, 1996), pp. 118–122; previously published under the title 'Making Little Monsters Walk', *The Agony and the Ego: The Art and Strategy of Fiction Writing Explored*, edited by Clare Boylan (Penguin, 1993), pp. 105–112 • 'Thou Shalt Not Kill', *Arguing at the Crossroads: Essays on a Changing Ireland*, edited by Paul Brennan and Catherine de Saint Phalle (New Island, 1997), pp. 133–142 • 'Speaks True Who Speaks Shadow', a review of *Selected Poems and Prose of Paul Celan*, translated by John Felstiner, and *Fathomsuns and Benighted*, by Paul Celan, translated by Ian Fairley (*The Irish Times*, 10 February 2001) • 'Fiction and the Dream', an address delivered at the Creative Writing program of the University of Philadelphia (September 2005); published in *Irish Studies in Brazil*, edited by Munira H. Mutran and Laura P. Z. Izarra (São Paulo: Associação Editorial Humanitas, 2005), pp. 21–28 • 'Beckett's Last Words' first published as a limited edition (Joe McCann, 2006); reprinted in abridged form in *Beckett at 100: Centenary Essays*, edited by Christopher Murray (New Island, 2006), pp. 122–131; broadcast as part of RTÉ's 'Beckett at 100' celebrations in their Thomas Davis Lectures series on 22 June 2006 • 'Living Ghosts', a review of Seamus Heaney's *Human Chain* (*The New York Review of Books*, 11 November 2010)

Fidgets of Remembrance

MEMOIR, 1989, 2003

'Lupins and moth-laden nights in Rosslare' (*The Irish Times*, 18 July 1989) • 'It was winter the first time I saw Prague', *Prague Pictures: Portraits of a City* (Bloomsbury, 2003), pp. 1–16; pp. 46–49; pp. 57–59; pp. 70–71

Firstlings

EARLY FICTION, 1966–1971

'The Party' (*The Kilkenny Magazine* 14, Spring/Summer 1966), pp. 75–82 • 'Wild Wood', *Long Lankin*, revised edition (Gallery Press, 1984), pp. 9–15 • 'On *Nightspawn*', first published as 'Second Thoughts: Greece wasn't the word: John Banville on his first novel, *Nightspawn*' (*The Independent*, 26 March 1994); *Nightspawn*, reissued edition (Gallery Press, 1993); p. 11

Begettings

IN PROGRESS/IN RETROSPECT, 2006/2009

'Of the things we gave them', from *The Infinities* notebook (2006) housed in Trinity College, Dublin: MS 11356-1-1, pp. 147–137 (the author has flipped the notebook over, treating the versos as rectos, hence the reverse pagination; a transcription of the title page on p. 447 should read: 'Amphitryon/— "a novelette" —/Quisque suos patimur manes (the spirits who haunt us are ourselves)/Virgil Aeneid IV (*sic*) 743/ A man is a god in ruins./Emerson') • 'First Light', *The Infinities* (Picador, 2009), pp. 3–29; an early version of these passages was previously published under the same title in a stand-alone volume (The Bridgewater Press, 2006)

Grateful acknowledgement is made to Trinity College, Dublin for permission to reproduce a page from *The Book of Evidence* notebook (MS 10252-9-2-15) on the endpapers.

About the Author

John Banville was born in Wexford, Ireland, in 1945. He was educated at Christian Brothers Schools and St Peter's College, Wexford. He worked in journalism from 1969, as a sub-editor on *The Irish Press* and from 1986 at *The Irish Times*. He was Literary Editor at *The Irish Times* from 1988 to 1999.

Banville's first book, *Long Lankin*, a collection of short stories and a novella, was published in 1970. His first novel, *Nightspawn*, came out in 1971. Subsequent novels are *Birchwood* (1973), *Doctor Copernicus* (1976), *Kepler* (1981), *The Newton Letter* (1982), *Mefisto* (1986), *The Book of Evidence* (1989), *Ghosts* (1993), *Athena* (1995), *The Untouchable* (1997), *Eclipse* (2000), *Shroud* (2002), *The Sea* (2005), and *The Infinities* (2009). His non-fiction book, *Prague Pictures: Portraits of a City*, was published in 2003.

Among the awards John Banville's novels have won are the Allied Irish Banks Fiction Prize, the American-Irish Foundation Award, the James Tait Black Memorial Prize, and the *Guardian* Fiction Prize. In 1989 *The Book of Evidence* was shortlisted for the Booker Prize, and was awarded the first Guinness Peat Aviation Award; in Italian, as *La Spiegazione dei Fatti*, the book was awarded the 1991 Premio Ennio Flaiano. *Ghosts* was shortlisted for the Whitbread Fiction Prize 1993; *The Untouchable* for the same prize in 1997. In 2003 he was awarded the Premio Nonino. He has also received a literary award from the Lannan Foundation in the US. He won the Man Booker Prize in 2005 for *The Sea*. In 2011 he was awarded the Franz Kafka Prize.

His most recent novel is *Ancient Light*.

Under the pseudonym BENJAMIN BLACK, he has published the following crime novels: *Christine Falls* (2006), *The Silver Swan* (2007), *The Lemur* (2008), *Elegy for April* (2010), *A Death in Summer* (2011) and *Vengeance* (2012).

kept getting

repeat the simplest actions

in my agitation I kept getting

repeat [things] the simplest

wheel was burning hot from

windscreen. [I let out the cl

like a lumbering predator]

I let out the clutch too qu

in a series of bone' shaking

down like the prow of a shi

watchers at the window

wrenching at the door handle

maid was scrabbling at the d

the gate, and when